Integrity

Noyes writes in first-person point of view like no other. This author made me see and feel everything through Lexie's eyes. Noyes' writing is beautiful and real, I loved getting lost in the main character's head and re-read several paragraphs because they were so poignant.

Noyes always writes witty, funny heartfelt dialogue and this book has all of that in bucket loads.

-The Lesbian Review

Noyes never fails to impress me with her talent. She is fearless in her storytelling, never hesitating to flesh it out and let the story take her where it will. Because she does, it feels organic to the reader. Scenes don't feel forced. They work. Furthermore, they advance the plot. It all works to prove Noyes is a master at producing stories that are pure, indulgent escapism. Readers get so caught up in the narrative that it's over before they know it and they're a little disappointed that it has. However, a true Noyes fan always knows that the reread is going to be just as good, if not better than the first time through... Book one of the Halcyon Division Series is a fantastic beginning; I have no doubt readers are going to enjoy this journey and sign up for more. This is heart-pumping, non-stop, page-flipping fun, and one heck of a ride! My recommendation: don't miss out!

-Women Using Words

Schuss

This is an absolutely charming first-love, new-adult romance between characters that I had already bonded with. Seeing how they have grown and matured in the four years is a treat and watching the two struggle with their feelings for each other just melted my heart... *Schuss* could be read as a standalone novel, but honestly, I think you should read both books together. They are wonderful stories, and I highly recommend them.

-Betty H., NetGalley

E. J. Noyes has this way of writing characters that you get completely absorbed into. When we were left with the Gemma and Stacey cliffhanger in *Gold*, I was hoping we'd get their story and it was phenomenal.

-Les Bereading, *NetGalley*

If I Don't Ask

If I Don't Ask adds a profound depth to Sabine and Rebecca's story, and slots in perfectly with what we already knew about the characters and their motivations.

-Kaylee K., *NetGalley*

Overall, another winner by E. J. Noyes. An absolute pleasure to read. 5 stars.

-*Lez Review Books*

Go Around

Noyes excels at writing both romance and intrigue and it shows in this book. Her characters might as well be real they are so well-written. I'm a pretty big fan of second-chance love stories, and I love the way this one is done. You get the angst you expect from the two women trying to get past the pain of their separation and work their way back to being a couple in love. The outside forces that had a role in their breakup are still around and have to be dealt with. Add in a nasty bad guy (or guys) who are physically and psychologically stalking Elise and you get a tale full of danger, excitement, intrigue, and romance. I also love the Easter egg the author included for her book *Alone*. I actually laughed out loud at that little scene. E. J. Noyes' works always get my highest praise and recommendation, and this novel is no different. You really need to read this book.

-Betty H., *NetGalley*

In *Go Around*, E. J. Noyes has dipped her toes in the second-chance romance pool and was masterful in blending angst, enduring love and suspense in it. The chemistry and dynamics between the pair were thick and palpable but what stood out for me throughout the book was the type of love everyone wished they had; fierce and protective, grounded in loyalty, passionate yet to be able to just be when you are with the other. Noyes also made Bennet, Avery's dog another highlight for me. He was the tension breaker and a giant darling.

-Nutmeg, *NetGalley*

Pas de deux

Pas de deux doesn't disappoint: the writing is excellent, the pace is ideal, the characters are layered and, yes, relatable, including the secondary characters, from Caitlyn's groom Wren, to Addie's friend Teresa and, of course, Dewey the horse. One of the many things I loved in this book is the way the MCs deal with problems. They do this very adult and very rare-in-lesfic thing: they talk to each other. This book is proof that miscommunication isn't required for drama. Neither is a breakup. Well-fleshed characters with very human hang-ups bring all the angst and drama necessary. It's all the more interesting here as *Pas de deux* is part enemies-to-lovers romance, part second chance, depending on whose point of view is playing.

-*Les Rêveur*

This story is not the traditional enemies-to-lovers romance, and I love that. Noyes really puts emphasis on how skewed memories can become as you get older, and how an experience may appear different to another person who had the exact same one. Even if you are unfamiliar with dressage, Noyes' writing is still spot-on and delivers the same compelling, fun, and intriguing story with loveable characters of both the two-legged and four-legged kind. This love letter to a sport she obviously has a passion for is so evident and I felt honored to have her share her passion with me and every reader who picks it up. If you love horses, enemies-to-lovers, or even just Noyes' stories in general, this one will definitely be a favorite on your list.

-*The Lesbian Review*

Reaping the Benefits

The story is quite eccentric with its paranormal context but in fact is a pure romance at heart with a nice dose of humor. The book is written in third person, from the point of view of both protagonists, which is not common for Noyes, but it is executed perfectly. With all main elements done well, this makes an awesome read which I could easily recommend to all romance fans.

-Pin's Reviews, goodreads

I've read many love stories that entertain the idea of soul mates, but this one does something even more interesting. This one explores the depth of love and its ability to transcend death. This story plays with the idea that love has no limits or boundaries. Its exploration provides a unique setting for this heartfelt romantic tale. At its core it remains a romance. The love story between Jane and Morgan is tender and sweet. It's so cleverly and delightfully done; I've never read anything quite like it before. Noyes possesses the ability to see a story where others don't and turn that into something unique and captivating. She uses rich storytelling and engaging characters to enthrall and delight us.

It's fresh and original. It's everything you crave when you want to dig into a great romance. I highly recommend it.

-Deb M., NetGalley

If you're looking for a lesbian romance, but with a twist of something different, I recommend *Reaping the Benefits*. It's sweet, sexy, and fun.

-The Lesbian Review

If the Shoe Fits

When we pick up an E. J. Noyes book we expect intensity, characters with issues (circumstantial and/or internal), and a romance that builds believably. Considering this is *Ask, Tell* #3 we expected all of the above layered with epic seriousness. We were pleasantly surprised and totally floored by the humor in addition to what was already expected!

-Best Lesfic Reviews

Alone

E. J. Noyes is easily one of the most gifted writers pulling us into whatever world she creates making us live and feel every emotion with her characters. Definitely, loudly, vehemently recommended.

-Reviewer@Large, NetGalley

Alone is an absolutely stunning book. This book is not a 5-star, it is well above that. You don't see books like this one very often. Truly a treasure and one that will stay with you long after the final page.

-Tiff's Reviews, *goodreads*

There are only a few books out there so compelling they seem to take control of you and force you to read them as quickly as possible. You can't put them down. You just want the world to go away and leave you alone until you can finish this story. *Alone* by E. J. Noyes is that book for me. This novel is absolutely wonderful.

-Betty H., *NetGalley*

Not only is this easily one of the best books of 2019, but it has worked its way onto my personal all-time top 10 list. There is not one formulaic thing going on, and it's "unputdownable."

-Karen C., *NetGalley*

I cannot give this anything more than five stars, but damn I wish I could. I would give it 15.

-Carolyn M., *NetGalley*

Ask Me Again

Not every story needs a sequel. *Ask, Tell* demanded it, and Noyes delivers in spectacular fashion. Sabine and Rebecca show us their fortitude and their strength in their love for each other…Thank you, Noyes, for giving us a great story, a great series, and amazing women that teach us the best things in life are worth fighting for.

There really is only one way to tell this story, and Noyes executes it perfectly. She gives us events from the first-person perspective. However, she alternates each chapter between Sabine's point of view and Rebecca's point of view. You're able to get the full perspective of their inner feelings and turmoil they hide from one another. In addition, you're able to get the complete picture of the unconditional love Sabine and Rebecca have for each other. It's this little light of love that propels the reader to keep going and hope these women will finally reach the end of the darkness.

-*The Lesbian Review*

Gold

This is Noyes' third book, and her writing just keeps getting better and better with each release. She gives us such amazing characters that are easy for anyone to relate to. And she makes them so endearing that you can't help but want them to overcome the past and move forward toward their happily ever after.

-*The Lesbian Review*

This book is exactly the way I wish romance authors would get back to writing romance. This is what I want to read. If you are a Noyes fan, get this book. If you are a romance fan, get this book. I didn't even talk about the skiing… if you are a skiing fan, get this book.

-Lex Kent's Reviews, *goodreads*

Turbulence

Wow… and when I say 'wow' I mean… WOW. After the author's debut novel *Ask, Tell* got to my list of best books of 2017, I was wondering if that was just a fluke. Fortunately for us lesfic readers, now it's confirmed: E. J. Noyes CAN write. Not only that, she can write different genres… Written in first person from Isabelle's point of view, the reader gets into her headspace with all her insecurities, struggles, and character traits. Alongside Isabelle, we discover Audrey's personality, her life story and, most importantly, her feelings. Throughout the book, Ms. Noyes pushes us down a roller coaster of emotions as we accompany Isabelle in her journey of self-discovery. In the process, we laugh, suffer, and enjoy the ride.

-Gaby, *goodreads*

The entire story just flowed from the first page! E. J. Noyes did a superb job of bringing out Isabelle's and Audrey's personalities, faults, erratic emotions, and the burning passion they shared. The chemistry between both women was so palpable! I felt as though the writer drizzled every word she wrote with love, combustible desire, and intense longing.

-*The Lesbian Review*

Ask, Tell

This is a book with everything I love about top-quality lesbian fiction: a fantastic romance between two wonderful women I can relate to, a location that really made me think again about something I thought I knew well, and brilliant pacing and scene-setting. I cannot recommend this novel highly enough.

-Rainbow Book Reviews

Noyes totally blew my mind from the first sentence. I went in timidly, and I came away awaiting her next release with bated breath. I really love how Noyes is able to get below the surface of the DADT legislation. She really captures the longing, the heartbreak, and especially the isolation that LGBTQ soldiers had to endure because the alternative was being deemed unfit to serve by their own government. I applaud Noyes for getting to the heart of the matter and giving a very important representation of what living and serving under this legislation truly meant for LGBTQ men and women of service.

-The Lesbian Review

E. J. Noyes was able to deliver on so many levels... This book is going to take you on a roller-coaster ride of ups and downs that you won't expect but it's so unbelievably worth it.

-Les Rêveur

Noyes clearly undertook a mammoth amount of research. I was totally engrossed. I'm not usually a reader of romance novels, but this one gripped me. The personal growth of the main character, the rich development of her fabulous best friend, Mitch, and the well-handled tension between Sabine and her love interest were all fantastic. This one definitely deserves five stars.

-CELEStial books Reviews

LEVERAGE

BOOK TWO
IN THE
HALCYON DIVISION SERIES

E. J. NOYES

Other Bella Books by E. J. Noyes

About the Author

E. J. Noyes is an Australian transplanted to New Zealand, which may be the awesomest thing to happen to her. She lives in the South Island with her wife and the world's best and neediest cat, and is enjoying the change of temperature from her hot, humid homeland.

An avid but mediocre gamer, E. J. lives for skiing (which she is also mediocre at), enjoys arguing with her hair, pretending to be good at things, and working the fact she's a best-selling and award-winning author into casual conversation.

LEVERAGE

BOOK TWO
IN THE
HALCYON DIVISION SERIES

E. J. NOYES

BELLA
BOOKS

2023

Bella Books, Inc.
P.O. Box 10543
Tallahassee, FL 32302

Printed in the United States of America on acid-free paper.

First Edition - 2023

Editor: Cath Walker
Cover Designer: Heather Honeywell

ISBN: 978-1-64247-497-8

PUBLISHER'S NOTE

Acknowledgments

Though writing can be a somewhat solitary experience, no author is an island, and I'm incredibly grateful for those who hold my hand, and give me little nudges or large shoves along the way. Every one of you (and that's you too, readers) plays a part in helping me get a project to publication. It's this mix of gentle and tough love, support, excitement, and encouragement that wraps around me and helps me open up my works-in-progress when all I want to do is play *Call of Duty* or engage in some other mindless, time-wasting exercise.

This series has been both pleasure and pain to write, mostly due to my own stubborn refusal to change my writing process, and I'm so thrilled that people have taken Lexie and Sophia into their hearts. Now, it's off to work on the next book in the series. I promise, everything works out in the end—I am a romance writer at heart, after all.

Kate, you read the alpha draft of this when you were dealing with a literal newborn. I think that's insane, but I'm so very grateful for your support, your thoughtful advice, and your friendship. WZ soon?

Friends, I am eternally grateful for your constant support. I don't know how you put up with my book whining when I'm trying to make something work during the ol' writing process, but I'm so glad you do.

Betsy, I can't thank you enough for your time and expertise. Not only did you lend Lexie authenticity, but you gave me valuable advice and insight for the rest of the novel. And you taught me things. I love learning things (as long as I don't have to research it myself).

Abby, again, many thanks for your yoga wisdom to make Lexie sound more real. But more than that, thank you for showing me I am a yoga person after all. Who knew?

Grandma… You won't see this because thankfully you don't read my books. But I'm realizing now, as I get older, just how much you shaped me into a decent (I think?) human. Thank you for saving me and giving me the opportunity to be the best me I can be. And that me just so happens to be someone who writes books.

Cath – what more can I say that I haven't said a million times already? Or, more specifically, in twelve books prior to this one. If you ever doubt how much I value our working relationship, please just go flick back through the acknowledgments in those other books.

Bella Books. All of you. I honestly can't think of the words to express how grateful I am for this team, so…thanks. A lot.

Pheebs, when I stumble, you pick me up, dust me off, give me a lil kiss on the forehead and a pat on the butt, and send me out to try again. And the only reason I can keep trying is because I know you'll be there when I falter.

Author's Note

This one is fiction too.

PROLOGUE

So, how did we get here?

You're probably curious about what happened before this, right? Though, if you're *not* curious or you're up to speed already, then you can skip forward past this quick explanation.

I'm Lexie Martin, a government intelligence analyst, it's nice to meet you. About three weeks ago, I was enjoying a regular day at work when I received some seemingly routine information about a chemical weapon attack in Afghanistan. It didn't take me long to realize that something seemed weird, and this attack looked suspiciously like one of our own, an American, illegally testing a chemical weapon. With Russia's help.

Yeah. Bad.

My suspicion of something being wrong was confirmed when a stranger let himself into my apartment for a "chat" that night. I was supposed to forget about the horrible intel, and go with him to debrief and delete all relevant files. No thanks—my parents taught me about Stranger Danger. After escaping the guy, I did what anyone would do.

I ran.

Once I'd hunkered down in a safe location for the night, I got a call from one of my bosses, the one who runs Halcyon Division. Oh yeah, sorry, I forgot to mention I *also* work for Halcyon Division. Think of Halcyon like…a hidden anti-virus for the government, keeping corrupt and tainted-by-foreign-influence people out of Congress. So, that intelligence I was ordered to forget? Turns out it was super important. My Halcyon boss, Lennon, ordered me to keep it safe, and see if I could unravel it. If I did, Halcyon could remove someone—I had no idea who—from the highest office. Someone who was actively working against the good of the country.

Because I am a doubly diligent government employee, I agreed. When I say "agreed," I mean I didn't actually have a choice. When you might hold the key to keeping your country safe, you can't really say no without looking like an asshole. And in case you've never tried it, let me tell you—running and hiding from the government is *hard*. Especially when they know you know a secret that they didn't want anyone to know.

I needed a human security blanket, someone with me to discourage governmental snatch-and-grabbing. Witnesses are awesome. So is someone to keep you company.

There was really only one option: Sophia Flores. Swoon. Yeah, I said swoon.

We'd only been on a few dates, but there had been a whole lot of flirty texts and interesting FaceTime conversations—can you say "chemistry and instant connection"? I can, and I'll add "off the charts." Thankfully, Sophia agreed to come road-tripping with me. Thankfully not just for the whole intelligence thing, but because I *really* liked her. Of course, I told her it was just a boring old road trip, definitely didn't mention I was fleeing from the government because I'd found out something that might be bad.

Long story short, it was an adventure. Sophia and I totally caught feelings for each other, which helped when I had to come clean(ish) about what I was really doing. And yes, I felt terrible about the lies and manipulation but some things, like the security and safety of the country, are a little more important than my love life. Fortunately, Sophia forgave me for not telling her the truth in the beginning (not that I told her the *whole* truth in the end but, you get the idea), and then kept me sane and grounded while I figured out the secret behind the intelligence—yay, me.

I sent what I knew to Halcyon, got a pat on the back for uncovering the secret, or the start of it, and after ensuring Sophia's safety I turned myself in because honestly—running forever, no thanks. Halcyon intervened to keep me from being incarcerated and branded a traitor and uh, well, it was kind of like an action movie. A painful one. But I survived, I'm free, and apparently I still have a job (or two).

So, here we are…

CHAPTER ONE

My oasis

In the fifteen days since it had last happened, I'd forgotten what it was like to wake up next to Sophia Flores. Or, more accurately, not so much *next to* as kind of underneath and kind of on top and kind of all entwined together. I squirmed my feet, trying to get some blood flowing back into them, but ended up trapped when Sophia shifted in response to my shifting. The position she now caged me in was comforting and familiar, though admittedly painful given my recent escape from custody. Or more accurately—having someone stage my escape from custody for me while I was just a helpless participant.

My job as an intelligence analyst is usually straightforward, and often mundane, but since I'd been given intel implicating the vice president in an illegal chemical weapon test in partnership with Russia, my life had been turned on its head. Hopefully my life was on its way to being set the right way up again.

Carefully, I brushed Sophia's dark, wavy hair from where it'd fallen over my face, but not before I'd inhaled deeply to remind myself of the scent of her shampoo. While waiting to see if I'd be thrown in jail as a traitor, I'd thought about the smell of her hair...the fullness of her lips...her laughing light-brown eyes...her low, husky voice...the way her breath hitched as my fingers mapped her skin…the way her body begged my body.

Her heavy curtains cocooned us from the world outside, and without a bedside clock, I had no idea of the time. Morning, based on the fact I was awake. I drew in a deep, slow breath and then exhaled, taking stock of my body. Broken fingers ached sharply, not-broken but still damaged and bruised ribs hurt, not-broken ankle ached and throbbed, right leg and hip felt like they'd been wrenched out of place and put back carelessly. And my head still throbbed like I'd gone twenty rounds with a professional boxer, the cut on my hairline pulling uncomfortably tight as it healed.

But… I was alive, free, and wonderfully tangled in bed with the woman who'd been with me through the stressful week that had preceded my short incarceration. The woman who I could easily and, scarily for me, never having been one for serious relationships, picture myself having a life with outside of all this. So, all in all, more pluses than minuses, which was a nice change after the last few weeks of mostly minuses.

Sophia shifted, her legs moving restlessly against mine. I knew from the eight days we'd spent together on our road trip, that was less fun driving adventure and more me hiding from the government and trying to uncover a huge secret, that the squirming meant she was thinking about waking up. Up until now, she'd stirred while I was doing my morning workout on the floor of a hotel room, but being in bed with Sophia meant I could finish waking her up. I smiled, remembering the one time that I'd woken her up. With oral sex.

I drew my foot up the inside of her calf and reached under the covers to slip my hand under her tee, lightly stroking the side of her breast. Sophia startled then jerked upright, freeing me and dislodging me all in one movement. She flailed, her limbs making contact with parts of my body that did not want that kind of contact. I grunted at the jolt of pain that burst through my torso, tried to move and failed, then tried not to hiss out an expletive and also failed. I lay supine, sucking in wheezy inhalations in a futile attempt to breathe through the searing pain and my spasming diaphragm.

Sophia rubbed her face. "Shit. Sorry, Lexie. I'm sorry," she mumbled against her palms. Her voice was rough with sleep and in any other circumstance, when I wasn't trying desperately to just inhale and exhale, I'd have found it sexy. She leaned over to look down at me. "Are you all right?" Her hand came to rest lightly on my hip.

"Mhmm." My response would have been a more convincing assertion if it hadn't come out as a strangled squeak. Technically I *was* all right, just momentarily rendered useless by the elbow she'd accidentally rammed into my bruised ribs.

Sophia's gentle hands raised my tee, her fingertips brushing my skin. She stroked lightly up and down my belly, murmuring for me to relax, until I started breathing more easily, instead of like a hyperventilating sprinter. She thumbed the underside of my breast in a gesture that was loving, almost possessive, instead of sexual. "I'm so sorry. I was dreaming and then woke up and forgot for a moment that you were back."

Back.

I *was* back from that place where I'd been held and debriefed. But was I back in her life? And if I was, was it for good or just temporarily? I bulldozed those worries aside for now. The pain had eased enough that I could talk again, albeit still breathlessly. "It's okay. I'm okay." I dropped my hand on top of hers.

"Where does it hurt?"

Smiling tightly, I said, "*Everywhere.*" When I realized how distraught she looked, I added, "But it's way better than it was a few days ago. So in a few more days I'll be good as new."

Sophia's hands came up to gesture awkwardly, like she just didn't know what to do or say. Eventually she asked, "What do you need, hon? What can I do?"

I bit my lip on a smile; I'd missed her *hon*. I took her hands and brought them back down, holding them against my chest. "I don't need anything except what I've got. You. And you can stay right here and help me go back to sleep." Wishful thinking. Now I was awake and uncomfortable, any chance of sneaking in a little more sleep was slim. But lying in bed with Sophia was a very close second to sleeping.

"Okay," she agreed quietly as she carefully eased herself back down beside me. A tentative hand moved lightly along the side of my ribs then down until it came to rest on my hip.

I could feel the tension, the discomfort, the desire to ask me the why and what and how. When I'd turned up at her pickleball gym last night, she didn't ask me anything, except for "Are you all right?" But she would have to be bursting with curiosity. After we'd spent those eight days closely quartered, taking a crash course in Getting To Know You, I'd left her in a hotel room just outside of Jacksonville. I'd told her she'd likely never see me in person again, because I'd fully anticipated being imprisoned for what I'd done, even though I'd been ordered to do it by Lennon, the boss of Halcyon Division, the secret government branch I worked for.

Yet here I was.

Last night, as she'd watched me change for bed, Sophia hadn't asked about the mess of healing bruises, cuts, and abrasions painted over my body. And I didn't know how to explain. How do you explain something as complex as my life, what had happened during those ten days where I'd been held in a secure facility, wondering what would happen to me, falsely accused of stealing top-secret intelligence? And even if we *did* talk about it, so much of what had happened was classified. And then there was the whole issue of Halcyon...

I could just imagine the conversation. Oh, hey, Sophia, so like, um, I'm totally a legit intelligence analyst and yeah, I gave you a bare-bones explanation of the deal with that intelligence I was working with during our weird road trip, but I also work for this secret bipartisan government division that helps keep all the corrupt and foreign-tainted bastards out of our government and that's why we had that fun vacation-not-a-real-vacation while I was trying to figure out the secret I'd been told to keep safe so that secret division thing could use it, and oh yeah, something exciting is coming up, so watch the news and hint-hint, the VP is a traitor and he's toast.

Yeah, right. Let me count all the ways in which that's not a good idea.

"How was your Halloween?" I asked, just for something to break the silence. "Did you do anything? Dress up, big party?"

She shook her head. "None of the above. Some friends tried to get me to go to a party but I didn't feel like it. I bought myself a massive bag of candy and watched the newest *Halloween* movie. How was yours?" The moment she'd asked, Sophia's mouth fell open. Apparently she'd twigged that I was most likely locked up on Halloween—I was—and she hastened to backtrack. "I mean...you know."

I kissed her palm, the base of her thumb. "It was good. I think," I added with a grin I hoped would ease her discomfort. "Not really sure what day was what but all the days were fine, so I feel confident saying my Halloween was okay." She still looked uneasy, so I continued, "Next year we should dress up in some cheesy matching outfits, like salt and pepper or Bonnie and Clyde and party until the small hours. Or, we could stay home and eat candy and watch scary movies and ignore all the kids in the building. Whatever you want."

"Deal," she agreed instantly. There was a long silence before she asked, "You really didn't know what day it was while you were gone?" I could hear the forced monotone in the question, as she worked to keep her emotions out of it. Clearly, my attempt to ease her discomfort had failed.

"I didn't, no. No phone or calendar supplied. Aside from the uncertainty and missing you like crazy, it was actually kind of nice to have zero responsibilities and a break from all the work stress."

Her teeth grazed her lower lip. "Will you tell me about it? Your time...locked up?" She'd also wanted to know the details of the 2017 event overseas where I'd been involved in a hostage situation that'd left my asset and three terrorists dead, and me with vengeance stab wounds after I'd killed a man in an attempt to escape. Those scars were a constant reminder of the job I used to do, of what I'd done. But Sophia's curiosity hadn't been voyeuristic. It was caring, as if she wanted to take on some of the trauma herself, carry some of its emotional weight. I sensed the same in her now.

"If it'll help you, yes, of course."

"I think it will." Sophia drew in a slow, slightly shuddery breath. "The whole time you were away, I imagined so many things, had started to deal with never seeing you ever again, but then you came back and you looked"—her whole face scrunched up like she'd smelled something bad and wanted to cry about it—"like *that*, and now I don't know what to think."

"I'm sorry," I said, hoping it was enough of a blanket apology for now. She deserved to know how I'd come to look like I'd been in a car accident—because I technically had—but what exactly could I tell her? How do you explain the unexplainable? I'd fought with that question during our road trip, and never came up with a satisfactory answer. I couldn't tell her about Halcyon. I couldn't tell her what I'd found out about our vice president and that he'd soon be removed from his position. I couldn't tell her the only reason I wasn't in jail for the rest of my days was because apparently Halcyon Division had almost limitless power over the White House and had assured them my release was in the country's best interests. So what *could* I tell her?

As much of the truth as I was able to. She deserved that.

I rolled onto my side, angling my sore right leg into a more comfortable position before fluffing her excess of pillows to lean against. Sophia moved with me, her hand falling from my body. I moved it back to rest on my hip. "Um, after they picked me up, we drove for a day or so. I still don't know where we ended up. It was fine, not much bathroom privacy but they were nice to me. And very quiet which gave me a lot of time to think." And think I did. "Uh—" I faltered and couldn't recover.

"It's okay if you're not ready," Sophia murmured.

"No, it's not that. It's just, I'm…" I paused. "Not sure how to word it." When talking about my job, ordinary things like mentioning an incident were never simple or straightforward. Thankfully Sophia understood the limitations my job put on sharing because she'd been with me while I worked through the intelligence that'd started this whole thing, and she knew I'd been dodging questions and telling some half-truths. Quarter-truths if you counted the fact she didn't know I technically had two jobs. But we'd come to an agreement—I'd share everything I could about the work stuff, and be an open book about my personal stuff.

"Ahh. Gotcha." She smiled tightly. "I figured, because you have The Look."

Frowning, I asked, "What's The Look?"

"You get an expression sometimes when you're trying to explain something. I've always assumed it's because you're doing mental gymnastics, trying to figure out how and what you can tell me."

My eyebrows shot up. "What's The Look look like?"

"First it's almost a little guilty, borderline panicky. Then you look like a kid who didn't do their homework but has been asked to give a last-minute talk to the class. Then your expression gets kind of faraway like you're hoping the right way to answer will suddenly come to you if you look at nothing for long enough."

"Wow." Laughing, I shook my head (and made a mental note to watch my expressions around strangers). "I had no idea. I…you're right, I am doing mental gymnastics, making sure I don't share something I shouldn't, while trying to be honest."

She squeezed my hip gently. "I know you can't share everything. But if you *can* share…"

What I could share wouldn't fill a thimble, but I had to give her what little trickle of information I could. "Okay. Um. I was debriefed a few times. It was…not fun. They didn't hurt me physically," I quickly added when I saw her horrified expression. "Only my ego, and we know how easy it is to bruise that."

Laughing quietly, Sophia pinched my hip. "Liar. Your ego is bulletproof."

"Not quite. More like…bullet resistant." I grinned cheesily. "I told them the truth. They didn't like it because they thought I was lying. Then I spent some days in my room by myself. Then more talking and alone time and that was that." This was where things got perhaps the trickiest, where I had to be careful not to let slip that I'd been *rescued* and maybe not entirely legally. "I don't know what happened exactly, but my lawyer was apparently very good at his job. They released me and on my way home, we got into a car crash, some guy T-boned our car. I spent a few days recovering, and then came to find you. And here we are."

"Mmm, yes. Here we are," she said. The little eyebrow scrunch told me she knew I'd omitted some parts and maybe been half-truthful about others.

I smiled sheepishly, genuinely remorseful that I couldn't share the things that might put her at ease. "Obviously, that's the bare-bones, nuts-and-bolts version."

The not bare-bones version included details where my agency boss, Derek—whose loyalty I'd been questioning through the whole process—rammed the transport vehicle in an attempt to stop it, but actually made it crash while I was chained in the back and getting flung around like a sack of flour. He set me free and sent me to a safe house with instructions to rest and heal, visit Sophia, and come back to work in two weeks. Oh, and then there was the bombshell that he was part of Halcyon Division too, and had been the whole time I'd known him. Talk about right under my nose.

Oh! Then there was something else Derek and Halcyon kept alluding to, where apparently I had "value," hence my rescue instead of waiting for the wheels of justice to slowly turn. I mean, yeah, I'm a great at my jobs, but… Valuable? I made a mental note to ask Halcyon if I was valuable enough for a pay raise.

Though Derek had assured me that everything would be okay when I went back to work, my short detention hung over my head as an ominous reminder that I'd been a Very Bad Girl. Not quite in the "stealing government secrets and leaking them all over the Internet" way. But definitely in the "I received intel, was threatened by a thug while I was naked in bed, got spooked and ran away, then accessed the intel not one hundred percent securely and discovered the vice president's illegitimate son had been in charge of an illegal chemical weapon test that'd killed three hundred and sixty-two innocent civilians" way. And also the "I discovered the VP was deep in Russia's pockets, and the president and a bunch of other people were pissed I'd found out their secret" way. They weren't pissed about the illegal weapon test or the murder of innocent people, only that someone had found out about it.

And now Halcyon Division was going to use the information to force the corrupt vice president to resign. Goodbye, Vice President Randolf Berenson, you treasonous sack of shit.

I hoped my explanation would satisfy Sophia. When I thought about it like that, laid alongside *actual* traitor deeds—in which I had *not* engaged—what I'd done didn't seem so bad at all. As an intelligence analyst, my job was to sift through intelligence, find relevant details, and put it into a format for policymakers to use. In this instance, I'd done my job and I'd done it well. Granted, I hadn't done it in a totally secure work setting or through entirely official channels, but when you took in the big picture, I'd done my best given the circumstances. Justifying one's actions was easy if you didn't dig too deeply into their nuance. My government had taught me that very recently.

I'd also received assurances from Lennon that Halcyon would do what they could to make things easy for me—without revealing themselves, of course. Halcyon Division operated deep in the shadows. So deep that, aside from those employed by Halcyon, only a select handful of high-ranking government officials even knew it existed. Super-secret government agencies designed to keep foreign operators and corrupt officials from ruining our great nation are *super*-secret.

Sophia thumbed the edge of my mouth, bringing my attention away from my thoughts and back to her and us in this bedroom, back to the place I wanted to be physically and mentally. "Did you see a doctor about"—she gestured vaguely up and down my body—"all of that?" She'd accepted my car crash explanation with nothing more than sweet concern, mercifully not asking how the hell I'd had the misfortune to be in a car crash right after being released from custody.

"Yep, I went to the ER. It's not that serious, it'll all heal up on its own just fine with a little time." I took advantage of her frowny disapproving face to ask, as casually as I could, "Did anyone strange come see you while I was gone?"

Sophia's eyebrows shot up. "No, nobody at all. Why?"

"Just wondering." Bastards. The lead debrief guy, if you could call an interrogation-esque conversation a debrief, had taunted me that he would break our deal, the one I'd insisted upon before I'd handed myself in—that Sophia and her family were to be left alone. He'd said that they'd been to see Sophia, and implied she'd spilled intimate details about our time together. I knew she'd seen none of the intelligence I was working on, or the reports I'd written, nor heard any of my phone conversations, and the thought they'd coerced her into sharing or made her uncomfortable had made my blood boil. Now my blood was boiling all over again, but for a different reason.

I set the boiling blood aside, forcing myself to think of something more pleasant. The woman beside me. "I thought about you a lot while I was…away."

Her eyes softened, her expression turning to a mix of relief and bashfulness. "I thought about you too."

"I'm glad." I kissed the tip of her forefinger. "But I mean, I *really* thought about you. As in dark of night all alone wondering my fate sort of thoughts. You really were a light in the dark, Sophia." Turning her hands over, I studied their shape, the taper of her fingers, her short nails, the rainbow Care Bear tattoo on her wrist. "They teach you that when you're in a situation you shouldn't be in, to focus on something, something that's not about where you are right then. Something nice, something good, something you want. It's an anchor point, an oasis you can send your mind to when someone is trying everything they can to make you do what they want or tell them the things they want to know. And you were my oasis."

"Spy training?" she quietly asked, a small smile lifting her lips.

I reminded her, yet again, in a teasing voice, "I'm not a spy. But we do receive some training for…" The words rattled around in my brain, separating and reforming into something that I could say to her. "Those questioning situations." Bravo. Very informative. I love my job (most of the time) but fuck, I hate the constant sidestepping and micro-deceptions and also the flat-out lies.

"I'm glad thinking about me helped. I thought about you too," Sophia said tightly. "So much. I was devastated that I was never going to see you again."

"I'm here now," I said, rolling carefully on top of her, both for my ouchies but also to gauge her mood. When her hands slid to my ass, I murmured, "And there's nowhere else I want to be."

As I slid my thigh between hers, Sophia went still. Not quite the reaction I'd been hoping for. But it made sense when she quietly said, "I don't want to hurt you. *And* you've got two broken fingers."

I held up my partially splinted right hand. "I do, but it's two unimportant fingers, pinky and ring. And I'm sure you can be gentle."

"Oh, I can be very gentle," she promised. "Except in the places you want me to be rough."

"And what places are those?" I asked hoarsely.

She showed me, until a knock on her bedroom door interrupted something I really didn't want interrupted. Sophia popped up from between my thighs. "Yeah?" she called.

An unfamiliar voice called back, "Sophia? You up? Are you still getting bagels this morning?"

"Shiiittt," she whispered. "Camila doesn't know you're here." She turned her head toward the door, raising her voice to say, "Just a sec." Sophia's older sister had been staying with her since she'd come home from Florida without me. Just some company, she'd explained last night. She didn't need to explain *why*; she'd been devastated when I'd left and didn't want to be alone. Sophia shifted from between my legs—sigh—patting the inside of my thigh as if reassuring me she'd return. "Are you hungry?"

I told my libido to put itself on ice for now and tried not to sulk. "Yeah, a little."

"Would you be okay here for a half hour while I go grab breakfast? Camila promised a Saturday morning bagel feast, with the caveat that I procure the bagels."

"Sure." I sat up. "I'll come too."

"Lexie," she said, slowly, patiently, the teacher explaining to the dumb kid. "Your walk is a limp. I think you need to relax and heal."

I thought about protesting but realized her jaw had set into stubbornness. "Okey dokey, you're the boss." I only just managed to stop myself from reminding her to be careful and to keep her eyes open for anything or anybody that looked out of place. We didn't really need to do that now.

Smiling, she kissed me. "And don't you forget it." She dressed quickly and left me with instructions to help myself to anything I needed until she came back. I heard a conversation—hopefully Sophia telling her sister I was here so she wouldn't freak out—before the front door closed.

I lasted two minutes before I began feeling antsy about lying around doing nothing. I stretched carefully, then eased out of bed. Sophia's apartment was on the top floor of a newish building near the university and when I glanced out the window, I spotted her jaywalking. Smiling, I found a space on her bedroom floor where I could have a short, gentle yoga practice.

Feeling much better in mind and a little better in body, I wandered into the living room and spotted an older, taller, darker-eyed version of Sophia in the kitchen, staring at the coffee maker. I offered an awkward wave. "Hi."

"Hello." Her appraisal of me was slow and measured, her statement even more so. "So, you're her new girlfriend," she said coolly.

Well… Girlfriend was an unexpected description for what I was, but sure, I was happy with that. The word made me feel warm and fuzzy inside and if not for the iciness radiating from Sophia's older sister, I'd probably have been grinning like an idiot. Instead, I smiled warmly in an attempt to offset the chill. "I am, yes. You must be Camila." I walked over, hand outstretched. "I'm Lexie. Sorry we didn't get to meet last night, but you were still at work when we went to bed. Nice to meet you."

She stared at my hand as if it were something toxic before she took it. Her overly firm grip was a power play as she confirmed her identity with a simple, "I am." Apparently it was not nice to meet me.

Camila wasn't cold or aggressive, more guarded. And with good reason. I was sure Sophia had told her about me, about us. It'd been a minute since I felt guilty about pulling Sophia into a mess then leaving her, but there that emotion was again. A deep inhalation and exhalation helped move the guilt to where I could deal with it later. I went with the best thing I knew to get past someone's defenses—keep them talking. Or in this case, get them talking. "Sophia told me you're a chef."

"Yes. At Manger."

"Oh! I've been there, a few times actually. You guys have a really great menu."

A dark arched eyebrow slowly rose. "Really?"

I nodded enthusiastically. "Mhmm. It's one of the few places I've found around here with multiple really good vegetarian options, at a restaurant that isn't purely veggie-focused that is."

"Thanks." She paused and I could see her weighing her words before she softened fractionally. "I craft the vegetarian menu."

I would have asked her for some recipes or a tip on how to get my *tartiflette* as good as Manger's, but got the feeling she'd tell me one of the main ingredients was cyanide or something. "How long have you worked there?"

"Four years." Camila peered over her shoulder as if she was worried Sophia might burst through the door with bagels in hand and catch us in the middle of a stare-off. "What's with"—she indicated me with a swirling forefinger—"all that?"

"Car accident," I answered as I poured myself coffee.

Camila slipped around to the other side of the kitchen island. "Looks painful."

"It was." I turned to face her.

She set her mug down. "Look, I'm just going to come out and say it. I don't know what happened during your 'vacation,' but I *do* know that when Sophia came back, it was like someone had just killed our parents and made her watch."

"Oh." My stomach dropped at the thought of Sophia's anguish. A gulp of coffee gave me a moment's pause to settle my own anguish and think of what to say to this stranger. No, while she was a stranger to me, she wasn't to Sophia, and I needed to remember that. "I'm not sure what she told you—"

"Not much," Camila interrupted.

"Right." Clearly, and thankfully, Sophia had kept her cards close to her chest. And obviously I couldn't tell Camila exactly what happened, but if I could smooth over her poor impression of me then I was damned well going to try. "We had a misunderstanding, one of those new relationship miscommunication mishaps. Then I had my accident, and after all that time had passed I wasn't sure how to approach her. So it kind of snowballed into seeming much bigger than it was."

"I see. Looks like you figured out how to approach her."

"I did." Smiling, I added, "Thankfully for both of us."

She moved around to stand by me, close enough to be uncomfortable without outright looming into my personal space. "I suppose this is where I tell you I'm keeping an eye on you. She's my little sister," Camila added, as if that explained everything. It did.

"Fair enough. I'm used to people keeping eyes on me," I said dryly. I'd had so many eyes on me in the last three weeks that I would have felt weird without someone watching.

"Also, I'll kick your ass if you hurt her." Based on her expression and tone I had no doubt she could and would.

"Honestly, I'll save you the trouble and kick my own ass." I set down my mug and raised placating hands. "Look, I don't intend to hurt her. And Sophia's a grown woman who's capable of choosing who she wants to hang around with. I'm hoping that's me. For a while yet."

"That she is, but she gets attached very easily. She's also got a heart the size of Europe and has a habit of adopting strays." The measured gaze made it clear Camila wasn't talking about bringing in a cat off the street.

"Um, thanks?"

She smiled broadly and if I hadn't seen the genuine amusement in her eyes, I would have thought it fake. Seemed there was a human under that cyborg bodyguard. "You're welcome."

The sound of the apartment door unlocking moved Camila to the couch where she flopped like she'd been sitting there all morning just drinking coffee and chilling, rather than threatening me to behave. When Sophia slipped inside, her arms laden with bags, I rushed to her as quickly as my throbbing leg allowed. "Here, let me help."

Sophia let me take one of the bags—apparently "getting bagels" meant "do a mini grocery shop"—studying me and then her sister with an expectant, slightly suspicious expression. "I see you guys have met." She unwound her scarf and hung it by the door.

Camila nodded vigorously. "We sure have!" She turned her toothy smile on me, which gave me a glimpse of what she might be like once she got past her wariness. *If* she ever did. "Right, Lexie?"

"Mhmm, we have indeed." I slid the bag onto the countertop and took the second from Sophia so she could take off her coat. "Getting along great."

"Like old friends," Camila agreed.

I smirked. I'd had a few people who were supposed to be my friends threaten me before, so the description fit just fine.

CHAPTER TWO

I don't want this bubble to burst

Once we'd finished her gourmet bagel breakfast, Camila left with a cheerful (or maybe faux-cheerful in my case) goodbye to each of us, citing she was superfluous to requirements now that I was there. I definitely caught a little snideness. Yeah, I'd screwed up, I get it. But it would never happen again.

We stayed at Sophia's place, just reconnecting, for another day and night before she quietly said she'd like to see my apartment. I mustn't have hidden my confusion because she'd been quick to say, "If that's okay."

I was so relationship-deficient that it hadn't even occurred to me that after everything we'd been through together that it was time to let her see my personal space. I almost stumbled in my haste to agree. "Sure, of course, no problem. We can go whenever you want." Frowning, I added, "Might have to grab some food though."

I'd only spent a few hours at my apartment after emerging from the safe house, and it'd been pretty hazy. All I really remembered was noticing that someone had cleaned my bedroom carpet where the guy they'd first sent to grab me had put his broken-nose blood all over it, that the wall he'd smashed into to receive said broken nose was repaired, and that my bed was neatly made with clean linens.

Because Sophia was a graphic designer and website builder extraordinaire who worked from home or wherever she wanted to, she packed her things in record time, and we were off on another adventure. To my house... Perhaps not quite an adventure.

After unpacking the groceries we'd picked up on the way home, and noting I maybe should have checked what was already in the fridge and pantry to avoid double-ups, Sophia claimed the rarely used small desk in my living room. And I tried not to fret about what she thought of my apartment. It wasn't artsy and eclectic like hers. It was...prosaic, like every place I'd lived in when I was growing up around the world with my constantly moving diplomat-father family.

I was suddenly struck by the realization that I was forty-one years old and dammit, I could decorate my place however I wanted. I'd kind of just always kept the same basic aesthetic I'd had in all the borrowed domiciles I'd inhabited as a kid—clean and modern, a.k.a sterile and boring. The only splash of color in my living space was the art I'd bought from all around the world, hanging on my plain white walls. My furniture could have filled the pages of an IKEA catalog. But now, maybe, Sophia would cast her vivacious, artistic eye over everything and leave her mark on my space.

My space. Would she find my mattress comfortable? Did I have enough towels for two people? Would we cook, or order in? Would she be okay with me disappearing each morning into my quiet room where I meditated and practiced yoga? Would we just...do what we'd done during our time in Florida, but now with added going out and not hiding from people trying to find me? What about when I went back to work in a week's time, how would that fit in with the existence we'd carved out together? This was different to the time we'd spent together holed up in hotels. Now it was real life. And real life was a little scary.

Along with a small bag of clothing and essentials, she brought her laptop and the portable second monitor she'd carted around on our road trip. As I watched her setting up to work, hanging clothes in the space I'd made for her in my closet, laying out her e-reader on the coffee table, I felt a twinge of sweet nostalgia, followed by a surge of certainty. I knew this woman—we'd already lived a small lifetime together in those eight days, and this could be our new life together, this existence of our regular, separate lives, and meeting in the middle for every other part. How wonderfully domestic. No sarcasm—it really was wonderful.

Discoloring my joy was my impending return to the office, the anxiety dangling over my head like a cartoon boulder teetering on the edge of a cliff. I tried replacing the anxiety with imagining the normality of returning to work: my morning workout and shower in the gym, the stroll from the gym to the main building, scanning my ID to open the ballistic-resistant front doors, scanning through the turnstiles, moving through the security and body-scanning stations, being confirmed as *clean*, the slow elevator up to my floor, settling at my desk with a cup of tea, reading taskings while I ate breakfast. That would be the same as always. And yet everything would be completely different. Because now I knew exactly the kind of government I was working for.

After almost a week of rotating between our apartments, Sophia and I had the girlfriends thing down pat and had reached "toothbrushes and clothing essentials at each other's places" stage. She'd also given me back the things she'd kept for me when I'd had to leave her in Florida. I'd taken gleeful re-custody of the premium Oolong tea, infuser, and Sasquatch mug she'd bought for me, the drawing of me as a superhero—Super Lexie—holding up the whole world, as well as a little black dress I'd bought on a whim during an evade-my-would-be-captors outing. That dress needed a maiden voyage, and a romantic date was just the thing—I just had to plan one, as I'd promised Sophia in Tampa.

A knock on my apartment door on the dot of three p.m., the day before I was due to return to work, made me feel like someone had plunged me into a hot bath. And despite knowing it was irrational, I couldn't rein in my fear. People didn't knock on my door, and the last uninvited visitor to my house had basically tried to kidnap me.

When I peered through my peephole, I saw a bland midthirties guy wearing dark-gray dress pants and a sharply pressed white button-down, standing back from the door. In one hand he held a small box wrapped in black plastic and in the other, a portable identification device. Squinting, I noticed the pin on his collar—a small gold kingfisher that could easily be taken for a fraternity or political affiliation insignia, but which I recognized instantly. I had one myself. I could relax. He was allowed to be here.

I opened the door. After glancing at the device, he looked up again and offered me a genuine, beaming, smile. "Good afternoon. Can you state your full name, please?"

I leaned toward his device-holding hand and raised my voice. "Alexandra Elizabeth Martin."

He held the device up to my face for a few seconds, then presented it to me like a sommelier presenting a bottle of expensive wine. "Left ring and right index prints, please."

I pressed the requested fingertips against the screen, underneath two photographs of me—one a passport-style ID photograph and the other from ten seconds ago—and the graphic of my matched voice wavelength. Once he'd confirmed I was me and not someone wearing a me-mask, he handed over the parcel. "Enjoy the rest of your day."

"Thanks, you too."

I closed and double-bolted the door. Sophia glanced up from her phone, her eyes straying to the box. She wrinkled her nose. "Dammit, I thought you'd ordered food."

I raised my eyebrows. "At three o'clock? And I thought I was cooking tonight?"

She shrugged, a smile building at the edges of her mouth. "You are, but I'm hungry and hopeful."

I leaned over the back of the couch and kissed her, careful to keep my parcel behind my back—not that there was anything that might identify it, but paranoia was a lifelong habit. "Once I've opened this, I'll make you a snack. And then I'll cook something amazing for dinner. I was thinking Indian, how does *aloo gobi* sound?"

"It sounds amazing." She twisted around to face me fully, put her hand on the back of my neck, and pulled me closer. "But I *can* make my own snack."

"I know you can, but if I make it, that means you don't have to get up." We'd been chilling on the couch for most of the day. The most vigorous thing we'd done was a standing quickie in the kitchen after loading the dishwasher.

"I like your thinking." After another lingering, toe-tingling kiss, she released me. She said nothing more about my visitor, apparently satisfied that if I was okay then she was also okay.

Safely inside my bedroom, and with Sophia safely outside my bedroom, I peeled the security tape with its stamped hologram H from the box, which otherwise displayed no markings. I knew who it was from, having received many parcels like this from Halcyon Division—mostly phones or credit cards and ID with not-my-name on them. The replacement Halcyon phone with its blue case was already set up with a SIM card and one number, which I knew by heart anyway, stored in the only app on the phone.

I opened up the encrypted communications app and pressed the number.

"Lennon," was the almost-immediate response. His familiar voice was soothing, as was the sound of him puffing a cigar. The world had not stopped turning while I'd been gone. Comforting, considering what I'd done to keep the world turning.

"Thanks for the new phone," I said. "I thought you'd make contact earlier." I hadn't spoken to him since the day of my surrender, when he'd given me permission to stop running, and told me I'd done good work.

"I thought you'd appreciate a short time to regroup and relax."

"Thoughtful, but neither of those things are going to happen. I assume everything is as it should be?" Like one of the worst VPs ever elected being kicked out of office, his illegitimate son arrested for his part in the weapon test, and illegal chemical weapon stockpiles destroyed.

"Yes. Thank you for your hard work. It's not gone unnoticed."

"Am I getting a promotion? A massive raise? A huge bonus?"

He chuckled. "Not quite. You're getting to stay free, which I'd say is a fair trade."

Not going to prison for the thing I did because I'd been asked to do it didn't really seem like that much of a reward. "Fine," I mumbled.

"I thought you'd like to know that thanks in part to your excellent work, the Halcyon Protocol is complete. It's anticipated Vice President Berenson will resign in the next few days."

"How exciting, and what a gift for my return-to-work week. What's the reason given for his resignation?" They couldn't say he was resigning because his illegitimate son worked with Russia to test a chemical weapon on innocent civilians and oh, just for fun, the vice president was also way too friendly with Russia. The citizens of this country needed to feel safe, and worrying about foreign influence lurking around every corner was not conducive to feeling safe.

"Health problems."

"Poor man," I said dryly.

"Indeed. How is Ms. Flores?"

"Better than ever," I said instantly, trying to slough off the annoyance I felt at that question. Lennon thought Sophia was a bad idea, that—among other things—she'd split my focus from my work. He'd made his feelings about my relationship clear while also praising me for having the foresight to utilize her to keep myself safe. Utilize was the *worst* word and I hated that it sat alongside attraction, interest, desire, lust, and maybe even…love. Sophia was the thing that'd made it possible for me to figure out the pieces of the puzzle I'd been assigned, but Lennon was still firmly glass half-empty when it came to her. And I didn't know why.

"Then I'm pleased for you," he said evenly.

"Whaaaat? No 'Be careful, Alexandra'?" He'd said it so many times in relation to Sophia during the great adventure that I'd almost thought he'd recorded himself and was just hitting playback.

"I always want you to be careful. But now that Halcyon's agenda is set in stone, I needn't worry about Ms. Flores distracting you from your tasks."

I let it go. Arguing with a man I'd never actually met about my love life was pointless. "She's not a distraction," I said firmly, congratulating myself for landing on *firm* instead of the *petulant* that had been at the back of my mouth.

Lennon ignored me. "I'll be in touch. I'll be calling upon you soon for something important."

"Oh! Is it my Lexie is the Savior of the World task dealio? That thing Derek said about me being valuable or some shit?"

He mhmmed his agreement.

"Exciting."

Having exhausted the necessary conversation, we hung up without goodbyes as we always did. Efficiency was probably in Halcyon Division's operating manual or something. I locked the phone in my closet safe and went back to the living room to show Lennon's Half-empty Glass some love.

She showed *me* some love after dinner, and once we'd officially gone to bed for sleep instead of sex, I passed out in what felt like minutes. And then woke again at 2:32 a.m. because why not have insomnia when I needed to be rested to go back to work?

Sophia shifted slightly, easing her weight off me, and I took the opportunity to slide from underneath her and slip from my bed. Before we'd first started sleeping in the same bed, we'd both admitted to sleeping like an octopus being exorcised and I'd thought there was no way two messy sleepers in one bed could ever work. But it did for us, and in those days without her I'd felt the absence of the weight of her limbs across my body as if a part of myself had been torn away.

I negotiated through the darkness of my apartment by memory, a skill honed while working overseas managing blackout curfews. The fear of all sorts of ammunition coming through the window because you made yourself a target in the light was a great motivator to learn how to see in the dark.

After collecting my laptop I settled at my kitchen table and hunkered in for some mindless browsing. Boring news, fearmongering news, vapid social media. I hopped up and paced slowly back and forth across my kitchen floor, but given its size it didn't take up much of my excess nervous energy about work tomorrow. A glass of wine might help put me back to sleep but solo insomnia drinking wasn't really a habit I wanted to start. Meditation was probably a healthier alternative.

I heard footsteps moving quietly along the hall and took a moment to assure myself it was Sophia, not someone who shouldn't be in my apartment. Fool me once, thugs. Sophia's silhouette appeared in the doorway, lit by the oven light and my laptop. "Lexie? Hon? You okay?"

"Yeah, just couldn't sleep."

The quick flicker of emotion was hard to miss, even in the muted light. Mistrust, resignation, upset. She thought I was keeping secrets from her again, up in the middle of the night as I had been in Florida. "Ah," she said quietly.

"Why are you up?" I asked.

"Because you're not in bed." She closed the distance between us, but paused a foot away. "Do you need to close that?" A flick of her fingers indicated the laptop.

I'd been so careful to keep what I was working on from her view, and it'd become second nature to her to avoid looking at the screen if I hadn't been as diligent with positioning as I should have been. I turned the laptop toward her, showing the kitten TikToks. Definitely not classified intelligence.

Sophia smiled. She stepped closer and slipped one leg in between my knees, nudging them farther apart so she could stand in the space between. "Do I need to put you to sleep again?" The nuance was clear.

Leaning forward, I wrapped my arms around her waist. "Maybe." When we'd made love earlier, she'd been sweet and slow, as if she'd sensed that my anxiously firing going-back-to-the-office nerves couldn't handle anything more than gentle lovemaking.

I pulled her closer and pressed my face to her stomach. She'd pulled on the pajama bottoms and tee she'd brought to my house— which were mostly used for presleep activities before their inevitable removal. The tee was soft and smelled like her distinctive laundry detergent, an organic sensitive-skin one that I, a "I wish I had more dedication to saving the planet" heathen, had never heard of before we'd met. Her hands came to my hair, fingertips sifting through the strands, gently sliding against my scalp.

My hands slid up under her tee to stroke the soft, warm skin of her back. The movement was soothing, comforting and I turned my head so my cheek rested against her belly. I wanted to burrow into the comfort of her and stay there like a kid hiding under a blanket, hoping it would magically be better upon emergence.

"Do you want to talk about tomorrow?" she asked, bending down to kiss my forehead.

And here I was thinking I'd done a reasonable job of hiding my anxiety. I disengaged slightly to look up at her, raising an eyebrow. "It just…doesn't make sense, and that makes me anxious," I said, exhaling loudly. "I hate things that don't make sense. I hate when I can't analyze something logically. I just can't figure this one out." Why had everyone just swept what I'd done out to sea? Halcyon was powerful, yes, but to have *zero* ramifications was really odd.

"Must be why you decided to be an intelligence analyst then, huh? So you can figure it out." She was trying for levity, but the tension around her mouth made it clear she had reservations too. Perhaps not of the same type or scale as mine, but she'd been there with me while I'd tried to work through the problem, and witnessed my frustration, my elation, my anger, my fear. However, she'd never know the whole truth of what I knew. Could never.

I made myself smile. "Must be." Drawing in a deep breath, I raised her tee and kissed her bare stomach. "It's just…I feel like I'm waiting for my own execution. Metaphorically," I hastened to add. "And how do you deal with that?"

Sophia took a small step backward, loosening my hold on her. "You'll deal with it the same way you did the other thing. Logically, one step at a time. I know you're all over this." She cupped my cheeks in her hands and tilted my face up to kiss me softly on the mouth. "You're the baddest-assed Not-Spy I know."

"I'm the only Not-Spy you know."

She grinned. "You don't know that. Secret identities are secret, right? I might know a dozen Not-Spies and be blissfully unaware." After another kiss she tugged my hand until I stood. Sophia slung an arm around my waist. "Let's go back to bed, babe."

"Another round?" I asked as I moved with her. My body and brain felt like they'd been through a wringer, but I'd surrender without a thought to have her again, let her have me again. And I'd love every second of it.

She smiled, and that smile said it all. She wanted me, wanted *that* as she always had, but there was something else more important to her at that moment. Sophia hugged me to her side, leaned over to kiss my temple. "No, hon. To bed, and to sleep."

I let her take me back to bed, resigning myself to more insomnia until I could meditate once she'd fallen asleep.

"You're different," she observed quietly once we'd snuggled back under the covers, settling until her head rested against my shoulder and her arm hugged my waist.

Funny, I felt exactly the same as always. "Good different or bad different?"

"Good. More relaxed."

"I told you the me in Florida wasn't the whole me. It was a…very stressed version of me. I'm glad to prove I wasn't lying about that." Just about a bunch of other things.

"I like this non-stressed version. But I also fell in love with the stressed version, so I guess I just love all versions of you."

I swallowed, trying to ignore how my heart rate had skyrocketed at those words. "Fell in love?"

Silence.

I let it go. As in I didn't push her, but I most certainly pulled those three words in close to hold them tight. "When I go back to work, I promise I'll be a perfectly balanced mix of a little bit stressed *and* chilled."

"I might swoon."

I pulled her closer and murmured against her ear, "Don't worry, I'll catch you."

CHAPTER THREE

I don't think hand amputation is an overreaction
AT ALL

I'd indulged in an extra-long yoga practice and meditation in my Zen room this morning, expunging most of my negative feelings about returning to work. Realistically, I was sure it would all be fine, despite my short stint on the other side of lawfulness. Awkward, maybe, but fine. I mean, what were they going to do? Let me get close to the building then yell "Psych!" and take my credentials away before dragging me back to that facility for more debriefs and incarceration for real this time? That's what the stupid part of my brain thought, at least.

Sophia decided to spend the day at my apartment, wanting me to come home to my safe space after my first day back. She'd extracted herself from bed while I was getting dressed—a big deal for someone who usually looked like she'd been told she had just twenty-four hours to live if she had to get out of bed before eight a.m. Like a mom, she asked me if I had my lunch and my gym bag and my work clothes, kissed me lingeringly at the door, lovingly patted my butt, then told me to have a good day and that she'd see me after work. Domesticity, even in its infancy, was amazing.

Reminding her I didn't have access to my cell phone during the day, I'd left my work number on the fridge in case she needed to call me for anything. Her mouth had quirked so mischievously that I'd had to amend it to, "Almost anything."

I was pleasantly surprised when I pulled into one of the parking lots close to my office building—not late and therefore not relegated to being stuck waaay back in "Parkistan," the lot farthest from the building—that everything seemed the same at work. It was stupid, but I'd expected something to be different. I took a deep breath, readying myself for a day apart from my girlfriend.

Girlfriend. Hmm. That word again. She *felt* like my girlfriend but we'd never actually explicitly discussed whether or not that's what we were. She'd casually mentioned it during the road trip, in a kind of "In the future when this hypothetical thing happens, you'll be my girlfriend" way. Her sister seemed to think we were, which was something, and I'd take being girlfriends any day of the week if that's what Sophia wanted.

I spun in a slow circle, then did it again, taking in the familiar sight. High secure fences, formidable boom gates with unfriendly tire spikes, and a whole lotta assault rifles and people I wouldn't say boo to—let alone make eye contact with—in guard huts dotted around the compound. The focal point was the huge bland building that housed a large percentage of the country's best intelligence analyst brains. Including mine, supposedly.

I was well aware that not only would the closest security checkpoint guys be watching me, but someone in a hidden surveillance room would have me on a monitor, waiting to see if my weirdness escalated. But I needed to take it all in, to remind myself why I was there, why I'd joined the agency, why I'd joined Halcyon.

To protect people.

I strode along the path parallel to the main building, and slipped around the huge concrete bollards pretending to be planters that would prevent anyone who managed to get past said checkpoints and spikes and assault rifles from getting a car close enough to damage us. The amount of protection around this building almost made me feel important. Almost.

I held my badge to the reader at the gym door, still half expecting to be denied entry, then let out a quiet "Phew" when the door flung itself open like it was happy to see me. Yes, I was anthropomorphizing a door. The security person sighted my ID and opened the second door for me. So far, I was winning.

I took my time stretching before hopping on the treadmill for a three-quarter-pace five miles. My injuries were niggling, but manageable, and I needed to run. I'd hardly managed anything vigorous, other than having sex, while I'd been traveling with Sophia, nor during my debrief detention, and there was only so much that yoga and meditation could do to calm my brain when I wasn't getting my usual running endorphin rush. I ran, I free-weighted, I stretched. Shower, dressed, hair, makeup. Just an ordinary morning at work.

I exhaled another quiet "Phew" when my ID opened the doors to the main building. I strode up to another badge scan at a set of turnstiles, and approached a security station to hand over my possessions for inspection. Kevin, one of the security personnel, seemed surprised to see me, and I hoped everyone had bought the story about me being absent the past month because of a particularly heinous bout of Covid. "Dr. Martin," he said warmly. "Glad you're back. I hope you're feeling better."

"Me too, and yes, I am." I placed my things on the scanning machine belt for inspection while I went through the usual routine— scrutiny of me and my ID before a metal-detecting body scan—that I'd done more times than I could count on all the toes and fingers of every person in the city. I sighed when my belt set off the metal detector, and yanked it off and handed it over before stepping through again. In all the anxiety about today, I'd done a poor job of choosing my accessories. "Covid's a bitch, I just couldn't shake it. I still don't think I'm quite right." There, that sounded convincing, didn't it?

"Sorry to hear that." He passed me back my belt, then my scanned bags. "My days haven't been the same without you and your fact of the day. I feel like my IQ dropped twenty points since I last saw you."

I stuffed the annoying belt into my gym bag to prevent an alarm repeat this afternoon. "I promise we'll bring it back up in no time." Smoothing the ID lanyard against my chest, I told him, "A bolt of lightning has enough energy to toast one hundred thousand slices of bread. But I wouldn't recommend making toast that way, even if you wanted to eat that much toast." I wiggled my fingers. "Zaaaaapp!"

His laughter followed me to the bank of elevators. My brief banter with Kevin had made me forget my jangling nerves but by the time I'd hit the button to call the elevator, they were back, and had brought friends. Nothing is going to happen. You're free. You did your duty.

I imagined scooping up all my anxieties and irrational fears and tossing them over a cliff. They might sproing back up later, like some Looney Tunes character, but for now—they were under control. I held the elevator to admit people I knew peripherally, but thankfully not well enough to warrant a deep conversation, for which I had no brainpower. We shared polite good mornings, then standard awkward elevator silence until I exited.

The second elevator had opened just before mine and Sam, my best work friend, fell out. He quickly closed the space between us and grabbed my shoulders, shaking me side to side. "You!" he cried. "I thought you'd died." We were work friends, not outside-of-work friends, and it wasn't weird that he hadn't tried to contact me during my absence. I'd have done, or not done, the same.

"Not quite, though it felt dicey." I turned, and gestured that he should walk with me.

Sam fell in beside me as we started up the hall toward our office. "You're feeling better though, right?" he asked. "You've been gone a month, gorgeous."

"Much better," I agreed. "How's Muffin?" The week before my life went off the rails, Sam's reason for living—his cat, Muffin—had been in rough shape after the local feline-Rocky beat her up.

"Fully recovered and now an indoor cat. No more neighborhood cat-bully bastard hurting her, and no more stress for me."

"Glad to hear it. Let's catch up at lunch. I want pictures of Muffin, *and* I have news for you…"

His eyebrows drew together. "Is it news about that woman you had that breakfast date with the day after I saw you last? Did she give you Covid? It's a *little* conspicuous that the last day I saw you was the day before you had your date, dontcha think?"

Laughing, I drawled, "She might have." I stretched the truth, something I was good at. "Let's just say I've had a very capable home nurse these past few weeks."

Sam held his badge up to the reader on our office door. The door clicked open. "I want all the details. Except the sexy ones. Just give me a broad overview of that."

"You got it." Final hurdle. I inhaled slowly. Once he'd passed through the door and it'd closed behind him, I scanned my badge. The door opened. Game on.

As I walked through cubicle town toward my own corner, a few coworkers expressed genuine pleasure at seeing me, and most expressed sympathies for my (fake) extended illness. If they knew what had really happened, their feelings toward me would probably change. Because even though I'd acted under instruction from a higher authority, I'd bent rigid rules to get to the truth.

At first glance, my cubicle looked untouched, though I knew someone would have rifled through my things and fine-tooth-combed my files. When I looked closer I realized my octopus mug was by my monitor and had been washed—thanks, Sam—and the piece of rock I'd picked up while hiking in New Zealand was in the wrong place. Someone had also moved my mouse from the right side to the left. Inconsiderate asshole.

I took a few minutes to rearrange everything back to its rightful place then settled in my chair. I'd fully expected to see an official government envelope with my employment termination letter inside, but there was nothing of the sort. Nor was there anything in my emails to cause alarm, just the usual CCs and Forwards, albeit quite a few more than usual given my absence. Derek had sent a calendar invite for a meeting tomorrow morning and I accepted it. That meeting would give some As to my Qs.

As I read emails, my confidence returned. This was my arena, the place where what I did mattered and where I'd earned the respect of my colleagues. That thought was part of what'd gotten me into trouble—the conviction that it was up to me to follow through, to keep what I knew safe. During my time away from the office, I'd realized that hubris could be a good or bad thing. In my case, I was unfortunately leaning toward the bad.

I'd never considered myself particularly egotistical or arrogant, but I knew I was very good at what I did. Instinct and learning had made me a *damned fine analyst*, to quote Derek, and I had a knack for sorting quickly through raw intelligence to find if it had value. Healthy egos were healthy, but I couldn't help the sickening dread that mine was a little too healthy and it was going to cost me.

I just didn't know what I'd have to pay.

I spent almost two hours sorting emails before logging in to check the agency's server-hosted email account used by old assets who liked to stay in contact even though I was out of the field. That account was where my contact Hadim had forwarded the video, photos, and voice recording of the chemical weapon attack in Kunduz Province, Afghanistan. Given ninety-eight percent of my work was handed to me by my boss, rather than the few leftover assets that still insisted on liaising directly with me, I didn't really expect to find anything new in my emails. But disappointingly, there was nothing from Hadim.

His email address had been deactivated in the twenty-four hours following his phone call that had changed my life, but he could still contact me if needed. I hoped he was okay. Surely the White House hadn't gone after him for what he'd sent me. No, Hadim had given me valuable and workable intel over the years and even the president with his single brain cell should know that. The most likely explanation was that something else had spooked him and he'd dived underground.

Quiet throat clearing broke my wandering thoughts and I looked up. Derek stood by the back cubicle wall, looking relieved. "Martin. Good to see you again. Are you okay?"

"Yes, sir. Fit as ever." This charade was hilarious. Not only had Derek and I seen each other on the night of my "escape," but he and I both knew full well that I hadn't been sick.

"I'm pleased to hear that. I'll see you this afternoon for our team meeting. Come see me if you need anything before our private meeting tomorrow."

"Will do."

I slotted right back into work, mostly just catching up on the goings-on from when I'd been away. I hadn't been assigned any taskings yet. Probably easing me back into it. Or…they didn't trust me. I mean, if they wanted to pay me to sit at my desk and read emails and then daydream for hours, they could be my guest.

I'd just sat down after a trip to the kitchen for my post-lunch cup of tea—thankfully nobody had touched my Oolong stash, or there'd be an office homicide—when Derek's voice boomed by my ear. "Martin! Let's go."

"Go where?" I asked, hating the fact he'd made me jump. His order sent an irrational fear coursing through me and my stomach flip-flopped uncomfortably. They wouldn't grab me at work and take me back to detention. Not in front of everyone. Unless I was being made an example of, which was entirely possible given the pettiness of our current leader. But why now?

No. It's nothing. Just a normal boring meeting or maybe another debrief. Meeting my boss's boss so I could explain myself yet again, or more accurately—lie, yet again, because of course I couldn't tell them Halcyon made me do it.

Derek lowered his voice to regular levels. "We have a briefing." At my confused frown, he elaborated, "Seventh-floor VIP. Look smart."

Oh yaaaay, a VIP. So the meeting wasn't about *me*, specifically. And there were only a handful of VIPs I could think of who'd come here, none of whom I wanted to meet. Derek had taken his own advice, rolling down and buttoning the cuffs of his shirt sleeves and putting on his suit jacket. The more important you were, the higher up you worked, so the seventh floor was basically for directors and those who had the ear of the President of the United States. All the big meetings happened up on the seventh floor. Yeah, I'd never been to the seventh floor.

I gulped a mouthful of tea, confirmed I hadn't spilled anything on myself, smoothed down my blouse, crunched a breath mint, and checked my makeup in my compact. After a quick lipstick touch-up I deemed myself "looking smart" enough for whatever VIP I was about to meet.

I fidgeted through the short elevator ride up, disappointed that the seventh floor looked much like every other in the building. Except for the dozen people in suits stationed all the way along the hallway on each side. Obviously Secret Service. Oh no, anything but this. Of all the people I did *not* want to talk to, the president and vice president were top of the list.

Like…what was I supposed to say? Sorry, Mr. President and Mr. Vice President. Didn't mean to ruin your reelection campaign and your political career and maybe your life, respectively, but to be fair, you kind of did that to yourself. What's that saying? Fuck around and find out. Surely the VP had to have known that eventually someone like us would find out about his ties to Russia.

The Secret Service men and women didn't move as we passed, but I felt multiple eyes on me at every step. Two solidly muscular guys guarded the door to the room marked Conference 1, and after checking our IDs, they opened the door. Too late to make a run for it then, I guess.

The room was a hive of activity, with staffers and Secret Service and who knew what roles half these people played all directed at one man. The president, Arnold Fletcher. I clamped my molars together. I'd have thought seeing him would make me anxious, considering people doing his bidding had made my life so unpleasant for a few weeks. But all I really felt was…disgust. Maybe a little mad. Yes, definitely mad.

A crisply pressed late-twenties guy introduced Derek and me. The president focused on Derek first. Derek's posture was ramrod straight. "Mr. President, sir. It's an honor to meet you." Liar. He hated the current administration almost as much as I did. Handshakes, photographs. Then the president's cool hazel eyes appraised me. I fought the urge to fidget as Derek made introductions. "Mr. President, it's my honor to introduce one of the agency's finest analysts, Dr. Alexandra Martin."

"It's an honor to meet you, sir." There, I got it out without stuttering, puking, or swearing. Go, me. Who cared if I'd just parroted what Derek said. "Thank you for taking time out of your schedule to visit us." Like he had just popped by for a social visit instead of to possibly make my life hell.

The president nodded, leaned down, and in a voice too low for anyone but me to hear, murmured, "You've caused me quite a bit of trouble, Ms. Martin." His breath stank of stale coffee and bad food.

Without thinking, I corrected a man who didn't like being corrected. "Dr. Martin, Mr. President."

"Doctor…" He took then shook my hand, his grip overly firm and rough. To cement the discomfort, he placed his hand over mine to trap it. Nice power play, asshole. I mean, *sir*. "I hope there won't be any more incidents like this one?"

I had to bite my tongue on responding, "I hope you won't be covering up bribery, diplomatic assholery, breaking humanitarian laws, manufacturing an illegal chemical weapon, and the fact that three hundred and sixty-two innocent people died because you chose a vice president who seems to love Russia more than America." Instead, I gripped his hand hard, though all I wanted to do was karate-chop it and yank my hand free from his dick-measuring grip. I flashed him the brightest and fakest smile I could. "No, sir. Of course not, sir." Assuming you and your disgusting sidekick don't do something like this again, of course. Sir.

"Good, because this was not something I wanted to deal with. I do hope it was worth it. This could have been very damaging and embarrassing for the White House."

What a baby. They'd covered everything up, and outside of his immediate circle, Halcyon, and the intelligence folk who'd had eyes on it—which was only Derek and me—nobody knew about the chemical weapon test and who was involved. It wasn't going to cost him shit. Oh…right, yeah, except for the resignation of his vice president. The fact he was more concerned about a second term than the other thing made me feel sick. Who cared about the Russian-compromised bastard standing behind him, undermining the country he was supposed to be leading, right?

I congratulated myself when, instead of vomiting on his shoes, I managed to say, "I'm very sorry you were embarrassed, Mr. President."

He stared expectantly at me, and I knew he was waiting for me to amend my statement. He'd be waiting a long time; I wasn't sorry

I'd embarrassed him. His grip on my hand tightened to borderline uncomfortable. I squeezed back.

"You must love your job," the president said.

Surely he knew I was with Halcyon. Though, on second thought, based on his demeanor, he probably didn't. Maybe he just thought I had friends in high places. I did, though I wouldn't call them *friends* exactly...

"I do, sir," I said emphatically. "A great deal. And I'm *very* good at that job." I raised my chin. "Of course, I'm also very committed to my government and the people of this country. Protecting them is my highest priority." It took every ounce of willpower I possessed to leave it there, to not add on that part of my commitment was wanting them to know the truth about what was going on in the name of *keeping them safe*.

"I can see that." His voice lowered again as his eyes narrowed. "Sometimes commitment can be mistaken for treachery. I'd hate to see you have an...issue because of your ideals, *Dr. Martin*."

Thankfully a staffer bustled up and started babbling about time and press commitments because I was utterly stunned by what the leader of the United States had just said to me. Too stunned to respond. He'd threatened me and hadn't even bothered to disguise it. What a dick. I was too disgusted and annoyed to be upset or afraid.

As if slipping on a mask of pleasantness, the president asked, "Are you ready?"

"Ready for what exactly, sir?"

His eyes were cold, though his lips smiled warmly. "We're going to have a photograph taken so we can show everyone that everything is just fine and business as usual and that my intelligence agencies are working hard to keep the country safe."

His intelligence agencies. What a fucking idiot. My smile felt so tight my cheek muscles pulled. "Sounds wonderful, sir." I had a feeling that sometime in the future I was going to regret this photograph, which felt a little like bribery.

The president looked me up and down and, apparently satisfied with my appearance, nodded and turned to face the center of the room, searching for something. "Peter! Where do you want us?"

A middle-aged man turned immediately and gestured to the far wall. "Just by the flag, Mr. President. Those patriotic colors are so flattering on you."

I had to suppress my gag at the sycophancy, and also at having to stand so close to the man I despised with every cell in my body.

And I'd despised him *before* the whole "government testing an illegal chemical weapon with Russia" incident. We posed side by side and thank fuck he didn't shake my hand again or put his arm around my waist or something equally as nauseating. If he'd touched me again, I might have found myself under a football-tackle crush of Secret Service agents after I'd punched him. I made myself stand up straight and smile, because there was no way I was going to look like an idiot in photos that could be distributed countrywide.

Peter checked the back of the camera, nodding vigorously. "All done, sir. Excellent photographs."

The photographer was dismissed and the president turned his attention back to me. "Now everyone will know you and I are on the same team, Dr. Martin. Don't forget what you're working for."

As if I could. "Of course not, sir."

"And have you learned a lesson from all of this?" he asked quietly.

"Yes I have, Mr. President." I knew he wouldn't ask what lesson I'd learned, and would assume I'd learned that I need to be a *good girl*, so I added, "I've learned I need a better security system so that thuggish gentlemen can't break into my house to threaten me for doing my job, thereby starting a chain of events out of my control that I did my best to get under control." I turned a bright smile on his rapidly reddening face. I'd probably just shot myself in the foot. Worth it.

He turned away, and ignored me. Doubly worth it. After a pointed look from Derek that drifted from me to the door, I realized with relief that I'd been excused from the briefing that was about to take place. For now at least. Given I was sure it was about me, I assumed I could be called back in to give an...*other* account of my movements and activities while I'd been AWOL.

Now I knew Derek was part of Halcyon Division, I felt somehow protected. But I still had no idea a, why I wasn't in custody and b, why I still had this job. Accessing secure servers and extracting intelligence, then working with that intelligence offsite was cause for disciplinary action, even if I ignored the underlying Halcyon directive. But there'd been nothing. "Come back to work and we'll act like it never happened" was the official line I'd been fed. It made less sense than the time I'd paired a tutu with combat boots, seamed stockings, a ripped Grateful Dead tee, and pink-striped hair. Derek had better be in an answering mood tomorrow for our meeting, because I needed to know what the hell was really going on.

I thanked everyone, genuflected to the president, then rushed out of the conference room and into the elevator back down to my floor where I shoved into the nearest ladies' room. I almost collided with Nicole, one of my colleagues. She braced herself against the wall, letting me rush past. "Whoa, where's the fire?"

"He shook my hand." Shuddering, I pumped soap into both hands, lathering frantically as I bumped the faucet with my forearm.

"Okaaaay, you're going to have to back up." She turned the water on for me when my forearm flailing failed. "Who shook your hand?"

"The president. Do you have any Lysol? Like a whole can? Or failing that, I need you to please amputate my right hand. This is an emergency."

"The *president* is *here*?" Disbelief made her voice squeak up. After a beat she mumbled, "Gross."

"Yep. Upstairs." I scrubbed my palm furiously with my nails. "And tell me about it."

"Right, well, I'll go get a bone saw," Nicole deadpanned. She leaned against the wall as I washed my hands again. "What'd he want? Did you brief the president?" She sounded appropriately curious. People like us did not meet presidents.

"God no. He just wanted to talk to me about something I was working on before I was sick. Tell me I'd done a great job," I lied, laughing to myself. I rolled my eyes and rinsed my hands, reassuring myself that I didn't need to wash them again, despite the feeling of bugs crawling over my skin. "Not exactly the highlight of my first day back."

"Lucky you," Nicole said dryly. She studied me. "You feeling better? We were starting to worry about you, thought you'd suffered some complications or something. Sam was complaining about maybe having to take over some work for you, and that he didn't have anyone to listen to him talk about his cat. FYI, *I* listened, and dispensed an appropriate amount of sympathy for an event that's long passed and had an okay resolution."

"Sounds like him. And sounds like you did some heroic deeds." I yanked an excess of paper towel from the dispenser, dried my hands, and slam-dunked the balled-up towel into the waste. "And I am okay, thanks, it just hit me hard."

"Well, I'm glad you're back. Derek's always an asshole when you're gone, but he was completely out of his head this time." She smiled fondly. "Teacher's pet."

I made myself return her smile. If only she knew exactly why Derek had been such a bear with a sore head. "You know it."

Nicole patted my shoulder and pushed out of the bathroom. I stared into the mirror. The bruising around my eyes had faded and the sickly yellow remnants were easily covered by makeup. I'd been "sick." Right. And as for my boss's attitude, it was less to do with missing me and more to do with the fact the Higher Ups had been riding his ass about my...transgression.

I wasn't happy that he'd had to deal with the stress and fallout from my jaunt out of bounds, but that's why he got paid the big bucks. We still hadn't discussed the fact that he and I were doubly on the same side, and I wondered if he was technically my boss in the Halcyon ranks too. Knowing my recent luck, he probably fucking well was.

I didn't see Derek for the rest of the day, and by the time I'd made my way out of the building and walked to my car, it was after five p.m. I'd promised Sophia I'd pick up dinner on the way home, and that I should be at my apartment around six. But now I knew that by the time I negotiated city traffic, I would be late. I unlocked the trunk of my car and pulled my phone from its secure, temperature-controlled lockbox bolted to the chassis. I powered it on and messaged Sophia to let her know I was on my way home, apologize for being late, and ask for her dinner order.

The tightening of my skin made me pause putting my phone into my handbag and on instinct, I scanned the parking lot. My gut feeling never lied. I was fairly close to the building, the lot was well-lit, and not to mention more secure than Alcatraz. You couldn't even get beyond the fences without a pass and if you tried, the assault rifle guys would quickly dissuade you.

But something felt off.

Trying not to appear too obvious, I scanned my surroundings. There. At my four o'clock was someone I'd never expected to see again—the guy I'd first dubbed Swarthy Man, who'd told me his name was Mr. Smith. The man who'd led all my debriefings after I'd turned myself in. Fuck multiplied by three. I held my ground and we made eye contact. His face held the same controlled expression as it had through most of our previous time together.

My face felt as if someone had frozen it in a mix of disbelief and anger. There was no point pretending I hadn't discovered him following me, because there really was no other reason for him to be in my vicinity. Well, screw him. I closed the distance between us and forced my face into something resembling hospitable. "We meet again, Mr. Smith." That sounded a little bit *Matrix*-y.

"Indeed we do." He held his hands clasped together in front of himself, his posture stiffly upright. "And how are you, Ms. Martin?" He'd shaved the black stubble from his cheeks, exposing more of his darkly tanned olive skin, but his eyes were the same coolly appraising blue they had been during our debriefs.

"Dr. Martin," I corrected him, and not for the first time. I'd busted my ass for my PhD and I was damned if I'd let these assholes forget it, even if it made me feel like an idiot every time I reminded someone of my title. "And I'm very well, thank you."

"I'm pleased to hear that." It didn't sound insincere, which surprised me.

"Why are you here?"

"I work here," he responded instantly.

"Right." I dragged the word out. "Then why have I never seen you here before in the five years I've been based at this location?"

"It's a very big building, Dr. Martin." Smith leaned in, while still keeping a perfectly polite personal-space bubble around me. His smile was conspiratorial. "But I have a feeling we're going to see one another more frequently from now on. Have a pleasant evening and say hello to Ms. Flores for me." He turned and walked away before I could think of a comeback.

By the time I'd thought of one, I'd decided it was for the best that he was gone. I probably would have punched him.

CHAPTER FOUR

A good result, don't you think?

Sophia looked up as I juggled work and dinner bags through my apartment door. Her eyebrows shot up, her mouth falling open before she snapped it closed on a smile. "I'm sorry, do I know you?" She made a slow up-and-down inspection, and her heated gaze made me feel suddenly self-conscious.

I unloaded dinner onto the counter and ran a hand down my stomach, smoothing the fabric of my gray silk blouse. I'd just nervously checked that the collar lay flat when it twigged. I'd left for work that morning wearing gym gear for my at-work workout and carrying a plastic garment bag of crisp office clothes, and Sophia had never seen me dressed for the office.

In our time together, I'd been mostly dressed casually in sweatpants or jeans, tees and hoodies with boots or sneakers. Thirteen-year-old-tomboy chic. On our three dates I'd obviously dressed up, but definitely not in skirts and heels with a full face of *take me seriously, men* makeup. The unashamed desire in her eyes turned my self-consciousness to confidence. "Do I need to give you the secret code word so you know it's really me?"

"I think a kiss will do."

I slipped an arm around her waist, pulled her against me, and kissed her like I hadn't seen her in a week, instead of just twelve hours. "Do I pass the test?" I asked once I'd pulled back, trying to rein in my flush of excitement.

"Yeah, you do." Sophia exhaled loudly, apparently as affected by the kiss as I was. "God, you in a skirt suit and heels is hot as fuck. How did I not know this about you?"

I divested myself of handbag and gym bag. "Is this where I say I look hot as fuck in anything?"

"And out of anything," she quipped.

"Smooth." I hung my coat, then tugged her closer for a hug. "Hi," I murmured. "How was your day?"

Sophia's arms stole around me and she burrowed her face into my shoulder, muffling her words. "Productive. But I missed you. God you smell good," she added absently. "How did I also not know your perfume is incredible?"

"I had to keep *some* secrets from you," I teased, and immediately regretted my careless wording. I'd kept many secrets from her. Necessary ones, but secrets nonetheless. "I mean," I fumbled, "you know what I mean."

She pulled back, her expression softening. "Yes, I do." Sophia stretched up to kiss me again. "Why don't you go change out of those incredibly sexy work clothes and into something comfortable and still sexy, and I'll set the table."

"Deal."

I changed into sweatpants and a hoodie and pulled my hair out of its ponytail, leaving it free, and came back to find Sophia rummaging around my kitchen. She'd made herself so at home in my home, and I loved it. We moved easily around each other, pouring drinks and setting out Turkish takeout. I'd imagined this, in an abstract way, while we'd been in Florida. It had been so easy being close quartered together and I'd wondered if it would be as easy back in the real world, while resigning myself to the fact that it would never happen. But it was happening and it was easy and I loved it.

Once we'd each dished up platefuls of food, I started the dinner conversation with, "So I met the president today."

Sophia's forkful froze midway to her mouth. "Are you serious? Wow. That's...um..." Her eyebrows furrowed as she fumbled for words. Eventually she gave up, shook her head, and forked falafel and rice into her mouth.

I decided to help her out, and finished off her attempted sentence with, "Shitty and gross. I know."

She covered her mouth as she chewed, then burst into laughter, loud and rich, full of genuine amusement. "I was trying to find the right words to express yay for meeting the leader of the country but no-fucking-thanks for it being that one. Are you okay?" she teased.

"I'll live. But I did consider amputating my hand after he shook it." I ate the forkful of food I'd been carefully compiling, savoring the tartness of my salad against the rich *cig kofte*.

Sophia's eyes narrowed as she stared at my hand like it was radioactive. "I hope you washed that hand, or it's not touching me."

"I did," I confirmed. "So many times. Scrubbed, in fact."

"Good." Her forehead furrowed, and remained furrowed through another mouthful of food. "Why exactly did you meet the president?"

There was no way I could tell her that he had basically made a personal visit to intimidate me. That he was incensed about someone blowing the lid off the Kunduz intelligence. "Work stuff," I said airily, then busied myself tearing my flatbread into small pieces and adding a dollop of *baba ghanoush* to each portion.

If Sophia suspected that our sojourn in Florida was linked to the president's visit, she didn't let on. Despite the time we'd spent together, we were still in the getting-to-know-you phase, learning new things about each other every day. And though I would say confidently that I knew her, I couldn't add *very well*. Yet. But I did know that she had very little guile, and I trusted myself enough to read her expressions. And trusted her to tell me what she thought or felt. Which she usually did.

That guilelessness was part of what made having to lie to her, or rather, distort the truth, so hard. I'd done it a fair bit in those early days. Early days... It felt like a lifetime ago, though it was only a month. Every time I'd told a mistruth, or an outright lie, I felt a stab of guilt and had to remind myself that not only was it necessary because of my job, but that I was protecting her. That which she did not know, could not harm her. But lying to Sophia always felt a bit like shooting Bambi's mom. I ate my bread and had to force it down around the dry, tight lump in my throat.

After another mouthful, and a sigh of food contentment, Sophia asked, "So, what's he like in person?"

"Shorter, more beady-eyed, and far more disgusting than on TV or in photos. Bad breath and he wears way too much cologne, so in addition to all that, being near him is like choking."

"So he's worse than what we thought. I'm shocked," she deadpanned.

"Exactly." I pushed kofte, mixed pickles, and rice around my plate and after a few moments realized I should eat instead of play. My mom's voice echoed in my head, exasperated and tired. *Alexandra Elizabeth, if you were meant to play with food you'd eat your dinner on the playground.* A bunch of random things made their way onto my fork and after a moment of deliberation, to my mouth.

"How was your day?" I asked once I'd swallowed.

"You already asked me that, babe," Sophia said gently.

Oh, right. I had indeed asked, during our initial "Hey, honey, I'm home and how was your day?" exchange. "Ah, yeah. Sorry. I'm, uh… just…really interested in what you did today?" I offered a sheepish smile.

My sheepish smile was met with a knowing one. "Like I said, I had a productive day. There was a happy client and an annoying client and a new client."

"That's good. Great. Sorry," I added after realizing how dense I sounded. "Guess I'm a bit spaced out."

"Meeting a dickweed of the highest caliber will do that," she said seriously. "Oh, I did talk to my parents this afternoon, so that's something moderately interesting."

"How are they? How's your dad?"

"He's fine. Mom said he'd been having some nightmares about being locked up, taken away from us and never seeing his family again. But they've been talking to a therapist, so I think he'll be okay."

"I'm so sorry, Sophia. I never meant for that to happen." I'd apologized so many times but it always felt so hollow. To force me into finally giving myself up, the government had taken her father away from his family and threatened him with deportation to Mexico. How could you express enough regret for being responsible for something as horrific as that?

"I know you didn't. It's okay, all over now." She cleared her throat. "Speaking of that. Um, you met the president but I might have something a little scarier for you."

"What's that?"

"Meeting my parents? And the rest of my family?" Her tentative smile grew bolder. "Mom has officially invited you to Thanksgiving."

"Oh. Uh, I've never done that before. Met the parents, that is. I've done Thanksgiving, obviously." I sipped a small mouthful of water that did nothing to ease my dry throat. So I tried a larger mouthful of wine, which was marginally more helpful. "But Thanksgiving sounds great. I'd love to meet them," I said with genuine enthusiasm.

Sophia exhaled, her shoulders dropping. The relief was evident in everything from her posture to her expression to the soft breathiness of her voice. "Great, that's really great. They keep asking about you and dropping hints about meeting you. When I told them about your parents, and how you hung out at home by yourself with television and a cheese board last Thanksgiving, Mom nearly cried."

"A solo wine and cheese board adventure is a legitimate way to spend Thanksgiving." Last year had been my first Thanksgiving alone after my parents' death, though it hadn't honestly felt all that different to my usual Thanksgivings with them. Their motto was "Everything in Moderation," even love, and Thanksgiving was just like any other day, except with different food and more stress from my mom.

"Oh I agree, except I think shared bottles and cheese boards are better."

"Then why don't we share a bottle of wine and a cheese board and find out?"

Sophia grinned. "Deal."

Despite our banter, there was a niggle of discomfort I couldn't shake. I ate more of my dinner, using the time to cause a break in the conversation so I could redirect it. After a minute, I quietly asked, "Do they know the whys of your dad being detained?"

She paused and I saw her nervous swallow. "No. As far as they know, it was a random mistake with Immigration. They don't need to know the truth, or even a variant of it. It would lead down a whole road of explanations and questions that neither of us will be able to answer. Me, because I don't really know the answers, and you, because you just can't tell them the truth." She turned her wineglass ninety degrees then turned it back again. "We both know you didn't intentionally do something that made it happen, and he's fine, and that's enough for me."

Her simple forgiveness made it easy to sweep aside the fact that things might not have been so easily resolved for her family. "Okay, then I'll stop worrying about meeting your parents." I reached toward her and left my hand resting palm up on the table.

Sophia didn't hesitate, slipping her hand into my palm and curling her fingers around mine. "They're going to love you, I promise."

I was glad she was so certain. "And I'm sure I'll love them too."

Part of Sophia's evening ritual included the Primetime news at nine p.m., which, ironically, was how I'd ended up figuring out VP Berenson's connection to the Kunduz attack. We watched the usual, nothing-special updates for almost ten minutes before an ad break was cut short. The anchor looked like someone had rushed up to her desk and slapped her during the ads. Oh. I sat up a little straighter, having a good idea of why her composure had changed. She took a deep breath, and the words I'd been waiting weeks to hear spilled out.

"Breaking news out of the White House tonight. In shocking and unprecedented scenes, Vice President Randolf Berenson has been arrested. Just moments ago, the vice president was escorted, in handcuffs, from his home in Washington, DC. It's unclear exactly what charges have been laid, but a spokesperson for the FBI has said the following."

Cut to a crisp late-thirties woman, who looked like a poster child for government law enforcement, stepping up to a lectern. "After a thorough investigation, we have sufficient evidence to arrest the vice president, Randolf Berenson, this evening. As this is an ongoing investigation, that is all we are at liberty to divulge. Thank you."

Cut to a reporter standing in front of a throng by the White House fence. She nodded then raised her microphone, looking like she'd just scored the biggest newsbreak of her career, which she had. "Though the actual charges are yet to be confirmed, our sources say that Berenson, the president's long-term political ally, allegedly accepted personal donations from Russian-affiliated sources in exchange for under-the-table munitions, and insider information about our military capabilities and intelligence agencies. If these allegations are true, this shocking crime will send ripples through Congress, US security and intelligence organizations, the entire country, and our allies.

"The White House Press Secretary has issued a statement that the president and vice president are cooperating fully with the investigation, and stresses emphatically that the president was completely unaware of the events that led to these charges. A White House press briefing has been scheduled for nine a.m. tomorrow morning, and it is expected that Vice President Berenson will resign soon after.

"I'm sure every American citizen is now wondering, as I am, just how deep does this betrayal go? Did the Vice President of the United States, a man trusted to uphold our values and ensure our safety, sell State secrets to Russia? Are we safe in our homes, in our jobs, on our vacations? Is a world war imminent? Stay tuned as we bring you live updates, or follow this incredible story as it unfolds, on our app or website."

The picture faded, replaced by an infographic scrolling updates along the bottom of the screen as the studio anchor came back on. She shook her head disbelievingly. "Again, breaking news from Washington tonight, the vice president has been arrested after allegedly accepting monetary donations from Russia. Stay with us for the most up-to-date news on this unbelievable story affecting every single American, as well as our allies abroad."

Someone had leaked the Russia connection. Interesting.

I muted the television then turned to Sophia. Time to have a conversation about Berenson, and peripherally—my role in all this. She was utterly motionless. So motionless that I gently nudged her. "Are you all right, sweetheart?"

Slowly, she rotated on the couch to face me. "I…I'm…Oh my god. What the actual fuck? Russia? Is this treason? I…it's…this…is…" She trailed off splutteringly, like a car running out of gas and coasting to a stop.

"Yeah," I agreed. "What the fuck, right?" A little squirmy excitement overrode my caution. "Do you remember how, before I left Florida, I told you to keep an eye on the news? That if anything big happened, that it was related to why I'd had to hide?"

Sophia still looked dumbfounded. She shook her head disbelievingly before her eyes found mine. "Yeah…?"

I raised my eyebrows, pressing my lips together as I inclined my head toward the television, hoping she'd connect the dots I could never explain.

She nodded, then suddenly stopped nodding. Her mouth fell open. "This…*this* is what you were trying to keep safe?" Her voice broke with disbelief. "*This* is what you were trying to work out that whole time we were in Florida?"

"Mmm." There. Not an outright yes but the inflection in my answer certainly indicated a big fat "YES!"

"Fuck. Oh my *god*. This is huge." She gaped. "*You* did this?"

"Some of it," I quickly corrected her. "I just…happened to have it handed to me to investigate but I didn't know this was what it was in the beginning."

"How? How did you even—" She held up both hands. "No, I know you can't tell me. And yes, I know the rules of 'never say anything' and 'I can't know the full story' still apply here." She took my hand, turning it over, studying it like she was trying to figure out how my hand, my body, my brain, had figured out the secrets hidden in intelligence that, on the surface, seemed so innocuous. "How the hell did you not have a complete breakdown?"

Shrugging, I said, "Because you were with me. You kept me sane, reminded me why I was fighting so hard. I already told you that," I added gently.

She fish-out-of-watered again then finally snapped her mouth closed.

I lightly touched her cheek. "Are you sure you're okay? You seem a little stunned. Do you need something?"

"No, I'm fine. Just shocked. And a million other things. And you're one hundred percent forgiven for lying and manipulating to get me to come along with you for protection. Fully."

"You mean I wasn't already?" I teased, still hating the reminder of what I'd done to get her to stay with me, even though I'd justified it a million times as necessary for the greater good.

Sophia wrinkled her nose, but her eyes crinkled too. "You were about…ninety-eight percent forgiven. Like I told you, it was hard for me to be butthurt when I knew you were doing something important for the security of the country—something *super* important I now know—but there was still a niggle at the back of my mind."

"Ninety-eight percent? Honestly, that's more forgiven than I expected at this point after our adventure." I leaned over and kissed her. "And I know. I hope you can make it to one hundred percent forgiven for real at some stage, but I'll understand if you can't." The level of manipulation and betrayal I'd engaged in to get her to come with me, to keep Them away from me, was monumental. And though she understood the why of it now, as much as someone could while not being told the full truth, it was still a huge emotional hurdle to overcome.

Sophia smiled knowingly, though it only lasted a few seconds before she seemed to remember what she'd just learned. "Fuck," she said again, this one ten times more incredulous than her first. "*This* is what your job is?"

Laughing, I assured her, "No, this was an anomaly."

"Russian influence," Sophia breathed. "Holy shit. Do we need to worry about like…spies and all that stuff?"

"No, sweetheart. The people who take care of that sort of thing are all over it. You don't need to worry about anything like that."

She shuddered. "I knew I hated the VP for a reason other than him being one of the world's worst humans. I just…I thought that thing you worked on was something like you'd found some new terrorist group or something. But this is *huge*. You protected us from this. From him."

I shrugged, suddenly feeling embarrassed about my role in Berenson's resignation. "I just did my job."

Sophia rolled her eyes. "Modesty doesn't suit you, babe. You know why?"

"Why?"

She gently cupped my face. "Because you really are Super Lexie."

CHAPTER FIVE

Getting some As for my many Qs

My unsecured work phone rang at 9:12 a.m., startling me out of reading emails. I hadn't had a call on that phone since my parents died, and when I saw Sophia's number on the digital screen, I felt a surge of warmth. What a wonderful distraction. I snatched up the handset. "Hey, you. Miss me already?"

"Hiii," she breathed. "I'm so sorry to bug you at work, I know you're kind of incommunicado during the day, but Mom is having a minor Thanksgiving freakout and has demanded I get her answers regarding you immediately. Apparently she's been up since before dawn, fretting."

I pointed out, "If I was truly incommunicado, I wouldn't have given you my work number, would I?" And oh dear, Thanksgiving freakout relating to me.

"True," Sophia mused. "They don't worry about people tracing these numbers?"

"Nobody can trace these numbers," I said instantly, laughingly. "Trust me. And I think Thanksgiving emergencies qualify as a genuine reason to call me at work, and talking to you is a nice interruption to my morning. What's up exactly?"

"Mom needs to know *right now* if you want something like Tofurky, or is there another vegetarian thing you like for Thanksgiving? Sorry, I told her it wasn't important and it could wait, but she insisted because she'll need to do a cooking test-run and then come up with plans B and/or C if A doesn't work."

"Oh, shit. No, no, don't make her do anything special for me," I begged. "Really. I'll just gorge on all the sides and stuff. I've rarely met a Thanksgiving side I didn't love."

There was a pause before her dubious, "Are you sure?" At my sound of assent, Sophia agreed, "Okay, hon. But I'll tell her or Camila to make sure there's a tasty vegetarian gravy. Nobody should be without gravy at Thanksgiving."

"You're the sweetest. Thank you."

"I know I am. Okay, second item of importance. What's your favorite Thanksgiving dessert?"

"You really have to ask? All of them," I laughed. "I love every dessert, Thanksgiving or not."

"I knew you had a baby sweet tooth but I didn't realize you were Thanksgiving dessert obsessed."

"Everything is worthy of obsession at Thanksgiving, even things you'd eat at any other time," I said seriously, smiling when she laughed. "What should I bring?" I asked. The holiday was in nine days. Plenty of time to figure out something to wow my new girlfriend's family, one of whom was a chef at a fancy French restaurant. No pressure.

"Just your lovely, personable, charming self. Mom has a strict policy of doing everything herself like a madwoman. It's kind of her thing."

"Her and my mom would have gotten along well then. Mine was the same, except she always acted like Thanksgiving was as stressful as a bomb disposal, despite there only being three of us. Thanksgiving memories aren't among my favorites," I admitted.

"I'm sorry." Sophia's voice softened. "We'll make new memories, together, and they'll be epic."

"That sounds like a promise," I murmured.

"It is," she assured me.

I was about to go gooey when the ten-minute reminder of my meeting with Derek popped on the screen. "Sophia, I'm sorry, but I have a meeting to get to."

"Sure," she said easily. "Have a good day."

"You too. Love you."

Silence.

Long silence.

Finally she spoke. "Okay." Her shock at what I'd said seeped through the phone in that one word.

Great. I'd shocked her. "Okay," I echoed brightly, trying to ignore how idiotic I felt. I didn't want to take back what I'd said, I just wished I'd said it to her in person first. "See you tonight." I hung up, and would have melted under my desk in mortification if not for my important meeting with Derek. I had a lot of questions, and it was time for a lot of answers.

The moment I knocked, Derek summoned me inside his office. I made sure the door was securely closed then sat in the old chair on the other side of his desk and got comfortable. Derek dropped heavily into his rolling leather chair, taking a moment to settle himself. His expression relaxed as he watched me watching him. "You have no idea how happy I am to see you back at work, Martin."

"You have no idea how happy I am to be back at work. Speaking of, am I going to get to do some actual *work*? Or am I being held on the outer rim for some reason?"

"You're not being held on the outer rim," he said immediately. "But we thought you might appreciate a few days to reacclimate."

I shook my head emphatically. "Hell no. Throw me in, coach. To the deep end. I'm ready."

Both Derek's eyebrows shot up as he leaned forward to rest his forearms on his blotter. "Are you sure?"

"Yes," I said firmly. "I don't need to reacclimate. It's not like I've been gone a year. I'm fine, mentally, emotionally, and physically. Cross my heart, I swear."

He nodded and made a note on the pad currently fighting for space with mugs, folders, pens, and an abnormal number of broken pencils. Good to see some things never changed. "All right then." Derek paused, settling back in his chair. "Sorry about yesterday, I tried to keep you out of it, but the president insisted."

"Of course he did." A look of shared dislike passed between us, then it seemed we both decided we didn't want to waste any more breath on the president.

"I would like you to talk to someone about what happened with the intel, and in Florida and after, but I'm sure you understand how that's proving difficult. And as you know, Halcyon won't be providing a therapist."

"Yeah, I get it." Halcyon Division had always seemed rather bare-bones to me. No medics, shrinks, or anything like that—just the agents, like me, collecting information and disseminating it to those who ran Halcyon. The Division probably lacked support staff because being physically injured was rare, and we all worked in other jobs—like intelligence—where we had access to psych consults if needed. Though, psych sessions where you omitted the part about being an agent in a secret government division felt a little pointless. What could I say? "Oh yeah, I'm super stressed about this thing that happened but unlike with my agency job, I can't even allude to it because hardly anyone knows about Halcyon Division. What's Halcyon Division, you ask? Can't tell you."

"You can always talk to me if you need to," Derek said gently.

"I know, thanks. I will if I suddenly start feeling squirrelly about things. It's just…it is what it is. Not something I ever thought I'd be involved with, but it's part of the job, right? Well, part of one job," I added with a wry smile.

"That's true. But the offer's still on the table, any time."

"Thanks."

"You…are important. I've not been privy to *why* exactly you're important, but Lennon expressed it explicitly. You are to be protected, at almost any cost."

Wow. I'm so special. I crossed my legs and relaxed into the upholstered chair that had probably been put in this office during Nixon's time in the White House. "Is it something aside from my charming personality and incomparable skills as both an ops officer and analyst that makes me important?" After the 2017 incident, I'd moved from being an ops officer—collection of intelligence through human sources—to an analyst—analyzing that intelligence. And I was very good at both my jobs. But I didn't think that was the golden ticket it now seemed to be.

"I'm not sure," he said, and I believed him.

"Right. Cryptic. But I'm glad my importance kept me out of prison."

Derek raised his hands. "If I knew and could tell you what it's actually about, I would."

"I know. I'll just bask in my self-importance for a while."

He smiled. "Don't you usually do that? Anyway, how're you feeling? Injuries healing up okay?"

"Mhmm. All fine, as confirmed by an exhausted ER doctor the day after you picked me up. Nothing serious or lasting, thankfully. I'm almost back to one hundred percent."

"Good." He dropped his hands to rest on his belt buckle. "So… what do you want to know about what happened?"

"Everything," I said emphatically. "How and why Halcyon secured my release, because I was under the impression Lennon would rather burn me than bring Halcyon into the light. How you managed to bury this so I kept my security clearance and my job. Why you never told me you were Halcyon. Just…like, all of it."

His mouth quirked at my rambling. "Where do you want me to start?"

"Anywhere. Just explain some things to me, please. Or explain it all, if you can."

"You still have your clearance and your job because Halcyon intervened and insisted upon it. Despite the confusion, and the White House thinking you'd taken the files, Halcyon obviously knew you hadn't stolen intelligence, and word from them was good enough to make this whole thing go away."

"I see. I'm starting to think Halcyon is more powerful than I'd imagined." I mean, any organization that could free a declared-treasonous prisoner (I really wasn't treasonous) who was about to be locked up forever, return revoked security clearance, and basically wipe away a week's worth of events was pretty high up in my book.

He nodded. "You already know they have the power to remove anyone from office, even the president. And if they say you are needed, that you're to keep your clearance and your job, then that's the end of it."

"Okay, but, I mean, they kind of left me hanging in the beginning there, because the president's lackeys kept chasing me. Why? Why didn't the president drop it if Halcyon was in the background, and why didn't Halcyon give me somewhere safe to work through the intel, instead of making me run around like a rabbit who's spotted an eagle?"

"The president didn't drop it because he's a stubborn, idiotic ass with small-man syndrome, and you embarrassed him. Once you'd uncovered the connections, he only backed down because Lennon reminded him of Halcyon's power. I'm sure Halcyon didn't want to tip their hand too early and show the president they were involved and the Protocol had been put into effect. And I don't know why you weren't given somewhere safe to work, but I can only assume that they didn't want you in the office where what you were doing could be monitored."

As far as I was aware, the Halcyon Protocol to remove a high-ranking member of government had only been enacted three times before this instance. Four times in over sixty years. And because Halcyon had the power to remove presidents, presidents tended to follow Halcyon orders. "It wasn't fun," I reminded him.

"I know."

"I had to pretend I was a traitorous idiot. Sophia thought that's what I was. Not a great look when you're trying to connect with someone."

Derek smiled. "Doesn't seem to have harmed things," he said matter-of-factly.

"No," I sighed. "I think we're okay." Except for my embarrassing, nonreciprocated, ILY verbal slip before. "Thankfully she's smart, smart enough to see through some of the lies I had to tell her. And now she knows the basics of how we got here, it's a little better. Plus, like she said—it's hard to be mad at someone when they need you to help them save the world."

"That's true," Derek agreed. "And you did help save the world, Martin. Imagine where we'd be if we hadn't found this and worked it through to its conclusion. With a Russian-backed vice president making decisions against our best interests. That's a nightmare scenario right there."

"Yeah, I know. I'm proud of what I did, even though it was one of the most stressful things ever, and I've been held hostage in a foreign country and beaten and stabbed," I drawled.

"Thanks for the reminder," Derek said flatly.

"You're welcome," I answered sweetly. "I think we should give it a name or something, like…The Berenson Boo-Boo or…Lexie's Big Mystery Solve, instead of just calling it 'the intelligence,' because that could be anything, and this one was special."

"You really are one of the strangest people I know. Let's just call it the Kunduz Intelligence because that's where it originated from."

"Works for me." I traced my fingertips over the pattern on the armrest of the chair. "I've been wondering, are you also my boss at Halcyon?"

"Technically, yes. Though, as you know, there's less of a hierarchy there than here."

"Goddammit," I griped. "Just once, it'd have been nice to be the boss. In that vein, I've always thought it weird you came here after I left field ops. Was that because of the Division and my…importance? Did you know I was Halcyon?"

"Halcyon suggested it, and it'd been in my mind for a while. Roberta wasn't thrilled with me being in the field or the military, so it was an easy decision. And no, I didn't know you were a Division agent until about a year ago."

"Admit it, you just really like me and that's why you followed me here."

"Caught me," Derek deadpanned.

"If you're Halcyon, what was with the whole 'I'm disappointed in you' speech at the golf course when you came down to Florida to debrief me?" He'd really made me believe that he was nothing more than a boss who suspected I'd stolen intel and run with it. And I'd been both devastated and furious at his reaction to what I hadn't really done, like he'd actually thought me capable of doing such a thing.

"We felt it in your best interests to not give you too much new information at once. Your focus was to be on keeping that intelligence secure and unraveling it without arousing suspicion. I was against not telling you my allegiance, but Lennon insisted that telling you I was Halcyon too early might put you off the course you were on, the course where you were figuring out the truth."

"I see. Well, I suppose it all worked out in the end."

"It did." Derek leaned forward. "I'm proud of you, Alexandra."

"Wow. My name. You really are proud of me." I pretended to wipe away a tear. He'd only ever used it a handful of times before. "What about my rescue? Seemed a bit black-ops and over the top to me."

He laughed. "I imagine it did seem that way. It was mostly for the benefit of those transporting you. Easier to explain away a 'black-ops' rescue or abduction than having you freed and allowed to walk out of a facility on your own."

My eyebrows shot up. "Really?"

"Yes. People aren't freed from places like that, Martin. Like I said, we had to move before you were sent somewhere off the grid."

"And you think it's less conspicuous for the van to have been involved in an accident while transporting me and me to have 'escaped,' than to pretend I had a good lawyer or I was innocent? You don't think they'll be worried that there's no news about escaped me?"

"No. Because you were at that facility under the radar, so no news is not unusual. They will forget about you and move on to the next person they have to detain."

"Okay. I just didn't expect to be in my own action movie."

"Halcyon does whatever is necessary to achieve its sworn objectives. This was what Lennon wanted." He raised his eyebrows in an unspoken "And what Lennon wants, Lennon gets."

"Wow, okay, Mr. Halcyon Recruitment Brochure. I get it, but it still fucking hurt."

Derek grimaced. "Lennon said you would be safely restrained, that he'd had confirmation of that fact. His instructions were very specific. You were to be alive and able to work."

Alive and able to work. Not alive and unharmed? I filed that away, along with the fact that someone had passed along incorrect information about my *restraints*. "But broken bones and stuff were fine?" I asked dryly, annoyed, and onto it like a dog with a bone. "Because I wasn't restrained, except for handcuffs and chains on my ankles, and I gotta tell you—they aren't nearly as good as a seat belt."

"I'm sorry," he said again.

I decided to let it go for now. "Did Halcyon leak the Russian connection?" News of Berenson's arrest had reached saturation point overnight, and the swirl of rumors about his ties to Russia was growing bigger and bigger. "Because I thought they'd keep that under wraps to avoid a national panic."

"Yes," he said, raising both hands, palms up. "I don't know why or how it was leaked exactly, but we both know that nothing they do is without meticulous thought and planning."

Like my breakout accident. Sorry, right, letting it go… "So what happens now? I just…wait around until someone tells me why I'm so important?"

"Yup," he agreed cheerfully. "Back to work, back to your life. And trust me, I'm just as intrigued as you are about this whole 'Lexie's immense value' thing."

"Lexie's Value. Sounds like a Lifetime movie."

He rolled his eyes at me. Guess it didn't sound like something he'd want to watch.

We'd moved to Sophia's apartment for the next few days, and when I let myself in after work, I was surrounded by the incredible smell of her cooking. Or, as I realized when I saw there were takeout bags from Manger on the counter, Sophia reheating someone else's cooking while she crafted a side salad with the help of what looked like a laminated instruction sheet. That made more sense, given Sophia was horrible at cooking (her words, not mine). I shed my work things and, rolling up the sleeves on my blouse, slipped into the kitchen.

"This looks fancy," I observed as I stepped behind her, lightly resting my hands on her waist.

"Camila put together a meal for us. My job is to make a salad, according to these very specific, Sophia-proof instructions." She turned her head slightly to kiss me. "Hi," she said softly.

"Hi. So, what's for dinner? Aside from salad." I squinted at the laminated sheet, but without my glasses, couldn't quite make it out.

"Pumpkin and goat cheese quiche, which I just need to reheat."

"Wow. Yum. What's the occasion?" I asked as I pulled a chilled bottle of sauvignon blanc from the fridge.

"The vice president's resignation," she said easily.

"Oh." Yeah, it was a big deal. Berenson had announced he was resigning—hard to be VP when you're in jail—during the White House press briefing, but of course had left out details of the whole Russian lackey dealio. Unfortunately, we didn't get to see him being handcuffed again and dragged off, but I'd gleefully imagined it. The president had stepped up to announce his regret at losing such a valued person—no mention of traitorous behavior, of course—and introduced his new vice president, who actually seemed to be a decent human. I wondered if Halcyon had anything to do with that, and if the new VP had been *suggested* by them as Berenson's replacement to temper the president.

Sophia turned slightly to face me. "I'm kidding. The occasion is us."

I swallowed. Asking her chef sister to create a dinner for us implied there was something special going on. Was she building up to some big declaration? If so, it kind of made my accidental "I love you" seem pretty fucking lame. Oh god, was Sophia going to propose? Shit. After a month? Shit. Did I want to get married? Sure. To her? Maybe. Now? No. Shit. I sucked in a deep breath and reassured myself that she wasn't going to propose, she was just being sweet.

I reached up to the cabinet beside the fridge for a couple of wineglasses. The love elephant wasn't just in the room—it was wandering around, swinging its trunk, breaking shit and crapping everywhere. I poured us each a glass and drank a healthy gulp of mine before setting it down out of reach so I wouldn't chug the rest.

"So, um, about that whole 'I love you' thing…" I trailed off, not sure where to go from there. I mean, the other night she'd let slip that she'd fallen in love with me, right? So my declaration shouldn't be a big deal? I'd been hoping she'd bring it up and I could just follow on and explain, rather than having to initiate the conversation. But she remained stubbornly silent on the matter.

"What about it?" she asked without turning around.

Even from behind her, I could tell she wasn't tense, but the fact she was refusing eye contact made me nervous. "I meant it. But yeah, it kind of just slipped out when I thought I'd say it first in person."

"Oh? I admit, it surprised me," she said lightly, and I caught a hint of amusement.

"Right. Okay. Well…" Are you going to say it back or have I moved too fast and do I need to get my shit out of here or what? "It's totally weird now. But I just wanted you to know."

"I do know, thank you. Because you told me this morning."

Nothing else? No? "Okay. I'm…just going to take a shower. How long until dinner's ready?"

She picked up her instruction card, which even seemed to have chopping diagrams for the salad. "I have to check the quiche in ten minutes and rotate the dish because Camila says my oven sucks. Then another ten minutes."

"Great. I'll…be back."

The elephant stopped stomping long enough for us to eat an excellent dinner, clean up, and take the remains of the bottle to the couch. But once we sat down, the stupid pachyderm started wandering around again.

"Should I not have said it?" I asked, picking at the edge of my cherry-red nail polish. I was *sure* she felt the same as I did, because even without her "fell in love" declaration in bed on Sunday, she showed me every day that she loved me, was in love with me. So why did it feel so weird for me to have said an official ILY when she hadn't yet?

"No. You definitely should have said it," she said, glancing at me before returning her attention to the television.

"Okay, but—"

She cut me off with a fierce kiss that pushed me backward until I was lying on the couch. Sophia quickly settled on top of me, her thigh between mine and her hands working their way under my top. My mood shifted from uncertain to horny in seconds when her hands cupped my breasts, thumbs brushing my nipples. The burn of desire was so intense I was stunned into immobility.

I lay on my back and stared up at her, taking in features that were already burned into my mind's eye. The full arches of her eyebrows over soulful brown eyes, the high curves of cheekbones, those lips… full, soft, sensuous. Sophia's expression felt like a reflection of my feelings, and my anxiety about what I'd let slip fell away.

As if she'd sensed me give in and let it go, her hands stilled and her face relaxed, a lazy smile curving her mouth. Then she dipped her head and kissed me like she hadn't seen me in years. Fierce, hungry, and full of pent-up emotion. I opened my mouth to her, met her tongue with mine as we kissed in a needy clash of lips and teeth and tongue.

There were no words as we wrestled out of our clothes and threw them to the floor, both of us desperate to connect skin-to-skin. When she settled on top of me again, I spread my legs to give her room to nestle between my thighs. I raised my hips, desperately seeking friction and Sophia ground her hips into me. She knew exactly where I needed her mouth on my neck, where I most wanted her touch on my body, and when she lifted herself up on one arm, angling herself to push her fingers deep inside me, I choked out a hoarse, "Yes. Please, yes."

She fucked me deep, but not hard, and every stroke had my arousal spiraling higher and higher. I wanted to bury myself in her and never come up for air. Sophia grunted when I bit her lower lip and I soothed my accidental wound with a gentle lick. I slung my arm around her neck, my other hand moving between us, past obstacles of writhing body parts, until I found her wet and wanting.

Sophia moaned against my neck and the steady, knowing stroke of her fingers became erratic. She came first, and the unmistakable gasping and panting, her hips grinding into my hand had heat and excitement rushing through me. "Lexie…" The way she said my name, low and almost moaning, sent me tumbling over the edge after her.

I pulled her closer, my hands slipping for purchase on her sweaty back and we lay on the couch, breathing steadying and limbs trembling. She shuddered and I wrapped her tighter in my embrace. "Are you cold?" I mumbled against her neck, stroking the hair falling over her shoulder.

"No," she assured me. "You keep me warm." After an eternal pause, she whispered, "Lexie?"

"Yes?" I whispered back, wondering why we were whispering.

She raised herself up slightly to look at me. Her entire face relaxed a moment before she smiled brilliantly. "I love making you squirm."

"I know you do," I said breathlessly. I'd been squirming since she'd pushed me back on the couch with the ferocity of her kiss.

"Alllll day…" she singsonged.

I frowned at her. "What—"

She dipped her head, brushing a soft kiss over my lower lip. "I'm sorry, I shouldn't have teased, but watching you wrestling with what you said has been amazing."

"Noooo, that's so unfair."

"Maybe a little," Sophia conceded. Her eyes burned with desire, lust…love. "I love you too. I knew I did from the moment I first woke up beside you, and every moment since then has only made me more certain of how I feel…"

CHAPTER SIX

No thanks, emphatically not, no way, no how

I'd just brought my cup of tea back to my desk when I was pinged with an alert on the intra-office messaging system.

DAWOOD: *Meeting in my office at 0930. Please confirm.*

Two personal meetings in two days. Lucky me. I quickly responded, wondering why the late notice for this one.

AEMARTIN: *Consider this my confirmation.*

A quick glance at the time told me I had twenty minutes to drink my tea, and complete my usual post-workout and post breakfast-at-work tasks before my presence was required in Derek's office. Again. Hopefully this meeting was about actual work instead of secret Halcyon business. My inbox was fuller than it had been yesterday, but still felt sparse.

I smoothed a hand over my still shower-damp hair as I opened a short intelligence brief I'd been sent. The lack of work, combined with the disconcerting and disgusting meeting I'd endured with the president on my first day back had me feeling antsy and out of sorts. And after my chat with Derek yesterday morning, I'd expected more normality. Maybe his assurance that all was cool wasn't as assured as he'd made out.

He'd told me everything that'd happened with Hadim's intelligence had been swept under a metaphorical rug, and I believed him. But maybe Derek wasn't as powerful as I'd thought. Whatever. There was nothing I could do about it, and driving myself nuts wasn't good for my mental health or my ability to do work—when I got work to do. Time to think of nicer things. Like…my impending Thanksgiving with Sophia's family. Okay, so maybe *impending* wasn't the right word.

In bed last night, Sophia had checked in with me again about Thanksgiving, and made me promise that I really didn't need a special vegetarian main. I'd stupidly blurted that I wanted to return her parents' hospitality and extend an invitation to them for dinner in a few weeks once things had settled back into a normal rhythm at work. Embarrassingly, it would be my first time hosting a dinner party type thing for a girlfriend's parents, but Sophia's assurances that she was sure they'd love to join us eased my discomfort. Sort of…

Look at me, so normal. Normal was not a word I'd ever applied to myself, but it actually felt pretty good in this instance. Since I'd met Sophia, I'd had so much normal, but she'd given me more than just normality—comfort, safety, love, trust… She'd made me feel that, despite my parents' indifference to showing affection or encouragement that wasn't related to me achieving something important, I was worthy of affection and encouragement and so much more.

I finished my tea, locked my computer workstation and checked my face in my compact. I looked exactly as a diligent and hardworking government employee should. So let me be hardworking, please…

Derek's office was a two-minute walk from my desk, through the maze of cubicles and convoluted hallways typical of our building. Expecting to be waylaid by coworkers along the way wanting to chat about a file or a briefing or something inane, I left at 9:23 a.m., was waylaid twice and arrived right on time. Ten points for punctuality. I rapped sharply on Derek's open door. "You wanted to see me, sir? Again? I feel special."

He'd been staring at the far wall—the one that had photos of his father with John Fitzgerald Kennedy when JFK was junior Massachusetts senator, and Derek's father one of his senior staffers—and when I spoke he startled and spun his chair around to face me. "Yes, come in."

I closed the door and sat opposite him, studying his expression. I couldn't recall the last time I'd seen him look so discomforted. A dozen possibilities ran through my mind, none of them good, and in a panicked blur, I asked, "Have they fired me? Did they change their mind?" No protection from my employer would mean a trial, more *debriefs*, fines, jail time, media attention, public scrutiny. Sophia and her family would probably be dragged back into the mess, only this time they'd know the reason why. Fuck.

Derek hastened to reassure me, "No, you haven't been fired."

"Ohhh," I breathed. Then I brightened, though my heart was still racing from runaway panic. "Well, all right then. So what's up?"

"I got a call first thing this morning. You've been reassigned."

"Oh." I un-brightened. A reassignment wasn't unexpected, and I wondered what dank basement they were going to send me to so I could read through transcripts for the rest of my working life. "Well then, I suppose I'll see you at the Christmas party or in the break room if they ever let me out of my dungeon."

"Alexandra." Again, that usage of my first name. He only ever did it when he was upset, uncomfortable, or emotional, and I'd heard it more in the last few weeks than in all the years I'd known him. "I'll get right to the point. You've been ordered on assignment out of the country. It's a pilot program and they want someone with your expertise to trial it. You'll be in the first team to go to this location under these directives. The program's primary function will be consolidating and filtering intelligence—weeding out bad or unhelpful intel before it comes to us—and also providing immediate onsite assessments for the ops officers in the region. You'll liaise mostly with the ops team, but also with this office as usual."

"I'm sorry. What?" Of course I'd heard him, but my brain was processing a million emotions and those three words were all I could manage.

"You've been reassigned into the field," he said simply.

"I—No, but I didn't apply to change roles or departments. They can't just move me to a completely different role in a different office, *overseas*, without my consent." I took a deep breath. "And besides, this whole thing seems like a pointless extra step to me. We analysts are perfectly capable of sorting useful from non-useful here in the agency offices, and since when have ops officers needed on-the-spot analysis?"

"I didn't make this decision, Martin. It's out of my hands."

I swallowed hard. "How long is it for?"

"Six months."

"And which out-of-your-hands person made this decision?"

"Those in charge," he evaded.

The rush of nausea was so intense I had to take a moment to get my stomach under control. "Those in charge," I repeated, my voice breathy and weak. "Like, *hypothetically*, the president who's angry at me for just doing my job and finding out he was hiding the vice president's dirty chemical-weapon-testing secret and that maybe he knew Berenson is in Russia's pocket? This screams pettiness and spite, so I know exactly who's behind it." The pettiest, most spiteful person I knew. The President of the United States.

Derek's stare was measured. "Careful," was all he said to my rant. "The official orders will be on your desk by the end of the day." He fiddled with his pen. Derek wasn't a fidgeter. "Do you have any questions?"

Only a zillion. "What if I say no?" The idea of going anywhere like where I'd been when I'd been held hostage set off a dozen alarm bells, each one ringing a different tune in harmony to make a song I called "No Fucking Way."

"You can't."

"Sure I can. No, I'm not going. I refuse this reassignment. There, I said it."

"Martin," Derek sighed. "You know the alternative. How do you look in an orange prison jumpsuit?"

"Okay then, at the very least, can I register my objection?" I fought to keep calm. Not only was ranting insubordinate as well as plain rude, it wasn't the right tactic here. "Please consider this a verbal objection, and I'll have my written to you once I see the documentation." I'd probably be disciplined. But at least I wouldn't be going back to a hostile area as a lesbian pretending to be a heterosexual tourist, teacher, nurse, Red Cross worker, or a dozen other false not-lesbian identities that would allow me to gather intel up close and personal and also be in a situation where I'd be taken hostage and—

Shut up, brain. Just shut up. Please, please shut up…

"Think about what you're saying." Derek's sigh was loud and slow, as if I were a dumb kid he'd already explained the same thing to a hundred times before. "Clearly they planned for your reticence, and they're ready for whatever you do. What do you think they'll do when you say 'no thank you, I'm not going and you can't make me'? Think, *really* think. You have two options. Accept this reassignment, or accept incarceration for an indeterminate period of time."

Jail or war zone. Neither option was a good choice. But at least I was guaranteed to come out of a government jail alive and unharmed. Assuming I ever got out. I closed my eyes and inhaled slowly, trying to find a neutral mental space so I could debate rationally. After a handful of deep breaths, I opened my eyes. "I thought mine was an unconditional release."

"You should know there's no such thing as 'unconditional.'"

So the president was a fucking liar. Color me not-shocked. "I'm not even an ops officer anymore. I'm an analyst. Office, not field. So I can't go. I'm going to call Lennon and ask him to intervene."

"I've already spoken with him about this. Halcyon won't intervene."

Suddenly, everything made perfect sense. "Right. Of course not. They won't risk showing their hand again, because they already bent the rules to pull me out of one *situation*. A situation *they* put me in, remember?"

"I know. But this is the way it is."

I tried another tactic. "Aside from the fact fieldwork isn't my job anymore, you know I'm no longer cleared to be in the field because of my incident." Hostage situations ending in beatings and multiple stab wounds tend to mess with a person's head and make them feel weird about returning to the situation that led to them being captured and assaulted. Such people are generally not considered a sound investment in a shaky market.

"I'm aware. Because it's only a temporary assignment, they've reviewed your file and cleared you for fieldwork." Though he relayed the facts calmly, Derek's expression was contorted with displeasure. Nice to know he was as unhappy as me about this development.

"What the fuck?" I spluttered. "I haven't even seen the shrink in the last two months. How the hell is this legal? You can't just suddenly say I'm doing a new job when I haven't consented or asked for it." The word *temporary* had stuck, and I couldn't help thinking it was temporary because I wouldn't be coming home… It would be a "clean" way to eliminate a troublesome embarrassment, taking what I knew about the administration with me.

"It's legal because they say it's legal. Everything from here on out is a consequence of your actions last month. I can't do a damned thing about it, and believe me—I'm as unhappy about it as you are. But it's over my head. You broke the rules, and technically the law, even if we ignore everything behind the scenes."

I leaned back in the chair, laid my arms on the armrests. "I have a theory."

"I'm all ears."

"They won't incarcerate me without provocation because they're still worried I have the intelligence ready to leak, even though I don't and I wouldn't. They won't fire me because Halcyon has basically forbidden it. So they're sending me to the hot zone where I'll be out of the way."

Derek's mouth had set into a thin line, and when he spoke it was forced through tight lips. "You're an incredible analyst, and you were an excellent ops officer, and they want you there because you'll do a good job setting up the bones of this program and ironing out the bugs."

"Bullshiiiit. They want me there because they're hoping I'll get killed in a drone strike or suicide bomb attack—unintentionally of course, just an innocent bystander who was sadly in the wrong place, at the wrong time—and then this problem that's tied to me will go away."

He looked nauseated and by his expression I could tell that he'd had the same thought. "The government doesn't make a habit of killing its citizens, especially not those involved in keeping us and our interests protected." He said no more on my morbid thought process. "Go, do your job, and come back. Without injuries this time."

Oh that one hurt. "Ouch. You make it sound like I intentionally got myself captured and held hostage and beaten, then stabbed six times," I snapped. "Just for the laughs."

He looked instantly contrite. "I'm sorry. I didn't mean it that way."

I felt bad for sniping at him, even though he'd deserved it, and softened my tone to assert, "This is ridiculous. Unprecedented."

"Well, you can consider it precedented." He looked to his computer monitor, and frowned. "You're also being assigned a partner for the duration."

Oh, right. *Team*. "Who?"

"I don't have that information yet. Someone from outside the office."

Working with a person I didn't even know sounded horrible. "Great?"

Derek's hold on his exasperation looked tenuous. "It's for your own good. As well as being someone to share the workload, they will be a support person for you."

"Great," I repeated. "So is it a support person as in someone to help me with my job and for me to lean on in stressful situations? Or is it someone to watch over me and make sure I don't do anything *silly?*"

He didn't answer. But his unmasked expression made it clear it was about thirty percent from column A, and seventy percent from column B. "Take some time to read over the assignment paperwork, and we'll meet again tomorrow and get the ball rolling on this."

"Derek," I quietly said and when he looked up, I reached over the desk to take his hand.

He stared at my hand as if were a thing he'd never seen before. "Yes?"

"I can't do this again, I can't go back to a place like that again. Please don't make me." My voice broke as I begged him and I felt the sting of tears, which I blinked away. I would not cry at work. "*Please. I can't do it.*" It was the first time I'd ever admitted such a thing to him, and the weakness of it felt awful but the honesty was liberating. "What does the president want? A public mea culpa? I'll do it. I'll do anything. I'll go on TV and lie about what I did if it soothes his ego. Just don't make me go back there, please. Please don't. *Please.*"

Derek's Adam's apple bobbed. "It's completely out of my hands, Alexandra. There's *nothing* I can do. And nothing Lennon can do. It's do *this*, or suffer *that*." The nuance was plain. Even Halcyon couldn't pull me out of this, even if they wanted to. He cleared his throat and when he finally met my gaze, he looked as if he was trying not to cry too. "I'm so sorry."

"So am I." There was nothing more to do or say, so I left his office, and hid myself in a locked cubicle in the ladies' room, crouching down with my back against the wall. I will not cry here, I chanted in my head. I will not cry here. I will not give that dickwad who leads the country the satisfaction. I will not cry here. I slumped back against the wall.

I mean…fuck. Just, fuck. I had no idea how to manage my mess of emotions, especially when I couldn't let them out here. How had this happened? Thirty minutes ago I'd been in lah-di-dah land, riding the wave of the prospect of work returning to normal and the joy of my going-awesomely relationship with a new girlfriend. Now I felt like someone had just run me over with a busload of sad and anxious. My brain finally caught up and looped back. One thought came to the forefront.

My girlfriend.

Shit. How the hell was I going to tell Sophia that my job was about to come between us again?

I sleepwalked through the rest of my day, unable—or maybe

unwilling—to process that I could be sent back to the place where I'd almost died. Obviously not that exact place, maybe not even that exact country or province, but hostile was hostile no matter how you sliced it. The reassignment paperwork arrived as promised, but it didn't explain much, just that I'd find out more at the meeting tomorrow morning assigned for that exact purpose. Great.

I called Sophia the moment I'd liberated my phone from the trunk of my car. When she answered, her voice was full of pleasure. "Hi, babe. You're done with work early?"

"A little, yeah. Hey, I know we were going to spend tonight apart, but would it be okay if we changed plans? Can you come around? I really want to see you, and I'd like to cook dinner for you." We'd spent every night together since I'd come back, and had tentatively agreed maybe we should spend a night apart and do boring personal things like laundry and housework.

Sophia laughed. "You read my mind. I didn't want to seem needy, but it feels wrong not seeing you at night, especially when I'm still adjusting to not seeing you during the day."

"It's not needy. It's normal and I love it." I started the ignition but didn't move, just sat in the car staring out the windshield at the impending sunset. "I promise a fabulous meal, great wine and excellent company."

"Sold," she said immediately. "When would you like me there?"

"Give me an hour? I just need to get home and take a shower before I start dinner."

"Done." She blew a kiss down the phone. "Can't wait to see you."

"Me too," I said quietly before I ended the call. I had to hang up quickly or I'd have blurted something about my news, and this was something she had to be told in person. The thought sent a flood of upset through my body. This was not going to be enjoyable. Big understatement there.

After a lightning-fast shower, I had time to pour myself a glass of red before starting on my old standby wow-factor-but-so-easy-to-make roasted mushroom gnocchi. Sophia arrived as I was pulling the tray from the oven. I rushed to meet her as she opened the door, kissed her quickly, and enjoyed that kiss so much I had to kiss her again. "Can you lock the door please," I called behind myself as I dashed back to the kitchen.

I had to dash, and not only because of dinner. If I lingered near her then I might break down right away. I wanted…no, *needed* some time with her to enjoy the calm before I had to tell her what was happening. Because once I told her, our lives would split again as they had in Florida—to "before she knew" and "after she knew" time. I wanted this normal time for as long as I could keep it, even if I knew everything was about to explode in our faces.

Sophia followed me at a more normal-person pace, flung her peacoat over the back of the high-top chair as she always did, and stood behind me, peering over my shoulder as I tossed spinach on top of the mushrooms and gnocchi. She slipped her arms around my waist, pressing herself to my back. After bestowing soft, lingering kisses to my neck, she said, "That smells so good. What is it?"

"Dinner," I answered, crumbling blue cheese over the top.

She swatted my stomach, then lightly slapped my ass. "Smart-ass." Sophia stole a sip from my glass, then with another ass pat—this one affectionate—left me to pour herself a drink. "Need a refill?" she asked, holding up the bottle of pinot noir.

"I'm good, thanks." Smiling, I added, "Even after your thievery."

"What's yours is mine, right?"

"I think that's only applicable for marriage."

"Are you proposing?" she shot back.

I almost choked on my, "Pardon?"

Sophia burst into a fit of giggles. When she could finally speak again, she hiccupped out, "The look on your face is priceless." She wiped under both eyes, then reached up to pull my face down for a kiss. "I'm messing with you. I don't think a month of dating puts us *quite* into marital territory, even by lesbian U-Haul cliché standards."

My heart rate slowly dropped toward its normal resting beats per minute. "Right. Of course. Don't mind me. Clearly I left my humor radar at the office."

"Clearly," she said, still smiling.

I popped the tray back into the oven. "Are you not into marriage?" Though I tried to make it sound like a casual query, it definitely came out sounding both hopeful and concerned.

"Of course I am. I want what my parents have, that gooey eye-rollingly sweet love that lasts forever." Her eyes softened. "What about you?"

"Sure. I mean my biggest marriage role models were Steven and Elyse Keaton from *Family Ties*, but it's always seemed like a good thing." Way to sound like an alien. Who the hell describes finding a person you want to tie yourself to legally, romantically, physically, and emotionally as *a good thing*? I cleared my throat, fighting down a powerful wave of embarrassment. "I didn't mean to imply you and me or anything like that now or soon or later or anything. I was just curious because we've never talked about it. That's all."

"No, we haven't," Sophia agreed amicably. Her smile turned mischievous. "How do you feel about kids?"

"Oh." I dropped the knife I was washing into the sink. "Fuck."

"Is that a fuck, no? Or a why the fuck did you just ask me about this?"

"It's a fuck, I just dropped a sharp knife. But no, I don't want kids." I carefully picked up the knife and resumed washing up. "I've never really considered myself maternal material."

"Why not?" she asked quietly. "I think you'd be an excellent parent."

Emotionally absent and having to lie to my kid? Sounds like a great way to bring up a child. Just ask my parents. I shrugged. "I don't know, I've just never thought about kids for myself. Never felt that great maternal desire. And I think I'm getting beyond the age where I'd want to have a child. I'll be like…sixty when they hit college." Glancing up, I met her eyes. "What about you?"

"Nah. I was maternal for about five minutes in my early twenties, but since then I've realized it's not for me."

"Good to know." Much to my relief, the oven timer interrupted a conversation that felt like it might stray into deep territory. One tough conversation was enough for the night, thank you. "Dinner's ready," I murmured.

She sidled up to me and slipped an arm around my waist, kissing the side of my neck. "Then let's eat."

Sophia declared dinner *so fucking tasty* and practically melted with glee when I Tupperwared the leftovers for her to take home in the morning ready for her lunch tomorrow. I added the dish to my mental shortlist for when her parents came for dinner. If they came. No, I should make something fancier. I swallowed nervously as I topped off our glasses. "Couch time?"

"You are the perfect woman. Fabulous meal, great wine, and now you want to snuggle?" She placed the lightest kiss at the edge of my mouth.

I made myself smile. "I try." We settled on the couch, and I raised my feet to rest against the edge of the coffee table. Tell her now? Wait a little? Wait a lot? No, waiting bad, forthrightness good. The sooner

I told her, the more time she'd have to process the news.

"Sophia?" I'd never had issues with communication before, not when it was information that I was clear to convey, but when I tried to say the words, they just…stuck.

She dipped her head, eyebrows furrowing. "What is it?"

"I, um…I—" A mouthful of wine helped unstick my tongue. Just say it, Lexie. It's not going to be any easier if you stall. "I've been temporarily reassigned. At work. To a new location. For six months."

The silence hung uncomfortably in the air. "Oh. Okay." Her face was impressively calm. "Where are they sending you? Are we going to have to do the long-distance thing?"

You could say that. Thousands of miles of long distance. I nodded. "I'm going back overseas."

Her face blanked, her complexion paling until she seemed as if she were about to pass out. I took her by the shoulders and shook her gently. "Sophia?" My hands moved up to her face, my thumbs caressing her cheeks.

"Where exactly?" she asked, her voice a hoarse whisper.

"I'm not exactly sure, but when I find out, I…can't tell you." After a quick pause, I added, "But I'm sure you can imagine a few options for where someone with my skill set might go."

"But…you only just finished that other thing. How can they send you overseas? I thought you said that's not your job anymore after the whole"—her hands flailed as she searched for the words—"hostage stabbing thing."

"I know," I said with calmness I didn't feel. "It's not my job. But it doesn't matter. I've been ordered to go somewhere, and I have to go." The delicious meal I'd made threatened a reappearance, and I had to inhale slowly to settle myself. I was not going to think about that dark, dangerous room.

Sophia's mouth worked open and closed before she spat out, "Fuck your fucking bullshit job!"

The venom in her voice was startling, and I let go of her.Quietly, I agreed, "You're right, it is fucking bullshit. But that fucking bullshit is what helps you to walk the streets safely, what keeps gas in your car, what helps you keep your freedom. So that's why I keep doing it."

"I don't care if you're saving the whole country yet again. I don't care. I want you to put *me* first, instead of everyone else." The corners of her mouth edged downward. "Why are you so annoyingly pragmatic?"

Smiling, I shrugged. "It's a flaw." It'd be fabulous to bury my head in the sand, but it wouldn't help, not in the long-term, big-picture scheme of things. And I didn't have two personas—professional and personal. I was who I was, all of the time. "I can't change what's happening so I may as well try to accept it. And I *have* to accept it." I swallowed hard. "Sophia...It's either accept this new assignment, or accept incarceration. One is for six months, the other is for maybe twenty or more years. It's a no-brainer, isn't it?"

"But, but...I don't understand." Her voice broke on that last word. "You did something incredible in Florida."

"Some people, people with power, don't think so."

She sagged, like she'd completely given up. I knew that feeling. Her voice dropped to quiet, almost childlike. "Is it dangerous?"

For the briefest fraction of a second, I considered lying to her and saying no, not at all, of course it's not dangerous going to a hostile war zone basically to spy on terrorists. But lying when lying wasn't needed was the fastest way to ruin our relationship. Especially when Sophia knew that my job would always require me to lie, and that I'd promised that I would always tell her the truth if I was able, even if I knew it could hurt us. So I pushed aside the urge I had to protect her, and respected her intellect with a truthful, "It might be. But I'll be as careful as I always am."

Her dubious expression made it clear she was thinking of what happened the last time I was stationed overseas. My throat tightened when I thought about those days and nights, and before I could stop myself I was crying. Not full-on, ugly, lost-it-and-can't-even-talk crying, just kind of gently weeping.

Sophia stretched over immediately to put her glass on the coffee table, and in the next instant, enveloped me in a tight hug. "Sweetheart," she murmured against my ear. "Hey...hey...talk to me."

"I don't want to go. I'm scared." The words came out cracked and tight around my crying. "I'm scared of being in that situation again." After a few gulping breaths I blurted the thing I'd been trying to smother before it overwhelmed me. "I don't want to leave you."

"I don't want you to leave either." She stroked my hair, kissed my temple, soothed me as I cried, and I could feel her tears against my skin, hear her convulsive swallowing.

There was an odd sort of comfort in sharing sadness like this, but it wasn't comforting enough for me to completely let go of my emotions and stop crying. When I could finally speak again, I pulled away slightly and said, "I'm so sorry. God, I've been holding on to this sick feeling all day and there was nothing I could do about it." I rubbed my palm over my sternum. "I didn't mean to just unload on you like that."

"I'm glad you did," she quietly said. "I'm glad you feel safe and comfortable enough with me to let me see you vulnerable like this." She tidied my hair, kissed under my eyes, and eventually asked a question in a voice that was barely above a whisper. "Why you? Why now?"

I ran my hands through my hair and dragged it back into a ponytail before releasing it again to fall against my neck. "It's obviously not something they're going to tell me, but I think it's because of what I did. I'm being punished. But for some weird reason they don't want to punish me the way they should, by firing me, taking my security clearance away or jailing me. They want to be underhanded about it so they don't have to tell anyone that they're breaking the rules." Rules... There were no rules when it came to this, when it came to me it seemed.

Sophia winced at that final option and her voice cracked up in disbelief. "Would they *really* do that? Can they?"

I gave her the upsetting truth, something she'd probably already gathered if she'd followed any of the news surrounding our terrorist detention camps or intelligence leakers and government whistleblowers. That truth made me want to curl up into a ball and cry until I was raw and bleeding. "They can do anything they deem necessary for the safety of the country." Including, I suspected, disappearing a government employee while they were overseas.

CHAPTER SEVEN

Just when you think it can't get any worse…it does,
obviously

Derek had beaten me to the morning-meeting punch, and already sat at the head of the conference table, reading a printout. He raised his eyes and acknowledged me with a small nod, then went right back to the apparently very important page.

"Morning," I said stiffly, taking a wide berth around the table to sit to his right.

"Good morning," he answered, equally as stiffly, as he passed me a quarter-inch-thick yellow manila envelope with the standard blue "CONFIDENTIAL" cover sheet telling me, as if I didn't know, that this contained classified information.

Well this was a barrel of laughs. I couldn't recall the last time, if ever, he'd been like this. Doesn't bode well for a fun meeting, does it? Though I doubted anything could top the shittiness of yesterday's get-together. Actually, maybe telling Sophia I had to leave—that was pretty shitty. Last night, we'd cried together, then she'd taken me to bed and loved me so thoroughly that it was both salvation and torture.

Now I had to set all that aside to focus on learning about the next six months of my life. My life was always full of setting aside, but this one was going to be difficult. I watched Derek, wondering if he was in such a foul mood because of my reassignment, or if it was something outside work, or if it was just because of me—though who knew why it would be me, because I was a bundle of sunshine and we'd *never* had problems. Then again, did it really matter why he was in A Mood? Just another issue to add to the list of issues this job had been causing me lately. I put my forefinger on the middle of the envelope and with my other forefinger, spun the envelope around and around on the table. "May I look through this?"

His response was a distracted, "Not yet. We're still waiting on one more." Derek indicated the second envelope in front of him. "Your new partner," he explained.

Oh right. That. I'd been trying not to think about it. I slumped back into the chair, crossed my legs and swung the chair from side to side. Who would it be? Sam would probably be the easiest, though I'd have to listen to him crying every day about how much he missed his cat. I'd probably be complaining about missing Sophia, so at least we'd be able to find comfort in shared missing people and pets boo-hoo-hoos.

What was I thinking? It would never be Sam. He was an analyst, like me, but unlike me he'd never been an ops officer, never been in the field. I had, but I shouldn't be going back in the field for even a day, let alone six months. But here I was, facing half a year without Sophia. I almost leaned forward to rest my face in my hands to have a feel-sorry-for-myself session, but the door opened and someone I did not want to see or talk to or be anywhere near ever again walked in.

The self-pity was instantly replaced by an undefinable emotion. Undefinable, but so intense I almost forgot to breathe. Thankfully that one was an automatic event or I'd have accidentally suffocated myself in shock. How was this happening?

Mr. Smith, the very same Mr. Smith who had been shadowing me lately, said a quick hello to Derek before turning his attention on me with a smile that, surprisingly, held genuine friendliness. Friendliness laced with a touch of *gotcha*. "Good morning, Alexandra."

Oh, you have got to be fucking kidding me. Unable to formulate anything cogent, I mumbled a few syllables, hoping he'd assume it was a greeting. Or maybe a bunch of expletives. Either was fine with me. Derek cleared his throat, and thankfully my brain finally decided to kick into gear.

I launched at Smith with, "Are you going to tell me your name? Given we'll be working together for the next few months, I should know it." Referring to him as Smith was not only annoying, but didn't bode well for trust and team cohesion. Still, I wondered how much I could bond and cohere with the man who'd debriefed me, put me down constantly, and made vaguely sinister threats to my girlfriend in the few hours we'd spent in each other's company.

"Jeffrey Burton," he responded. "And it's not *a few* months, it's six." He said it calmly, but there was no mistaking the tinge of delight at his correcting me.

Don't remind me. "It's going to take a while to get used to your real name instead of *Mr. Smith*."

"It's okay, Alexandra. I'm sure even you can manage," he said dryly as he sat down opposite me.

Did he mean to be snide and demeaning or did it just slip out? I raised my chin and smiled. A fake smile but hey, at least I'd tried. Sort of. "So, do I call you Mr. Burton?"

"Jeffrey is fine."

Even this concession to a first-name basis seemed to pain him, so I decided on a little payback for the misery he'd inflicted upon me. Sure, he'd only been doing his job as interrogatey debrief guy, but mistitling me on purpose, threatening me, and threatening Sophia were so not on. I grinned. "Okay, *Jeff*."

His returned grin was sharklike, and not in the cute *Finding Nemo* way. "Oh, isn't this going to be a fun assignment."

Derek held up both hands like a referee trying to keep boxers apart. "Can you two do this another time? There's a lot of material to cover to get you both up to speed before your departure. You can find a way to get around your differences on your own time."

I spluttered, huffed, and blurted out, "Our...differences? You're kidding me. We have more than just *differences*, Derek." My boss would be aware of everything that was between Burton and me. That said, I wasn't sure he'd know the intimate details of what had happened during my detention, though given our occupation—he could use his imagination. I looked between the two of them, and for the second time in as many days registered my objection. "I'm not happy about this."

"You're not the only one," Jeff said, but it seemed more like he was saying it because it was the expected comeback, rather than because he actually thought it. He seemed the same as he always did—irritatingly composed.

I turned to stare at Derek, trying to read his neutral expression. "You expect me to work with him? With everything that happened in Florida, and after Florida." Part of this work, especially spending time in the field, was trust. I had to trust my coworkers and a partner to be honest with information, and to have my back—emotionally, professionally, mentally, and sometimes even physically. I didn't trust this man at all, and even if I got to know him during our time in the field, I doubted that sentiment would change.

"I know your history, Martin," Derek said tightly. "All of it," he reminded me. "And again, your reassignment is out of my hands. So I suggest you find a way to deal with it, and fast. Or accept the alternative consequence."

I ignored the pointed raised eyebrows he sent my way and looked back to Jeff, who sat calmly across from me, watching the back-and-forth between Derek and me, with his hands resting on top of his special yellow envelope.

I wanted nothing more than to fold my arms over my chest, slide down in the chair and pout-snarl at both of them. But that was giving away too much when I'd already stupidly shown my hand. So I straightened up, placed my hands flat on the table and said simply, "Okay. I've dealt with it." I was going to have to learn to deal with it, so why not pretend I'd skipped to the end result so we could move on and I could get out of this room.

Jeff's immediate surprise at my surrender was almost worth giving in. Almost. It would probably be the only time I'd ever surprise him.

Derek nodded. "All right then." He gestured to the envelopes in front of us. "Those packets contain all the pertinent information for this assignment. Take some time now to read through the documents, then we can discuss any concerns or queries or suggestions you may have."

I almost put my hand up. Excuse me, but I have concerns, queries, and suggestions. A lot of them. But instead of expressing them, I kept my mouth shut, opened the envelope and scanned the first page of the document. My name and the tiniest notation of "Reassignment" cut me to the bone. As if I could forget.

When I saw where I'd be spending the next six months of my life, bile rose up my throat. I swallowed it back down. I'd been to this country before, when I was an ops officer. I'd been there a few times. The last time was in 2016 through to 2017. I'd left on a military medevac flight.

It was a different region this time, but that was a minor detail. I was still going to the country where I'd been badly wounded. The country with a new, unstable government and so much civil unrest that there were travel advisories against going there. An unstable government our government had helped install—unofficially—because it suited our interests, even if they'd promoted a despotic regime.

Cold sweat stuck my blouse to my back.

Inhaling deeply, I slid a neutral expression onto my face, not wanting Burton to see my reaction. Suitably calm on the outside, I kept reading. Basic operation details like mission goals and targets, accommodation, daily living allowance, blah blah. It seemed cobbled-together, almost—dare I say it—last-minute. But aside from the location, which had my stomach churning queasily, it was all fairly standard, and nothing that gave me any cause for concern over and above the obvious. Annoyance, sure, but not concern. I noted they were sending me in with the old identity I'd always used in the field—Ellen Jackson, schoolteacher. She'd seen some stuff, let me tell you.

I turned to the second page. There it was. The thing that *did* give me concern. Oh, wonderful. My departure date. I was leaving on Thanksgiving Day. I looked up, not bothering to close my gaping mouth. "You're kidding me. I leave in seven days?"

Derek's expression said everything his lack of words didn't. No kidding detected.

"So, just checking, in case I'm the only one who knows this, but… you do realize that due to its unstable political climate, this country is in a heightened state of political and civil unrest and that terrorist attacks are frequent in both major and minor cities?"

Derek's response was a clipped, "We're aware."

"Okay. As long as you know we're being sent right into the middle of a terrorist-attack hotbed that might erupt into civil war within the next six months."

His look told me I was about to push his buttons. I wanted to keep pushing them, hard, slam my fist down on them, have a tantrum all over them, but instead, I clamped my mouth shut and listened as Derek went over the assignment.

The three of us sat around the table without making eye contact for the rest of the briefing. I swear I listened to everything Derek had to say—which was basically just going through what was in the document—but most of my brain was trying to process things. I was now absolutely certain the president was punishing me for my work on the Kunduz Intelligence, and in the pettiest, cruelest way possible. Why else would they partner me with this man? The guy who'd debriefed me, tried to humiliate me, tried to break me into telling him what he wanted.

This version of Mr. Smith—sorry, Jeffrey Burton—felt almost like a regular guy. He was, dare I say it, nicer than the blank slate who'd dealt with me repeatedly in custody, but his underlying snide condescension was still there. Everything he said felt like it had double meaning, a hidden agenda. Or maybe I was just looking for reasons to dislike him, even though I already disliked him plenty.

After almost two hours, Derek consolidated his papers into a neat pile. "Okay, I think we'll wrap up there. Contact information for the department overseeing your insertion is in the document if you need specific answers, but you'll meet with them in the next day or two to discuss your travel and whatnot." He forced a smile. "It's been a few years since I worked with field ops, so I'm probably not the best person to ask, but if I can help you, then of course I will."

He didn't need to say how unusual this all was. Rules were being bent for me, but not in a nice way. His expression softened, and for a moment he looked more like the guy I'd known for over a decade, instead of this surly shell of himself. "Even if it's just telling you to contact the ops office." Derek attempted another smile, but it fell flat, and we all stared at one another like each of us spoke a different, unknown language.

I didn't know what else to say that wasn't an endless scream, so I just nodded, stood up, murmured my thanks so I wouldn't be rude, and left the room, trying not to crumple the envelope of my worst nightmares as I walked out.

Jeff caught up with me as I was skulking back to my desk. "Alexandra." He said my name with surprising gentleness, and the lack of snarky condescension threw me off guard.

"Yes?" I responded crisply. He was lucky he got crisp and not a teeth-bared snarl—I'd spent an entire meeting smooshing my emotions down and was fast approaching my tolerance for holding in emotional discomfort.

Jeff pulled out my chair and sat down, leaving me standing up in my own damned work cubicle. He was fast catching up to the president on my dislike list. He picked up my New Zealand rock, raised it to eye level, then turned it around, studying the smooth surface.

Exasperated, I raised my hands. "Sure. Make yourself at home."

A toothy smile. "Thanks, I have. I know we just had a lot of information thrown at us, and the preparation for this new assignment is short and far from ideal, personally." For some reason, I expected him to follow up with "Are you okay? If you need to talk…" or something that showed he cared, or had even thought, about my mental health and well-being. Instead, he said, "I wanted to remind you to get your permit so you can take alcohol into the country."

The bristling at his inference that I didn't know one of the most basic things about where we were going, even though I'd been there before, was instinctive, and I fought to keep the *no fucking shit* tone from my voice. "Thanks for the reminder, but I don't need it." Sure, I loved good wine, a frosty craft beer, a well-crafted botanical-rich gin, but in situations where I didn't feel entirely safe, drinking made me feel sketchy. Half a year without alcohol was the least of my worries.

"Great. If you're not bringing any alcohol with you for you, then I'll take your allowance in bourbon, please. Either Booker's or Maker's Mark will be fine."

I stared blankly. "Do I look like an alcohol store to you?"

"Alexandra," he said, with all the exasperated patience of a parent trying to convince their kid of the importance of homework. "If you're not going to use it, then at least let me. Show some compassion. I'm sure you're capable of it. We're going to be in country for six months. Roughly one hundred and eighty-eight days. If I only have my allowance, then that gives me…" His forehead wrinkled, lips moved soundlessly. "Ten milliliters of bourbon a day which is barely a taste, not even an actual shot of liquor. But! If you bring in another two liters then I can have twenty milliliters per evening which is *almost* a respectable amount of bourbon for my evening unwinding which is a very important part of my day that helps me to process what I've been doing during my waking hours. Or I could even have a drink every second day and make it almost like an actual two fingers of bourbon, which would improve my mood greatly."

"Are you some sort of creepy math genius? Did you spend that whole meeting calculating from our departure date to our estimated return date, and then dividing the amount of liquor we're allowed?"

"No. I'm just a regular genius."

"You've been nothing but an asshole to me from the moment we met. Why should I help you?" The promise of his mood improvement bonus alone was tempting. Not that I'd ever really found him to be in a bad mood, but more that his general state was so sharp that I often felt cut to ribbons. And I'd spent hardly any time with him in the scheme of things. Having to live and work with him for half a year might just kill me.

"Because I asked you to." He grinned cheerfully. "And I even did it *nicely*."

Exhausted by the latest development of Jeff plus our imminent departure and the ramifications of me leaving so soon, and wanting nothing more than to remove myself from his presence and the reminder of what was coming, I relented. "Mmm, okay. I'll see what I can do."

"Thank you." He slapped his palms lightly on my desk and stood. "That wasn't so hard, was it?"

I offered what I hoped was a withering look in response, but I had the feeling that in the face of his imperturbability, he probably thought I looked constipated. "Just like pulling teeth."

His smile showed most of his teeth. "Well, all mine are still here." Jeff paused, his expression impassive. "How are you feeling about being intelligence analyst trailblazers? A new position, just popping up out of nowhere, with nobody lined up to fill it, and you just get tossed in? You sure are special." Without waiting for me to answer, he barreled on. "Personally, I think the timing is a little poor, as is the short lead-up to our departure. I'm going to miss Thanksgiving and Christmas with my family."

"Me too," I pointed out. "Both of those, and also my birthday, with my new girlfriend. Try again."

He didn't, just stared at me, a slight smirky smile twisting his mouth. "Have a good day, Alexandra. I'll see you at our next briefing."

"I can't wait."

The rest of my day went along with much the same vibe that'd accosted me during the meeting—frustration, annoyance, and a mild dose of anxiety. Jeff caught up to me again as I was powerwalking to my car so I could go home to Sophia and break the news to her that not only would I miss Thanksgiving, but we'd have hardly any time before I left. He told me, in a voice that was completely steady and sincere, that he hoped we could move past our past to work together safely and efficiently. My immediate thought was a sarcasm-laden *Sure thing, Jeff.*

In that instant of my bitchy internal comeback being let loose, I realized how toxic and unhelpful the thought was. The Kunduz Intelligence, Jeffrey Burton, my "reassignment," the fucked-up conditions surrounding my imminent (though temporary) move to a foreign country—all of it was stifling me. It was trying to drag me down to a place where my anger and frustration would overwhelm me so much that I couldn't function in my usual (generally calm) brain space.

I *needed* my calm brain space. I had worked damned hard after 2017's attack to get through my trauma and find my Zen spaces, and fuck me if these bastards were going to steal it from me. Or more accurately—goad me into letting it go.

So, I decided right then and there that I should let it go, and shed the mental toxicity associated with the reassignment. Not all the way let go and not *all* the annoyance and frustration, because I had to hang on to *some* of my rage. But I would let most of it go. Feeling this way wasn't going to help me when I was in a foreign hostile environment, trying to gather information from people who wouldn't think twice about murdering me in the name of their cause.

I could put aside my anger and frustration toward Jeff for the time we were living and working together. Or, at the very least, I could stuff it down into a place where it wasn't eating at me. I had far greater things to worry about, and allocating brain space to being pissy at this man, who really was nothing more than a representation of that which had caused me so much grief, was pointless. He'd only been doing his job, as I'd been trying to do mine—in a slightly unorthodox way. "Okay," I said. "Why don't you send me a calendar invite so we can meet up and consolidate a list of groceries and supplies to ask for."

His eyebrows bounced upward in surprise. "Sure. Will do."

"Great." I made myself smile, actually felt better for it, and walked away. My newfound resolution to not be an asshole to him was a start, but it still needed some work. Luckily I had six months to work on not disliking him…

CHAPTER EIGHT

*Time flies when you're frantically prepping to leave
your girlfriend to go to a hostile foreign country
with a guy who isn't your friend*

Sophia's reaction to my imminent departure and the fact I was missing Thanksgiving with her family was basically what I anticipated, and also mirrored my feelings. Upset, furious, resigned, sad, and a dozen more all fighting for space. We moved through yet another round of trying to work through our emotions about me leaving.

I lost count of the number of times I apologized for not making Thanksgiving or meeting her parents, because I couldn't carve a full day and night out of my preparations to travel there and back on a non-Thanksgiving day, and her parents were no longer comfortable driving the distance to come here. Sophia pointed out she could collect her parents for me to meet, then drive them back again afterward. In the next breath she mumbled that it was a stupid idea and trying to make it work was too hard.

There was no way around the ever-present atmosphere of how fucked-up the entire situation was, but I was battling to stay positive and hold myself together for her. It was all happening so fast that there was no time to stop and have real feelings about leaving her, about going to a place I never wanted to go to again. I was just pushing through, trying not to dwell. Couldn't wait for all those repressed feelings to anvil-drop on my head when I was thousands of miles away from my safe place and safe person.

And as if it wasn't enough to give me barely any time to prep for my first overseas assignment in five and a half years and to send me so I'd miss Thanksgiving and Christmas, I now had to cram in as much time with Sophia as I could in just one week, while trying to deal with the myriad things I needed to do before I left. She put on a brave face, but I could tell she was as devastated as me at the thought of being separated, and so soon. How do you condense preparing to be apart from someone for six months into just a week?

A few days later, I tentatively and stupidly and unwillingly asked if she wanted to take a break—*not* a breakUP—while I was gone, hinting that I didn't expect her to commit to me while I was gone for half a year when we'd only been dating for a month-ish. She looked like I'd suggested she commit homicide.

Once she managed to stop gaping at me like I'd sprouted another eye, she flatly said, "No. I don't want to take a break, breakup, or *anything* like that."

"Good," I breathed. "Me either, but I didn't want you to feel… stuck." Especially not after the trip to Florida, where I'd given her every opportunity to leave if she wanted to, but had used subtle psychological cues to guide her toward wanting to stay with me.

"I won't. Lonely maybe, sad definitely, but not stuck." Sophia clasped both hands in front of her chest, fluttering her eyelashes at me as she Southern-drawled, "I'll be true to you, Alexandra Elizabeth Martin. Will you be true to me?"

I matched her accent. "You know I will, Sophia Emily Flores. I'll wait for you until my return in the spring of the year next."

She leaned over and gave me a chaste, 1920's movie kiss. "Good." Sophia grinned wickedly, then pulled my face down for a very not-chaste kiss. When she pulled back, the grin had faded. "I *hate* thinking of you spending Thanksgiving traveling and Christmas alone. Well, not alone, but not with me."

"Me too." I held back my long, sad sigh. I'd held back a lot of sad sighs these past few days.

"Will you guys celebrate Christmas while you're gone?"

"Mhmm, I'm sure we'll do something to mark the day." No idea what, because the place we'd be wasn't big on Christian holidays. "Even if it's just a quick meal together. Maybe we can get a tree of some sort to decorate. I really don't know. Maybe I could video call

you and your family while you're all together at Christmas?" Maybe…
maybe…maybe.

Sophia exhaled loudly. "I would love that. And so would Mom and
papi. They texted today to tell me how much they loved meeting you
over FaceTime yesterday, and how they can't wait for the real thing."
We'd compromised on my whole bailing-on-Thanksgiving thing by
video-calling with Sophia's parents after dinner last night so we could
at least meet, albeit not in person.

She'd once told me her dad looked like a Latino Clark Gable
when he was younger, and I agreed with the resemblance. Sophia's
mother was a serene-looking woman with warm blue eyes and long,
curly, silver-gray hair. The conversation was light and easy, and after
almost forty minutes, it had come to its natural conclusion. We made
plans for when I came back to the States to make up for missing the
holidays, and I promised I'd take care of myself.

Once we'd ended the call, Sophia had asked, "You okay? I know my
parents are kind of full-on, even not in person."

"Absolutely. And they're not full-on, they're both adorable." I could
see pieces of Sophia in each of them, from her father's eyes and sense
of humor, to her mother's nose and deep compassion. Her parents
acted as if we'd met years ago, and I was already part of their family,
easing the mild anxiety that I'd felt when Sophia had suggested out
of the blue that she was going to call her parents and maybe we could
make it a joint video call.

She gently cupped my cheek, her thumb stroking along my
cheekbone. "Will you get your work partner a Christmas gift for while
you're away?"

Jeff was low on the list of people I wanted to give gifts to. "Maybe?
Probably not," I hedged. "I don't know him very well, and with all
the hectic preparation, we haven't discussed Christmas properly, let
alone gifts. I don't want it to be weird." What did Burton even like?
Mentally torturing me. Being a dick. High-and-tight haircuts. Running
marathons and lifting weights, if his physique was any indicator. Not
exactly good ideas to use as a basis for what to gift him.

Her eyebrows-raised, pursed-lips look made me reconsider. "Lexie.
He's going to be part of your support system for months. I think it'd
be weirder if you *didn't* get him something."

I couldn't exactly tell her about the background between Jeff and
me, so I smiled and nodded. "Okay, yes, you're right. I'll go after work
tomorrow and get something small and pointless and a complete token
gift." A giftwrapped turd. Expired, melted chocolates. An ugly tie.

She smiled knowingly. "Good. It might help break the ice a little, even if it feels pointless."

Doubtful, but she was the queen of treating people well, and she was right. I agreed with a quiet, "Okay."

"Are you still on to meet us at the bar after work tomorrow?"

"Shit, yes. Of course." I took her hands and squeezed. "I'll be there. I'll get a gift the day after." Fuck knew when exactly the day after, which was my last day before I left. And I still had to find something to give to Sophia. Or, more accurately, to leave for Sophia to open. By herself. I still had no idea what, and hoped I could pen some poetic words to supplement whatever gift I found.

Meeting up with some of Sophia's friends was just one more thing to squeeze in before my departure, when I was trying to spend as much time with her as possible. The past week had rushed by so quickly that I felt like I'd just been standing by, watching myself madly prepare for a trip I didn't want to take. But she'd asked and it seemed important to her, and it would only take a few hours—unlike a full day-and-night adventure to meet her parents—so I'd agreed to meet them at a hip queer bar after work tomorrow.

Maybe Sophia just wanted her friends to see I was really real before I possibly disappeared. Maybe she wanted me to see another part of her life before I possibly disappeared. Maybe this was just a logical step in a relationship. Relationship. It still felt so weird to think that we were officially together. But we were, and I was going to hold on to that with every bit of strength in my body while we were apart. It was all I had.

I was on the cusp of sleep when I felt her shift and slide closer to me, pressing herself tightly to my back with her arm wrapped around my waist. "I don't want you to go," she whispered against my neck.

I stayed still, feigning sleep because I had absolutely no idea what to say to her that I hadn't already said. "Me either," "I know," "It's fucked," "I hate it," and every possible variant of these had been expressed dozens of times before, and expressing them again wasn't going to fix anything. And I knew if I answered, I'd just start crying again. I felt like such a coward as I smothered my grief, and left her alone with hers.

* * *

As I was halfway through my prework five-mile get-all-my-wiggles-out run, an unexpected and unwanted person appeared in the gym. I bit back my sigh—but only because it would have interfered with my breathing.

"Hello, Alexandra." Jeff, dressed in a suit, hopped up onto the treadmill next to mine and began a slow walk.

"Hello," I said, without looking at him.

I ran. He walked. We said nothing more.

It was clear he wasn't going to leave me alone until he'd said what he needed to, so I slowed the treadmill to half pace and gave him my attention. Or most of it, as best I could while running on a treadmill that required my attention to avoid being shoomped off the back. "What can I help you with, Jeff?"

"You all set for your departure? Sorry we won't get to be travel buddies." He was leaving the next morning to liaise with the ops team and make sure everything was set up in our living and working space when I arrived few days later.

I gave him a quick, grim smile then turned my head forward again. "As I'll ever be. Even packed my favorite teddy bear."

"How cute."

I strained my eyes looking sideways at him. "You're not going to be getting in my face like this while I'm trying to work out or do my daily yoga and meditation, are you? Because that's really not going to work for me."

Jeff looked scandalized. "No, Alexandra, I would never interrupt that," he said sincerely, and I believed him. "I recall how important those moments are to you." Oh, right, he'd probably watched me doing calisthenics and yoga and meditation in my small room during my time locked up in his little facility. "I won't be getting in your face during your mental and physical health rejuvenation time, as I expect you'll leave me to mine."

"Deal," I said instantly.

"Good." Jeff bopped his fist on the Stop button and stepped off the treadmill. "Safe travels and I'll be seeing you soon." Then he walked out of the gym with his usual cat-burglar silence, which was both creepy and admirable.

I supposed at least he wasn't going to be stomping around the place, annoying the shit out of me by being loud. I mentally added one point into the Tolerable Coexistence column. The next few months were going to be interesting enough as it was, but every time we interacted I felt less and less like I was going to spend the entire time worrying about him cornering me for an "interrogation." Still, I wondered if I would ever let my guard down around him and have a conversation where I didn't feel like I needed to weigh what I was going to say in case he turned it against me.

I pumped the speed back to my full pace and increased the incline a fraction. At this stage, I'd need to run to Tibet and back to work out all my anxiety and frustration about my new assignment and my new work partner.

Honestly, the last thing I felt like when I was done with work for the day was being social. But I knew my meeting Sophia's friends was important to her, so I left my work stress at work, and made my way to the bar. Late. Quick makeup touch-up in the car, pull my hair out of its micro bun, stress that I was still wearing the dress I'd worn to work and that it screamed corporate instead of casual or cool. While I wasn't trying to impress anyone, I didn't want Sophia's friends thinking I wasn't good enough for her. I'd already had that thought enough times myself.

I'd just opened the car door when the blue phone rang. The timing of a call from Lennon was rarely convenient, but in this case, it felt like he'd deliberately called me at the most annoying time possible. I hadn't heard from him at all since Derek had told me about the Great Motherfucking Reassignment. I closed the door again and answered without a greeting. "I was wondering when you were going to call." I exhaled loudly. "I thought you'd want to talk to me sooner about my exciting news."

"Yes. And before you ask, we did try to have the decision overruled." So Derek had said, I thought. "But we were unsuccessful." Lennon sighed. "Despite Halcyon's strong objections, the president thinks his personal vendetta is more important than your worth to us."

That again. "My worth? I'm really struggling to connect the dots of my 'worth.'"

"Then don't try to connect the dots. Just know we need you to continue excelling in all aspects of your role within Halcyon *and* the agency, and that Halcyon will have another task for you when you return."

"Another dedicated assignment? Careful, the other agents might start getting upset that you're paying me so much attention."

Lennon chuckled. "I'm sure they recognize that you've earned a few accolades after the…Berenson situation."

The Berenson Situation. It sounded like a bad drama series. Lexie's Value would out-rate it for sure. "So why me?" If they wanted to give me accolades, Halcyon could start by giving me some time off and a substantial pay raise.

"Because this is something only you can do."

"Ohhh, right, yes. Any hints?"

"No. You'll know what you need to know, when you need to know it."

"Yay, vague answers." Though he couldn't see me, I still rolled my eyes.

"It's the only answer I can give you at this moment. When the time comes, I promise I'll have answers that should satisfy you. Just get through this assignment first."

"I hope so. You know I hate this wishy-washy shit." I didn't expect to be in the loop for everything. In fact, I expected the opposite—my job wasn't to know all the details behind the scenes, it was to assess information. But I didn't like being jerked around like this with allusions to things about me. It felt like being back in elementary school and some snotnosed kid taunting me because they had a *secret*.

"I know," Lennon assured me. "And I'm sorry, but it's necessary at the moment. Halcyon will be in touch in due course. I'd been hoping to start you on this new project soon, but your reassignment complicates matters."

"How?" My role within Halcyon remained the same regardless of where I was based or what my current agency role entailed, and I'd expected to continue to keep an eye out for any relevant intelligence to pass on to the Division.

"It's quite possibly one of the most important and highly classified things you'll ever work with, and it's not secure enough outside our facilities. But we will keep it safe until you return."

Exciting. Cryptic. Trademark Halcyon. "Bigger than Berenson?" And obviously not time-sensitive.

"Much. So, be careful, Alexandra. With *everything*." The emphasis he'd placed on "everything" made me pause. *Everything* seemed kind of broad, more than just "don't get killed by terrorists."

"I will." I craned my neck to peer up at the neon rainbow bar sign. "And if you don't need anything more from me, I have to go. I have a personal social event that I'm already late for."

"Yes. Very good." There was a long pause before his stilted, "Have...fun."

"I will."

I stowed the blue phone in a hidden inner zippered compartment of my purse and climbed out of the driver's seat, setting aside the call with Lennon to focus on more important things. Like meeting my girlfriend's friends. I buttoned up my long wool coat, fluffed my hair, and made my way into the bar. Inside, the vibe was upscale casual—warm lighting, rustic wooden tables, greenery galore, hipster bartenders—and as I peered around the packed space, I spotted Sophia sitting with four women at a high table nestled in the back corner.

Deep breath, time to impress the friends-slash-support system. Smiling, I threaded my way through the crowd, and as I approached, one of the women at Sophia's table made eye contact with Sophia then pointedly looked to me. Sophia spun around, a delighted smile already lighting up her face. "Hey, you made it," she murmured.

"Hey. I sure did, so sorry I'm late." I leaned in and kissed her cheek. Cheek. *Cheek.* Cheek! We did *not* kiss cheeks. But the moment I'd seen four sets of strangers' eyes turn expectantly to me, I'd panicked. Trying to recover, I looked around the table, making brief eye contact with each of the women. With an awkward wave, I introduced myself with a friendly, "Hi. I'm Lexie."

Sophia slipped her arm around my waist, her hand squeezing reassuringly. "Hi, Lexie, I'm Sophia." After a wink at my smiling eye roll, Sophia went around the table, introducing each of her friends— Gina, Steph, Alana, and Jada—before pulling out the empty chair to her right and sliding a glass of red over to me. "Already ordered for you."

I hadn't thought about what I was going to drink, but the moment I saw the deep burgundy of the wine, I realized it was exactly what I felt like. "Thank you, sweetheart." I picked up the wineglass, surprised when everyone else at the table raised theirs as well for an enthusiastic "Cheers."

After those initial, expected, appraising looks, without exception, each of Sophia's friends acted as if I was part of the circle with none of the usual awkward, trying to figure out who-fit-where vibe. It was almost as if they'd decided anyone that any of them brought to meet the group was worthy of inclusion unless they proved otherwise. My anxiety about assuring them I wasn't a sociopath eased a fraction. We quickly ordered another round of drinks, as well as appetizers, then settled in for some superficial get-to-know-you chat. Deeper getting-to-know-yous would have to wait until after I returned from…that place.

They were a mixed group of women—fashionably grungy, casual, designer-dressed, eclectic—but one thing they all had in common? They were super nice, and all seemed to genuinely care about Sophia. It made me feel marginally better about leaving her, knowing she had both a loving supportive family and a solid, albeit small, friendship circle.

Gina, an artist who favored flowing, brightly patterned clothing smiled warmly at me. "Lexie, Sophia tells us you're a business consultant."

I quickly swallowed the mouthful of wine I'd just sipped—sipped, very politely, though all I wanted was to gulp the entire glass—and smiled back at her. She'd made it sound like I was some benevolent humanitarian saving businesses in trouble, and you know what? I'd take it. "I am, yes."

"What does that entail, exactly?"

Thankfully Sophia and I had gone over my fake job beforehand, so I had a plausible response. "Cocktail napkin version? Either I help new businesses with plans for success, or I travel wherever I'm needed and hopefully stop struggling businesses from going under."

She mock-shuddered. "Sounds busy and stressful. We hear you're off for another save-a-business assignment soon." Murmurs of concerned agreement around the table. "When do you leave?"

I glanced at my girlfriend, and her tight smile conveyed everything. "Thanksgiving Day." At the collective groan of disappointment, I raised my hands. "I know. It's pretty dire, a last-ditch effort to save an offshore multi-multi-million-dollar company, so they're expecting to need my hand on the rudder for at least six months."

Everyone conveyed their horror with murmurs and facial expressions, and it was Steph who asked, "Wow. How do you cope being away for so long?"

Smiling, I said truthfully, "Badly." After a quiet sigh, I added, "But it's been a while since I drew the short straw for one of these overseas save-a-business assignments, so I suppose it's only fair that I go this time." There, convincing and not too convoluted.

Sympathetic nods all around.

The conversation moved easily around the table as we talked acquaintance-style—getting to know each other but not sharing anything deep or particularly meaningful. I got the feeling that even though they'd accepted me, it still felt like they were all still figuring me out, deciding if I was worthy of dating their good friend, just as I was figuring out if they would keep her safe while I was gone.

Gone.

I was trying so hard to not think of it, but that thought intruded into every corner of my life, and at the worst possible moments. Maybe being apart from Sophia would be easier once it had actually happened and we'd settled into staying connected in new ways. Or maybe it was just going to suck.

As I was about to order another round for the table, my phone rang. I cursed inwardly when I recognized the number. Outwardly, I smiled apologetically. "I'm so sorry to be the workaholic asshole who didn't mute their phone, but I need to take this."

"Sure," Sophia agreed amicably. By now, she knew that any phone call I received was something or someone important.

I stepped away from the table and answered the call with, "One moment," then continued out the door. When I was safely outside, away from ears and eyes, I raised the phone again. "Jeff. Always a pleasure. How'd you get my personal number?" It was pointless to ask. Though I still didn't know exactly what Jeff did, I knew that he was someone who always got the resources he needed when he wanted them.

"Nice to hear from you too, partner," he said, ignoring my question and tone. "I've just had a call from the leader of our insertion team and they've asked us to come in for a briefing immediately."

I suppressed a groan. What the fuck could they need to discuss with us now, on a Tuesday at seven thirty p.m. "Why *now*? And why didn't they call me directly?"

"Now, because I'm leaving tomorrow morning, and they didn't call you because I said I would and save them the scowling through the phone. I'm used to your scowls now."

Yeah… I knew it wasn't the fault of the team helping us prep for our assignment, but their association with the thing that was causing me so much anxiety made it hard to control my snark-face whenever I was near them. "Work is over and I'm out at a social thing right now."

"Wow, well isn't that the event of the century. Congratulations. There's a chicken roasting at my house and I'll be eating it cold once we're done, *and* it's my last night at home with my family for a long time. We all sacrifice things, Alexandra. I'll see you at the office in thirty minutes."

Fuck. "Sure," I muttered.

Maybe I could just quit. Fuck this whole thing. Fuck the president. Fuck the mind games and the manipulation. But that stupid, rational, knows-what's-best part of my brain chimed in to remind me *If you quit, you'll probably go to jail*. And not one of the nice ones that lets you have visitors and learn some skills and get online degrees and shit, but the one where they put those who have betrayed their country and everyone thinks you're worse than dog shit on their shoe.

Instead of hurling my phone across the street, I put it in my purse and went back inside to break the news to my girlfriend that I was bailing early on our social event. As I approached, her expression telegraphed that she suspected what I was about to say.

So I just said it, in as contrite a tone as I could summon. "Sorry, but I need to go put out a forest fire before everything burns down. I'm so, so sorry." I ran my hand down Sophia's back, and she reached around behind herself to rest the flat of her palm against the outside of my thigh, pressing me into her. "It was so wonderful meeting you all, and hopefully we can do it when I get back and I'll be able to stay for longer than just one and a half drinks. I'd love to get to know everyone better."

There was a cheerful, if not slightly inebriated chorus of "Sure!" and "Of course," and "No problem!" before I left some cash on the table to cover the next round of drinks that I wouldn't get to enjoy.

"I'll walk you out," Sophia said.

"No need, sweetheart. Stay here where it's warm, with your drink. I'll call you when I'm done with this brie...meeting."

She inclined her head in agreement, a knowing smile twitching the edges of her mouth. I smiled at her, squeezed her hand, then walked away.

As I moved away from the table, I heard whispers and murmurs from the group—the words indistinct in content, but very distinct in tone—and it took barely a second for me to twig to the reason for both the chatter and tone. They weren't telling Sophia how great I was, what a catch, how attractive, how funny and charming. They were implying I was an idiot, because...oh...I hadn't kissed her. Why didn't I kiss her goodbye? And also, I'd given her that crappy no-intimacy cheek kiss when I'd arrived. We'd PDA'd in public before. Plenty of times.

So why hadn't I kissed her properly when I'd arrived, or at all when I'd left? Was I subconsciously distancing myself from her because I was leaving? Did I think she was ashamed of me for some reason which even I couldn't figure out because she'd never indicated anything like that? Was I worried she didn't want the general public knowing we were a couple, even though neither of us had ever said we didn't want that?

And now I was totally overthinking it.

So, instead of pushing through the door into the cool evening air to rush off for something I had no interest in, I let the door fall closed again, spun around and strode back to the table. Sophia's back was to me, but the surprise of her friends made her turn slightly at my approach. She set down her drink. "What did you forget?" she teased, the words catching around a laugh.

I shook my head, and without saying anything, stroked my hand from between her shoulder blades to the small of her back. Slipping my hand around to grip her hip, I tugged gently, helping her spin all the way around on her barstool. Sophia's eyebrows arched in surprise, but dropped back down when I placed a hand on each of her knees and gently pushed them apart so I could step into the space I'd created.

The insides of her knees brushed my hips and once I'd settled, she slowly closed her thighs until her knees pressed into me, trapping me there. Even with the lack of frontal contact, my heart rate still tripped for a few beats. Sophia's hands came to rest lightly on my waist, and she watched me carefully, expectantly.

The room fell away, the whispers of her friends receded, my focus narrowed to Sophia—her eyes, bright and loving; her cheeks, blushed pink; her lips, full and parted slightly. I cupped the side of her neck with one hand and her cheek with the other. My thumb traced the soft lines of her mouth, then brushed over her chin. Sophia's lips parted in anticipation as I leaned in and brushed a light kiss over her lips. Her groan of frustration was barely audible, but I felt the small vibration and suppressed a laugh. A pause, still lingering within a breath of her lips. Then I kissed her properly and perhaps a little too intimately for a public location, but I didn't care—I only had so many kisses before I left. Her fingertips dug into my waist, her knees pressed harder into my hips as we kissed like lovers who hadn't seen each other all week.

She pulled away first, but it was me who spoke first. "That," I breathed. "I forgot that."

Her eyes fluttered briefly closed, then opened as a slow grin turned her lips up. "I like it when you're forgetful."

"I know."

From behind her, I heard a mumbled, "Fuck, I need a cold shower" and quiet agreements from the rest of the table.

Sophia turned slightly to face her friends, and agreed hoarsely, "Me too" before she spun back to me. Her eyebrows arched in an expression that told me I was going to be punished and rewarded for that kiss when I got home—punished for the teasing torture, rewarded for the anticipation.

I smiled smugly. "I love you, let me know when you leave the bar, and I'll see you at my place when I'm done with this work thing." I kissed her again, quickly this time, and with a second goodbye, left her in the care of her friends and went to try not to stab Jeff in the eye with a pen.

CHAPTER NINE

So…I guess this is goodbye

Numb.

It had been my overriding emotion as I'd prepared to leave Sophia, but in a horrible twist, the numbness fell away on my last day, leaving me feeling much like a bleeding, gaping wound. Everything at work was laced with an uncomfortable underlying vibe, all my coworker interactions tinged with that "You're going away for six months and we all know what happened last time you went to that region and we'll miss you and please don't die" feeling.

Nicole had baked a luscious chocolate cake and my team took some time from their afternoon to sit in the break room and share cake, drink coffee, and chat in what was probably one of the most awkward social experiences of my working life. These people were analysts, not field operatives. Like…what do you say? We're not close, and it's possible I'll be killed while I'm gone, so…it's been nice knowing you? As the shindig wound down, Sam pulled me aside and hugged me, seemed to realize that maybe it wasn't work appropriate—not that I minded, because he was a work friend—then dropped me like a hot potato and made a lame comment about sending me Muffin updates every week so it'd be just like I was here at work.

"Then you'd better send me two-hourly updates if you want it to be just like at work," I rebutted, trying to sound light and easy.

"Don't tempt me." He squeezed my forearm, leaning down to murmur tremulously, "Take care of yourself and I'll see you when you get back." Sam blinked a few times, offered me a wonky smile, then left the break room like a swarm of bees were chasing him. The man was terrible with goodbyes and was probably running to the men's room to bawl.

After wading through the goodbyes and well-wishes from those who remained in the break room to demolish Nicole's cake, I managed to extricate myself from the discomfort and went in search of Derek. When I knocked on his office door, he gestured for me to come in and close the door, and abandoned the contents of a manila folder he was leafing through. In an unexpected move, he also abandoned his chair behind the desk and came to sit in the one beside me. "How're you doing, Martin?"

I shrugged. I'd said everything I could say on the subject of how I was doing.

"Is there anything you need?"

"Plenty, yes. But is what I need anything you could actually do? No. But thank you."

He nodded slowly, and thankfully didn't push. "Stay in touch outside of work communication. I want to know how you're doing. And you know I'm here to talk if you need me. And if you think of something I could actually help you with, please let me know."

"I will. Do you think it's safe over there for communication?" I hoped my raised eyebrows conveyed what I was getting at: "Ya think they're going to be spying on me while I'm gone?"

Derek's answer was a calm, "I'd exercise caution with all forms of contact, especially while you're in the office or your home space." The spaces set up by Them.

"Right." I'd had no illusion that they would afford me privacy with my work, but common decency (and privacy laws) should surely have given me privacy with my personal communications. But, as I'd learned recently: all bets were off when it came to this whole situation and I just had to grit my teeth and bear it. "Try not to burn the place down while I'm away."

Derek snort-laughed. "No guarantees." He leaned over to pat my back fondly, which was his version of a tight hug. "Take care of yourself, Alexandra," he said seriously.

"I'll do my best." I forced a smile, and left his office before I started crying. As I walked back to my cubicle I tried to suppress my rising unease. Because I was still technically working for this office and my team, my role wouldn't be filled and my workspace would remain empty until I returned. But I just couldn't shake the feeling that something was going to happen to me and I wouldn't be returning.

I spent my last hour in the office making sure there was nothing left undone on my workstation, and emailing the few people who would need to know I wasn't in the office but was still contactable through usual channels. Once I'd packed up the few personal things I didn't want to leave sitting around, I shut down my machine, and said a collective goodbye to everyone.

Goodbye, office.

Goodbye, team.

Goodbye, work security.

Then I left the building and sent up desperate pleas to the universe that it wasn't for the last time.

We were spending my final night in the States at my place and when Sophia suggested Mexican for my Last-Supper-of-sorts, I agreed right away. Eating Mexican food with her always reminded me of the first dinner on our quasi road trip, and I imagined she was as nostalgic about it as I was. Knowing I'd want to do nothing but be with her for our last night together, I'd been packing in fits and starts for the past few days and all that was left was to toss a phone charger, toiletries, and medications into my bags in the morning.

We'd also been through pretty much everything I could think of to tell her about the logistics of my being away—staying in contact, sending things to me, the possibility of me being incommunicado for (what would seem to her) long periods, a few things about living in my apartment if she wanted to stay over for whatever reason, and a bunch of little pointers that might make it easier for her to be separated from me. Easier for her… Nothing would make it easier for me.

While we waited for dinner to arrive, I took a shower and washed my hair, shaved everything that needed shaving, tidied my eyebrows, then pulled on underwear and sweats. I heard Sophia opening the front door to greet the delivery person and hastened to shrug into a long-sleeved tee, skipping a bra in my rush to eat.

I stepped up behind her and kissed the side of her neck. "Mmm, smells great."

"Me or the food?"

"Both."

As I helped her unpack the takeout containers, I realized she'd bought exactly what she'd ordered us that first time in a tiny hotel in Rocky Mount, North Carolina. Vegetarian *pozole*, plantain *enmoladas*, rice with vegetables, grilled corn, and chips and guac. That first night, we'd enjoyed dinner and beers, then whiskey afterward, and she'd told me all about how her parents had met.

As if she was trying to re-create that same atmosphere, Sophia set out two bottles of Modelo Especial alongside the numerous containers. We passed things back and forth and even though my stomach felt like a stone, I dished up a kaleidoscope of food for myself. "This smells great, babe. Good choice."

She smiled winningly. "I thought so."

Sophia attacked her dinner like she'd not eaten all day while I picked at the corn, and the rice and vegetables, then moved on to the pozole. Pinto bean pozole… In North Carolina she'd found a place that made it vegetarian instead of with the usual pork, then told me her mother made excellent pozole, as taught by Sophia's abuela. In the next breath, I'd been assured her mom would love to figure out how to make me vegetarian pozole. Would… I hoped one day I'd get to taste her mom's cooking.

After the first delicious mouthful, the food stuck in my throat and I had to chase it down with a huge gulp of beer, which made me burp like a college beer-pong bro. "Sorry," I mumbled.

Sophia's fork paused in midair. "You feeling okay?"

"Yeah. I mean…no, but yeah." I ran my spoon through the pozole, turning it on its side so the stew dripped back into the bowl. "It's great, but I guess I'm not as hungry as I thought I was." Smiling, I looked up at her. "Means there'll be more leftovers for you, though."

"That's true," she agreed, forcing a small smile. "Leftovers for daaays."

Yep, things weren't strained at all. It wasn't us—it was the situation, my departure lingering in the air like the stench of rotten food which would remain even after I'd gone. I ate another mouthful, then pushed both bowl and plate aside. Sophia kept eating her enmoladas, alternating between studying her plate and studying me. I picked at the chips and guac, because chips are addictive which means they don't fill you up even if you're full, and that's a scientific fact.

We didn't talk any more. She finished her dinner. We packed up leftovers. She put them away. We cleaned up. She poured us both a glass of wine. We moved awkwardly around each other at a time when

I most wanted us to feel connected. It was almost like I'd already gone, and we'd completely forgotten how to communicate.

"I don't know what to say," I finally admitted, as we stood in my kitchen like neither of us had any idea where to go or what to do next.

Sophia closed the gap between us. "Me either." She stretched up on tiptoes and kissed me, her hand cupping the back of my neck.

For a few minutes, we said nothing at all.

I would have taken her to bed then and there, but I wanted to make sure she was satisfied with what was happening and how to get around the logistics of my absence. I reached up to hold her hand that was against my neck, gently pulling it down and kissing each knuckle, then her palm. "I'm sorry this past week has been so hectic and we haven't been able to spend more time together."

She reached for her wineglass. "I know it's not intentional, you've had to prepare for your new job. But I think we've made pretty good use of the time we've had." The smirk as she drank made it very clear what "good use" she was talking about. My eyes were drawn immediately to that smirk, her mouth, those soft pillowy lips, and I remembered the way she'd indulged herself with me last night, taking her time, her lips and tongue exploring every inch of my body.

I drank a slow, indulgent mouthful of wine, storing away those memories alongside the cache of Sophia that was already in my brain. "Yes," I agreed hoarsely. "We definitely have."

The smirk faded, replaced by a frown and furrowed eyebrows. "You'll stay in touch while you're traveling, right? Like when you're waiting during layovers?"

"Of course," I said immediately. God, I couldn't believe this hadn't come up yet, and that we were still going through such basic details hours before I was due to leave. "I'll text as soon as I can at each layover."

"When will you get to...where you're going?" Sophia asked neutrally. She'd been silent on the topic of my actual travel arrangements, probably because she knew I couldn't share many details with her, and in the maelstrom of getting ready, giving her a vague itinerary had been way down my list and had never happened. What could I even say? I'll leave, then after a bunch of flights, arrive in an unspecified country. She had no idea where I'd be, and had expressed her concern about it a few times, wondering if she should worry if she heard about "events" overseas. Understandable, but my hands were shackled on sharing that information, and I couldn't break out.

I groaned at the thought of the travel monstrosity awaiting me. "It'll be your Saturday morning, assuming no delays." And there were always delays. "I'll text when I'm cleared at my final destination, but probably won't call you until I've at least taken a shower to make myself feel somewhat human again." Final destination. Nice one, cyborg.

"That's fine. Just when you can, so I know you've arrived and I'm not worried."

"I will. I promise." I pressed my forehead to hers. "I'm not sure what comms will be like where we are, and it's possible there will be cell issues initially. If you're worried, you can call the number on the info sheet I've left on the fridge."

"Good. Not the phone issues, but me having someone to call." Sophia kissed the tip of my nose then pulled away so we weren't quite so eyeball-to-eyeball. "What time do we have to leave for the airport again?" She'd insisted on coming to see me off, and I'd agreed, even though we'd also both agreed that public goodbyes were shitty. She'd leave the airport and drive straight to her parents' for Thanksgiving, which I'd objected to—driving while upset was not a good idea—but she'd shut me down.

I pulled a face. "Early."

"Oh." Sophia didn't mask her disappointment. "So you need to go to sleep early tonight?"

"No." I quickly finished my wine, took her hand and began pulling her out of the kitchen, through my living room, toward my bedroom. "I can sleep during my flights and layovers. I want as much of you as I can before I go. I need to saturate myself with everything that I'm going to be missing while I'm gone." I wanted to fill myself with her, keep her in all the places that would hollow out with anxiety and frustration and fear while I was gone.

Sophia came willingly, and as she walked along my hall, her free hand trailed along the wall. "Saturate? That doesn't sound very sexy, honestly."

I paused at the door to my bedroom to turn on the light. "It's very sexy," I argued teasingly. "*If* you do some mental gymnastics about saturation and being wet and how it could be a euphemism for arousal."

A dubious eyebrow rose. "Then I'd better give you something good to saturate in." Laughing, she wrinkled her nose. "Nope. Sorry. Can't do it."

"What a shame. I suppose I'll just have to go the old-fashioned way and ask you how wet you are." I pushed her shirt up, briefly cupping her breasts before slipping my hands around to unhook her bra. But she slithered away as soon as I'd undone the clasp.

"Nuh-uh. Not until I say so." She shimmied the straps off, threaded her bra out through the sleeve of her tee, then handed the garment to me. "Put this on the chair."

I inhaled sharply. Dominant Sophia was hot as hell, and she knew it. She'd only brought out Dominant Sophia a handful of times, and each time it was clear she'd noticed my (very favorable) reactions to this aspect of her. I took the bra and as I draped it over the back of the antique Chippendale chair in the corner of my room, Sophia moved to stand by the bed. My heart hammered with anticipation. I wanted to ask her what she wanted me to do next, but didn't dare.

Her expression was smug as she studied me like she knew exactly what I was thinking. "Take off your top. Slowly."

I raised it over my head and dropped it to the floor, waiting for further instruction. My nipples tightened as Sophia's slow, lusty gaze traveled over my breasts and down my torso. I saw her quick inhalation before she murmured, "Now your sweats."

I hooked my thumbs in the waistband, but didn't move, except for my eyes which traveled up to meet hers. Sophia nodded, and I complied immediately, pushing my sweats down and standing on the cuffs, hooking my foot in the fabric to kick them out of my way.

I shivered, not from the cool air, standing before her in nothing but my panties, but at the appreciative, appraising look she gave me as her gaze traveled up and down my body. Sophia closed the space between us and without a word, wasted no time divesting me of my underwear. Her hands moved slowly over the skin of my thighs and ass, lightly, teasingly, and my shiver turned to a shudder.

Sophia cupped my breasts, and as her thumbs stroked my nipples, she began maneuvering me toward my bed. "Lie down. On your back."

I dropped onto the bed and shimmied back until I lay against the pillows.

"Spread your legs for me."

I did as I was told.

"Wider," she commanded. "Let me see how wet you are."

I now had absolutely no desire to make a joke about saturation. My legs fell open, spreading for her. Within seconds, Sophia dove between my thighs, settling herself against me with her hipbone pressed against my most sensitive places. Her mouth moved over my collarbone, my breasts, down my ribs. And when I went to tug at her clothing, she carefully moved out of my reach, while still keeping contact with my bare skin. She held my eyes, her expression serious but at the same time, so soft. "I need this, Lexie. Please. Let me have this first."

Swallowing hard, I nodded. She could have whatever she wanted, whatever she needed. I knew that she'd let me take the same when she was satiated. Sophia held herself up on an elbow and pressed her fingers deeply inside me. Her groan covered my muffled, "Oh my god" then her open-mouthed kiss smothered my, "Oh, fuc—"

She fucked me hard and deep, but not roughly. Every stroke, every thrust, felt like love, and my back arched in response, hips rising to meet her. Her lips remained within a whisper of my skin, licking, sucking, kissing, nibbling. I was facing months without this, without intimacy, without her, and I had no idea how I was going to do it. I clung to her, unable to do anything but let her give me pleasure so intense I felt it in every cell of my body. The heat built until it felt molten and as my breathing hitched she withdrew her fingers and scrambled down until she was snuggled between my spread thighs.

When the warm wetness of Sophia's mouth covered my labia, my thighs clamped around her shoulders and as her tongue circled my clit, I took a fistful of her hair. Sophia murmured something against my clit, the subtle vibration sending a heavy pulse of arousal through me, and when I tugged her hair a little harder, guiding her, the reverberation of her deep moan nearly sent me over the edge. The insistent press of her fingers reentering me pushed me closer. When she stroked inside me as her tongue and lips softly worked my clit, I couldn't hold on to my climax, nor my loud cry as I came.

Sophia kept her mouth on me, her fingers lightly stroking until I stopped twitching and shuddering. I reached for her and she gently climbed up the bed, bestowing kisses over my inner thighs, hipbones, belly, ribs, breasts, until finally she kissed my mouth. She stayed there, looking down at me, her eyes shining with tears she kept blinking back. "I love you. Promise me you'll come back to me safely in one piece."

It took a deep inhalation and shaky exhalation before I could speak, because I needed her to hear me, to know I meant each word. "I promise."

"*Promise* me," she said again. "Because I need you. I need *this*. For many more days. Months. Years. Decades even." She swallowed hard, blinking rapidly. "I've never felt like this before about anyone, Lexie. Ever. And I don't want to know what life is like without you."

I pulled her face down to mine. "I promise," I said solemnly. I'd never wanted to keep a promise so badly. As I began to untie her sweatpants, I murmured, "I need you too."

And until dawn peeked through my bedroom windows, I showed her just how much.

CHAPTER TEN

My new home sweet home

I'd hoped I might get to travel business class, or at least some kind of premium economy section instead of being shoved at the back of the plane with all the crying babies and lavatories. No such luck. I was smack-bang in the middle seat at the back of economy class for every single flight. It was like whoever had arranged my travel had purposely chosen the most annoying combination of flight legs and seating positions—almost forty-five hours of travel, flights departing and arriving in the small hours of the morning, and one stupid eleven-hour layover in the UAE. But I had to suck it up, because if I didn't, you know…jail, or worse.

So my trip was basically many hours feeling stiff, cramped, and annoyed with people encroaching upon my physical and mental space, and when I disembarked from my final flight, I had to stop myself from throwing double middle fingers at the plane. Honestly, I'd need these six months just to recover from that journey. I'd texted back-and-forth with Sophia at each stop, until she'd fallen asleep midconversation while I'd been waiting to board my last flight. Bless her.

My travel documents passed rigorous inspection at every step—thanks, Identity Team—and I moved through Customs and Immigration with only the regular level of scrutiny, which I'd expected. But I had no idea where I was going beyond the airport and, of course, Jeff was ignoring all my calls and texts. It was midafternoon in a foreign country and I was, for all intents and purposes, alone. Great. I mentally listed my options and decided upon the most logical one—napping in an airport chair until Jeff answered.

I sent a quick text to Sophia to let her know I'd arrived safely and confirming I'd be in better contact once I'd settled in. No answer. I double-checked my time conversion. Even though she knew this was about when I should have arrived, it was still not even seven a.m. back home, which sat firmly at "way too fucking early in the morning" for Sophia. I smiled, wishing I was still at home in bed with her.

After making sure my headscarf covered my hair and draped nicely around my shoulders, I shrugged into my backpack, slung my duffel over one shoulder, and wheeled my suitcase through the terminal, searching for a safe place to camp out. As I meandered, trying to not look scared and desperate, my phone buzzed a text alert. Not Sophia—an unknown number.

Come outside.

Well, I was either about to walk into my very own horror movie, or catch a ride. I did as the text instructed, and saw the most unwelcome welcome face leaning against the hood of a sedan that looked like it'd fall apart after a few miles. Jeff. He raised a hand in a jaunty wave, and I picked my way through the crowd amassed outside.

"Thanks for coming to get me. And for telling me you'd planned to come get me." Dammit. I'd promised myself no snark, and I hadn't even made it thirty seconds. Do better, Lexie.

Jeff smiled broadly. "My pleasure. How was your trip?"

"So many crying babies. So many people with airsickness. So many elbows in my sides. So many manspreaders."

"What a shame. My trip was the most relaxing I've had in a while," he enthused. "Business class the whole way, which was nice, considering it's a work expense and they usually barely spring for coach. I've never slept so well on a long-haul flight."

I unclamped my molars to grind out, "Lucky you."

"I know."

I rolled my eyes at him and thankfully remembered my no-snark resolution. "Okay, Jeeves. Let's go."

He held out a hand for my bags. I dropped my duffel from my shoulder and passed it to him. After stowing my two bigger bags in the trunk, he chivalrously opened the passenger door for me. Once he'd settled in the driver's seat, Jeff turned to me. "I've had some time to acclimate, so I'm ready to take you into the office so we can get cracking with this assignment." Without waiting for me to answer, he pulled out into traffic like he was driving a stolen car.

Inhale for three, exhale for six. Lose your murderous intent. "Can I at least go home and take a shower? Unpack? Eat some food that isn't of questionable freshness, outright stale, or from a vending machine that operated in a language I don't speak." The candy had been weird, but surprisingly tasty. "I also need to call Sophia." And do an hour of yoga until my body resembled my body again, not the Picasso painting it currently felt like.

"Home is also the office. Our apartment is a few blocks from the main city *hub*"—he raised one hand off the steering wheel to air-quote—"where the action is. It's a new apartment building, modern and quite nice. Shared bathroom, sorry, but with a Western toilet thankfully, because I have old knees and my squat ain't what it used to be. A bedroom each, obviously, with good-sized living area. They converted part of the living space for our workstations." He glanced at me, eyebrows bouncing upward. "Not ideal, but at least it's a short commute from home to work."

Jeff cracking a joke? How novel. I decided to play along. "But commuting is when I listen to podcasts and audiobooks."

"Break it into thirty-second blocks up and down the hallway. You'll finish a podcast episode every few weeks and maybe one book before you go home."

"Marvelous."

He weaved expertly through the traffic. "I've been working with the local ops team to get everything set up. I think you'll be happy with the work and living spaces. We have a building-supplied housekeeper, but I've already told them we won't be needing any services. We have to do cooking and housework ourselves because of the sensitive nature of our work, but if we need help with grocery essentials then the option is there."

"Wow, I could get spoiled having someone do my grocery shopping for me." I glanced out the window as we sped away from the airport. "But I'll be fine procuring food and other supplies, thanks."

"You're not spoiled already?" he asked. "Doesn't Ms. Flores take good care of you?"

I bristled at his insinuation and turned away to check my phone for a message from Sophia. Nothing. "She takes very good care of me," I rebutted indignantly before my brain engaged, and I snapped my mouth closed. This man was the last person to whom I should be giving personal information. The last person around whom I should drop my guard. I trusted him because I had to, but I wasn't going to invite him over for tea, cookies, and hair-braiding.

"I'm glad." He smiled at me. "And don't worry, Alexandra, I'm domesticated. I'm also excellent with a vacuum and toilet brush."

"Lucky me."

"You don't know the half of it," Jeff said steadily.

I watched him for another ten seconds, and when he said nothing and I still couldn't figure out what I say, I looked out the window again. The scenery was mesmerizing, and I stared at the mountain ranges with sprinkles of snow on their peaks, and the swathes of dust swirling in the unceasing wind out by the airport. The sparseness gave way to gentle gentrification and then after a few more kilometers, the city. The bustling city center looked much the same as all cities I'd visited in this country, a strange juxtaposition of modern and old, traditional and nontraditional, high-rise buildings nestled alongside houses and mansions and a presidential palace and barely standing housing structures that could only be described as shacks. Dotted amongst this chaos were buildings in all stages of construction—though "half-finished" seemed to be the norm.

So many people. Cars loosely obeying the road rules. Bicycles holding up proceedings. Motorcycles weaving precariously through traffic. And the occasional weapon in plain sight. Good times.

"Where'd you get the car?" I asked when Jeff paused to let a mass of people cross in front of us. "Let" was perhaps a generous term. They stepped onto the road as a group, and it was stop or run them over.

"The local field office helped me buy it yesterday from our budget, not that we *really* needed a car. Everything we need is in walking distance and if there's anything heavy, then we can pay someone to deliver for us. But it's nice to have, just in case."

"Great." I turned back to staring out the window, memorizing the route, taking in the surroundings, trying to spot anything that looked out of place. Nothing did, of course. That would make things far too easy, because who'd hang banners on their homes saying "Terrorists Live Here"? A mosque was being built and when we stopped in traffic next to workers laying the beautiful stone foundations, they glanced our way then went back to their task.

Deep in the city, after traversing a maze of streets, Jeff stopped on the opposite side of the road to a twelve-story—we were stopped a while, I counted the height—apartment building, ignoring the honks of displeasure as cars swerved around us. With a tilt of his chin across the street, he said, "Here we are."

The building was a pleasing orange, black, blue, and cream color, a balcony on each side pressed around the exterior on each level. Four balconies meant four apartments per floor, so…lots of neighbors, easy to blend in. It was a nice area, all things considered, and I was grateful for the location which should provide both relative safety as well as central convenience. An illuminated sign proclaimed this was Tala Tower. My new home sweet home.

Finally, a gap—barely big enough for a motorcycle it seemed— opened up and Jeff gunned the poor old car through it, ka-dunked over a drain and then a speed bump before slamming on the brakes at a security arm. The glass-enclosed security hut was manned by a bored-looking thirty-something guy who gave us a cursory glance and when the swipe card Jeff held up to the scanner raised the boom gate, turned back to his book. Security present, check. Capable, yet to be proven.

We drove down two ramps before Jeff expertly executed a three-point turn to squeeze us into the tiny space. I hoped the parking spaces weren't indicative of the apartment sizes. "Do we have our own parking spot, or is it first come, first served?" I asked.

"Own spot. Which isn't great."

I mmm'd in agreement. If someone figured out we weren't who we said we were, they would watch us and learn our routines. It would be easy to tamper with the vehicle. I reminded myself that the likelihood of any of that happening was almost nonexistent. This wasn't my first time in the field, nor Jeff's, I imagined, and I got the feeling he was good at being a chameleon, part of the scenery.

"I think the parking garage is secure enough but I'd still check things before I got in the car. You never know who knows what, and if that's slipped our notice." It was a loaded statement.

Oh good. Car bombs. Why not add another thing to the list of things to worry about? Sophia's question rattled around my brain. *Is it dangerous?* Just a whole lot, sweetheart. But only if we're caught. Otherwise it's just every-day-in-a-terrorist-hotbed dangerous. I tried to keep the image of her in my head but it kept sliding away, leaving me with nothing more than just a sense of her, of the feeling I had being near her, thinking about her. Whole. That thought had to be enough for now.

The car only just fit under the concrete roof of the parking space and I instinctively ducked. Jeff peered at me, seeming satisfied about something I didn't know, and murmured before he cut the engine, "We're on the sixth floor. Your garage swipe card, keys, and some other goodies are upstairs."

"Okay, thanks." A little higher up than I liked—getting out quickly in an emergency was my jam—but higher meant no through-the-window visitors, and six was still in reach of fire department ladders. I opened the door, careful not to scrape it on the pylon next to me. I didn't know why I bothered, because the car's paint job was basically one great big scrape. "This is a nice building. Nicer than where I was living the last time I was here."

"If you want to find accommodations like what you had last time, be my guest, but I'm staying right here with my amenities."

"I rather enjoyed cooking on my wood stove, thank you very much," I said imperiously as I hauled my suitcase and duffel from the trunk.

It was the truth. Elaheh, my ex-girlfriend—if she could be called that—had taught me how to prepare local dishes, and we'd cooked around frantic fucking sessions and then eaten our creations to refuel during moments of rest. I wondered what had happened to her. Married off to a man? Killed in drone strikes? Escaped somewhere where she could live the way she wanted?

It'd been attraction then flirtation then seduction before I'd realized Elaheh's younger brother was a person of interest who was quickly working his way up the local terrorist cell hierarchy. Talk about rock and hard place. I'd thought about asking someone to track her down once I was safely back on home soil and recovered, but wondered what the point would be. Though I'd cared for her, I didn't love her, and most importantly—I'd murdered her brother in self-defense during my hostage event, and my rescue operation had also killed her uncle. There was nothing more to say to her.

"I'm sure you did enjoy cooking on your wood stove, and maybe you were even good at it." There it was, another compliment wrapped in a slap.

"Thanks?"

"You're welcome. Now try to look like a schoolteacher wanting to establish a school for the young women of this region."

I quickly checked my appearance in my compact, ensuring I looked presentable and my headscarf was still settled neatly and tightly over my hair and around my shoulders. Jeff took my suitcase and duffel and started walking toward the bank of elevators set into the polished concrete wall, leaving me to hurry after him.

"And what did we decide you were again?" I asked when I drew level, trying for a withering tone and falling short to somewhere around disparaging. I knew what Jeff's cover was, but was in a snicky mood. I held the strap of my backpack tightly and tried to look as casual and not "hey I'm an intelligence analyst here to gather information on people you might know" as I could.

"Your long-suffering husband, also a schoolteacher, relegated to the shadow of your brilliance in a nonteaching position this time." He adopted a hangdog expression as he pressed the elevator button.

I raised an eyebrow and, as best I could from my three-inches-shorter position, looked down my nose at him. "You'd better remember that."

"I never forget my place, Alexandra. And it's the perfect complement—I'll say I'm looking at assisting with infrastructure and whatnot, related to your school. And I couldn't bear to be apart from you for months on end." That last bit dripped dry sarcasm.

"Solid." I raised a clenched fist. "The dream school team."

As we waited for the elevator, I pulled my long-sleeved linen top away from my body, annoyed that I was sweating through the cool, airy fabric. The weather was much as I recalled when I'd been in the country around the same time of year—cool and dry—and I tried to ignore the fact the sweat trickling down my back had nothing to do with the climate and everything to do with nervousness.

The elevator was empty when we got in, but stopped at the lobby floor to admit a young couple. I peeked out through the closing doors, taking in the lobby and noting that, like the interior of the elevator, on the surface it looked elegant and well-crafted. But if you looked closer you could see evidence of quick, shoddy work. I hoped the shoddy work was only cosmetic and didn't extend to important things like the structure and electrical stuff.

I offered a polite nod to the couple then averted my eyes and kept them down as we rode the elevator up. Thankfully, it was sans shitty elevator music. When we stopped on six, Jeff took my bags again, and gestured for me to go ahead. "Six-oh-three," he said once the elevator doors closed behind us. "End of the hall on the left."

Standard apartment hallway, and the doors were surprisingly well-spaced. Maybe we weren't in for cramped living quarters after all. Cooking smells from 601, television sounds from 602, a quiet argument from 604.

"Home sweet home," Jeff declared as he opened the front door of our apartment, and after peeking inside, ushered me in.

I dropped my backpack onto the kitchen counter just inside the doorway on the right, and stared at what would be my home for the next six months. The apartment was a medium-sized two-bedroom with soundproofing on all the walls and ceiling. "What about the floor?" I asked as I pointed to the tacked-up foam material, which would keep our conversations private, but also made home-ifying the space with artwork hard. "Or are we only worried about what's above and beside us?"

He set my bags down by the door then closed and locked it before engaging the deadbolt and super-heavy-duty chain. "It's under the flooring."

A small table with two chairs sat on a shiny linoleum patch beside the kitchen, a couch was wedged against the far wall facing a television set on a small entertainment unit. The rest of the living room was taken up with two desks laden with computers, laptops, telephone and electronics equipment. The desks were separated by a partition which had maps and photographs and assorted documentation pinned to it. It provided a small amount of privacy so we could work without the distraction of someone right beside us.

"You did all this in just a few days?" Organizing the rent or purchase of the apartment and kitting it out would have been a huge, time-consuming job.

"No. I just made a few modifications. The ops team had been utilizing this apartment as a second office. They're not particularly happy to have lost the space."

"What a coincidence, because I'm not particularly happy to have gained the space." I unwound my headscarf, folded it in three, and draped it over the back of a chair.

"But it's a great space. With a great view." He pointed to the kinda-cubicle farthest from the apartment door. "That's your workstation."

"Thanks." I'd deal with that once I'd taken a shower, eaten something that wasn't snack food, done something about the fact my body felt like a knotted rope, and spoken to Sophia.

I checked out the couch, which was barely a two-seater, and the television that was more like a computer monitor but was better than what I'd expected, which was nothing. Actually, the whole apartment was better than I'd expected—new, clean, and surprisingly light and airy. I realized immediately that the windows were bullet resistant. Comforting, but I wasn't worried about bullets; I was worried about something bigger and boomier. Surprisingly, given the fortresslike feeling of the whole place, the door to the balcony worked. I unlocked the sliding glass door and peeked out. Jeff was lying about the view, unless you were an urbanophile.

As well as the plethora of small buildings and houses, I could see two embassies, the Presidential Palace, a school, a few other apartment buildings, and a handful of restaurants. Green spaces—parks and rudimentary sporting fields—broke up the immense sprawl of buildings, but the press of so many high-rises felt stifling.

When I came back inside, Jeff double-checked the sliding door lock, and I grumbled internally at being treated like a five-year-old until he explained it was a weird one, and I discovered I hadn't locked it as I'd thought.

"Thanks," I mumbled, suitably embarrassed at my reaction.

He nodded. "I've taken the first room and left the one at the back closest to the bathroom for you."

Seemed he'd jumped in and grabbed the good stuff first—workstation, bedroom. My brain mercifully ran the scenario before I accused him of that, and realized he'd actually taken the worst of both. They were closest to the door, which would put him in the metaphorical line of fire. Interesting. "Great, thanks. I pee in the middle of the night, so…close to the bathroom is good."

Jeff's eyebrows rose fleetingly. "Good to know. I'm a light sleeper, when I actually manage to sleep, so I'll make a note to train my brain into 'that's Alexandra peeing, not someone who shouldn't be in here.' Also, there's something in the closet for you."

"Is that supposed to be a joke?" I asked dryly. That was going to get old fast.

His laugh was quick and loud. Still chuckling, he assured me, "No, that's just where I thought it'd be safe and out of your way until you needed it."

Chivalry personified, he took my bags to my room, placing them outside the door, then mumbled something about leaving me to settle in before slipping away, now mumbling something about food.

My bedroom was about ten-by-ten and consisted of a bed, unmade but with linens folded neatly on the full-sized mattress which looked mercifully clean and new, a bedside table, and a freestanding closet and dresser. The walls were covered in the same soundproofing material as the rest of the house, and my immediate thought was that at least I could have phone or video sex without worrying about being overheard. All the furniture seemed new and when I sat and bounced on the mattress, I discovered it had a pleasing firmness. Great sex mattress. Pity I had nobody to have sex with.

I opened the closet in search of what'd been left for me. Jeff's closet gift was a Heckler & Koch handgun case. Nice to have but still, something I hoped I'd never use here. I clicked it open and peered inside. An HK P30—the same model as my personal, rarely used, firearm. Creepy that he or They knew that.

I got to work putting clothing and shoes in the closet and dresser, and setting out my Kindle and laptop before making the bed with the pale-blue linens provided.

The bathroom was surprisingly spacious. Half the cabinet behind the mirror and also the space under the sink had been left for my stuff. Jeff had sensitive teeth. I packed my personal bathroom items into the spaces provided, magnanimously didn't leave tampons strewn everywhere, and left the area as neat as I'd found it.

There. I was all moved in. Still no answer from Sophia.

I took my mind off that fact for a few minutes by adjusting the time and date on my wristwatch. The Longines was a gift from my father on my thirtieth birthday and was, like most things I'd received from him, flashy but not really my style. A quick shower and clean clothes helped me feel somewhat human, and I further humanized myself setting up the Zen space in the bedroom with my yoga mat and props, a scaled-down version of my altar from home, my portable speaker, and a picture of calming forest scenery stuck to the closet. I'd need to find some healthy greenery and gorgeous scented candles at the market to complete the vibe.

Still nothing from Sophia.

I wasn't worried, but I was…yeah, I was worried. I didn't think anything had *actually* happened to her, but it was unlike her to sleep this late. Unlike her, but still not completely outside the realm of possibility, especially not given the stresses of the past week. I'd soften my brain and body with some yoga, otherwise I'd be projecting my anxieties and stress onto her, then I'd call.

I changed, put on my yoga playlist, and settled in for a practice I'd been anticipating for days. Everything outside my body receded as I moved through Sun Salutations, Cat-Cow, deep Forward Folds and back-stretching Head-to-Knee Forward Bends, energy-focusing Warrior Two, and long, gorgeous minutes in Pigeon to open my plane-and-airport-stuck hips. I took my time in each pose, letting the movement and breath calm me, then lay down on my back for a long restorative Savasana. Finally, my brain and body felt like mine again, like I could inhale a full breath into my belly and move my limbs without them sticking.

My practice had settled the worry I'd felt about Sophia and when I picked up my phone again, and saw her message on the silenced screen, that worry left me completely.

Sorry! I was dead asleep. So glad you're there safely, call whenever? The group of emojis that followed looked like she'd smashed everything that might convey love.

I responded to her message on Signal that I was about to video call, and received a heart emoji in response. I hadn't tried the Internet yet, and crossed my fingers it'd work. Sophia accepted my call within seconds and after a heart-stopping connection lag, her face appeared. She sat on her couch, with the laptop on her coffee table. I closed my eyes and imagined the space she was in, warm and comforting, the ever-present scent of vanilla from the candles she kept burning whenever she was home.

When I opened my eyes again, Sophia's expression of worry and delight and relief made my eyes burn. "Hi," I breathed. "Can you hear me okay? See me?"

"Yes! I can. I'm so sorry, I've hardly slept since you left and I got super tired so I set an alarm to wake up when you were supposed to land, and then I slept through it. I'm a terrible person. How are you? How were your flights? You look tired, baby. God, I love you. I've missed you. I can't believe I survived two days with you a million miles away."

What was I supposed to say? I love you so much that it fills me with indescribable joy and I miss you so much my chest hurts. And how am I? Terrified, anxious, and missing you. Smiling at her expectant expression, I answered, "Tired. But I'm doing okay." It was true, just a slightly abbreviated version of how I was.

She propped her chin in her palms. "You look exhausted. Have you eaten and relaxed at all yet? How's your accommodation? Are you in a house?"

I looked around the room. "I haven't eaten yet, no. That's next on the agenda. We've got an apartment. Pretty new and nice, actually. I've showered and had a short yoga practice, so I'm as relaxed as I can be." I pushed up off the bed, raising my phone up high. Contorting out of the way of the front-facing camera, I did a slow three-sixty spin around the room so she could see my bedroom.

"What's with the padding?"

"For when I feel like throwing myself at the walls." I grinned, then grinned wider when she smiled and rolled her eyes in response. "It's soundproofing. Which will come in handy when you and I want to talk about something other than my new digs." I bounced my eyebrows, hoping she'd catch my drift.

She did. "So noted," Sophia murmured. After a charged pause, she said, "It looks…cozy."

Laughing, I agreed, "That about sums it up. But it's got enough space for everything I need in a bedroom. Just."

She gestured over my left shoulder. "I see you've already got the Zen Zone set up."

I flopped down onto the bed, lying on my back with the phone held above me. "Yeah. I think I'll really need some Zen."

"I'll bet." She let out a soft groan of frustration, then shook her head as if forcibly shaking whatever thought she'd just had out of her head. "What about your work partner? Are you guys getting along okay?"

I paused. "He's fine. I may have misjudged him slightly and he's not actually the vilest thing to walk the Earth. But it's only the first day, so there's still plenty of time for him to let me down."

"Well, that's a positive, right?"

"Right." I sat up and settled back against my pile of pillows, raising my knees to rest the hand holding my phone against my thighs. "How about you? How was Thanksgiving? How'd you sleep last night?" These questions, ones we'd ask each other if we were in the same city and had spent the day apart at work, now felt like polite small talk between new friends, not deep conversation between lovers.

"Thanksgiving was the same as it always is," she said lightly, and I could tell she was being evasive, probably worried about upsetting me because I'd missed it. "And I slept like shit. Kept waking up, until I forgot to wake up. I just…miss you. And it's only been a couple of days." The unspoken "And we have nearly two hundred more" lingered unpleasantly between us.

"I know, sweetheart. I miss you too. It's shit, and I hate it. I hate being here. I hate being apart from you. I hate knowing we have to schedule talking to each other. I hate that we had no time before I had to leave, and that everything felt so stilted and like we'd forgotten how to communicate with each other." And I hated that it still felt like we didn't know how to communicate. I blew out a noisy breath as the weight of the situation finally settled on my shoulders. "I…I think it's finally hit me. That this is really happening. That we're separated and it's for a while."

"Yeah," Sophia agreed glumly. "I've just been trying not to think about it, but…we need to think about it, don't we." She swiped her palms underneath her eyes. "How the hell are we going to do this?"

I had no idea.

After Sophia and I said our goodbyes and confirmed timing for a video call the following night, I took the two bottles of bourbon I'd carted from the States into the kitchen, where I found a glass of water and a PB&J waiting for me. A pot of fresh-smelling coffee sat on the warmer—so tempting—but drinking coffee would mess with trying to reset my circadian rhythms. I just had to ride out the sleepiness and go to bed at my usual time in my new time zone.

I murmured my thanks for the snack and set the bottles down without officially handing over custody. Jeff leaned against the kitchen counter while I ate, studiously ignoring the bourbon until I'd finished half the sandwich. With a casual gesture at the paper-bag-wrapped shapes, which were clearly bottles, he asked, "Say, is that that bourbon I kindly asked you for?"

"Mhmm," I said around my mouthful. "But it's going to cost you."

He reached into his back pocket, affecting a heavy, fake sigh. "How much?"

"Some common decency? I think that's a fair trade for two liters of bourbon." I bit off an aggressive chunk of my sandwich.

"I think I'd rather pay you in dollars."

"You're a bastard, you know that?" I said cheerfully. Cheerful means I don't really mean it, you see? I'm just kidding around, my friend.

"Believe it or not, I have been told that before."

"No, I believe it. Why not both? Reimburse me *and* stop being a dick to me."

He huffed out a sigh. "Look, Alexandra. I am who I am. We have a job to do, so let's do it and accept that you're you and I'm me and we have to find a way to work in close quarters without antagonizing each other. It's as simple as that." He held out three fifties and shook them when I just stared. "I'll try for some decency, but no promises. I made you a sandwich, didn't I?"

"Trying is good enough. And yes you did, thank you." I pocketed the cash and pushed the bottles toward him. "One liter of Booker's, one liter of Maker's."

"Thank you." He hugged them to his chest like a precious pair of newborn twins. "You know, we might actually get along after all."

I raised an eyebrow. "What? You mean we aren't already?"

"Like a house on fire, Alexandra."

I laughed and stuffed the last of the sandwich in my mouth. A house on fire. Yeah, and I was trapped inside the inferno...

CHAPTER ELEVEN

Just when you think you know someone—you don't,
obviously, is what I'm getting at

I spent the rest of the day familiarizing myself with the apartment, the contents of the pantry and refrigerator which Jeff had partially stocked, putting my important Oolong tea stash, mug and infuser out on the counter, and going over home and work expectations with Jeff. As the parameters stated, part of our job was "quick" analysis of raw intel collected by the ops team—some of which we already had here waiting for us—but after a cursory glance, the work mostly seemed like sit and wait. I loved sitting and waiting. I was *so* good at sitting and waiting. Sarcasm over.

"When can I meet the ops team?" I asked Jeff, who was clacking away beside me on the world's loudest keyboard. Guess this was going to be a headphones-while-working office space.

He popped up over the partition. "Tomorrow? I thought we could go for a walk first, so you can stretch your legs and get the lay of the land and fill up the pantry and fridge with things you want. Then drive over to meet the ops team, I'll make some introductions and we can talk to them about what they'd like from us, and vice versa."

"Sounds good."

He grinned. "No, it sounds like we're all crash test dummies for this wonderful new *initiative*."

I found myself returning his grin. "Glad you're finding it as bullshit as I am."

Dummy or no, I was excited by the prospect of digging in, even if it meant going over all the files with a magnifying glass and fine-toothed comb to check all was as it should be. I needed to immerse myself in the work, ridiculous as it might be, stuck out in the middle of nowhere. Otherwise it was going to be a horribly draggy time here—the whole keeping busy to take your mind off being in a hostile country with a man who isn't going to hurt you but may or may not be an ally and you're without your brand-new girlfriend actually works. And I *needed* my mind fully taken off the situation, because while the logistics of prep and travel had kept my brain busy, now that was over, the dread was back and had brought its friends.

The first file I clicked on was labeled "The Cleaner." The ops team had mostly been focused on gathering intelligence on a local cell, homing in on one of the suspected lieutenants, doing the usual digging into his dealings, trying to spin the web out from him to see who else would be caught in it. The Cleaner, real name Basir Mohammadzai, had turned up on our radars four months ago and was proving to be intelligent and brutal—the worst combination—*and* it seemed he had ties to funding from cells in America. Part of our job would be figuring out those ties, as well as where this cell fit into the larger network.

I pushed my chair back to peer around into Jeff's cubicle. This partition was going to get old really quickly. "Did we name him The Cleaner, or is that what he's officially known as?"

"The officer whose asset first gave us the intelligence about Mohammadzai called him that." Jeff's shrug was accompanied by a tiny eye roll.

"Original," I said dryly. "You know, this is the fifth time I've seen an ops officer nickname someone The Cleaner."

"Maybe they're all just really clean," he deadpanned.

"Mmm." Let's go with that rather than the more likely gruesome explanation behind that nickname. I used my feet to wheel my chair back to my desk and resumed skimming the details of Mohammadzai's file. After I finished the biographical stuff, it was time for the meat. When I got to the meat, I saw instantly that it was rotten.

Intelligence suggested that The Cleaner had been at the top level of planning four of the last six terrorist attacks originating from this region. He was ambitious, I'd give him that, and it was interesting that we hadn't really picked him up until recently. Where had he come from and when? Was he recruited—late—by family? Had he moved from another region where he'd been learning and watching, while staying under the radar? Or had he joined on his own to further his ideology?

I clicked over to look into the family segment of his file. Wife, one three-year-old son. A woman in the ops team had tried to make contact with the wife a few weeks ago, with little success, and now it seemed they were figuring out their next tactic for approach. I kept scrolling until the picture of Mohammadzai's wife came into full view. The moment I saw the face, framed by hijab, I froze. I recognized her instantly. My whole body felt like I'd stepped into an arctic blast. Oh no no no.

Elaheh.

A flood of memories washed over me, trying to drag me under, and I struggled to draw in a breath. Air rushed in raggedly, then out just as roughly. I tried again, managing a slightly more controlled breath, just enough to mutter, "Oh my fucking god. Oh fuck. Fuck. Oh no." I covered my mouth with both hands, my heavy, uneven breaths echoing in the space made by my palms.

Jeff was by my side in seconds. "What is it?" he asked calmly.

I dropped my hands and pointed at the screen. "I—I know her." Elaheh looked the same as when I'd last seen her in early 2017, except she maybe had a few more fine lines enhancing her face. Huge, intelligent, deep-set gray—true gray—eyes, heart-shaped face, smooth skin, razor-sharp cheekbones. In this surveillance shot, her expression was intense, with a concentration I recognized. What I didn't recognize was the flash of anger in her usually serene eyes.

Jeff leaned over my shoulder, staring at the photograph of Elaheh. "Who?"

"Mohammadzai's wife. Elaheh Ahsan. She's…uh, well, I think she's…*technically* my ex-girlfriend?" The admission was nauseating.

"*What?*" he exclaimed.

"Maybe ex-lover is a better description? I don't know. We didn't *date*. We just slept together occasionally for about five months. So yeah, not my ex-girlfriend. Just a woman I've slept with. And it was years ago, I ended it in 2017, not long before the hostage thing. Fuck," I exhaled. How was this happening to me?

Jeff picked up his dropped jaw. "Please explain to me how you were sleeping with a woman whose husband is part of a local terrorist cell? No, not part of, but one of its *leaders*."

"Because, obviously, she wasn't either of those things back then. She was widowed young, still to be remarried." It had been a huge deal, her brother and uncle haranguing her about finding her a new husband when that was the last thing she wanted. But finding her a wife was even more out of the question than remaining single. "There were no signs of her being involved in any of the local cells or having any terrorist ideology at all. The thing with us just happened. And it was good while it lasted." I frowned. "You've read my file, you should know the details."

Jeff's eyebrows shot up. "That a woman you'd been intimate with and were considering talent-spotting had a younger brother in a terrorist cell who you'd tagged for close surveillance and maybe collection, and that you then killed him in self-defense during your hostage situation? Yes. I know that." He shook his head. "That's a whole other issue, and I can't believe I didn't see that connection or recognize that name from your file. But I'm talking about the relationship between you and this woman. Alexandra, you're not dumb. How did you not realize what was going on here?"

"Because there was *nothing* going on back then," I said immediately. "We were just sleeping together, we talked about inane things. I wouldn't have even called her a friend." His eyebrows still looked like they were being held up by pieces of string. Deep breath, calm down. "I learned about her brother through other channels, not through her. I know the signs from someone who has that ideology, I know what to look for. And there was nothing from her." I made a frustrated gesture. "You can't honestly think I would have slept with her if I'd thought for *one moment* she was in any way involved in local cell activity." This was insane. Completely and utterly bonkers.

His expression softened. "No, I don't. But you never considered she might have taken in some of her family's ideology by osmosis?"

"Honestly? No. She always seemed opposed to the violent aspects of it all."

"People change," he pointed out.

"It's only been…five and a half years since I last saw her. Surely that's not enough time for her to completely change who she is." Maybe if I deluded myself enough, I could rationalize what I'd just discovered.

"Yeah, well…" He reached over for my mouse, scrolling down to show a series of photos: Elaheh leaving a handbag by a building. Elaheh walking away. The building exploding.

Fuck.

Jeff met my eyes. "Looks to me like it's plenty of time."

By six thirty p.m. I was fading—a combination of jet lag, not having eaten a proper meal in a few days, exhaustion, and all the underlying stress that I was trying really hard to ignore. Elaheh was just the icing on a cake made of shit, and I had no idea how I was going to unpack that whole mess, personally or professionally. I'd finished skimming The Cleaner's file—taking note of the section on Elaheh, where they were deciding if she was just an "innocent" puppet or deserved her own file—and set it aside for tomorrow when I could allocate it the attention it needed.

Tomorrow... I stood and slowly stretched my back and legs. Tomorrow I'd take some time to figure out a game plan for how I'd approach the whole "the woman I'd slept with is apparently now a terrorist" thing. I started dinner without consulting Jeff, and he seemed surprised when I told him I was making a veggie frittata, and if he didn't like it to speak up now.

"You cook?" Incredulous, wary.

"Yes, I cook. I love cooking, and I'm even okay at it. So unless you're secretly a Michelin star-awarded chef, I'm happy to make dinner every night if you're happy to clean up. I'll even cook meat for you if you order it. But you need to make sure it's already butchered, please."

"Deal," he said immediately, then made a gesture like he was passing me something delicate. "I hand the reins of chef for the duration over to you. I can't cook."

"Can't cook, or won't cook?"

"Can't," he said instantly. "I burn water. My wife sweats any time I walk near the kitchen, and breaks out in hives when I go into it." His smile was fleeting, but unmistakable.

Ah. A clue. Married, clearly loved his wife. But most importantly? He was actually a human with emotions. Amazing. That would make it easier to keep this truce we needed if we were going to get through this assignment without a complete meltdown.

"Well, you've proven you can make coffee, though I can't speak to the quality yet, and a perfectly edible PB&J, so I'm happy for you to be near the kitchen."

He brought his hands together in front of his chest. "So benevolent."

"You might change your mind about dinner-for-dishes when you see how much mess I make when I cook."

Jeff shrugged. "I'll wear it."

I rechecked the spices in the pantry and deemed them satisfactory, for now. But I needed to visit the markets ASAP. "Any allergies, or anything you hate or refuse to eat?" I asked as I scribbled down a few additions to my spice shopping list.

He leaned his elbows on the counter. "I struggle with offal, and I don't love eggplant. Give me raw onion or scallions and I'll pick every single piece out. Other than that, I'm easy."

"Good, because there's no way in hell I'm cooking offal for you. Scallions are just window dressing, so I can do without them. Raw onion is essential in some dishes, but I can *try* those with cooked onion, no guarantee it will work though. But…may I try to convert you to eggplant?"

"You may try," he said magnanimously.

"Thank you. Is it the texture or taste that you don't like?"

"All of it. It's repulsive."

"Easily fixed." *Borani Banjan* was amazing and would convert even the staunchest of eggplant-hating weirdos. "I even promise you probably won't hate it when I serve it up."

"That's so comforting," he said dryly.

"Prepare to be comforted. I'm going to introduce you to some amazing local dishes." At his raised eyebrow, I added, "You've told me fuck-all about yourself, Jeff, so I have to assume you've never been here or tried regional cuisine?"

"I have been in this country before. Many times. The last time, which was quite some time ago, I either ate at the mess on base, or what they supplied us for covert ops."

The mess on base. Covert ops. He was ex-military. "MREs?"

He nodded and after a long pause, added, "Some of the guys would go out and buy food from locals, or bring something back to barbeque, but I was usually too tired to leave my rack."

I shrugged. "I mean, I'd happily eat vegetarian MREs every day, so I see the appeal. But for you, I'll make the effort to give you a new set of food memories to replace the old."

His mouth fell open. "You…like MREs?"

"I do," I admitted. Holding up both hands to ward off his revulsion, I said, "And yes, I know they're disgusting. But I still love them. The last time I was in the field, a friend used to smuggle me some every week."

"I spent ten years eating that shit while out on missions and if I never saw even a picture of one ever again, it would be too fucking soon." He indicated the chopping board. "So where'd you learn to cook regional cuisine? Was that part of your talent-spotting strategy? Playing the part of the Western woman wanting to take fresh menu items back home?"

"I learned from Elaheh."

His expression turned carefully neutral. "So you were close enough with her that she taught you how to cook some of her country's traditional meals?"

"Our relationship wasn't exactly deep, Jeff," I said matter-of-factly as I cracked eggs into a bowl. "Like I said, we slept together, she taught me to cook her favorite meals which she tweaked to be vegetarian, I taught her to cook some of my favorites. Sometimes we talked about superficial things, or mostly—she talked. She was lonely and I was there." I was lonely too, and the sex had scratched an itch. A purely physical one. I'd never felt completely comfortable with her, never felt I could fully let down my guard the way I did with Sophia.

Sophia... In a normal world I'd have to wrestle with myself about whether or not to tell my girlfriend that an old sex person had made her way back into my sphere. But my world was not a normal world. I poured the beaten egg mixture over the sautéed vegetables I'd carefully arranged in the skillet, sprinkled split green olives over the top, and popped the frittata into the oven. "I want to talk to her."

"Who?"

"Elaheh. I want to see her. I want to talk to her, maybe see if I can recruit her, or at the very least, get some information from her. The ops team has started a strategy for approaching her, so it's clearly a good call. If I can't recruit her then I'm sure I can find out *something* we can send up the chain." I didn't need to go through the talent-spotting process with Elaheh—I'd spent enough time with her to know I could get to her, get information from her.

"She's too far gone, Alexandra," he said gently. Gently, but clearly. "You saw the photos. Even if she's just casually involved with the cell, or was forced into it, she's still involved."

"Okay, then let me just talk with her for old time's sake. I killed her brother." I didn't have any illusions that I could just waltz up to her and talk to her about that, but I already had the groundwork laid because I knew her. Intimately.

"Talk with her about what? To tell her you're sorry? Explain yourself? Out yourself as an intelligence analyst?"

I rolled my eyes. "No, of course not. I just...I think I can work on her."

"I have to caution against that," he said calmly. "It's possible she knows who you are after your capture and her brother's involvement. And that can only end badly."

Of course anything was possible, but I was sure that, "She doesn't know who I am. All the men who were involved were killed during my rescue. I'm sure I can get her to talk." She used to love to talk, especially after we'd been to bed. Obviously I'd have to think of a new way to get her to open up to me now. I couldn't invite her over, but I was sure she'd invite me to her house for tea if we happened to bump into each other, accidental-like.

"She might not know that it was *you* specifically, but you would have to assume that she would know what happened to get her brother killed. She could know it was an American woman. Perhaps even know it was a blond American. And you know, even if she wasn't involved back then, her family was part of your capture. Families talk."

I shook my head. "Nuh-uh, not her family. Not to her. She complained about that often. And there's plenty of tourists who fit that description. Foreign aid workers too. Blond American women aren't exactly unicorns."

"They are in this country." His eyes narrowed slightly. "Is this truly about your certainty that you could gain something useful for us or even recruit her, *or* because you feel you have some unfinished business with her?" he said steadily. "Because your hubris could get you killed. Could get me killed."

"Any unfinished business I might have with her doesn't matter. This is because I know her and I think that could be valuable in utilizing her."

There was a long pause, not exactly a standoff, but we both stared at each other without moving. He sighed. "I think you should take some time and look more closely at what the ops team have gathered on her husband, read the notes they have for her and then decide if you think this is a smart idea."

I already knew it probably wasn't smart, assuming I could even make contact with Elaheh without it seeming forced. "Fine." I yanked the dishtowel from my shoulder and tossed it onto the counter. "Dinner will be ready in half an hour."

Jeff seemed surprised that it was not only edible, but tasty. I made a show of leaving my dirty dinner plate in the sink for him, then grumpily excused myself to meditate before bed. I needed to quiet my mind and calm my body. And I needed to get rid of the irrational annoyance that had flared at Jeff's insistence that trying to find, then talk to, Elaheh was a bad idea. I knew it was a bad idea but I couldn't shake the feeling that if I could pull it off—which I was sure I could— then the rewards would be worth it.

But if I couldn't pull it off...

Despite the soundproofing cocooning us, outside noise still seeped into the apartment, and from my bedroom the sound of cars and mass conversation was faint, but still there. It felt obnoxiously oppressive, except for one sound that had permeated the walls—the call to prayers. I'd heard them during the afternoon and early evening and had paused to listen, feeling instantly calmed by the familiar sound. The multiple calls broadcasting from the mosque loudspeakers had been part of my daily life every time I'd been on a field assignment and they were beautiful, calming, peaceful.

I was desperately hopeful that I could find that same calming peace this time around.

CHAPTER TWELVE

The things I do for this job…like pretending to be heterosexual

I woke a few minutes before the call to early morning prayers began emanating from mosque speakers. The sound echoed through the surrounding buildings and I lay motionless, eyes closed, in bed until it had ended. I spent longer than usual with my morning yoga practice, trying not only to set myself up for a good day but to calm the anxiety that'd greeted me upon waking. One day down and nothing had happened. Now I just had to make it another one hundred and eighty-five or so in the same vein. Talking with Sophia yesterday had helped, but one helpful thing fighting against a sea of terrifying things was a big ask.

When I made my way into the kitchen and found the kettle whistling on the stove, I decided Jeff was a five out of ten on the Okay Scale. Evidently he'd heard me showering after yoga and calisthenics and had decided to be nice.

"How's the jet lag?" he asked from his position at the small kitchen table. By the smell of it, he'd also made coffee and the pot was full ready for later, when I'd be ready for it. I moved him to a five-point-two-five out of ten.

"Bearable." I filled my tea strainer with Oolong, dropped it into my mug and poured boiling water over it. The breakfast offerings were an oatmeal-type cereal, bread, or fruit—all of which suited me. I'd noticed the day before that the fridge had been stocked with eggs, meats, some dairy, and vegetables, but the thought of anything more than the most basic of meals at that moment fried my brain and made my stomach protest indignantly.

I'd slept. Not well, or long, but I had slept. My night had been broken by the inevitable I-shouldn't-be-awake jet lag, but even after reluctantly taking a pill, my attempt at sleep had been fitful and stuffed with nightmares about being late for important meetings or going to the wrong place, and then a doozy about Sophia suddenly arriving here and wanting me to show her the sights. It didn't end well.

I dropped a handful of dates onto a plate, collected an apricot and a knife, and decided some carbs were probably a good idea. The bread was a traditional flat kind, and I cut one of the large squares in half and added it to my plate. The bread needed something and after a long search inside the quietly humming refrigerator, the slab of goat's cheese caught my attention. Don't mind if I do. Within a few minutes I had a goat's cheese and apricot sandwich with dates—not quite chips, but good enough—on the side.

The first mouthful was a revelation and my flat mood morphed into something more like a normal status. My tea further equalized me and within minutes I felt like myself. Mostly.

Jeff waited until I'd finished my breakfast before speaking. Up to a five-point-five there, Burton. "You still feel up to getting out this morning for some recon work? I'd like to get some personal surveillance photos of the area, see who's around the public places, give ourselves a feel for the streets and whatnot. Maybe we'll see something interesting. At the very least, we can stretch our legs."

"Sounds good." I had a basic idea of the immediate neighborhood and surrounding blocks from studying maps yesterday, but nothing beat getting down onto the streets and finding out all those hidden things that satellite imagery couldn't show you. I ate a date, and held back a sigh of pleasure at the sweetness of it. I'd forgotten how good the food was here, and I couldn't wait to get out and explore and find the food stalls at the local street markets.

"You good with our cover in public?" he asked carefully.

I nodded.

"And you're okay with nonintimate touching to make it believable?" he continued, as if he thought I hadn't picked up what he was putting down.

Joy, fake heterosexuality as a cover. Though it was better than being murdered for being queer. Thankfully PDAs weren't the norm here or

I might have to amputate my hands by the end of the assignment. "It's fine." I glanced at the not-wedding ring on my wedding finger, swapped from my right hand. I'd decided to wear it as a 24/7 faux marriage token in case I had to leave the house in a hurry and forgot to swap it from right to left. And, I admitted, I liked how it felt, and may as well get used to it, just in case, you know…

As I fiddled with the band, I stared at Jeff's hands. "Why don't you wear a wedding ring?"

He looked up from his coffee. "What do you mean?"

"Exactly what I said. You're married, right?"

"I am. Twenty-six years at the end of the month."

I felt a twinge of pity for him missing his wedding anniversary. "Right, so why no wedding ring? I've noticed a lot of men don't. I mean if you're working manual labor jobs, it makes sense, but you don't." I gestured to my own left hand. "If I was married for real, nobody would be able to get that thing off my finger."

Jeff fished inside his neckline and pulled out a thick gold band on a solid chain. "I do wear it, just not where anyone might see." He tucked his ring back down his shirt. "I *don't* wear it for the same reason you're wearing that ring while you're here. Because you need to present an image, because you want to control the narrative."

"Well, yeah, but mine's to keep me safe. I don't see how you hiding that ring does anything in this scenario we're in now." The image that'd just been comfortably hanging out in the background leapt to the front. Me and Sophia. Rings. Oh shit. Thanks, brain. A normal leap to make, even though we were nowhere near that stage, if we *would* ever reach it.

"I actually don't enjoy keeping it around my neck instead of on my finger," he quietly said. "But it's easier to keep it off all the time than off, on, off, on, which I learned makes me feel worse when I have to remove it."

"What's wrong with wearing a wedding ring?" Especially here and now when we were fake-married in public.

"Think about it, Alexandra. Imagine our debriefing. You see me wearing a wedding band and then you know things about me, you ask about my wife, do I have children and then you're controlling the questions, even if only for thirty seconds, which is still too long." He smiled wryly. "And I know that's something that you would have done."

"Obviously. Because I'm not dumb. But I like to know things and sometimes mindless banter helps in tense situations." I shrugged. "Mostly I just really like to know things about people. That's why I was so good in the field."

"I'm sure you were. But in my job, if I'm performing that specific role, a subject thinking they might gain something from me, or wanting to be familiar can be disastrous if not properly managed." Jeff shrugged. "So there you have it."

I leaned back in the chair until it tipped onto its back legs before rocking it down to the ground again. "What is your job exactly?" He seemed like a buffet—doing a little of this and a little of that.

"I wear a lot of hats," he evaded.

I stared.

He stared.

I won. But it took almost three minutes.

Jeff sighed, but he was smiling. "Perhaps I should reevaluate my opinion of your tenacity." He settled himself more comfortably, leaning forward with his elbows on the table. "I'm a contractor. I do the things that need to be done, mostly when the government or certain organizations need to operate slightly outside the lines of accepted operational parameters. And at the moment, what I need to do is a job that complements your job. Sometimes I gather intelligence, sometimes I evaluate those who give us intelligence, sometimes I evaluate those who analyze intelligence, sometimes I keep people safe. We're working for the same team, Alexandra. You seem to forget that."

One of the same teams. "I guess I'm still scarred by the threats to me and my girlfriend when I was wrongly incarcerated. I haven't forgotten *that*."

"I think I'd like Ms. Flores," he said, the statement seemingly genuine, but still giving me a what-the-hell pause at its out-of-the-blueness. "She seems like a lovely person, who fits you well."

"Okay, that's bordering on creepy territory."

"Is it? Part of my job was to learn about you, Alexandra, and I learned that you snagged yourself a good one. And so did I. Though god knows how for either of us, given our natural disinclination toward truthfulness. Finding a partner who accepts what we do is hard. And when you get that person, someone who understands the necessity of everything we don't say or can't do, you should do everything possible to keep them in your life."

"Wow. Life advice from Jeff?"

"Cherish it." Smiling, he picked up his empty coffee mug and walked into the kitchen, effectively declaring the conversation over.

Breakfast finished, I went back to my room to change for the big outing. Jeff wore chinos and a dress shirt but no tie—casual enough to not look out of place, but dressed-up enough to be taken seriously. I'd decided that while I was "at work," it would be jeans or casual slacks, flats or loafers, and casual blouses. But now I was leaving the building, I had to change again. My blouse had to go, replaced by the one full-length, long-sleeved green tunic top I'd brought with me from the last time I was in the field.

The last time.

I took a moment to acknowledge the expected discomfort that surged at the solidified thought, then pushed it aside to focus on something pleasant. Shopping. I'd known I'd could purchase clothing while I was here, and spending money, even tourist money, generally made you likeable. And it made me happy. I picked a light-blue headscarf and draped it around my hair, tucking stray pieces back into the fabric.

I grabbed my phone, sunglasses, shopping bags, and a fistful of cash. I thrust the wad of money at Jeff. "I need some new clothes. This is the only tunic I have for being in public and it's going to get old really fast." Not to mention the possibility of purchasing beautiful scarves and trinkets for me, and also to send as gifts for Sophia. "And I need to visit food and spice vendors," I reminded him.

"Okay." He tucked the cash into the front pocket of his chinos, picked up a well-thumbed translation book from his desk, and slung a camera around his neck. "Then let's go see some sights."

We walked through the city, pausing for a few "tourist photographs," until we came upon a neatly kept park filled with people. A playground gym was occupied by young children while groups of women chatted and tended to the kids. Jeff gestured to the tree-lined pathway and we detoured to walk through the park rather than around it on the road. At the far end of the green space, we passed a group of elementary-school-aged kids playing a ragtag game of soccer and Jeff slowed to watch the group roughhousing. After a Hail Mary attempt at goal missed by a mile, the soccer ball bounced over to us, and Jeff scooped it up with his foot. I expected him to kick it back, but he started dribbling the ball on his foot and knee, bumping it up to his chest then head before letting it fall back to his foot. He even did some fancy moves flipping the ball behind himself that had even me impressed.

I clapped as the kids came running over, laughing, yelling, and gesturing that Jeff should come join in. Jeff kicked the ball up high then caught it, and as he was preparing to throw it back onto the pitch, I said, "Go on, Ronaldo. Give them a run for their money."

"Fine," he sighed, but he was grinning. He handed me his camera and the translation book then jogged over and kicked the ball around with the kids for ten minutes, and once he'd scored a goal for each side he jogged back to me. He looked jubilant, relaxed, and happy, and I made a mental note to send him out to find some kids or soccer whenever he started looking stressed.

I raised an eyebrow. "Well, that was not something I had on my bingo scorecard."

"My mad soccer skills, or playing with kids?" He turned back and waved to the group before taking custody of his things, then my arm to guide me gently back down the path.

"Both." He'd seemed so at ease with them all, playing around and joking while still interacting with each one like they were the most special kid on the field. I glanced up at him. "Do you have kids?"

His expression turned instantly from light and breezy to closed-up and distraught, and I felt horrible for the obvious pain my casual question had caused. Jeff shook his head. "No. We can't have kids. We tried everything, for years, but it's just not meant to be."

I lightly touched his arm. "I'm so sorry, I didn't mean to—"

He patted my hand. "It's okay, you wouldn't have known. We wanted to foster or adopt, but with my job, every application was met with an instant no. But! We do have the world's best dog." He shuffled away from the stream of people moving toward the city center, pulled out his phone, and handed it to me.

I stared at the picture of Jeff and his dog, smiling at the softness. "Wow I really didn't pick you for the white-fluffy kind."

"Benjamin," he said fondly as he swiped through pics of his dog sleeping, eating, playing, swimming, and doing basically every canine activity known to man. "He's a great dog." Jeff cleared his throat. "Come on, let's keep moving."

As I approached the bustling market, the distinctive sounds became even clearer, separating out into hundreds of conversations rather than one indistinct noise. The moment I stepped under the rough stone arch, I felt my heart lift. I inhaled deeply, taking in the warm scents of spice and roasting foods. Beside me, Jeff laughed. "You look like you've just stepped into Nirvana."

"What can I say? I love markets."

"Then let's get into it."

I posed dutifully by stalls, picking those that showed good segments of other parts of the market in the background as well as the lanes, while Jeff took pictures. I picked through the scarves and tunic tops, pretending I barely spoke or understood the language. The vendors, without fail, told us effusively in broken English that everything I looked at was lovely, very pretty, the garment was perfect for me and the best quality.

I smiled and thanked them in fake slow and broken words, then stood by while Jeff pretending to consult his translation book so he could barter over the prices when I'd made my choice. When they'd agreed on a price—too high in my opinion, but who was I to have an opinion—Jeff paid. I ended up with four tunics in beautifully patterned blue, yellow, green, and purple. He offered his opinions while continuing to photograph everything, just like a tourist would, and waited patiently while I bought herbs and spices. No part of his demeanor screamed "long-suffering husband" and I wondered if he took his wife shopping as part of his normal day-to-day life.

We continued around the market, and I relaxed fractionally as my body and brain remembered places like these that had been so special to me in the past, even when it ended in something so horrific. We purchased more clothing, jewelry, and trinkets and when I paused to study a stall filled with silk scarves Jeff stood behind my right shoulder. I selected a scarf in varying shades of red, orange, and yellow, shot through with strands of gold thread and turned back to show it to him. "What do you think?"

"It's very pretty." Despite his words, his nose wrinkled.

"Then why do you look like you just smelled something bad?"

"I'm not sure the color scheme suits you," he said diplomatically.

"Of course not. But what about for a dark-brunette with light brown eyes?"

Jeff's eyes softened. "Ah, then yes. I think it would suit Ms. Flores very well." He spoke with the vendor via his translation book, then dug into his front pocket and handed over more of my cash. I was going to have to visit a bank to withdraw more money soon.

Once I'd tucked the scarf into my now-bulging string bag, I told him, "You know, I'm sure Sophia wouldn't mind if you called her by her first name."

"That's a negative, Alexandra. I haven't met her, and it would feel wrong for me to use her first name."

A surprising answer, almost chivalrous. "Okay, that's fair. Are you going to buy anything for your wife?"

"Of course. But I'll get my gifts another time so we've got a legitimate reason to come back to the markets again. A reason other than you loving the atmosphere." He gently took my arm. "Come on, I think we've exposed ourselves enough for one day."

We took a different route home and I stood by more buildings, street signs, and intersections to have my photo taken. I even smiled, like a real tourist excited to be in a new place and wanting to document my trip. Documenting the location as a fake tourist was a happy side effect of our surveillance. I'd have to vet the photos before showing them to Sophia, but it'd be nice to prove to her that I really was out there doing good work as I'd promised.

Good work… I was keeping people safe. I was keeping her safe. Maybe if I reminded myself of that often enough, I'd be able to rid myself of this lump of concrete that seemed to be permanently stuck inside my chest.

We dumped my haul of stuff at home…home…yes, it was home for now, then collected the car. Different parking garage gate security guy, marginally more interested than the one yesterday, though still not what I'd call a paragon of security. The twenty-minute drive to the outskirts of the city where the local ops team were holed up was uncomfortably quiet.

Our meeting with the team went as I'd expected. A lot of talk that made it clear they thought they were in charge of the operations in the region and that Jeff and I were nothing more than secretaries fetching them metaphorical coffees. Jeff made it clear what he thought of that directive, both to their faces and then again during the drive back to our apartment. "Some people aren't team players," he grumbled.

"No they are not," I agreed. "Seems they're as happy with this new integrated team as we are. Fuck this stupid demotion." Because that's what it felt like. "I know, I know. I'm still part of the chain of intelligence, but this is bullshit. I want my own cases, not just wasting everyone's time checking shit for other people."

"It does seem like a waste of time," he agreed.

"I'll contact Derek and let him know that stage one of merging these departments into one happy family in the field may not be going so well. Maybe he can talk to their supervisor and get some asses kicked."

"If you like." Jeff grinned ferally. "Though I've always thought it's better to kick asses for yourself…"

CHAPTER THIRTEEN

And I don't think ear amputation is an
overreaction either

After a week away from Sophia, little chunks had started breaking off that concrete lump in my gut, making it slightly easier to deal with. If I kept up my emotional chip-chip-chipping, in another few months, it might be down to a fist-sized lump I could ignore. And, after a week of living and working with Jeff, we'd settled into a solid routine and hadn't even come close to fisticuffs. In fact, dare I admit it, things were actually…fine? We'd developed a casual back-and-forth of trading barbs and snipes, but instead of piercing me, they bounced off like lighthearted relief, which I sorely needed.

I was respectful of his personal time and space, as he was of mine—keeping quiet inside the apartment during my scheduled Zen times. Soundproofing did a great job of not letting sounds out or in, but it sometimes felt like it amplified every noise inside. I'd practice yoga and calisthenics as soon as I woke up, and after my shower would emerge refreshed and ready for the day. Jeff always had the kettle boiled when I came out, and after a cup of tea, I'd cook us breakfast—usually eggs with flatbread and pickled vegetables—and then we'd settle in for our workday.

We'd work, I'd use my late-morning brain break to email Sophia something sweet for her to wake up to, we'd work some more, then before dinner we'd take a walk around the neighborhood, varying our route each day. I'd cook, he'd clean up, then it was time for Jeff's tiny evening drink. And for me? Either reading or watching one of the zillion TV shows I'd downloaded before I'd left, or more work if I was bored, or hoping the Internet held up enough for a call with Sophia instead of being down as it frequently was in the evenings. What an annoying coincidence. Just a coincidence. Because of my connectivity issues, my contact with Sophia had been…sparse. We'd managed at least one email and solid text exchange each day, but only two more video calls—one of which cut out after three minutes—instead of the daily face-to-face we'd promised to strive for. Not exactly keeping up the romance communications.

Jeff hadn't been lying when he'd said he didn't sleep much, and I'd often see the glow of his screens, or hear a quiet and indistinct conversation if I woke in the middle of the night. And as predicted, the analyst work was basically what I would have done back home. It was noticeably less busy, even with the extra steps of dual reporting to both the ops team as well as the agency back in the States. Fine by me—if they wanted to punish me by paying me normally plus a living-away-from-home allowance to do less work, they could go right ahead.

Less work to do meant I had more time to figure out what to do about Elaheh. So far, more time hadn't produced more epiphanies. I was hopeful of a lightning-bolt brilliant idea hitting me soon, especially now that I'd kind of made peace with the woman my ex-sex partner had become. I still didn't know why I'd been so surprised, so reluctant to accept it—her brother and uncle were part of a terrorist cell, the cell that had captured me. She'd been surrounded by it probably her whole life and had now been absorbed into it.

People change, and not always for the better.

Just before lunch on Monday, Jeff barreled into my cubicle, mug in one hand, a manila folder in the other. He had an annoying habit of coming to talk to me during call to prayers, and I'd decided after the second or third time that he did it on purpose because I'd made an offhanded comment about how I'd always enjoyed the beautiful sound echoing through the city. His mind games were insidious, rather than overt, and I wondered for the hundredth time what purpose they served.

He leaned against the partition where I had relevant intel—photos, maps, transcripts—pinned on my side. "Why don't you have any personal photos up in here?" he asked out of nowhere.

"Hi, Jeff. My morning is going well, thanks, and yes, I slept okay except for the random gunfire at three this morning, how about you?"

"No, seriously. You've got a girlfriend, correct?"

So it's going to be a pointless question day, is it? I sighed and decided to not answer, because he knew Sophia and I were involved. He knew more about me than I was comfortable with, and most of it was things I hadn't told him.

He looked around my workspace, feigning surprise. "Why no photographs of you two? I know if I didn't have family pictures up, my wife would kill me."

I smiled up at him. "Is that the only reason she'd kill you? And I have all the photos of us I need on my phone and laptop. Plus, I have that." I pointed to Sophia's Super Lexie drawing pinned to the wall behind my desk. "And you *don't* have family pictures up."

"Yes I do."

"What? No you don't. I walk past your cubicle every single day and I've not seen any pictures."

He motioned me over and pointed to the wall behind his monitor. "There."

In the corner, hidden behind a set of filing trays and the edge of his monitor was the world's tiniest photo frame. I made a show of raising my glasses, then resettling them on my face. "Wow, if that's your definition of 'having a picture up,' I gotta say, you need to reevaluate your life."

He grabbed the frame, holding the picture of a gorgeous Asian woman up to me. "Alexandra, look at my wife. She's beautiful. And having her staring right at me while I'm reading about depraved acts committed by depraved humans is not only very distracting but is also not two things that I want living next to each other in my brain. So she's on my desk, but not *on* my desk."

I leaned in closer to look, as he'd told me to, at his wife. The photo was a candid shot at the beach, showing her pushing windswept hair back away from her face, generous mouth smiling, steady intelligent gaze fixed on the camera. "Fair. And yes, your wife is very attractive."

"Inside and out," he said gently. "Inside and out."

"What does she do?" I asked, trying to ignore the achy tug in my chest. No brainer why it'd suddenly appeared—I'd just thought of my own beautiful-inside-and-out girlfriend. Who was nowhere near me.

Jeff's chest puffed. "She's a human rights lawyer at one of the biggest firms in our state. Brains, beauty, and benevolence."

"Wow, how long have you been waiting to use that slogan?"

"Decades." After a fond look at the photograph he set it down, before sitting in his desk chair. "How's your report into Mohammadzai coming along?"

"It's coming along. I..." Frowning, I bit my lower lip. "I need to look deeper into Elaheh Ahsan." I set wistful thoughts of Sophia aside. Like Jeff, I wanted to keep her separate in my mind, especially away from Elaheh, as much as I could. "I'm just trying to unravel the threads so I can figure out how and where to send resources to collect the information."

"Yes, we do need to look more closely into her," he agreed. "My gut feeling is she's not a 'contractor' her husband is bringing in, but that she's a newer, permanent, addition to the cell."

That was my gut feeling too, but aside from that one photographic sequence of her planting a bomb, there'd been nothing further to confirm my gut feeling. Look at me, casually thinking about a woman I know murdering and maiming people with explosives. "I want to know why she's working in the cell at all, and why someone who'd shown no obvious signs of terrorist ideology would change so drastically? My obvious personal curiosity aside, I think we need to look at whether there's been a shift in their recruitment operations."

Jeff nodded slowly. "Good idea to look into recruitment. We know one of the most obvious motivations for terrorism is that the terrorists are unhappy, with either their own country, or what they perceive to be opposing ideals in foreign countries. Given this cell is focusing attacks on their home soil, against citizens of their own country, my gut feeling is that it's retaliatory action against the new crappy government."

"Makes sense. But...is that really a reason for Elaheh to have completely one-eightied her core ideals, even if I factor in the possibility that she doesn't care about her socioeconomic status and she's actually being completely manipulated by her husband? And some of these attacks have wounded or killed foreigners. That goes beyond targeting your own government."

"I don't know, but I can see how you would turn against a government that doesn't care about you, especially one put into power with the aid of a country you despise on principle. Killing foreigners as well as your fellow citizens sends a message, and can disrupt tourism cashflow. I was quite the anarchist in high school and college and if I grew up in this country, perhaps this is the road I would have ended up walking. These people have something they believe in, Alexandra, even if we don't fully agree with it, or understand them on their core level."

"I know," I said, irritated at him lecturing me about something I already knew. Terrorists were people too, even if I despised their methods of getting their messages across. "It's just…her. I don't understand how she, of all people, could be involved in terrorism."

"Push someone enough and sometimes they push back. Violently. You have to remember she's lived here her entire life, and you know the social and economic situation for these people isn't great. And now it's even more so. Desperate people will do anything to better their situation."

I frowned. "I don't know. Elaheh's situation seems…fine compared to a majority of this country's citizens."

"Maybe it seems *fine* because she's fighting for it, in her own way. Perhaps she's a socialist anarchist trying to make the country better for her fellow citizens." He raised an eyebrow. "Not unlike you, except for the anarchy part."

I bristled, biting off my words. "Please don't ever compare me to Elaheh Ahsan again."

"Sorry. But you know what I mean. And until we receive hard evidence, then we have to go with assumptions for her motivation."

"Her motivation is the squeaky wheel gets the grease? Or in this case, the bombing terrorists draw attention to their cause in the hopes it might change something."

"Exactly."

"I should do it." I exhaled loudly. "Approach her," I elaborated at his querying look. "I know her."

Jeff looked like I'd just told him I thought I should go outside naked. "Aside from the fact that it's not your job, if you want to fuck up an investigation because of your bias, go right ahead."

"Fine. Maybe I'll do that," I shot back, battling annoyance at his accusation of my bias.

"It might be your funeral," he cautioned me, then turned back to his monitor.

I'd gone to the bathroom before starting dinner when Jeff called out that he was ducking down to check our locked mail box in the lobby. When I came back out, there was an item on the counter. Nice drop and run, Jeff. His "gift" was an eight-by-ten photo, and though it was clearly a surveillance shot, it wasn't grainy or distorted. In fact, it almost looked like a perfectly in-focus posed shot. There was a yellow Post-it stuck to the print with a single sentence written in Jeff's blocky hand.

Thought you might like this to brighten up your space.

I stared at the photo, trying to make out the exact location. Tampa. The day I had an altercation with a goon for following Sophia and me. We were outside the burger joint, holding hands, talking before we went in for lunch. Sophia was laughing. I was grinning at her. It was the perfect candid shot—we looked happy and like we were having a good time.

We *had* had a good time that day up until about an hour after the moment documented in the picture. We'd had a good time most days really, if you set aside the main reason for the trip. But the photo was such a gross violation of our privacy that the lighthearted image made me feel vaguely nauseated. I studied the image of Sophia, the lift of her mouth, her free hand pulling dark hair away from her face. Stunning. My discomfort morphed into desire.

Fuck Jeff and his mind games. I pulled some pins from my desk drawer and stuck the picture to the soundproofing material on the wall behind my monitor, next to Super Lexie, right where he would see it every time he came into my space, or exited the hallway connecting the working area to our bedrooms and bathroom. When he came back from collecting our mail, I thanked him effusively. His mouth twitched into a smile, then his face went blank.

"What?" I asked. "You've got your 'I'm psychoanalyzing someone' face on, and I don't like it when it's directed at me."

"No no, no analysis. I was just thinking that you're not as... facetious, as irreverent and disrespectful as you were during our debriefing. You seem to have lost some of your bravado, Alexandra, almost as if you've accepted your situation. I'm not sure if it's good or bad that you seem to have stopped raging."

He was probably right. Being sent to a hostile environment with a work partner who may or may not be as equally hostile, leaving a woman who I'd been enjoying getting to know and had fallen in love with, and being a woman attracted to women in a place where that could get you murdered will do that to you. I shrugged. "Figured I wouldn't waste my time. You didn't seem to appreciate my wit and talent during our little locked-up chats."

He laughed. "Oh I appreciated it. It's always funny to watch someone who's been backed into a corner use every skill in their arsenal to get out of the corner."

"Skill? Wow, coming from you that almost sounded like a compliment."

The edge of his mouth twitched before he regained control, but I could see the amusement in his eyes. "Don't get used to it."

"Don't worry, Jeff. I wouldn't dream of it." I paused. "Also, why?"

"Why what?"

"Why can't you compliment me every once in a while? I mean, the banter is fun, but would it kill you to toss out a 'Doing a good job, Alexandra,'" I said, imitating him, "every once in a while? Or even just, you know, be kind to me a little more? I'm an African violet, not a rose bush." At his raised eyebrows, I explained, "You know, African violets grow best with a little care, but roses love being hacked up, that makes them grow best. I prefer care, not being hacked."

He sighed, but it wasn't a sigh of exasperation, more of resignation. "I'm sorry if you don't feel like I'm coddling you, but I don't think I'm being cruel." I made a musey, noddy kind of eeyyeah, no, you're not being cruel exactly gesture. Jeff rolled his eyes. "You're an intelligent and capable woman and a very good analyst. Coddling isn't going to get the job done, and it's demeaning to both of us. I understand you're feeling out of sorts being away from Ms. Flores. As I am being away from my wife. Every time you feel that, you have to remember what you're here for, what and whom you're fighting for and why." His expression softened. "I'm here to help you, Alexandra, remember that, no matter what it might seem like."

A notification on his phone prevented my response, if I'd even been able to think of one. Jeffrey Burton was possibly the most complex man I'd ever met, as if he had dozens of different men inside him and could pull one out for every situation, a magician pulling endless handkerchiefs from his sleeve. Jeff stuffed the phone into his back pocket. "I need to duck out for a short while."

"You were just out. Or…down."

"I know. And now I need to go out again. I'll be back soon. Do you need anything?" he asked.

"Okay, Captain Vague. And no, thank you. Oh, wait, no, yes I do want something. If that vendor with the *gosh-e fil* is out there, can you get me one please." A sweet fried pastry sprinkled with pistachios and smothered in powdered sugar was just what I needed for after dinner. "Actually, you better get me two, please. Or, you know…if there's a special on three, I'll take three."

"Sure. Three it is, because let's be honest—that's what you want, regardless of price." He was so right. Jeff nabbed his little translation book, scowling at it before he tucked it under his arm. "God I hate pretending I don't speak the language. It makes me feel like a dunce."

I bit my tongue on asking him how did he think I felt, pretending for a week that I was an idiot who'd run off with classified intel. Instead, I smiled. "Think of the good side. People who think you don't understand them might talk about things they wouldn't normally talk about in front of strangers."

"Yeah, I know," he mused. "See you in a bit."

I waved him off and had just sat back down after engaging the deadbolts and chains when the secure VoIP landline on my desk started ringing. Derek. What a happy surprise. I wondered if he had somehow alerted Jeff that he was going to call and discuss potentially classified things, and told him to scram. We needed to come up with code words for *Halcyon Division* and *Lennon*.

Even though I knew who it was, I still answered, "Lexie Martin."

Derek's answering greeting was warm. "Martin. How are you?" Hearing his familiar, calm voice sent a rush of relaxation through me. I'd only spoken to him once since I'd arrived, to fill him in on the friction that'd made our first meeting with the ops team less than enjoyable. Thankfully they'd found some grease, and relations between us had eased somewhat. Probably because I was fun, friendly, and really fucking good at my job.

"Wonderful," I monotoned. "I haven't had this much fun since I got my first period while away at school camp."

"That's more information than I needed about your childhood. I'm fine too, thanks for asking."

"I was getting to it," I assured him.

"I'm sure you were," he said dryly. "Nothing else to report?"

"No, nothing. Everything you need to know has been passed along in our daily briefing communication. But I'm sure you didn't call just to confirm something you already know. Do you have news for me? Am I coming home early?" Five months and three weeks early. I could dream.

The long pause made me suspicious. "No," he said finally. "I have a VIP call for you."

"Okayyy…and this VIP couldn't just call me themselves?" My stomach turned. The last time he had a VIP thing for me, it was the president. Gross.

"Yes, but to ensure call security this requires confirmation of parties involved, hence me acting as a go-between."

I snorted a laugh, though all I wanted to do was wail with frustration. The list of people who would require ID-matched security to speak with me was very short and yep, included the president. "There are only two people who have access to the apartment and therefore the phones, Derek. It's either me or Jeff and I'm pretty sure whoever wants to talk to me could tell the difference between us."

"I know that," he said indignantly. "You've become curmudgeonly since you left. But I was required to confirm it's really you before I transfer you, and now I can do that."

"Thanks, personal secretary. I appreciate you."

"Brat," was the last thing he said before the line went silent.

After twenty seconds, a bland male voice stated, "Please clearly say your name and date of birth for vocal matching and identification."

I did as I was asked.

The voice didn't change as it said, "Thank you. Please hold for the President of the United States."

Fuckity fuck fucker fucknut.

The last voice I wanted to hear in any context boomed in my ear, "Dr. Martin?"

One point for getting my honorific right, dickface. "Mr. President. An honor to speak with you, as always." I was shit at many things, but goddamn, I was a good liar. "How may I help you, sir?"

"Just checking in on our new program. How is it going?"

Riiight, sure. The fact he'd called about *our* program made me utterly certain that it was his decision to fling me to the far corner of the globe. "It's going very well, sir. Though it's still very early days, we're doing excellent work here and anticipate continuing in that vein."

"Good," he grunted. "See that you continue to do excellent work. I don't want this pilot program to fail because of you."

"If it fails, sir, it certainly won't be because of me."

A long pause, probably uncomfortable for him. Not for me. I love long pauses—really gives you time to get into someone's head, you know? "Dr. Martin, I'm sure you can understand how your actions have led to your current relocation."

How was he still passing blame onto someone else for his poor choices? If I told him to go fuck himself and that I hoped he'd go die in a deep hole, would they relieve me of this duty? Might be worth doing it and going to jail, honestly. "Mr. President, as I said during our meeting, I was just doing my job. I take national security very seriously, as does the rest of the Intelligence Community."

"I know you do. And it would be a shame if you couldn't continue doing that job for…whatever reason."

"Is that a threat, sir?" I shouldn't have asked it, but fuck him. He already held all the winning cards and I'd been dealt nothing but losing hands since I'd come into possession of the Kunduz Intelligence. Except for Sophia. She was a royal flush.

He chuckled condescendingly. "No. Just a word of advice."

"I appreciate that, Mr. President," I said through my teeth.

"How are you finding being away from your...girlfriend?" He sounded like he'd almost choked on the word. "Sophia Flores, isn't it?"

I had to forcibly unclamp my molars. Inhaling sharply, I answered quickly, not wanting to give him the satisfaction of knowing his arrow had hit. "It's difficult, sir, as I'm sure you know from your vast travels being away from your family."

"Yes," he mused. "That was a most regrettable incident with her father. I hope there are no more *regrettable incidents*." Nice downplay, you asshole.

They'd dragged Sophia's father—born in Mexico but a bona fide US citizen since early childhood—into detention to force me into giving up. That wasn't a regrettable incident. That was the dickest of dick moves. But it had worked. "She and her family had nothing to do with my actions, Mr. President. Sir, if you're set on punishing me or teaching me a lesson, then go ahead. But if you continue to drag innocent American citizens into...whatever this is, then you may find my cooperation waning."

Leveraging my girlfriend and her family against me was so uncool, and also questionably legal.

"Is that a threat, Dr. Martin?"

"Of course not, sir," I said calmly. "Just a word of advice. I'm sure you've got many advisors, but my job is to provide you with relevant information, Mr. President. I consider what I've said relevant."

"Clever," he said tightly. "I've known many clever people in my time. Be careful over there, Dr. Martin. I'd hate it if someone with your intellect and skill set became unable to do the job they love so much, as you've assured me that you do."

Ohhhh, now *that* was a fucking threat. I exhaled a long breath, taking a moment to compose my answer so I really didn't just tell him to go fuck himself. "Of course I will, sir. I simply want to ensure your safety and the safety of all Americans."

"Good. Don't mess this up."

Then I was listening to silence. I calmly replaced the receiver and stood up. Then I stalled completely, not knowing where to go.

God, I wanted to break the world. Fury at his blame and refusal to acknowledge and take responsibility for the Kunduz Intelligence, at his threat to me and then to Sophia and her family *again*, boiled under my skin, clenching my knuckles and grinding my teeth. How fucking *dare* he. That small-brained imbecilic motherfucker. I closed my eyes, and bent forward slowly, letting myself hang with my folded arms dangling, my head low and relaxed. Or trying to be relaxed. I pressed my trembling fists into the opposite crooks of my elbows until I'd melted into Rag Doll Pose. Twisting myself side to side helped loosen up a little of the tightness, but I still felt so fucking furious that I wanted to scream.

So I did.

I straightened up, and screamed as long and as loud as I could until I had to gasp in a sharp, ragged breath. Thank you, soundproofed apartment. After gulping in more air, I screamed again, smaller this time, weaker. A little better. I folded to the floor and into Embryo Pose, blanking my mind in the safety of my body until enough tension had left to allow me to think somewhat clearly. When I stood again, I had a little more clarity.

I needed to talk to someone about the call, the threat, the insinuations, and had picked up my cell to call Sophia, unthinkingly, when I remembered I couldn't tell her anything. Even if I'd been able to allude to the conversation, which I absolutely could not, I still couldn't burden her with it. But the conversation had left me panicked that something was going on behind the scenes, and I sent her a quick message: *I love you. Are you doing okay?* There, that sounded like a general "how're you doing?" concern rather than an "I think something specific might be happening" one.

Sophia answered within a minute. *Aside from you not being here, everything's fine. I love you too.*

Phew. One minor hurdle leapt. Knowing she was okay calmed a little more of my fury.

I couldn't talk to Jeff—he wasn't even here and even if he was, he was basically the same as Sophia, except he understood larger parts of it. Derek was one of the only people who understood the whole situation. He answered after a few rings, by which time I was calm enough to talk without gritted teeth. "Calling to share your conversation with me?" he asked casually.

"The president threatened me," I spat out. "Not explicitly, but he made it very clear that I'm walking a thin line because of the Kunduz intel and Berenson and the whole fucking mess that I got dragged into that I had no wish to get dragged into, but I did and I did my job and I did it well, and fuck I wish I'd never answered that call. I wish I'd just said no, I'm not doing it."

"Whoa, whoa. Calm down. Take a breath." He paused to let me do as he'd instructed. "What? How?"

"Both excellent questions. But it's true. Oh, and not just me, but also Sophia and her family. Again. They're leveraging me. Holding everything I did over my head, even though it was supposed to have been scrubbed from my record. Even though it was at Halcyon's instruction."

"I know," he said tightly. "Do you think he was bluffing? Just reminding you that he's the little man in charge?"

"I don't think so, no. I think he's serious, even though it's unconstitutional. You know I'm not safe here, and I can't live like this for the rest of my life, Derek," I said, fighting to hold back my tears. "Always wondering if I'm going to be forced into doing something or persecuted because of the Kunduz Intelligence. Always wondering if they're going to go back on their word about leaving Sophia and her family alone. I need Halcyon to protect me. I need Halcyon to make this go away." There'd been no signed confessions, no paper assurances that my supposed transgressions had been forgiven. Because anything that could be touched and seen risked exposing the one secret branch that could never be exposed.

"They did." He paused, clearly measuring his words. "But coming forward again to pull you out of a fire, if the president chooses to go further with this, risks exposing them."

Only a few select high-ranking members of the government knew about Halcyon Division, and I knew what Derek was saying. But it stunk. "Maybe the president should stop holding my feet over hot coals for doing my job. Just because he doesn't like the outcome of that job, which was performed with the highest accuracy and integrity, doesn't mean he can just throw a tantrum about it."

"I'll talk to Lennon and see what he thinks and if there's anything we can do."

"Thank you. Then can you please ask him to make contact when he has good news for me? I really need some."

"I will."

I let out a long sigh. "This isn't fair. I'll quit the agency before I let the president make my life miserable for the rest of his term. This isn't the Hoover era where they thought it was okay to spy and hold things over everyone's head to keep them in line. I won't let myself be manipulated by that stupid fuck."

"He is a stupid fuck," Derek agreed. "And Halcyon might just need to show him how much of a stupid fuck he is."

CHAPTER FOURTEEN

Tread(mill)ing water

I'd slept terribly all week, partly thanks to my lingering annoyance at the president's not-so-idle threat and partly because I'd been plagued by bad dreams that I couldn't make sense of, and more unusually for me—struggled to recall in deep detail when I woke. The only thing I knew for sure was that they had a recurring theme of fear and anxiety, which then remained in my subconscious long after I'd woken up. Yay…

I felt like I was just treading water, too far from land to swim, but not ready to give up and drown yet. Time to meditate and reflect and breathe through the discomfort. But first? So desperate to pee.

As I approached the bathroom, I heard a low buzzing sound and when I peeked through the open door, saw Jeff with his back to me. I cleared my throat loudly to compete with the buzzing. "Did you borrow something from my bedside drawer?" I asked when he turned to face me. "Because it's not a neck massager…" Of course I hadn't brought any such thing. Not really a culturally accepted item, and drawing attention to myself at the airport with sex toys was a no-go.

"You're hilarious." He held up a set of hair clippers, waggling them at me. "It's haircut day." Jeff twisted back around and brought the clippers toward the base of his neck, but with the angle in the mirror, he misjudged and almost gave himself a reverse mohawk.

"Whoa! Wait. You're going to cut something you don't want to cut if you're not careful. Which would be hilarious but also, I don't want to listen to you complaining about your self-inflicted bowl cut, or look at some weird-ass haircut for the next few weeks. Do you want me to do it?"

Jeff's eyes narrowed suspiciously. Fair. I'd be suspicious too. "Why should I trust you with my hair?" he asked, thumbing the clippers off.

"Because happy you means happy me. And this is not the first clipper haircut I'll have given someone. In fact, you could say I'm an expert, for a not-hairdresser."

"Do tell."

I almost told him to mind his business, but quickly decided against being antagonistic for antagonism's sake. "In college I dated a butch woman. Drummer in a band, bartender, the epitome of butch chivalry and swagger. One night she got called in to work this huge, important event at the last minute and she didn't have time for a haircut so she asked me to give her a buzz-trim. Long story short, she talked me through it, said it was the best haircut she'd ever had, and I cut, or clipped, her hair from that night forward, for many months, until she cheated on me with the lead guitarist from her band, like a ginormous cliché, and we broke up. Oh, and I smashed the lead guitarist's guitar. Like a ginormous cliché."

He raised his eyebrows. "So what you're saying is…your haircuts were so good they made your ex-girlfriend so hot that she got attention from other women and cheated on you? Hmm. I love my wife, Alexandra," he said seriously. "Don't make me too dapper."

"Don't worry. I promise you'll look as ordinary as you always do. But before I cut anything, I need to pee." I made shooing motions with both hands.

"Wash your hands when you're done, please," he said as he backed out of the bathroom.

"Thanks for the reminder, Dad."

I made sure to run the water for an extra-long time so Jeff could hear me washing my hands and when I opened the bathroom door, he was hovering in the narrow hall. "Do you need tea or coffee before we start?" he asked.

"Nah, it won't take long. I'll manage. Thanks."

"What about your workout? Yoga?"

"I'll do it afterward to recenter myself after touching you."

"Copy that." He moved past me to stand next to the bathtub, and by his expression, it was obvious he wanted to say something and either wasn't sure how it would be received (like that'd ever bothered him) or he didn't know how to phrase it.

"Spit it out," I said.

"I know your yoga stuff helps you feel centered, but is it helping at all with your bad dreams?"

I stared dumbly at him. "How do you know what I'm dreaming about?"

"Because you're very loud when you're dreaming. Or nightmaring."

I was? Sophia had never mentioned anything about me talking in my sleep. "Mmm," I conceded after a long pause. "And I don't know. I feel okay, all things considered but I'm still having weird, sometimes bad dreams every night. I'm not really the nightmare type, you know? Like I might have one here or there if I'm stressed but not most nights like I am now."

"Probably not unusual given the circumstances. If you want someone to unpack things with, you know where to find me."

"Thanks." I gestured to the bathtub and changed the subject. "Sit on the edge of the tub so I don't have to reach up."

He carefully settled on the edge, leaning to the side to make room for me to slip in behind him. Jeff wrapped a towel around his shoulders and sat completely still as I began clipping. There wasn't much to trim—the man did not like letting his hair grow out—and I made sure to do a good job. As I checked the clip lines, I had a mental image from what felt like a lifetime ago.

Me trimming my hair the night I'd gone on the run, then Sophia fixing the asymmetrical cut while we'd been holed up in Florida. The concentration frown between her eyebrows as she'd watched a haircutting instruction video. The soft glide of her fingertips over my skin. The careful way she'd trimmed millimeters at a time off the hair I'd already butchered myself. The way we'd made love afterward, soft and slow, sensuous and sweet.

"All done," I said, my voice a little husky from that memory. Hopefully Jeff would just attribute the roughness to morning voice.

"Not bad. I'd tip you if you were a real hairdresser." He ran his hand over the top of his head, brushing away loose short hairs. "You mind doing that every few weeks?"

"Sure." It'd give me something interesting to do, and if he was being an asshole I'd just shave lines, or a dick and balls, into the side of his head. I indicated the hair mess in the bathtub. "But you're cleaning this up."

"I'm sensing a theme here. You do something, I clean up after you."

"I do something *for you*," I reminded him as I snapped the guard off the clippers and handed it to him to clean. Waving the clippers near his face, I asked, "Need me to trim that growth on your face too?"

Jeff recoiled. "Fuck no. This is my working-away-from-home beard."

"As opposed to…a regular being-at-home beard?"

"Yes. My wife hates facial hair, thinks it's scratchy, and she barely tolerates me having stubble if I've been working nonstop days and nights and haven't had time to shave. The problem is, she never lets me get beyond scratchy stubble to soft and luxurious beard stage." He stroked his cheek. "So here I am, growing a beard while I'm away."

At least I didn't have to worry about beard hair in the sink. "You had stubble during our debriefs."

"Yes. Your situation kept me away from home for five days."

"Why not go home with the beard when it's all soft and show her what it could be like if she let you grow one at home?"

"Because she doesn't like beards," he said, as if it were obvious. He carefully took the clippers from me and shooed me out of the bathroom. "Thanks for the trim. Now go do your happy brain things."

* * *

I'd been trying to ignore the mental and physical side effects caused by a lack of vigorous movement, but by day nineteen, I felt like a grenade someone was holding with sweaty fingers. Nobody had explicitly said it wasn't a good idea for me, a single white woman, to be out sprinting through the streets, but the thought of what *might* happen was a niggle that refused to leave. And Jeff had made it clear that his knees did not appreciate anything high impact, so asking him to join me was out.

He tolerated my grumbling and squirming and getting up to pace every thirty minutes for a few days before he finally asked, "What is up with you?"

"I can't get any sort of proper cardio workout here," I griped, shifting in the chair. Pressing my fingers hard into my shoulder didn't help shift the knots. "I hate not moving. And I've got all this energy and no place for it." I'd been hammering myself with movement inside, but there were only so many jumping jacks and so much running on the spot or pacing that I could do. Taking walks with Jeff helped, but strolling just wasn't cutting it—my morning floor workout of calisthenics, stretching, and bodyweight strength training wasn't enough without some heart-pumping cardio as well.

"What did you do while you were in the middle of your little jaunt to Tampa? There were no reports of you running outside."

I forced down the bristle at recalling not only that point in my life but that he'd had people watching me and reporting back to him. "I sucked it up for the good of my country. And I did get in a few runs at hotel gyms, and I have my bodyweight floor routine thing that I did each morning. And, it was only a week. But here, I'm missing a very important component." My morning routine helped keep me sane. Wake up, stretch, forty-five-minute yoga practice, ten-minute meditation, then into the work gym for cardio and weights if I felt like it, relaxing shower, breakfast and cup of tea at my desk while I readied for the workday. Of course, since Sophia, I'd added *occasional morning sex* to my rotation. And for the better.

"Ah." He shuffled through some papers. "You know you *can* go outside unescorted, and run around the park."

"I know that. I'm just…still getting used to the vibe of the city," I said, trying to ignore how small and scared my explanation sounded. It was ridiculous to think what had happened in 2017 would ever happen to me again, but fears were dumb and irrational, and those fears kept telling me that if I didn't go out alone then I wouldn't get snatched again.

I'm pretty sure Jeff knew why I was reluctant to go out alone, but he didn't push. "I'm always happy to take walks with you, even twice daily. It's good for my back, and after all, you *are* supposed to be out and about, looking at sites for our 'school' and talking with the locals to keep up your cover."

"That's true. And I accept the twice-daily offer. Thanks." I took a deep breath. "Maybe I'll go around the park a few times a week to get started with my cardio again."

"You're welcome. Now, do you think you could stop fidgeting for an hour so I can finish reading this report?"

"No, sorry."

Jeff had gone out to meet an old friend and have an evening meal with them, so I ate canned soup and a protein bar for dinner, took a shower, then settled on my bed with my laptop to catch up on some of my shows while I waited for my call time with Sophia. In the twenty-three days since I'd left, we'd only had eight video or voice calls that lasted longer than a few minutes. *Eight.* So much for the "we'll talk every day" I'd promised. If I thought it'd get me anywhere, I'd complain about the Internet service but I was still harboring doubts that it wasn't intentional.

The knock on the front door interrupted the last ten minutes of my show, but was at the time Jeff said he'd be back, so I jumped up right away. When I peered through the peephole I noticed Jeff had company in the form of two late-teens boys and an indistinct contraption. I paused, waiting for the verbal signal that things weren't as they seemed and that I shouldn't open the door, but it never came. No duress for Jeff.

I opened the door, and saw the boys rushing back down the hall, laughing and joking with each other and talking about what they were going to spend their money on. The contraption was a treadmill, which they'd apparently hefted from who knew where, into the elevator and along the full length of the hall to our door.

"I brought you an early birthday present." Jeff ran his hand over the frame, avoiding the spots where the paint was flaking. "She's not much, but she'll do. I don't think I've seen one like this since my twenties. Maybe earlier…"

I put my foot on the conveyor, testing the cushion. Could be worse, could be a whole lot better. "Thank you, this is great. How much do I owe you?"

He waved me off. "I used part of our budget. Mostly because I'm sick of the sight and sound of no-cardio Alexandra, but also sometimes I just don't feel like going outside, so I can just walk inside. It's a win for all." He frowned. "Or it will be a win. We still have to get it into the apartment and into position, and we're working with one-and-a-quarter functioning backs here."

"I assume I'm the fully functioning back." I bent down to check for wheels, relieved to see a set at the heavy front end. "You want to push or guide?"

"Guide, please, if you don't mind."

We cleared a path into the living room and to a spot by the sliding doors, then I hefted the back while Jeff steered. "How the hell did you find it?" I asked as we guided the treadmill into the apartment. It wasn't like there was Craigslist here.

He came around behind me to close and secure the door. "I asked my friend if he knew where I could get some cardio equipment, he made some calls, and here we are. Plus paying a couple of local teenagers to bring it here is good for business. They'll remember us as people who pay for things. Including information."

Information. They were still young, maybe not involved yet. But kids heard things. "Good plan," I said, and meant it. "Careful, don't trip on the edge of that rug."

Jeff smiled. "Sometimes I think of smart things."

"A good plan," I repeated. "Even if we're not supposed to be paying for information…" I raised my eyebrows. "What was it the ops team said?" I lowered my voice to gruffness. "'We all have our jobs and if we stick to that, we'll get along fine.'"

"Well, *my* job is broad in scope, Alexandra, and I refuse to sit idly by, doing a job I can do in my sleep, while good information is out there floating around just waiting to be snatched up." He shrugged, mouth quirking. "So what if it happens to be us that snatches up the information first? Cut out the middle man, remember? Isn't that the whole reason for us being here?"

"You're devious." I stuffed down my annoyance that he was apparently allowed to go off gathering information, but I'd been "banned" from approaching Elaheh.

"No, I'm efficient. Careful, bend your knees. Let's get this set up so you can get running." After dubiously eyeing the dusty, basic electronics panel, he added, "Slowly to start with, I think. Maybe only ever slowly…"

"Slow running is better than no running. Thank you. I'd hug you if I didn't think I'd vomit from the disgust of touching you," I said dryly.

"Me too," he said flatly, though it was clear he was trying not to laugh. "So it's a good thing you haven't."

Once we'd tested the treadmill and confirmed Jeff hadn't bought a complete dud (just a slight dud), I dusted myself off and went back into my room to call Sophia. The planets aligned, weather conditions were favorable, satellites shifted into the right position, and my murmured, "Come on, come on, you bastard" had the desired effect. The video call connected, and held.

The moment I saw her, pleasure flowed through me, spreading warmth all the way to the tips of my limbs. It was like the sun peeking from behind a cloud after a month of storms. "Hey, you." I was surprised by the press of tears, and blinked hard to push them away.

"Hey, yourself. God, I'm glad to see you."

"Me too." I could see enough of her torso to tell she wasn't wearing her usual home clothes, but a nice top. And she wore makeup, which she never did when working at home. The question slipped before I could think about what I was saying. And implying. "You look great, are you meeting someone?" She did look great, she always did, but this wasn't just her usual "I'm hanging out at home" great.

"Mhmm. Gina and I are going out for lunch after this call." Sophia pulled a face. "Work's quiet enough that I can take a break, and she said she was sick of me moping around missing you, so she's forcing me out into the public for, and I quote, a cheering-up session."

"I miss you too. Like I knew I'd miss you but I didn't realize I'd *miss* you." Not having family now or a real friend network, I was clueless about how much I'd be affected by having someone back home waiting for me. Someone I wanted to see in person, to touch and smell and taste. But I couldn't do any of those things, and it was torture.

"I think that's a compliment," she deadpanned.

"It is! So...if you're going out, does this mean video sex is out of the question? I even put on my sexiest sweatpants for you."

"Now I'm imagining your ass in sweatpants..." Sophia licked her lower lip. "Maybe I should cancel this lunch and we can spend some quality time together. That would qualify as a cheering-up session, wouldn't it?"

"It would," I agreed. "But I like the idea of you spending time with friends. It makes me less worried about you being lonely."

"Fine," she grumbled. "Maybe I should call when I get back from lunch and we can talk some more about your ass in sweatpants."

"Maybe you should." We both smiled at that. I'd be dead asleep and we both knew it.

Sophia hmmed. "So, what's going on? How's work?"

"Work's good." If I ignored the whole Elaheh situation, that is. "We got a treadmill tonight, so I can run!" Frowning, I amended, "Kind of run. It sounds like a plane struggling to take off and I think it's going to be rough as hell on my joints, but it's better than nothing."

"Oof, be careful then. Please," she begged, mild panic lacing her expression. "I don't want you coming home with a broken ankle or wrist or nose or something."

"Noted. Though the idea of you playing nurse is appealing."

Sophia's rich laugh filled my bedroom. "If you're lucky, I'll do that for you anyway when you come back. Uniform and all."

My libido sat up. "Then I hope I'm lucky."

Her mmhmm of agreement made my libido roll over and beg. The image tilted for a moment then settled again, now showing a little more cleavage. Damn. Sophia smirked, obviously aware of the effect the view was having on me.

Her expression went dreamy, faraway, and when I asked what she was thinking, Sophia said, "I was thinking about you and your morning workouts last night. That first morning when I woke up and you were on the floor and you looked so sexy, all flexible and strong."

I hadn't felt anything but stressed at the time, but I was glad she'd enjoyed it at least. "I could film a workout for you," I offered. "Or we could flip our call times by twelve hours and we can video call the whole thing." Laughing, I admitted, "Though it's not so much sexy at the moment as it is clumsy in my small space."

"I'll take clumsy. How're things working out with having a roommate?" she asked. "You two still getting along okay?"

"Yeah, it's fine." I'd given her some bare-bones of my current living and working situation, but I couldn't tell her anything about Jeff. I hadn't even told her his name, because I didn't know how private he was about his identity. I made myself smile. "He's pretty inoffensive, but definitely not who I'd have chosen for a roommate."

"Well it's not who I'd have chosen for you either." She opened her mouth, then just as quickly closed it. A quick headshake and she tried again. "What else is happening?"

"Nothing much. Working, eating great food, thinking about you. Basically just like when I'm home." But I wasn't home. And the constant reminder of that was a sharp ache that I couldn't rid myself of, no matter how much I tried or how much I thought things were getting easier.

"Have you done any more exploring or shopping or anything like that?" She asked me that question nearly every call, like she was desperate for me to be enjoying myself.

"There's not really much time for me to do that," I said evasively, and also a little snappier than I'd meant to be because I'd had to quickly think of something softer than "It's not safe and my secret boss told me to stay alive." I tried for a gentler tone. And a touch of honesty. "It's not really the kind of place I like to be out and about alone. I mean I'm sure it's fine, and I see local women out alone all the time. I…it's not that I feel unsafe so much as uncomfortable, untrusting because of… last time I was in the region." I smiled, stretching my cheeks to try to make it seem less forced. "And I've had my fill of discomfort for this decade."

"That's understandable. Do you want to talk about how you're feeling?"

I waved her off, not wanting to spend our brief time together dissecting my feelings, which were vast enough to fill a galaxy. "It's fine, really. I mean, we go out together, hit up the markets, take walks and stuff."

"That's good. Do you guys have your Christmas figured out yet? You're doing something special, right? Even just one thing?"

"Yeah, we are. I think we're going to try and have a special dinner, and I have his gift."

"Good. And don't forget to open mine too, okay?"

"I won't. And you'll have to collect mine from my apartment where I hid it in a very secret safe spot that I'll disclose the night before."

"Oh, a Christmas treasure hunt. I like it." Her teeth grazed her lower lip before she smiled tremulously. "I wish you could be here with us."

I exhaled a long breath, trying not to sigh too loudly. "Me too. But we're still on for a Christmas family call?"

"Absolutely," she said immediately. "Already talked to Mom and papi about it. They're on board and excited."

"That's great. I'm excited too. So, what else is happening on your side of the world?"

"Not much," she answered quickly. Almost too quickly.

Maybe there was not much going on, but her haste made me ask, "What is it, babe?"

"Nothing." Her eyebrows creased. "Probably nothing."

"Come on, Sophia. Everything is worth talking about even if you think it's *nothing*. I want to know all about what you're doing."

"It's not what I'm doing. It's what I've been seeing. Look, I'm probably just being paranoid but I'm pretty sure there's been someone following me the past week."

My stomach dropped. "Someone following you how?"

"There's this same car that I keep seeing, and I'm sure there's been a guy I've spotted a few times around the building and while I'm at the gym and pickleball and the supermarket." She forced a smile. "I'm sure I'm just being weird, maybe it's just subconsciously thinking about you, and us, in Florida with all the sneaking around and spying."

"I'm not a spy," I corrected automatically, smiling in an attempt to break the tension I felt at her revelation.

"Shush," she said, laughing. But she sobered pretty quickly. "It just feels weird, and one of the many things you've taught me is that if it feels weird, it probably is."

"I don't think you're being weird. I'll talk to someone, see what's going on. And I'm sorry if it really is someone checking up on you." But why was someone tailing her? That fuckery aside, there was the matter of Sophia now feeling like she had to look over her shoulder all the time because being with me and my stupid government secrecy plot had turned her from someone carefree to someone worried.

She shrugged. "Honestly? I kind of expected it with you gone."

My stomach dropped even more. "What do you mean?"

"I…this whole thing just felt wrong and rushed, hon. It makes me think something else is going on. I know you said that everything was clear with you and me and my dad and stuff, but I have this weird feeling I can't shake."

"Nothing is going to happen to your dad, sweetheart. I promise. That's one of the few things I'm certain about with all this mess." They wouldn't dare get me offside, not with what I knew. I made myself smile. "I'll call my boss and get this sorted out. I'm sorry," I said uselessly, for the millionth time.

"I know you are. And I know, and I want you to know, that it's not your fault." She held my eyes, her gaze fierce. "Don't give me that bullshit 'technically it is my fault because if it weren't for me…' line either."

I exhaled loudly. "You're right. Thank you. I'll get this mess unmessed right away."

"Thank you. Shit." She glanced down. "Hon, I have to go. Sorry to cut this call short, and right at the deep conversational part, but Gina just texted that she's on her way up." She wrinkled her nose. "Why is she early for the first time in her life at the most inconvenient time?"

I tried to disguise my disappointment that this was all the face-to-face time we'd have tonight. "Oh, of course. Sure. No worries. Are you sure you're all right?"

"Yeah, I am," she said, and I believed her. "I'm not scared, just annoyed. I swear."

I had a feeling she was downplaying for my benefit, but let it go for now. I knew my girlfriend well enough to know that if she needed to talk about something, then we were talking about it. "Okay. Have a great time, okay?"

She grinned. "I'll try."

"I love you. Try again to video call tomorrow?"

"Nothing could stop me. Except your Internet. I love you too." She blew me a kiss, and then the call disconnected with an incongruously cheerful tone.

I stared at the laptop background image of her that I'd sneakily taken while we'd been watching a movie. She'd looked up and smiled just as I'd snapped the picture, and I loved her expression of pleasure, the easy joy in her smile. I let that joy in to push out the anger I'd been trying to suppress. This really was a nightmare merry-go-round, and I was wondering when I'd get flung off this damned thing.

Derek answered my call after five infuriatingly long rings. "Martin, what's up?"

"Hi," I said quickly, then launched my attack. "Sophia thinks she's being followed. She's seen the same car and the same guy a few times in the past week, and I don't think it's a coincidence. The fact she's seeing him makes me think they don't care that she's seeing him and they're sending me a message." A message that they could do what they wanted.

I didn't make out what he said, but from the sound of it, it was an expletive. "I am so sick of this bullshit."

"You're sick of this bullshit?" I scoffed. Try to imagine how Sophia and I felt...

"I'll make some calls. This breaks the agreed-upon rules."

"They'll deny it."

"Of course. But if they know we know, that should be enough to make it go away."

"Thank you."

"Did you want me to keep an eye on her?"

"No, I think that'll just make it worse and draw even more attention to how fucked-up this situation is." I sighed loudly. "She already thinks there's more going on than just me being reassigned out of the blue."

"You picked yourself a perceptive one, Martin."

"I sure did." I loved that perceptiveness, the way she somehow managed to see past the necessary layers of my life to the real me that I'd hidden away out of years of habit. But of course, the flipside was the awkwardness when she knew I couldn't tell her something and she had to make peace with that.

"I'll make the call as soon as we're done. Is there anything else you needed?"

I paused, then decided to tell him about Elaheh. "Yes. I need your advice. I have a conflict and I'm not sure how to proceed."

"What is it?"

"Do you recall how I was seeing that woman while I was on field assignment in 2017? And I found out her younger brother was of interest to us. He was part of my...situation."

"I remember," Derek said calmly.

"Well...surprise! She's here and she's remarried, to the man we're calling The Cleaner. Basir Mohammadzai."

Derek exhaled loudly. "A conflict indeed."

"Yeah," I muttered.

"Do you think it's more than a coincidence?"

"No," I said instantly, emphatically. "There's absolutely no way she would have known I'd be coming back to her country, let alone to a city that she's new to herself."

"Have you seen her?"

"No. The team is aware of her potential value and had started planning an approach in public. But I don't think it's going to work. She's not going to just talk to anyone, especially not if Mohammadzai has made her paranoid because of his activities." His activities that were also her activities. "I want to talk to her, see if she'll open up to me again, see if she knows anything about her husband that could help us." At his silence, I hastily added, "Not like that. I've got no illusion that I'm going to recruit her, but if she thinks she's talking to an old friend, old…lover, then she might share things without realizing." Or she might be hardened and suspicious and hurt, or kill, me.

"She might. So what's the conflict, aside from you knowing her? And that talent-spotting and management of assets is not actually your job now."

"Lennon told me I was to return safely. He was explicit about that one thing. Blah blah, importance, you know the deal. And if Elaheh realizes who I really am, then it's going to get dangerous. But she could be a valuable source, so…"

"Yes, she could be," he agreed. "But she could also be a dead end. Perhaps you need to investigate further, speak with the ops officer in charge."

"The team investigated. There's…damning photographic evidence that she's involved."

His voice softened. "I'm sorry, Martin."

Though he couldn't see me, I waved him off. "Whatever. That's the past. I need to know what to do about the present."

"If you're uncertain how she might react to you, why not send Burton to talk to her?"

"Bad idea," I said immediately. "What good will that do, a strange American guy approaching her? She'll suspect something right away. Whereas with me, it'll just be kismet, a coincidence." It was a massive coincidence, that I'd turned up in the city she'd moved to, almost six years after I'd told her I could no longer see her. But I knew my cover, and my ability to lie to preserve it, was ironclad and could withstand the heaviest scrutiny.

He asked a question I'd known he would. "Was she involved in the cells when you were sleeping with her?"

"Not to my knowledge, no. Nothing at all about her behavior gave me the slightest inkling of anything like that at all. I think this radicalization is new. Perhaps tied to her second marriage. Of course, I can't be sure she wasn't involved before, but my gut never gave me *any* indication she harbored that ideology."

"Okay." He believed me. I could hear it.

"She trusted me then. There's no reason she wouldn't trust me now. I just…I really think this is something I'm the best person for."

"What are the chances of her connecting, or perhaps already knowing, that you're American intelligence?"

"Miniscule, but of course nothing is ever completely out of the realm of possibility. I just don't think her brother and uncle would have come around during the period they had me in captivity and had a conversation with her, especially not one that started with, 'So hey, we caught this American woman we're sure works in intelligence, blonde, hazel-ish eyes, about five-eight, likes to talk back,' and then Elaheh thinking, 'Oh yes, that's the exact American woman I've been sleeping with.'"

"Probably not," Derek said carefully.

"From the conversations we had, the only time the men in her family spoke to her was to tell her she needed to marry, and that it was hard for them to find a new husband for her because she was widowed, and older, and what a burden she was to the family."

Derek huffed out a loud breath and I could tell just by that sound that he was about to turn me down. "I agree that you would be the best person to approach, but this isn't your job, Martin. You're there to analyze intelligence, not collect it."

"Even if I'm the best person for the collection?"

"Yes. Liaise with the lead ops officer and assist them with profiling her to ensure the best outcome. You're in a position to do good work here, given your intimate knowledge of this subject. Focus on that, rather than your other feelings about this and about her."

Intimate knowledge. I suddenly felt really dirty. Yeah, I was sure she hadn't been involved in terrorism when we'd been sleeping together, but had there been some part hidden in her that butted up against my core ideals? People changed, I reminded myself for the hundredth time. But could they change overnight? Whatever the answer, I'd been intimate with her. Intimate with…that.

And it made me sick to my stomach.

CHAPTER FIFTEEN

Conversations with your ex can be awkward,
especially when she's now a terrorist

I spent Christmas Eve morning working through raw intelligence sent over by the ops team, and engaging in back-and-forth emails with one of the officers about an "on the spot" analysis of intel one of his assets had brought him. Around all of that Jeff and I had been having an on-off conversation about gin versus vodka martinis. Gin wins, obviously.

By lunchtime, I had a headache brewing, tight shoulders from being stuck at my desk, and that all-too-familiar tension that seemed almost constantly in the background now. An unexpected message from Sophia was like a balm for all my shitty body and brain things, as if she'd sensed I was struggling. *Can't sleep and just wanted you to know I'm thinking about you, I miss you, I love you.*

I quickly typed out: *How did you know I needed to hear that right now? I love you too, and I miss you so much.*

We spent fifteen minutes catching up, and reconnecting as best we could over messages before she gently disengaged with her usual diplomatic *Okay, I'll let you get back to saving the world.* It was as if she knew that my capacity to initiate our goodbyes over and over was limited, so she'd taken on that role for us. The woman was a goddess saint.

We signed off with more I love yous, promises to attempt a video call that night, and so many kiss and heart emojis that I would have been mortally embarrassed if anyone had seen the exchange. But the moment I set my phone down again, the tension started creeping back in. The cubicle walls felt looming, the apartment cramped and stifling.

I pulled off my glasses and after rubbing fatigue from my eyes, popped over the divider between our workspaces. "Can we go out? I need some air."

Jeff threw down his pen, exclaiming, "Yes! Thank god. I've been holding off asking for the last hour, but my back is killing me sitting here. Let's go get lunch. And didn't you say you wanted to pick up some groceries?"

"I do need to grab a few things, yes." I feigned shock. "Is it possible we're starting to get mentally in sync or something?"

"I hope not. Your brain seems like a really weird place to be."

I shrugged and made a noncommittal gesture. "Sometimes it has clever thoughts."

Jeff raised his eyebrows, and for once didn't come back at me with a snide or disparaging comment. Instead, he stood, groaning, and carefully stretched. "Let's go. Fuck me, I hate desks."

We went exploring and found a new café on the edge of the city for lunch, lingering over the chai I was borderline addicted to and had also converted Jeff to, before Google Maps-ing our way to the largest supermarket of the neighborhood. Jeff followed dutifully, looking around at the offerings in a way that would seem casual if you didn't know him. He was always alert, even more so than me. I was grateful for his vigilance, even as I'd started feeling more settled in our "Western-leaning" neighborhood, the place that held the highest percentage of foreign workers of all the nation's districts.

I sorted through fresh fruits and vegetables, dropping them into the cloth sacks Jeff held. Like a pro, he swapped the sacks as I picked out bread, nuts, and dried fruits. Of course I had to stop by the homemade cookies and candies, and popped some cardamom and rosewater milk fudge, and almond and cardamom brittle into my bag. I'd been slowly taste-testing every bit of candy or batch of cookies I came across so I could figure out which to take home for Sophia, trying to look at them through the lens of her not-as-sweet-as-mine tooth.

I pointed to the dozens of buckets of different dried pulses and grains. "Can you please grab me three cups of dried red kidney beans? I thought I might cook—"

"Ellen?" The interruption, in that familiar voice, low and melodic, saying a name few people called me, had my head spinning.

Those thoughts of Sophia and her candy flickered like a dying bulb.

A cool shudder ran down my back and it was only Jeff's steadying hand on my arm that kept me from completely losing my calm. I feigned surprise—not difficult, because I was *really* fucking surprised—then turned and moved closer.

"Oh my goodness. Elaheh?" Her name came out as a tight, squeaked, whispery word, and I hoped she took it to mean I was fighting emotions, not shitting myself. I'd wanted to initiate a meeting, yes, but I hadn't gone as far as to prepare myself for how I wanted to control the narrative, because everyone had said it wasn't on. Well, it was certainly on now.

Jeff's fingers tightened fractionally when he heard me say that name.

"Yes. Yes," Elaheh breathed. She spoke English, though she knew I was more than conversationally fluent in her first language. A nervous hand snaked up to smooth the fabric of her hijab across her neck. "It's me." She looked like she'd seen a ghost, which was probably not that far off the mark after how I'd ghosted her.

"What are you doing here?" I asked. "Did you move? When?" I lightly touched my throat. "Goodness, I'm sorry, I just...I didn't expect to see you again."

Her eyes furtively scanned the space, taking in other people casually going about their grocery shopping. "It is a long story. And that is a question I will turn back upon you. I also did not expect to see you again. Why are you here?"

The lie came easily. "Trying to set up a school for girls."

"Ah, I see. I'm glad. We were very sad when we heard the one you'd planned could not be built."

"Nobody was sadder than I was, trust me." I smiled, taking the pause to exhale the huge lungful of air I'd panic-breathed.

Elaheh looked up at Jeff, who was standing silently next to me, then immediately away again. Awkward. I moved slightly to the side to open up the space a little, while still keeping myself between the two of them. I gestured to Jeff, hoping my smile looked relaxed and friendly, instead of forced and like I was panicking inside. "Elaheh, this is my husband, Mark." I'd never explicitly discussed my sexuality with her—it'd been unnecessary because at the time my sexuality as it pertained to her was "interested in women," but I could see Jeff's presence startled her. "Mark, this is Elaheh, an old friend from the last time I was here scouting school opportunities."

Avoiding eye contact, he dipped his head in greeting, then shuffled a few steps away from Elaheh, who was alone. He remained close enough that if need be, he could act. If need be… The thought brought a surge of nausea so strong that I had to swallow convulsively to rid myself of it.

Elaheh lightly touched my arm. "Are you all right, Ellen?"

"Yes, sorry. I think my stomach is still adjusting to the food." A bright smile helped the untruth. "It's nothing like the last time I was here." God, why had I just said that?

Something like fear flashed in her eyes and I wondered if she was thinking about all the times we'd cooked and eaten a meal together, what had always come before and then what always came afterward. "No, I'd imagine not," she said evenly. Elaheh looked around again. "I really must be going. But I would love to see you again. Perhaps you could come by for tea?"

Declining would seem strange to her. So I didn't. "I'd like that. Very much," I added in an attempt to seem more enthused than apprehensive.

She pulled a small notebook from her handbag, scribbled down an address, then ripped out the page and passed it to me. "Tomorrow morning? Ten thirty?"

I glanced at Jeff, pretending to ask silent permission, and he nodded. I took that nod to mean he was okay—relatively speaking—with this turn of events, and turned back to Elaheh. "I'll be there," I said warmly. A second later it twigged. "Oh, wait. Sorry, no. I can't do tomorrow. It's Christmas," I explained. "The day after?"

"Yes. That would be perfect." Her eyes lit up with genuine enthusiasm. Okay, so it seemed she didn't know who I really was. This might work out okay after all. "I look forward to it. Now, if you'll excuse me, I must finish my shopping."

"Of course." I stepped backward to allow her to pass. "See you the day after tomorrow."

Her eyes creased with a smile as she reached a hand out to grasp mine. At the last moment, she snatched her hand back, tucking it inside her sleeve. After a gaze-averted nod for Jeff, she left us. I deliberately didn't look after her, standing statue-still as my mind whirled, trying and failing to land on one coherent thought about what had just transpired.

After a few moments, Jeff lightly touched my shoulder, murmuring, "She's gone."

"Oh my god," I wheezed out. "Oh my god. I think I'm going to puke."

"No you're not. Take a breath and let it all go. It's out of your control." He gently took my arm and tugged me toward the cashier to pay for our goods. "Come on, let's go home."

As soon as we were back in the apartment, and after I'd calmed down enough to have a rational thought, I called Derek to let him know the latest turn of events. He agreed that I couldn't have refused without it looking suspicious, and ran through a laundry list of rules and precautions for my meeting with Elaheh. I was still struggling to process the unexpected invitation, and Jeff offered to call the lead ops officer to apprise him of what had happened. I could hear the outrage through the phone, and mentally applauded Jeff for telling him calmly, yet with a distinct get-the-fuck-over-it tone, that this was what had happened, it had happened organically, and we made the best call we could under the circumstances.

I honestly didn't know how I felt about seeing Elaheh again, about our social event. I spent the afternoon putting together a plan for my approach, certain points I would try to bring up, and directions I wanted to steer the conversation in which might lead her into either giving me information or guide her to invite me to meet again.

The thought of having to manipulate her was nauseating. I'd done that with Sophia, guided her to outcomes to help me keep the Kunduz Intelligence safe, and it had felt fucking terrible, even though it had been the only way to move forward and even though I'd already been falling for her when I'd brought her along with me. Blaarrrrgh. I shook myself out, hoping to dispel the spiraling thoughts about what I'd done to solve that intelligence puzzle, thoughts I'd thought I'd moved past.

Jeff's head popped up over the partition, startling me out of my head. "How's that transcript coming along?"

I craned my neck to look up at him, smiling tiredly. "It's done. I'll get you to read it and see if I missed absorbing anything while I was having a little heart attack at the grocery store. I'm just skimming over the Airborne surveillance pictures now to see if there's anything near her apartment that we should worry about." I needed to be as prepared as possible, not just with what I was going to do and say, but in case there was anything unsafe near her apartment.

He nodded slowly. "Put it away, Alexandra. We've both been over the images already. It's tight. Any other checks can wait until tomorrow. Come sit and talk, have a Christmas Eve drink with me before dinner. I'll even share my bourbon with you."

"Um." I really don't love bourbon. I don't hate it either but it rates low on my list of last-beverage-before-I-die. Apparently my face gave away my bourbon apathy.

His expression turned to little-boy earnestness. "Come on. Indulge me."

I sighed. "Okay. Pour and I'll save all this work. Extra ice, please." Maybe that would dilute the taste a little.

"You wound me."

"Good. I meant to."

Smiling, he shook his head and went off to fix our drinks. As we settled at opposite ends of the couch with our respective predinner drinks—mine thankfully nothing more than two tiny sips of bourbon—he said, "Strange day. How are you?"

"Are you some kind of shrink now?"

Jeff laughed. "Actually, yes I am. I have a psychology degree. In Iraq and Afghanistan, part of my role was…extraction of intelligence. I've worked at a lot of black sites," he said grimly.

"Oh." I didn't want to think about the way he'd phrased that— extraction of intelligence—because I knew what happened at black sites. Frowning, I shook my glass to settle the ice. "I suppose that makes sense." Then I admitted something I probably shouldn't, but given we were now partners not Debriefer and Debriefee, I didn't see the harm. "You knew how to get right inside my head when we were having our little chats." And it had infuriated me, because I thought I was above that.

Jeff shrugged. "It wasn't hard. I knew your background, and I'd been watching you from a distance for a while, watching how you conducted yourself, watching you with Ms. Flores. And there was no real urgency to extract information, I was simply confirming what we mostly already knew, which always makes it easier." A smile broke through his thoughtfulness. "Time deadlines, and cases with no background information are the hardest. You were easy."

I ignored the references to how he'd been watching Sophia and me. Watching us at the time when we were just figuring out if we could make things work as an Us in the most absurd circumstances. "Why do you do it?"

"The same as why you do your job, I imagine. Because someone has to, and I'm good at what I do. We both know it's not for the benefits." He raised his free hand, palm up. "And so here we are."

"Here we are," I echoed.

"You shouldn't be here," Jeff murmured into his glass. After a small mouthful of bourbon, he added, "I've read your file."

"I know." It didn't really bother me as much as I'd thought it would. "What exactly does it say? I've always wondered."

"Lays out what happened during your hostage event, goes into stuff about your psych evals and your post-traumatic diagnosis. Also, I don't know why they keep asking you the trolley question, unless they think you're going to turn over to the other side. Seems a little redundant to me."

The trolley question… The needs of the many outweigh the needs of the few. Sacrifice one to save many. It had always been an easy choice for me. I'd talked to Sophia about that exact thing while we'd been in Tampa, and it'd been the basis for most of my life—including taking the Kunduz Intelligence and hiding with it when I'd thought it was in danger of being compromised. My throat felt tight when I asked, "What else? That's a pretty boring file."

"Confirmation that you're a good analyst. Not that I needed it." Jeff set the glass down. "Sending someone who experienced a traumatic event back to where it happened isn't good OPSEC. This right now, putting an analyst with your background in this situation, when this isn't their job anymore, just feels petty."

"I'm glad I'm not the only one who thinks so."

He was nowhere near drunk on his meager self-allocated ration of bourbon, but he was still far more open than he'd ever been. "I just want you to know it wasn't personal. The debriefs. I was told to do a job and I did it."

Ah, here it was, we'd reached some kind of truce and understanding. "Thank you. And I was just doing mine."

Jeff eyed me, and I could see the mental cogs turning as he tried to decipher that statement. "You still haven't answered my question."

"Oh, right. How am I?" I swirled the glass, watching the bourbon slide lazily up then down the sides. "Honestly, I don't know. I just really need to talk to my girlfriend."

"Understandable." He checked his watch. "Soon, right?"

"Mhmm." I sipped a tiny amount of bourbon, and though I didn't enjoy the sweet woodsy taste, I did relish the burn. Sophia loved bourbon and whiskey, and I'd indulged in a few fingers—mind out of the gutter—while we'd been road-tripping.

The road trip.

The bourbon burn turned unpleasant.

I inhaled shakily. "I—"

"What?"

After swallowing hard, I managed to talk again. "I just got...stuck on this thought, this...horrible thought, that I manipulate women who are close to me, because I *have* to manipulate them for some other, outside purpose. Sophia. Now I'm going to do it to Elaheh."

"Yes," he agreed quietly. "I think sometimes you do."

"Thanks..."

"Let me finish. You don't do it for personal gain. You do it because this job demands it of you. Because we all manipulate in some way to get what we need. Do you regret any of the talent you guided to the outcomes you wanted, guided toward a life being an asset for the agency?"

"No. But they're compensated. And they were just tools." I hated how impersonal it sounded, but it was the truth. I knew each person I'd recruited as intelligence-gathering assets during my time as an ops officer. I knew them intimately—their families, their hopes, their dreams, their fears—and I'd cared about their emotional and physical well-being. But none of them was a friend. None was an ex-lover. They weren't my girlfriend who I was deeply, desperately in love with.

"So why is it different now?"

"Because I *know* these women. I spent almost every hour with Sophia, every day for a week, while I lied and lied because I had no other option. It's different because I love Sophia and I hate what I did to her, even though she knows about it, or some of it now, and she knows why and forgives me. I always hated being asked to do this, it was the one part of fieldwork that never sat right. I hate lying." And I was starting to hate what this job was turning me into.

"You're good at it," he pointed out.

"Thanks," I said glumly. My brain snapped back to what he'd just said versus what I knew from things he'd already said. "Wait, what? During our debrief you said I was terrible at bluffing. You were super mean about it."

He shrugged. "I had no idea whether or not you were bluffing but I assumed you were because I didn't think you'd gone sideways or were stupid enough to release that intelligence." At my dumbfounded expression, Jeff shook his head. "It was a psych out, obviously. I'm surprised you didn't realize that."

"Forgive me for not picking up the nuance, I wasn't at my best. So I'm a good liar, great. But I still hate it. And now I'm going to do it again. And I know Elaheh is a terrorist, or at least involved with terrorists. I *know* that, but the stupid hopeful side of me wants it to be wrong."

"I'm sorry, Alexandra, but we're not wrong." He leaned forward. "And if you can't make peace with that, then you're going to make a bad decision and maybe get yourself killed. So please, for your sake. For Ms. Flores's sake. For my sake. *Please*. Make peace with it."

"I will," I said tightly.

I'd never counted down to anything the way I counted down to my call with Sophia that night, and when I saw her, I almost cried. "I am so happy to see you, baby. I have had…" I swallowed hard. Had what? One of the weirdest, most confusing, potentially frightening run-ins I'd had in a long time? "…a really weird day."

"Yeah?" she asked gently. "Weird like purple skies and flying dogs, or weird as in work weird."

"Work weird."

"Ah. Well, purple skies and flying dogs I could help with," she teased, "but I'm afraid I can't really help with work weird. Unless you want to talk about it in metaphors or in a roundabout, not giving away details, way?"

I loved that I didn't have to explain that I couldn't talk details with her, that she simply accepted this part of me. "I'm just…a little stuck."

"Physically? Emotionally? Ethically or morally?"

"Probably all of the above."

"Well…" she said carefully. "I guess the only thing I can ask you is kind of what I asked myself over and over when I was struggling to come to terms with what happened in Florida. Is what you're doing or going to do necessary to do your job, and is it for the greater good?"

"You mean, am I going to push the fat man in front of the trolley car?"

Sophia laughed. "Right. Is it a fat-man scenario?"

I smiled at the question. "I believe it is, yes." Not me sacrificing myself for the best outcome—at least not intentionally. But I was going to push a woman I'd once cared about under that trolley in order to save who knew how many lives.

Her expression softened. "Okay, then you know you have to do whatever it is to save that station full of people. And you know that you have to be okay with that because it's the right thing to do, and you just have to make peace with how you get there."

Sophia was right. Jeff was right. I had to make peace with it, I had to set aside my bias when it came to Elaheh. I had to forget the woman I used to know, or thought I used to know, and focus on the woman she'd become and how that was going to help me help others. If I couldn't do that, then I might not get to go home to Sophia.

CHAPTER SIXTEEN

Merry fucking Christmas

Even though it was almost midnight Christmas Eve back home, when I woke up I texted Sophia with a *Merry Christmas! Drive safely, say hi to your family for me and I'll talk to you all later. Love you.* I'd received a line of heart emojis and a *Merry Christmas. Love you, falling asleep, talk soon.* in response. I allowed the expected upset about what I was missing to flood in, let it stay for a few minutes, and pushed it out so I could start my day. We'd taken Christmas Day off work and after breakfast and cleaning the apartment together, Jeff and I took turns on the treadmill. Yay, Christmas celebrations.

We ate a relaxed lunch, then took a short walk through the park to get some air before it was time for me to come back and prep for our Christmas dinner while Jeff broke the no-work-on-Christmas rule. I divided marinade into two Ziplock bags and got to work slicing eggplant (my Christmas dinner) and cubing lamb (Jeff's Christmas dinner) to put into their separate bags. Camila had assured me her marinade recipe was perfect for both foods, and I hoped my effusive praise would further break some of the ice wall she'd erected between us at our first and only meeting.

The call to prayers had me pausing my dinner preparation. Each recitation by the *muezzin* brought a small dose of calm, and I closed my eyes to soak it up, letting it flow through me, washing away all my fear and anxiety and self-doubt. Tomorrow I was going to do something I dreaded, but today...today it was Christmas, even if I was without my girlfriend in a country that didn't recognize it, and I was going to enjoy it.

I'd never been a big celebrator of "important" events: birthday, Thanksgiving, Christmas always just felt like regular days to me, but Sophia loved celebrations and I'd been trying to adjust my thinking to be more in line with hers. I didn't hate celebrations, but having parents like mine had definitely influenced how I felt about them. I set the marinade bags in the fridge, and pulled out ingredients to make snacking platters for us to while away the afternoon until dinner.

I set a platter on the coffee table and poured us both a fresh glass of rosewater and lemon shrub I'd made that morning. Jeff raised his glass. "Merry Christmas."

I echoed the sentiment.

"This is a good batch," he said appreciatively, twisting his glass to peer at the bright yellow drink.

"Thanks."

"I'm taking all these recipes home for my wife. Can you write down any adjustments you've made to them?"

"Sure," I said, pleased that not only was he tolerating my cooking, baking, and drink-making, but that he wanted to continue consuming my creations when he went home.

We picked through the platter of nuts, dried fruits, olives, and flatbread slathered with soft cheese and in Jeff's case—cured meat, until both of us collapsed against the back of the couch, satisfied. I dropped my olive pit into the shallow bowl and wiped my hands on the cloth napkin draped over my thigh. "So...we didn't talk before we left about how we were celebrating Christmas and if we were doing the coworkers-in-close-quarters gifting or not. But Sophia said it would be nice if I got you something for Christmas. I mean, it's kind of my fault you're here on Christmas instead of with your family. So I have a little something for you, if you wanted to open it now?"

"Thank you. And it's fine. We're Thanksgiving people more than Christmas people." He paused, smirked. "Oh, wait...We missed that too, didn't we...?"

"Thanks for the reminder," I said flatly.

"You're welcome." His smirk turned to a devious smile, which made me instantly suspicious.

"What?"

"Nothing, just that my wife basically said the exact same thing. About giving you something for Christmas. So I have something for you as well."

"Oh?" I squeaked out. "Okay then. Great. Give me a sec."

When I came back from retrieving Jeff's Christmas gift, he'd collected a small, neatly wrapped and ribboned box from somewhere. As he offered it to me, he said quietly, "Our women are better than us, Alexandra."

"Mine sure is," I said glumly, as I passed him his present. "Thanks," I murmured.

We engaged in a small stand-off about who should open their gift first, when he set his down on the coffee table, and signaled I should get to unwrapping. As I moved to peel back the tape, he stopped me with, "Wait a moment, I forgot there's something else for you. You want the big gift or the little gift first?"

"Which one is this?"

"Little."

"Then I'll take the big one first."

He grinned. "Of course you will." He left the room and came back with a medium-sized, seen-better-days cardboard box with nothing on it except a blocky VEGETARIAN written on the side and top in Sharpie. "Sorry, I didn't have time to wrap this gift."

"You got me a vegetarian?" I exclaimed. "Thanks! It'll be nice to have a friend around here." I peeled back the packing tape and ripped the top flaps back. "MREs!" I exclaimed gleefully. "Yesssss. How did you manage this?"

Jeff worked to contain his smile, like he wasn't quite ready to let me see that my happiness made him happy. "You'd be surprised at the number of backdoor deals that used to happen on our military bases. I just happen to know local guys who bought cases of this shit while we were still here, because a bunch of them are halal and they're good for emergency rations."

I pulled out a single ration pack, and turned it, holding it at arm's length so I could read the printing. Cheese tortellini in tomato sauce. "Yum," I said, sifting through the box. Three each of the cheese tortellini, cheese pizza, creamy spinach fettuccine, and veggie crumbles with pasta in taco sauce. "Well, I know what I'm having for dinner tomorrow night."

"You're disgusting."

"I am," I agreed. "And thank you. This is a very thoughtful gift."

"I know. I'm a very thoughtful person. Are you going to see what other thoughtful gift I bought for you?"

"I'm not sure anything could top MREs, but I'm willing to accept another gift." I carefully unwrapped the smaller one, revealing a rainbow-striped lavender-scented soy candle and a small singing bowl. "Wow. This is great, and also something far more personal than I'd expected, so, thank you."

"Full disclosure, my wife bought these after submitting me to a questionnaire about what you liked, which I honestly couldn't answer with any certainty. Buying gifts for people you don't know well is a nightmare."

"Thank you, Jeff. And please thank your wife as well. She did an excellent job with what I'd imagine would have been very little information from you."

"Less than very little. And you're welcome."

"Are you ever going to tell me what your wife's name actually is?"

His eyes widened. "What? I haven't?"

"No. She's always 'my wife,' which I get, but I'm not the person you're debriefing anymore. I'm your work partner."

"It's a genuine oversight, Alexandra," he said earnestly. "Certainly not a deliberate exclusion. Her name is Dominique."

"Beautiful name."

"She's a beautiful woman, inside and out, remember?"

"I remember. Every time you say things like that, I'm reminded that you might actually be a real, compassionate human."

He rolled his eyes at me, but said nothing.

I picked up the neatly wrapped parcel from the coffee table and put it on his lap. "Well, full disclosure time from me. I bought you gifts myself, but very last-minute and Sophia did all the wrapping."

"That explains why it's so neat."

"Asshole."

He unwrapped the gift slowly, carefully pulling the tape free and folding the paper. First he picked up the TENS machine with inbuilt heat pad I'd bought him, staring at the box from all angles.

"It's for your bad back," I explained at his blank look.

"How did you know in November when you bought this, when we'd hardly interacted, that my back was crappy?"

"During our first debrief, right after they brought me to the facility, you said you wanted to get it done quickly because your bad back was playing up. It seemed like you were being truthful, which I thought was weird but I was grasping at straws for gift buying and it was one of the few leads I had about you."

"Well, as you know, yes, I do have a bad back." His mouth quirked. "This job is killing me slowly, Alexandra. Years of football, and then years of special ops missions, and now years of sitting at a desk."

"I'm sorry about your bad back, but I'm grateful you really do have a bad back so my gift is useful. If you didn't, I was going to point out it's also good for period pain or cold nights and I'd take it off your hands."

"Period pain isn't an affliction I suffer from, but I do suffer from cold nights." He studied the box. "Does it work?"

"My dad, who had a slipped disc or something and refused surgery, swore by his TENS and heating pads."

"Interesting," he said, nodding thoughtfully. "Thank you."

"You could also try yoga," I suggested. "I'd be happy to show you a few things to help alleviate back pain."

"Thanks, but I don't need yoga. I have this now"—he held up the box—"and also a pathological fear of anything that might make me examine my inner feelings too much."

Smiling, I assured him, "I get it. I used to feel like that. Avoid anything that might make me think about my feelings, who needs all that airy-fairy get in touch with your inner self shit, right?"

"And yet you do yoga every day," Jeff pointed out. "What changed?"

"A coworker who was just getting into it dragged me to a class to check out the hot instructor." Unfortunately, Sam deliberately didn't mention that what he really meant was that the male instructor had caught *his* eye, not that it was one who'd catch mine. But I'd been hooked after that one class, well beyond just the "insane flexibility" he'd sworn I'd get. And Sam's heart was broken when Yoga Sergio moved back to Venezuela after they'd dated for six months. "The instructor was far too male for me and therefore not my type, but it turns out yoga was." I'd been raised by cerebral parents, who weren't exactly emotionless, but science and logic and that type of thinking were king and anything that hinted at "mindfulness" was deemed wasteful. I'd absorbed that mindset and lived with it until I was old enough to realize that wasn't how I wanted to live my life.

A smile twitched at the edge of Jeff's mouth, but he reined it in. "I see."

I fiddled with a veggie taco crumble package. "It…helped, with the aftermath of the hostage thing. I was so angry, afraid, frustrated, and a million more negative emotions that were just pushing out any chance of finding a place to relax and deal with it. Therapy helped a little, so did admitting the situation might have given me a touch of something like PTSD, but…I needed more. And it just came at me out of nowhere. Meant to be." Smiling, I added, "But, I'm still a work in progress."

"Aren't we all," he said. "If it helped you, then I'm glad."

"It helps a little with being here, too." I folded my legs underneath myself. "You could just ignore the parts that might make you *feel* things, and just try the parts that help in whatever way you need. Maybe the feeling stuff will sneak in, in a good way."

"Thanks. Maybe I will." Jeff pulled out the second part of the gift, his eyebrows reaching dubiously for his hairline. "A comic book?"

I smiled sweetly. "I thought you'd enjoy it, considering how childish you were toward me during our briefings."

"If I'd known we were giving gifts based on our first interactions, I'd have bought you a Bratz doll."

I snorted. "Because I was a brat? Funny…"

"I know I am." He carefully put everything except the TENS device back into the gift box and set it by his feet. After reading the instructions, Jeff fiddled with the TENS and finally got it situated correctly on his back. "Heh, that feels funny. Wait, no…it feels good." He exhaled a long sigh. "Oh my god. Why have I never used one of these things before?"

I deepened my voice, imitating him. "Because you're just not that smart, Jeff."

Dinner was ten kinds of delicious, and once we'd finished eating then inhaled the rustic peach cobbler I'd tossed together, Jeff cleaned up while I showered. Once I'd dressed, I picked up my phone to check if I'd had any messages from Sophia and realized instantly that I had no cell service or Internet connection.

I leaned out of my bedroom and called out, "Is the Internet fucked-up for you too, or am I just special?"

Jeff appeared in the hall and a moment later his furious eyes made contact with mine. "Not just you. And my cell service isn't working either."

"Same." I rolled my eyes. "Merry fucking Christmas."

"Ho fucking ho," he said sarcastically.

I stood in my doorway, staring down the hall, trying to convince myself that this wasn't deliberate. I was unsuccessful. It was too big a coincidence to not be deliberate. Jeff stalked down the hall and into our workspace. He picked up the VoIP handset on his desk. "Nothing." He moved to the landline on the kitchen counter. "Well, this works, so we're okay in an emergency. But I will not be making a personal call on this line."

I nodded. There was no way I was calling anyone except a food delivery service on an unsecured local landline.

After fifteen minutes of sulking, and doing the ol' turn it all off and then on again, I realized we really were without comms. I dropped heavily onto the couch. "Well, fuck. This is fucking perfect."

Jeff sat down too, with far less flounce than me. "Wanna play cards? Watch a show together? Talk about our feelings?" He asked the questions casually, like he didn't give a shit if I said yes or no, but I sensed that he didn't feel like being alone for the night.

With the prospect of retreating to my room to think about the fact I was not talking with Sophia on Christmas Day, I agreed.

We'd been playing rummy for twenty minutes when he quietly asked, "What's up?"

"Hmm? Oh, nothing." I put down a run of cards. "Nothing except this amazing meld."

"Well done. You're good at fooling most people, Alexandra, but not me. So, what's up?"

Mentally cursing Jeff's almost telepathic ability to read me, I took a few moments to consider what was actually bothering me, other than a general malaise about my situation. "Aside from the fact I hate being here and I hate the current administration and I hate that I hate this stuff because it's fucking with my mental health to be so negative, it just...it feels like Sophia and me are kind of, not drifting apart, but maybe that we're not as connected as we were when I was home. I think it's finally starting to sink in, it really feels like we're separated."

"You are separated."

"You know what I mean, you asshole."

He smiled gently. "Yes. I do."

"How do you do it? I mean, if you've been married forever, and you used to do special secret ops shit, then you'd have been apart from your wife for big chunks of time, heaps of time before, right?"

"Right. You do your best to make it feel not separate," Jeff said simply. I'd overheard him the other morning talking with Dominique, and the gentle "Yes, my love. I will. I love you too with all my heart" had honestly melted me a little.

"We're trying, but it's *so* hard, and all the work we're doing to make it work kind of makes me feel like it's doing the opposite." I didn't think our relationship was in danger, but it didn't feel quite right either, and that had me worried given we were only one month into my posting. Maybe a communication blackout on Christmas was skewing my thinking a little, but also...it didn't feel skewed.

He nodded slowly, thankfully not commenting on the waffly disjointedness of my answer. "Relationships can be tough and they need both parties to work at making them solid." He said it as if he were teaching a class on how to relationship. If he had any advice, then I was going to take it, because at forty-one-and-two-thirds years old, I was a relationship novice.

"I'm getting that." I exhaled, imagining all my anxiety going out with the air. "I think it's just...like...we started this whole thing in such a weird way, and that connection felt so intense. Feels so intense. And then we've been separated right when everything was starting to get really amazing. I feel like we're having trouble staying connected, communicating everything, even the most basic conversation just feels so hard, like we're both overthinking every single thing we say."

"Being away from your lover for a week is tough. Six months? It's borderline unbearable. And when you add in the secrecy of our job, you've just doubled all that difficulty. But you do what you have to so you can make it work, make it fit in your life so it doesn't affect you too negatively, because the people we choose to have in our lives are worth that."

"Did you really just say lover?" I asked, eyebrows raised.

"Yes," he said firmly, and without a trace of embarrassment. "That's what my wife is. She's my lover as well as my partner, my support system, my strength, all my hopes and dreams, and so much more. As I am for her."

"Jeff, do you write pseudonymous romance novels in your spare time?"

He snorted a laugh. "No, but it'd be a heck of a lot less stressful than this job."

Laughing, I shook my head. "Who knew you were such a good husband."

"My job doesn't preclude me from being a good man and a good husband, Alexandra. You should know that better than anyone. What we do, who we are when we step into the office, is not all-encompassing. We are not our jobs, we simply do our jobs."

"Profound."

"That's me. How are you feeling about seeing Elaheh again tomorrow?" He laid down all his cards. "That's rummy."

"I hate you."

"You're a sore loser."

Not untrue. After tallying our scores, I piled up the cards and started shuffling. "I'm nervous, but not scared. I think it's just…Elaheh being *here* and her new ideology and the fact she murdered people because of that ideology? It's muddying the water. I *never* loved her, we were just fulfilling a physical need for each other. But I cared about her because of who she was and her situation, because she kept me from being lonely. But…" I exhaled. "She's not that person anymore, and that's making me confused and making me question why I chose two women who are so opposite to each other."

"I think you're overthinking your previous relationship with Elaheh and how that might relate to your relationship with Ms. Flores."

I frowned. "Probably. But trying to separate those two in my brain is not fun. What does it mean—that I have these two women, one good and one…bad."

"It means you're human, nothing more," he said firmly. "It's natural to want to compare the two, to find how you fit in amongst those things. But it's apples and oranges, Alexandra."

I shrugged. "Maybe it's extra hard today because it's Christmas and Sophia loves Christmas and I was trying to love Christmas but now I just fucking hate it." I eyed him. "Do you think they're doing things like messing with the Internet and cell service on purpose to punish me further? Make it harder for me to stay in contact with my girlfriend? And yes, I know it sounds paranoid. But I wouldn't put it past them."

He shook his head. "No. Because that's cutting me off too. And I'm the Golden Child."

"Jeff. Think about it. Why wouldn't they? I know their whole reason for putting me here is to make me miserable and to teach me a lesson. You know, they sent people to shadow Sophia. Recently. Why would they do that, except to mind-fuck me? I'm assuming you know the details of my arrangement with the president." The arrangement where he was supposed to leave me the fuck alone. I started dealing cards.

"Parts of it, yes. I can't speak as to their rationale, or what they hope to achieve, but…" He frowned. "If it were me? Yes, I would have people shadowing her, noncontact, just because I could and because I would want to remind you of that. Because they want to make sure you're doing what you've been told to do. That you stay in line."

Exactly what I'd thought. The president's warnings reverberated through my brain. "They don't need to do that. Actually, them doing this makes me want to step *out* of line."

Jeff chuckled. "You have the biggest fight reflex of anyone I know. Most people back down but you're always jumping in front of the enemy, imagined or real, fists up."

"The enemy in this case is unfortunately real." Of course I meant the president and his cohort of corrupt disgusting men. "And why wouldn't I fight them? They're immoral, for starters." And maybe as corrupt as Berenson.

"You don't need to fight. That's not the point here."

"Then what is the point?"

"To play out the long game. That's how you'll win against them."

"Who is *them* exactly?"

Jeff picked up his cards. He sorted them for a maddeningly long time before he answered, "The people who sign your paychecks. And sometimes mine."

I stared at him until he elaborated, "The same people who sent someone to collect you in the middle of the night. The same people who were following you to Tampa. Our government wants what it wants and few things will get in the way of that."

"Don't I know it," I mumbled. "How do I get them to back away from her? Like really leave her alone, forget she even exists?"

"I don't know. When you did what you did with that intelligence, you stuck a massive target on your back."

I asked him a question I'd asked Lennon early on. "Do you think they're going to kill me?"

"No," he said immediately, "of course not." He seemed almost appalled by the suggestion. "But you put Ms. Flores and her family on their radar, aligned them with you, and they know how important she is to you. Now they're going to do everything they can to make sure you never do anything like that again. Including holding something or someone over your head."

"Merry Christmas," I grumbled.

CHAPTER SEVENTEEN

Playing dangerous games

In a move that did nothing to ease my suspicions, the Internet and cell service returned at exactly the same time, early the next morning. What a lovely coincidence… The moment services came back, Signal went nuts with notifications ranging from *Are you there? Did you get Christmas drunk and pass out?* to *I'm really worried about you, call me or something PLEASE.*

The slew of messages was a timeline of Sophia's panic—she'd even contacted Derek to ask if something had happened and been assured there was no indication of anything like that—and with every message, I could feel her desperation, her rationalization, her resignation. It was late for her, but I hit the video call button as I was walking down the hall, and she answered as I closed my bedroom door, her voice and face pure relief. "Oh my god," she choked out. "Lexie. Are you all right?"

"Hey, I'm so sorry. We lost all comms just after dinner yesterday. Shit timing, huh? And I'm okay." I drew in a deep breath and exhaled my frustration, trying to focus on the present where I was okay and she was okay and we were talking to each other. "How are you?" I fumbled on the bedside table for my glasses. "There. Good. I can see you're still beautiful."

"I'm…Now we're talking, I'm breathing again. But this has been the worst twelve hours of my entire life. I've been so worried about you. Are you *sure* you're okay?" Her voice broke on the question.

"Aside from being seriously pissed off that we didn't get to talk on Christmas Day, I'm fine. Really," I added when her eyebrows shot up. I worked hard to moderate how upset I really was—now wasn't the time to dump all my emotions on her—and to instead show her how much talking with her right now was keeping me afloat before my meet-up with Elaheh in a few hours. "I'm so happy to see you, babe. Did you have a good Christmas?"

"It was nice, yeah. Just the usual food and family stuff. Everyone loved their gifts. But…I really wanted to talk to you and so did Mom and papi." Dejection seeped from her like a heavy, oppressive rain cloud.

"I know. Me too." I forced cheer into my voice. "No matter, next year it'll be in person and we'll celebrate extra hard to make up for this year."

"For sure." She smiled sweetly, and I could see the change move through her as she collected herself. "How was your day? How was your Christmas food? Did your partner like his gift?"

"It was pretty chill, actually, aside from the communication issue. The food was great. Can you please tell Camila that her marinade was delicious? And he did like his things, yes."

She smirked. "And did he give you something?"

"Yes, he did. You were right about the gifts thing."

"Of course I was right. Did you open mine?"

"God no, of course not. I was waiting for you. But then you never happened, but now you are happening, so…" I leaned over and snagged the gift from my bedside table where I'd spent the night staring at it, hoping she was okay and that somehow she knew that I was too. "Did you open mine?"

"I did. Sorry. I got all freaked out when I finally went to bed, thinking you'd died or something, so I opened it. That book looks really interesting! And the necklace is beautiful, thank you. I'm wearing it now." She pulled the neckline of her sweater aside to reveal the gold necklace and its small world globe pendant—a perfect gift for the avid traveler, the saleswoman had assured me while I'd been dithering.

"Oh, it looks great on you. And you're welcome, and I'm so sorry it wasn't something better or more thoughtful, but time was not my friend this year. But next year, expect gift extravagance." A necklace, and a book on the history of codebreaking weren't exactly exciting, but I knew how much Sophia loved puzzles and riddles and codes, as well as travel, so at least I'd managed to hit the "personal" note.

"Oh I will," she assured me. "And no apologies, I love your gifts. Also, don't get too excited, I had the same issue with the timing crunch."

I set the phone on the bedside table, propped up against a pile of books, and kept talking as I slid my thumbnail underneath the tape of Sophia's gift. "I'm sure whatever you got me is amazing, time crunch and all." I peeled back the paper and pulled out a purple octopus squeeze toy and some small temporary tattoos of cartoon octopuses. "Ahaha, so cute. God, I can't remember the last time I had a temporary tattoo. Maybe elementary school?" I held one against my shirt sleeve then set it down to squeeze the octopus. Mmm, stress relieving. "I love this, thank you. It's adorable, and it makes me think of our road trip."

After she'd found out what was really going on, she'd asked me to tell her some truths, and I'd blurted random things, like how I loved octopus—they were cool and clever and camoflaguey—and Sophia had laughingly compared me to one. I'd left a small plastic octopus in her car to show her that I was free and safe, and it seemed octopuses were now my thing.

"Me too," Sophia murmured. "What about the other one?"

It felt like a frame under the butcher's paper wrapping, and once I'd torn it back I was staring at a pencil drawing. Of Sophia. Completely naked. I swallowed hard. "Jesus," I managed to croak out. "I'm glad I didn't open this during a video call with your family."

Sophia cracked up. "Yeah that would have been a little awkward."

The drawing was erotic and tasteful, and I lightly traced the line of her hip, along her side and up to her breast. Based on the bedframe at the edge of the drawing, she'd positioned a mirror and drawn her reflection as she'd reclined on her bed. Her legs were slightly open, the shading between her legs enough to hint at what was there, but indistinct enough to make me desperate to see more. The full curves of her breasts and hips flowed like a meandering stream, graceful and elegant.

I swallowed hard, trying to suppress the ache of want. "Fuck me, you're so beautiful."

Sophia rubbed her palm over the blush creeping up her neck. "Thank you. Drawing yourself naked is…an experience. I was trying very hard to not rose-tint my self-portrait."

I whistled. "Baby, you did no such thing." Desire and arousal mixed together low in my belly, and I took a deep breath to settle the quiver of excitement. Reality was an unfortunate intrusion, and further settled my arousal. "And I would love to compare this drawing with the real thing in slow, intimate detail, but, sweetheart, it's the start of my workday here and I need to go out and meet with someone. Sorry to run off. I just had to call you and let you know what happened. Can we try for a video call tonight?" I did my best not to think about the fact that if I'd misjudged Elaheh, that there might not be any more calls in my future.

"Absolutely. Assuming the Internet and cell service works," she said, trying to tease, but I caught the flat effect of her annoyance. "Are you actually in some cave somewhere with no reception?"

I held back my choked laugh. "No, we're in a city full of technology. It'll work." I hoped.

"Good. I…I need a real, long conversation with you. I feel like we need to reconnect."

My breath caught. So it wasn't just me who felt like we'd drifted. "Me too, and I know. I love you," I murmured. "And I miss you."

"Me too. I mean, I don't love and miss me. But I love and miss you."

I laughed. The sentiment brought a warmth that quickly cooled and my laugh turned to a sigh. "You know what?"

"What?"

"Whoever said absence makes the heart grow fonder was a liar. All it's doing is making me really fucking sad."

Jeff was in the living room when I exited my room after my all-too-brief call with Sophia. "Everything okay?" he asked.

"Mhmm. She was scared shitless that something had happened but I think she's calmed down now we've talked. How's Dominique?"

"Same. And now that we've assured our respective better halves that we're okay, I need to show you something."

"I'm not squeezing a back zit for you."

"I thought women loved doing that shit, but it's not that." Jeff picked up something from his desk, then turned around, keeping his hands behind himself and the item hidden. "So, it made me suspicious that both the Internet *and* cell service went out at exactly the same time, *and* on Christmas Day which is a day we both would want to connect with family and partners. Then I remembered you asking if I thought they were messing with our personal comms on purpose.

Which I didn't. But, curiosity is my job, so I went digging around the apartment to see what I could see." He brought his hands out in front, holding up a small electronic device with wires extruding from the end. "And look what I've seen."

I leaned closer, my gut sinking as I realized with dread what the device might be. "Is that—"

"A signal blocker with remote access? Yes. Which means the services didn't just go down." He paused for effect. "Someone blocked them. Someone who is probably back in the States. Or…maybe headquartered just out of town and doing nefarious things because someone back in the States told them to." Jeff dropped the plastic box into the sink, plugged the hole, and turned on the water. He spun back to face me, arms crossed casually over his chest. "Who exactly did you piss off, Alexandra?"

"I'm sure you know."

He raised his chin to stare me down, but the edges of his eyes crinkled with amusement. "You did a damned good job of it."

"Trust me, I know. If I was as good at everything else as I seem to be at infuriating the president, then I'd be happy."

Jeff laughed. "Keep trying." He seemed unfazed by my revelation. "Are you ready for your meeting? Anything you need to talk through before you go?"

"Yes, and no."

"Good. We'll leave to do our recon walk in an hour."

"Mhmm."

It was almost game time. Yay.

Elaheh lived in one of the newer apartment buildings similar to ours, a twenty-minute stroll away. The recon walk Jeff and I took around the surrounding blocks confirmed what the satellite imagery had shown—nothing was obviously amiss, and I felt very little anxiety about something untoward happening from outside during my visit. My anxiety was tied to my feelings about seeing her again after the way I'd ended things, and the whole "your brother and uncle were terrorists, and I killed your brother and was responsible for your uncle's death soon after that." Plus, there was the normal underlying awkwardness of talking to someone you'd broken up with abruptly, having planned to leave the country so they couldn't contact you.

I still couldn't shake the lingering, unfounded, unease that she knew what I'd done, and who I really was. But in the next thought stream, I realized how ridiculous that was. I was as certain as I could be that they'd taken no photographs of me while I'd been held hostage, my cover had been secure—or as secure as it could be with a novice asset who'd blown it to the people who'd captured me—and in the years since, the name Ellen Jackson had never come up in any intelligence briefs. And to be certain my cover wasn't blown, a cleanup crew had come in after my rescue and scoured the premises, making sure no trace of Ellen had made it into the network.

Jeff had positioned himself in a café kitty-corner from Elaheh's building to wait for me and keep an eye on things, and having him there eased some of my nervousness. Less than two seconds after I'd knocked, as if she'd been lingering on the other side, waiting for me, Elaheh answered her door. She wore hijab in a beautiful emerald-green pattern, her smile was warm, friendly, and she held out her right hand to me, squeezing mine as she murmured, "Ellen." She pulled me toward her and kissed me lightly on the cheek. "Please come in. Welcome."

"Thank you so much for the invitation," I said as I passed her the flowers I'd purchased on my way over. I removed my shoes and lined them up neatly in the entryway as Elaheh examined the bouquet.

"Orange tulips. My favorite. You remembered." She lifted her eyes to meet mine. "Thank you."

"You're most welcome." The formality of the conversation felt so strange after everything that had transpired between us. "This is a beautiful apartment. So light and airy. You must have a beautiful view of the park from here." The spiced scent of brewing tea wafted to me, and I inhaled deeply.

She smiled knowingly for a moment before the smile turned mischievous. "It is a world away from my old apartment, isn't it?"

I recalled the cramped space, the worn furniture, the homey feeling of the apartment where I'd spent so much time. But I felt nothing as I recalled that time together. "It is," I agreed.

"Please, make yourself comfortable. I have chai brewing. Are you hungry?"

"No, but thank you. I had a late breakfast." I glanced around furtively as I followed her through her apartment, though I didn't know what I was expecting to see. Plans for an upcoming terrorist attack would be nice. Okay, not *nice*, but...you know, good for the Intelligence Community. Elaheh guided me to the living room just off the kitchen, and gestured to the large, ornately decorated cushions on the beautifully patterned rug covering almost the entire room. "Please, sit. Make yourself comfortable."

I took a seat on a soft cushion, where I could see into the kitchen. Ever the gracious hostess, she came back almost right away to set a plate of freshly baked *khetayee* cookies on the low table in front of me, each one perfectly shaped with a generous pinch of ground pistachios in the dimple on top. After a warm smile, she went back to making tea. I watched Elaheh stirring chai in a battered old saucepan that I imagined had absorbed decades worth of spices into the metal. Probably why the chai I made for myself at home never tasted as good as it did here.

"You still wear the same perfume," she said casually. "I missed it when you left."

I had no idea how to answer, so I said, "You do too." As well as the spice from her tea, I'd been surrounded by the scent of English rose the moment I'd entered her apartment, and had pushed down the wave of sad nostalgia. I gestured at the drawings on her refrigerator and asked a question to which I already knew the answer. "You have a child?"

One corner of her mouth turned upward. "Yes. A son. He is almost three years old."

"He's not here?"

Her gaze was steady. "With my husband's family. I thought it best while you visited."

Interesting. Best because she didn't want me to meet her child, or vice versa? Best because she wanted to discuss something with me away from a child's ears? Best because she knew I struggled with children, especially young loud ones? Or...best because she thought something might happen between us, that we'd shift back to the place where we'd been before? Elaheh turned back to the stove, standing with her back to me as she slowly stirred the chai.

The silence expanded to fill the space, moving between us like mist. "What are your husband's and son's names?" I asked casually, just a friend making polite conversation.

"Basir. And Basir, Junior," she added with a smile that didn't touch her eyes. Elaheh strained the brew, and brought the teapot and two yellow glass cups into the living room, bending at the waist to set them down. After carefully pouring chai into both glasses, she passed one to me. I took it carefully so she didn't accidentally trap my fingers underneath hers.

I waited until she'd sat opposite me, gracefully folding her legs beside her, before I raised the glass, inhaling deeply before sipping the aromatic milky tea. The warm cinnamon, clove, and nutmeg melted over my tongue. "Oh my goodness. Thank you. That's wonderful. I've tried making tea the way you do, but I can never get it just right, even with a recipe."

Elaheh curled both hands around the mug, cupping it tightly as she raised it to blow across the surface of her tea. A faint smile raised the edges of her mouth. "So it was worth coming all this way just for my tea?"

"Yes." I decided to just push through into the heart of the conversation and see where it would get me. "How long have you been married?"

"Almost five years. Not long after you left, my family found Basir for me to marry. We moved here soon after the wedding." She said it completely without inflection, completely without facial expression, which gave me no idea how she felt about her second marriage. Though, I'd have thought if she was enthused about her new husband, she would have shown it.

"Do you like the city?"

"Yes. It suits me well. I feel…useful here."

Useful. An interesting and odd way to frame her feelings. I made a mental note to probe that further if the opportunity arose. "Then I'm pleased for you."

"Thank you." Though I'd only had a few mouthfuls, she topped up my tea.

"It must be a big change for you, moving here." I adjusted my tone to caring, yet tinged with neutrality as I tried to gauge her feelings. "There have been a lot of changes since I was last here. How is the new government working for you?"

The skin around her mouth and eyes tightened. "They do not work for anyone but themselves. I did not think anything could be worse than our previous government, but I was wrong."

Jackpot. Maybe.

"I'm so sorry, Elaheh. Are you and your family okay? Do you have what you need to live comfortably?"

"Yes," she said instantly, almost defensively. Then she softened a little. "We are fine, much more privileged than some."

So noted. I was grateful I'd had so much practice at not reacting to things, because I would have given myself away right then. The Robin Hood ideal Jeff had mentioned—that she was crusading against the establishment to better the lives of the poor—seemed to fit. "I'm very pleased to hear that."

Elaheh inclined her head. Then she deftly changed the subject. "How is your school planning coming along?"

"Slowly." There was no need to remind her of the disdain her government had toward educating girls. "There were whispers that they might allow girls to resume schooling, and we decided to press forward. Perhaps they think it will help their image." We actually had had some brief meetings with local low-level government officials, set up by one of the team's assets and aided by a financial incentive, just to help keep our covers intact. We'd keep up the charade, and then close to the end of our assignment, our funding would be "pulled," and we'd disappear like we were never there.

Elaheh scoffed, "They think allowing girls to educate themselves will make us like them?" She'd gained a new confidence, but also a coolness that didn't suit her.

Offering a placating smile, I tried to smooth the rough edges of her mood. "Regardless of their reasoning, if we're successful then it's the young women of this country who benefit. I'm hopeful we'll succeed, even if it takes a while," I lied smoothly.

"I'm hopeful too," Elaheh said, calmer now.

"I'm glad."

"I thought I'd never see you again," she said quietly.

"Neither did I, but I'm very pleased I have. Are you happy?" I asked.

"Yes." She offered the plate of cookies to me. "And you?"

"I am." After selecting a cookie and biting off a generous chunk, I said, "This is amazing. And you remembered too." She had made khetayee cookies for me before, and I'd fallen in love with them.

"Yes," she said quietly. "I remembered."

We sat in companionable silence, drinking tea and eating cookies until Elaheh broke the quiet. "What does your husband…Mark, do?" she asked. I recognized the desperation for answers hidden behind the nonchalance.

"He's also a teacher." I turned it back on her. "And Basir? I would love to meet him."

There was the slightest pause, one I only noticed because I was so finely tuned to her. "He works for a local company, managing a team of builders. He's very busy," she said easily before changing the subject again. "I admit, I didn't think you'd ever marry, especially not a man."

I shrugged and at the last moment, remembered to smile. "Neither did I, but it just happened. Sometimes I think we're powerless to resist an attraction." My mind went immediately to Sophia, to the immediate, intense attraction and connection I'd felt to her, the love we shared, and I was instantly soothed by the thought of her. I lightened my tone. "And, he's a great cook."

"Yes, I have experienced that feeling before." Elaheh laughed lightly and I tried not to think of the undertone in that laugh. "Do you still cook?"

I acknowledged the memory of us together, and how those memories lingered in her question. "Yes, I do. I've been cooking a little here, but I really don't have as much time as I'd like. Do you have any recommendations for restaurants in the city?"

"Basir always enjoys Aber."

"Oh, we've walked past there a few times. We'll have to go in."

There was a long pause as she looked around the room, and when she finally returned her gaze to me, her eye contact felt tenuous. "I've always suspected that restaurant had cockroaches." Elaheh pulled a face, sticking out her tongue in disgust.

I laughed at the expression. "I see. Well, thank you for the advice. We might just keep walking past, then."

"I think that's wise."

I reached across the table and lightly touched the top of her forefinger near her fingernail. "Your nails look gorgeous."

She peered down at her hands, pulling one from the mug and splaying her fingers wide. "Thank you."

"I need to find somewhere to get my hair cut, and my nails done." I held up my hands, wrinkling my nose in distaste. "I didn't have time for a manicure before I left. Can you recommend anywhere?" It was a dual-edged question—I really did need a haircut soon, and a manicure even sooner. If the woman I used to know was still in there somewhere then she'd offer to take me to her salon. And it was likely we'd have tea or a meal afterward, which meant another chance to meet with her in a casual setting where we could talk.

Elaheh took my bait immediately. "Yes I can. You must give me your phone number, and we can go together." The edges of her eyes softened. "I would very much like to see you again."

"Me too," I said honestly. I gave her the local number I was using for things that didn't require deep phone security, and she put it into her phone.

"How is next week?" she asked. "Monday? I can make the salon appointment."

Hook.

Smiling, I agreed, "Monday is perfect. Just text me the time."

I'd have to bide my time before I went for line and sinker. Good thing I was a patient fisherwoman.

CHAPTER EIGHTEEN

She's on Fire

Though I knew it was ridiculous, as soon as I got back to the apartment, I took a scalding shower, washing my hair and scrubbing my skin until Jeff knocked on the bathroom door to ask if I'd passed out.

"No," I called back as I reluctantly shut off the showerhead.

"Okay. Then, are you all right?"

I wiped water from my face. "In a broad sense? Yes."

"Good." He tapped the door once, decisively. "When you're ready, why don't you come out, have some coffee, and we'll talk."

I took my time drying off, attending to my facial routine, brushing out my wet hair, and moisturizing everything that could be moisturized, before I bundled myself up in my favorite feel-better sweats and long-sleeved tee. Comfort trumped appropriate workday attire. Despite the long, hot shower, and being snuggled in my comfy clothes, I couldn't shake the chill that'd wrapped around my body.

I slumped at the head of the kitchen table, pulling my hands into the sleeves of my tee. A strange numbness had crept in and I fought against the mental fog as I struggled to understand why I felt like I'd been hit by a truck. Jeff set a steaming mug of coffee in front of me then sat opposite with his own.

"Thanks." I wrapped both hands around it, grateful for something to hold on to.

"Are you sure you're okay?" he asked gently. "Did anything happen?"

"Aside from talking, drinking tea, and eating cookies? No, nothing happened. I'm being ridiculous. I don't know why I'm so freaked out by having tea and talking with a woman I know."

"Because that woman is no longer the woman you knew, Alexandra. And the change she's undergone would shake anyone up, even if they didn't have to sit in her house and act like nothing was amiss."

"I know, but…you know." I shook myself out. Get a grip.

"I know," he said kindly. "We're superhuman." Jeff turned on a cyborg voice as he said, "No weakness allowed, only strength."

Smiling, I shook my head at his funny attempt to cheer me up. After a careful sip of hot coffee, I fished my phone from my pocket, set it on the table, and started the recording app to capture what I was going to tell Jeff about the conversation with Elaheh. Luckily I had an excellent memory because I hadn't worn any sort of recording device, nor kept my phone recording, in case she discovered it.

I took my time recounting the meeting, telling him not only what we'd said, but some of my feelings about it, like her "useful" comment. Jeff's forehead wrinkled. "She said her husband eats at Aber a lot, but she thinks there's cockroaches?"

"Yeah. That's what she said. And it made me wonder if she meant *actual* cockroaches, in which case—why let your husband eat there? Or if maybe her husband and his friends are the cockroaches, which makes me wonder if she's not as invested in the cell as we thought."

"Interesting. Put it in your report for the ops team, they can follow up and maybe mark Aber for surveillance." He stood and refilled our coffee mugs, adding some rock sugar to mine. "And she said nothing else about Mohammadzai at all, except for the construction job comment?"

"Nothing," I confirmed. "I didn't get the sense there was marriage tension, just that she was private."

"Understandable. You know, if you're involved in terrorism you're probably not going to blurt about your life."

"Yeah," I said ruefully. "I'm going to keep gently probing about Mohammadzai when I see her on Monday for our salon appointment. I don't think that's a weird thing for an old friend to do, right? If she pushes back, then I'll just back it up a step and try another line of inquiry."

"Are you sure you're okay to continue doing this?" The unspoken lingered heavily in the air—was I going to have a meltdown after every time I had to talk to her, and was that meltdown going to compromise me.

"Yes. I can do it," I said firmly.

"Okay, if you're sure. If nothing else, assuming you come through with something after all this, the ops team might pull that stick from their ass." Jeff cracked a faint smile. "Maybe they'll finally invite us over for a social event."

"Isn't that the dream," I deadpanned.

I took my second coffee—oh boy was I going to be wired tonight— to my desk and after sending Derek a quick update email, put my AirPods in and transcribed the recorded conversation as a base with which to write out my report about my meeting with Elaheh. Jeff wordlessly set a PB&J and cup of canned tomato soup by my elbow somewhere near dinnertime, then removed my dirty dishes and replaced them with a generous portion of yesterday's peach cobbler. No mention of me making or not making dinner, he just went ahead and put together something from his limited repertoire. Nice work, Jeff, you're now at a solid eight on the Maybe You're Not An Asshole Scale. I was on my first editing pass of the report when my phone lit up with a message. Sophia. I snatched it up.

Is everything okay?

Why wouldn't things be oka—Fuck! 8:37 p.m. I was late. I'd been so caught up in Elaheh and trying to work out my moves for our next meeting, that I'd completely blown past my video call time with Sophia.

Sorry! Caught up with work. You still okay to chat?

Always :)

I saved my reports and speed-walked into my room. Meeting Elaheh had left me feeling more than a little off-kilter, and I needed to get out from underneath the weight of it. Needed to reconnect with my life back home. Needed to reconnect with Sophia, the calming counterpoint to everything shitty here. That need became suddenly desperate. I wanted to be with her, near her in any capacity, nonsexual, or very sexual. I wanted to touch her, watch the way her eyes seemed to darken as she'd hold that intense eye contact with me while she kissed and licked and sucked her way down my body before spreading my legs and—

I locked the bedroom door, flopped onto my bed, settled against the headboard, and said another silent thank-you for the soundproofing.

Either they thought we'd be working in our rooms, or they realized that people living away from significant others needed some time to, uh...connect. I yanked open my laptop and started a video call, fumbling to get my earbuds in before she answered. Sophia accepted the call, her face pixelating for a second before stabilizing. "Hey, you."

"Hey, sweetheart, how are you? I love you," I blurted, then paused a moment to take her in, ground myself in her. "And I'm so sorry. I caught a break and totally lost track of time."

She grinned, her eyes and nose wrinkling adorably. "I forgive you. Only because it reminds me of you being obsessed with work in Tampa, which makes me feel warm and fuzzy."

"You really enjoyed the weird road trip that much?"

"It's nostalgia," she said with faux indignance. "It was where we fell in love."

Fell in love. God I loved hearing that. "That's true," I agreed, smiling like a goof.

"So, work is going good then?"

Good wasn't exactly how I'd describe things but...now that I stopped to think about it, terrible wasn't the right word either. "We're getting there," I said cheerfully, too cheerfully. Dial it down, Lexie.

She was also in bed, propped back against her mountain of pillows, and in the corner of the video I could see the edge of her metal and wood bedframe. She'd removed her leather restraints from the bedhead. My libido went skipping merrily off along memory lane, recalling the few times we'd played with Sophia's handcuffs. The delight on her face, the way her fingers had trembled as she'd buckled one around my wrist, the slow and sensual way she'd touched me. I swallowed hard and tried to ignore the throb of arousal so I could have an actual conversation with her first.

She smiled softly. "That's great, hon. How was your work thing earlier?"

I thought about everything I wanted to tell her, then set it all aside to say, "Productive. Hence the late." I wished I could explain instead of hiding behind the ten-foot-high chain-link barbed-wire-topped fence erected around what I did for a living.

"My little hard worker."

"That's me." I was about to check in with her about her follower, if she'd seen them again after Derek had promised he'd take care of it, but as I shifted to get more comfortable I caught a glimpse of her drawing where I'd hung it on a wall hook—thankfully, Jeff never came into my room. My body's reaction was instantaneous, and I crossed my legs, clenching my thighs together to try to stave off my arousal. Conversation first, sex second. My attempt at a calm inhalation netted a sharp intake of breath instead.

"What's going on?" Sophia asked, an eyebrow arching. "You look like you just had a naughty thought."

"I did," I admitted. "I just saw your drawing."

"Ohhhh…" Her smile turned devious as her fingertips traced a line across a collarbone. "Didn't you say you wanted to compare the drawing with the real thing?"

"Mhmm," I squeaked out, my eyes following the path of her fingertips. Okay, looked like our catchup was done. Commence sexy time.

"Fingers crossed the Internet holds this time," she teased as she smoothed her hands down over her belly.

"Yeah," I agreed dumbly. The Internet had crapped out during our last video-sex session, right as Sophia had spread her legs to show me how wet she was. Most unfortunate and most annoying. But so far, so good with connectivity.

The view tilted then resettled slightly farther back and a little higher, giving me a sightline along the length of Sophia's body. I let my gaze wander the smooth skin of her bare legs, the line up to her hip and the seam of her panties. She wore a pale green tee, *my* tee, that skimmed the top of her hips and clung to breasts that were most certainly braless. "You're wearing my clothes," I said inanely.

"I am," she said. She pulled the shirt off, confirming that she was indeed not wearing a bra. "And now, I'm not…"

My whole body pulsed with desire, and I inhaled a shuddering breath as I stared at her almost-naked body. Fuck, she was gorgeous, a perfect complement of curves and swells and smooth planes of skin. "Touch your breasts for me," I whispered.

Sophia reached up and cupped her breasts, fingers lightly scissoring her nipples. "Like this?"

"Yes," I said hoarsely.

She gently pinched her nipples, then dropped a hand to lazily stroke her belly above the waistband of her underwear. "Seems unfair that you're still fully dressed, doesn't it?"

"A little." I evened the field by pulling off my tee and tossing it aside. My hands moved without thinking, reaching up to cup my breasts.

"That's better," she said tightly. "I wish those were my hands on you."

"Me too." I swallowed hard. Pinching my nipples sent a delicious current through my belly, down into my clit. I bit back an audible moan. "This being-separate thing isn't *all* bad," I managed around my attempts to draw in a full, deep breath.

"No?"

"I wish we were together, obviously," I said as I lazily stroked the inside of my breast. "But this anticipation makes me so fucking horny."

"Same." Her fingertips moved back and forth along the thigh seams of her panties. "How much do you want me to take these off?"

"Right now, more than anything." The anticipation of seeing her wet and wanting, of watching Sophia touch herself, bring herself to climax, had me squirming.

She hooked her thumbs in the top of her panties and carefully wriggled out of them. I leaned forward, trying to see the familiar landscape of her labia. Sophia let her legs fall open. My mouth went dry.

"So?" she asked as her hand moved between her thighs. "Does the drawing compare with the real thing?"

"I'm not sure," I murmured, tugging my sweats down over my hips and kicking them off. "I think you need to give me a closer look…"

* * *

Remembering that video-sex session carried me through the next few days of bickering with the ops team about Elaheh—good—but it also made me ache for the real thing—not so good. Soon. I would be able to see her, touch her, taste her, soon… If you measured "soon" in decades, not days.

Sophia had a meeting with a client that would overlap with our regular call time, and rather than skip our call attempt for the day, we'd moved it forward. I'd told Jeff dinner would be late, then locked myself in my bedroom for some quality time with my girlfriend. Slouching on her couch, coffee mug in hand, plate of peanut butter toast on her knee, it looked like she was enjoying a normal morning.

"Morning, sweetheart," I said. "I didn't know we were having a breakfast meeting or I would have made myself tea and an omelet or something."

Her nose wrinkled, both at my teasing and with annoyance. "Sorry, I've got this client call in half an hour and I need to eat beforehand because I just know he's going to blather on and on and I don't want to be hangry at him." She bit off a huge mouthful of toast, licking the corners of her mouth before she started chewing.

I decided to jump right in with a question that'd been hovering at the edge of my consciousness. "I meant to ask you the other night, but you distracted me with nudity—that guy who was following you. Did that stop?"

She paused, but her expression never wavered. "Mhmm."

The pause made me pause. As did her expression. And her short, noncommittal and not-an-actual-yes-or-no answer. "It did?"

This time there was no pause. "Yes."

I decided to take her at her word, because she'd never kept something this important from me before. That I knew about, at least. "Good. But if it starts up again, tell me right away and I'll kick some asses."

She smiled as she assured me, "I will."

"So what else is new, aside from blathering clients?"

"Pickleball is canceled tomorrow. Well, not canceled but Alana broke her ankle in a mountain biking accident and I can't get anyone to fill in."

"Oh shit, she going to be okay?"

She swallowed her mouthful of coffee, nodding. "Yeah, apparently it'll heal up fine. I think she's secretly pleased to have everyone doting on her."

"Phew. Does that affect your New Year's plans at all?" Sophia and friends had a bar crawl planned. Jeff and I hadn't even talked about celebrating the event, which was in two days. I'd probably be asleep by ten p.m. as usual.

"Nah," Sophia said nonchalantly. "We've hired her a wheelchair. When we're too drunk to push her, it'll be time to settle down for the rest of the night in whatever bar we're in."

The image of Sophia and her group drunkenly pushing their friend around on New Year's—and the associated shenanigans—made me laugh. "Solid plan. I'm expecting many drunk New Year's calls."

"I'll try to limit them to two per hour." She bit back a grin. "Oh! And the funniest thing happened while I was trying to organize the chair for her. I was almost going to text you about it right then and there, even though you would have been asleep."

Her mirth was contagious and I smiled with her. "Yeah? What hap—" A dull orange flash of light in the corner of my eye caught my attention a second before a deep shock wave of sound and vibration rattled my bedroom window.

"What the—" I said at the same time as Sophia blurted, "What the fuck was that?"

"I'm not sure," I said, though I was very sure what it was, just not the specifics of what had exploded. I picked up the laptop and moved toward the window to peer out into the city, hoping to catch a glimpse of what had happened and where. The window was intact and the building wasn't shaking or rumbling or cracking. All good signs.

Not good signs were the smoky, fiery cloud marking the location of the explosion, the muted, muffled car and building alarms going off, and people screaming. God I hoped Sophia couldn't hear that through the earbuds mic. This was exactly what I didn't want her to be thinking about while I was away, and I'd been lucky that none of the semi-frequent attacks in the city had happened when we'd been video or voice calling. My luck had to run out some time, I supposed.

"Was that an explosion?" Sophia choked out.

Before I could answer, there was a sharp tap on my bedroom door. "Alexandra? Are you all right?"

"Sorry, babe. Just a sec." I turned to the door to answer Jeff's question. "Yep. You?"

"I am. I think we'll need to get involved with this." Of course. "This" was our job.

"Okay. Be right out." I turned back to the laptop screen and smiled as reassuringly as I could. "Sorry, sweetheart, but it looks like I need to go see what's going on. It...might be a work thing."

Sophia looked like she wanted to cry or hurl, or both. "A work thing?" Her voice cracked up on the last word.

I nodded.

"Was that an explosion?" she asked again, her voice a little steadier now.

"Yes," I said calmly. "But not close enough to us to worry. We're fine." I grinned. "See? Intact and not worried at all. I'll text soon, I promise. I'm safe here at home, I swear."

As if sensing I couldn't tell her anything further, she nodded, but it was a reluctant, unhappy nod. "Okay," she said on a shaky exhale. "Keep it that way."

"I will. I love you." The wail of sirens accompanied my sign off.

Jeff was scrolling frantically on his phone when I emerged and walked straight to the balcony. I opened the door just enough to squeeze my torso through so I could look out and get a better idea of the situation. The smell of explosives and dust filled my nostrils, making me want to sneeze and choke all at once. The sound of citizens panicking made my breath catch and my heart race, and I almost fell in my haste to get back into the apartment and lock that terror outside.

Jeff's steady voice calmed me a little. "The ops team just messaged. They're not sure of specifics but it was in the street behind the big bank."

"Dammit. Is there a casualty or damage report?"

"Well, no, it's only just happened. But it's dinner time, and there's a lot of restaurants on that street so I expect there to be quite a few."

"Right, of course." *A lot of restaurants on that street...* "Jeff."

"Yeah?" he said without looking up from his furious texting.

"Isn't that street where Aber is?"

His fingers stilled, his face falling as he apparently put together the same pieces that I just had. "Oh no. Fuck."

"Yeah. Fuck." I felt sick as I realized exactly what Elaheh might have meant. It felt like too great a coincidence that Aber was in the area that'd just been attacked. "I think Elaheh was warning me to stay away. I need to talk to her." If she was warning me, then she obviously didn't want me dead. That was as good a starting place as any to begin recruiting someone.

"Do you really think that's a good idea? What if she was involved?"

"All the more reason to talk to her then, don't you think?" A worse, and sickening, thought flooded my consciousness. What if she was the perpetrator? What if I *couldn't* talk to her, not because it wasn't a good idea, but because she was dead? I began to gather my phone and purse, suddenly panicked about the explosion in a way no other attack in the city had affected me.

"Just wait a moment. Wait, please." Jeff blew out a loud breath. "You can't just go charging through the city now, especially not after an attack, and turn up on her doorstep. You'd be lucky if you even made it with all the mess out there at the moment. It's not safe for you to be getting in the way of rescue and investigation right now."

His calm rationality made me pause. "Okay, that's a fair point. I'll call her instead. I have her cell number now after she texted me about the salon appointment."

"I think we need to talk with the ops team, Alexandra, and get information first."

Given Elaheh's weird comment and my report, I'd expected the team to confirm at our weekly briefing tomorrow that they'd pay closer attention to Aber. These attacks, while not on American soil or against Americans specifically, were still troublesome. Because they could be test runs, and could easily escalate to attacks in the States, or injure or kill Americans on the terrorists' home soil. "Maybe I *had been* given information already, but I just didn't know what to do with it because I didn't know it was information. It wasn't clear that that was what she was saying. Fuck, *why* didn't I dig a little deeper? I should have been suspicious of everything she said, I should have been looking for links, for clues." Was I so out of practice at being in the field that I'd missed the obvious? "I need to go see her and talk to her about it. If not now, then first thing tomorrow."

"Just stop and take a breath. Please. If you contact her right after this has happened—assuming this is what it looks like and she's involved—then it will be beyond suspicious. Imagine if you turn up at her apartment wanting to talk about this so soon after the event, just randomly, as a tourist. The ops team will have their feelers out and we'll get information coming in soon. Wait for your nail-and-hair get-together on Monday and if there's an opening, bring it up. And in the meantime, we'll all be digging. I'm sure we'll know who pressed the button soon enough."

I tossed my things back onto the desk and walked over to collapse onto the couch. The shaky nausea I'd been trying to suppress rose up again and I had to close my eyes and concentrate on my breathing to settle it again. "Okay," I agreed quietly. "I'll wait until Monday." Then I could go in armed with information.

Oh, hi, Elaheh, yeah I think I'll go with *She's on Fire* on my nails today, probably just a little trim and tidy for my hair, and by the way, that whole cockroach thing—were you actually trying to warn me to stay away from the restaurant because there was an attack planned by the local terrorist cell that your husband, oh wait, sorry, your husband *and* you too, are involved with? Yes you were?

Cool…

CHAPTER NINETEEN

Rocks and hard places; it's all uncomfortable

Jeff waited until I'd filled my tea infuser and dropped it into Sophia's Sasquatch mug before he spoke. "Have you looked at this morning's news? They've set a date for Berenson's trial."

I brightened instantly. "Oh good! I can't wait to see how he tries to squirm out of this," I said cheerfully. "Do you think he's going to jail?"

"He *should* go to jail." Jeff raised his eyebrows. "You did excellent work with that intelligence. I'm not sure many people would have seen the connection so quickly."

Continuing the conversation about what I'd done would take us down the road of lying about Halcyon, and Jeff would be hard to mislead. So I deflected. "What do you think about the events surrounding the Kunduz Intelligence?"

He shook his head and confirmed he wouldn't answer by drinking a huge gulp of his coffee.

"Really? Nothing? Do you really have no opinion about what happened with Berenson?"

"I'm not allowed to have an opinion. Publicly," he added with a grin.

"But you *do* have one," I said matter-of-factly.

"Yes, of course I have opinions. About everything. Berenson, you, them, this assignment. Just because I don't express my opinions out loud, doesn't mean I don't have them, Alexandra."

"I'd really rather you called me Lexie."

"I'd really rather you didn't call me Jeff."

"Okay, deal. No more name antagonism." I leaned over and offered my hand.

He shook it. "Look at us, so mature."

"Right?" I pulled the infuser out and dropped it in the sink. "Well, *I* have opinions about him and about this and…about everything really."

"I know you do."

I took that as a "please share your opinions" invitation. "I'm sure you're aware that I don't have family. And before Sophia, I'd never had an actual relationship, just casual stuff. I don't have close friends. Maybe a few acquaintances that I see every few months when they reach out to meet up for coffee or something. Other than that, it's just work and my few hobbies."

"I did know this. And I don't know how you stand it." Smiling, he raised his coffee. "You probably can't believe it, but I'm quite the social butterfly."

"No, I can't. But I'll take your word for it." I inhaled the scent of my tea, then drank an indulgent gulp. "So here I am, trying to be in a relationship with someone, trying to be not alone, and they're using that against me."

"How do you think they're using Ms. Flores against you?"

"I thought it was obvious, even for someone of your limited intellect."

"Point to Lexie," Jeffrey drawled. "Indulge me."

"They already know the lengths I'll go to in order to protect her and her family. So I've outed myself with that. Sending people to watch her? It's just reminding me that they can and I'd better behave myself." I sucked in a deep breath and commenced my annoyed rambling. "Like, what is *this*? A pilot program to do something that doesn't need to be done? Really? It's my punishment and nothing more. It's taking me away from the personal security I wanted to build and making me *in*secure. It's telling me that no matter what I do, they can pull the safety net out from underneath me. This is not my job. They could have anyone do this. This is pointless and a waste of my time and talent."

Oh, and let's not forget Elaheh. I found it hard to believe that nobody had made a connection, and that it was just a coincidence that I'd ended up in the same city as her.

"I'm here too," he said dryly.

"I know. Sorry. It's just…if I'm here, then I want to go out and do what I'm good at in places like this. I mean, I'm very good at being an analyst, but I'm wasted here. We live in an age of instant communication. Round-the-clock intelligence services. Us, here, is dumb. We could do this job back home. I mean, if they wanted *me* specifically then set up another little office at the agency and call it whatever you want and tell me this is my job now. But don't send me, and you, off on pointless assignments just to punish me."

"Why do you think you're being punished?"

"I don't think, I know. It's because of what I did with the Kunduz Intelligence. I'm sure you can connect the dots, and it has nothing to do with me hiding, and everything to do with President Fletcher and ex-VP Berenson."

Jeffrey leaned back against the table, settling his hands in his lap. "Punishment is usually loss of employment and privileges and then incarceration. Not a reassignment."

"That's one form of punishment," I agreed. "And this is another." Huffing out a breath, I said, "Look, I don't expect you to get it, but trust me—this assignment is my punishment. And I'm actually kind of sorry you got dragged along with it."

"If it eases your conscience at all, I'm not sorry. I'm exactly where I'm supposed to be." He pushed off the table and patted my shoulder. "Let's go over the plan for your girls' day out."

After Thursday's explosion, Jeffrey had offered me a thin ballistic vest to wear underneath my ankle-length, long-sleeved dress, but after a lot of internal back-and-forth, I'd decided against it. If I was going to be spending hours with Elaheh—getting our nails and hair done, and then sharing a meal—I didn't want to be uncomfortable, or seem like something was off, and have her getting suspicious. I had no idea what she might think, or if she might be looking for something under the surface, but I had to assume. Assumptions might save my life.

After texting that I was there, I waited on the street outside Elaheh's apartment building, and tried to look relaxed as I surveyed the shopfronts opposite. The city seemed surprisingly unaffected by the terrorist event, probably because it was such a regular occurrence that they'd learned to pick up and move on. As usual, Jeffrey waited in a café nearby, and I made a note not to take Elaheh there for lunch.

After five minutes of standing around trying to act casual, I spotted Elaheh walking through the lobby of her building, chin up, shoulders back. She looked like a confident woman going about her business, not a woman afraid of her past. As soon as she saw me, Elaheh waved and walked quickly to me. "Good morning, Ellen."

"Morning. Are you ready for pampering?"

"I am, yes."

I feigned confusion. "Is Basir Junior with your parents-in-law today too?"

"Yes he is. I'm enjoying my time alone so much I think I will have to pretend to have some more appointments." Mirth danced in her eyes, and my breath caught as the woman I'd known six years ago peeked through this cool façade. She touched my arm. "This way."

Our path took us toward the city center. I waited for a few minutes before I lightly probed again. "Did your in-laws move to the city at the same time as you? Or did they already live here?" It was a pointless, leading question. Based on what I'd read of the family dynamics, I knew the answer, but I was trying to get her to elaborate on their background without asking outright.

"They moved here with us."

"Where is Basir's family originally from?"

She glanced at me. "The south-eastern provinces."

My heart thudded. The name Mohammadzai. The region her husband and in-laws had originated from. The irrefutable evidence of her husband's involvement which may have led to Elaheh's involvement. When you put it all together, it kind of looked like they were part of a big ol' terrorist family. What the fuck was I getting myself into by continuing to push this? I kept my face neutral and my voice pleasant. "A beautiful region."

"Yes it is." She gestured across the street. "We are here."

I smoothed my headscarf over my shoulders. "Wonderful. Let's go get beautified."

Despite the looming confrontation with Elaheh, I felt better after some therapeutic self-care at the salon. Plus, my hair and nails really did look fucking fantastic, so if she murdered me for pushing too hard or making her suspicious then at least I'd leave a gorgeous corpse. Always look on the bright side. We walked side by side, moving deeper into the city, and I let her guide me as she expertly threaded her way through the crowds going about their business, until she paused outside of a medium-sized café set back from the main road down a wide alleyway.

I noted right away that while this was a sex-segregated restaurant, it was filled with tables and chairs rather than the more common dining arrangement of being comfortably seated on the floor. The women's section of the eatery was completely empty and I threw up a thanks to the gods of privacy for giving me a chance to ask her questions without anyone overhearing. Once we'd been seated with tea and had ordered meals, I glanced around again. Still just us. I held out my hand. "Show me your nails."

Elaheh extended her hand, but didn't place it in mine, and it hovered awkwardly in the air between us. I leaned closer. "This is a beautiful color."

"Thank you. As is yours."

I took a moment to study my nails—it was an excellent manicure— before I looked around again, pretending to suppress a shudder. "I'm so glad you were with me today. Honestly? I felt a little afraid to come out into the city and I probably would have canceled if it'd just been me going to the appointment."

"What do you mean?" she asked, and though her tone showed her interest, there was also an underlying wariness in her voice.

"The attack at Aber on Thursday. So scary. I mean, it's always scary when that happens, but this one was so close."

"Yes, it is," she said neutrally.

Is scary? Is close? Is...something else? No "That's terrible" or "I hope nobody was badly injured" or "I'm praying for those who were wounded"? Nothing. It hit me then, like a sucker punch in the gut. I really didn't know her at all anymore. She was a stranger to me. A dangerous stranger. Deep down I'd known that, but it'd finally risen to the surface to float like a disgusting lump of flotsam.

"You don't seem bothered," I said, in as calm and nonaccusatory tone as I could muster.

Elaheh paused as the server came back into our dining room and set platters of food on the table before us. She waited until we were alone again. "No, perhaps I'm not," she mused. Finally she looked up to meet my eyes, and I was surprised by their complete lack of expression. "This has been my life for many years, Ellen. I suppose I am used to this in one way or another."

My life for many years... I didn't know if she meant her life because she was involved in these terrorist activities, or her life because she lived in a place where attacks were common. I forced a small smile. "I suppose you must be. And that makes me really sad for you."

Elaheh didn't verbally acknowledge what I'd said, yet her expression made me think she was desperate to talk more, but for whatever reason—she was silent on the matter. Instead, she turned her attention to the masses of food. Without me saying anything, she'd kept everything vegetarian. She served me as if I were a guest in her house instead of us being out together in a public eatery, scooping food onto my plate and topping up my tea. We ate quietly, her seeming to deliberately avoid looking at me, and I waited until we'd finished a decent portion of the meal before launching my attack.

"Elaheh."

She looked up, and for a moment I caught the panic in her eyes as she swallowed her mouthful of bread and curry. "Yes?"

"Something's been bothering me. When I saw you last week, you cautioned me against going to Aber. Then there was an attack there on Thursday. The restaurant was destroyed, as were the shops around it. People died. You knew something was going to happen, didn't you." I deliberately phrased it as a statement rather than a question. "How did you know?"

She didn't hesitate. "I didn't."

I rushed on, hoping she didn't think me questioning her was odd. "This just seems weird, that's all. And an attack so close to my apartment? That's scary. I'm worried about you. I feel like you're not telling me something."

"That sentiment goes both ways," she said quietly as she refilled our tea.

"You think I'm not telling you something?"

"I think…you have always had secrets, have always withheld part of yourself when it comes to me."

An astute observation, and a correct one. "I'm sorry. Maybe you're right. It's a habit to be a closed book, even with people I…know well." That's a good euphemism for someone you used to sleep with, right?

"I know it is your habit. And I understand, especially now after so many years apart, that you might feel you can't trust me anymore."

"No, it's not—"

Her raised hand stopped me dead. "Please. Let's not go down this path. I'm sorry I brought it up. I don't know what I was thinking." Under her breath, she muttered something I didn't quite make out, but it sounded like a quick prayer.

"Elaheh," I said quietly. "Please, look at me." Her reluctant eyes found mine, and held. I wanted to look away, but made myself keep eye contact. "Is something going on? Are you in trouble? I might be able to help you."

"No, you could not help me." No denial that there was something going on. My heart hammered at my ribs. She inhaled deeply, and almost as an afterthought said, "Thank you. But I do not need your help."

"Are you sure?"

"Yes," she said firmly, but without annoyance.

"Okay," I murmured. "But if you find that you do, at any time, you have my number."

"Yes, I do." She picked up her tea, then set it down again. "I have been helping myself."

"How so?" I asked.

She looked just off to my left, staring into space. "Since moving to this city, I realized that the life I was living before was not a good life. And I have worked very hard to correct my mistakes."

My heartbeat sped up. "What do you mean?" I asked as casually as I could, desperate not to give away my excitement. Her allusion to "not living a good life" felt like she was on the cusp of sharing why she might have changed so radically.

But as if realizing what she might share, Elaheh pressed her lips together. After an awkward pause, she asked, "Are you happy in your relationship, Ellen?"

"Yes," I said instantly, and honestly. "I've never been happier in a relationship." She didn't need to know that the relationship she thought I was referring to wasn't the one I meant. Sophia was everything I wanted and needed, and had never known I wanted or needed. Sophia... I let the thought of her in to soothe me, then put her in a safe mental place so I could focus on this conversation.

I didn't want to ask Elaheh that same question, because I realized that I feared her answer: that she was happy, that she enjoyed this new life and all that it entailed. So I kept quiet.

Her expression softened fractionally. "Then I am happy for you. But you must remember that you and I, we are not who we were. And we will never be those people again."

That sentiment lingered, floating back into my consciousness every time I managed to push it out again. Of course we weren't the same people we used to be—one of us was definitely not the same person they used to be—but for some reason, Elaheh pointing that out to me had gotten under my skin. I knew I'd changed, but I liked to think that it was for the better, especially because of Sophia's influence.

And because of that stupid thought, I spent the rest of the day twitchy and upset, even after Jeffrey's genuine compliments about my hair and nails when I got home. We went through our usual recorded debrief about the session—sorry to report no big breaks, I did not crack this cell wide open while I got beautified—then he left me alone to write up a report.

The whole time I worked on the report, all I wanted was to speak with Sophia. Speaking with Sophia recentered me, focused me, reminded me that I was something apart from the work I was doing. I needed the calming reminder that what I had with her was real, and right, and that being with her, even if only in cyberspace, made me feel safe and safe was what I needed.

The parallel or whatever you want to call it was not lost on me: every time I spent time with my ex...whatever-she-was person, the desire to cancel out that interaction, to cleanse my brain of all the background thoughts that swirled when I was with her, became overwhelming. I needed to convince myself that Elaheh was the old and Sophia was the new and they could not be further apart.

Sophia knew about Elaheh in an abstract way—that I'd been seeing a woman the last time I'd worked overseas, and that I'd broken up with her not long before the hostage incident. And that was it. Of course I couldn't tell Sophia about seeing her again because Elaheh wasn't *just* my ex-sex person—she was now a person of interest in intelligence gathering. And a terrorist. Sophia could never know any of what I was trying to juggle, so what was the point of mentioning that Elaheh had suddenly reappeared in my life? I didn't feel like I was cheating or anything like that, but I obviously wasn't telling Sophia that I'd met my ex-sex person a couple of times, and would surely meet up with her again. And those omissions made me feel as sick as if I were actually being unfaithful.

Rocks and hard places. That's me. I added the Elaheh Situation to the list of necessary lies or exclusions of truth that I had to employ with my girlfriend. Necessary didn't mean I liked it. In fact, I fucking hated it.

I video-called Sophia on the dot of eight p.m., unable to wait a minute longer—I'd barely made it to our regular call time as it was. The instant I saw her, I was soothed, like every ounce of tension had flowed out of my body and washed away. "Babe, hiiii," I breathed. "How are you?"

Her lips quirked into a crooked smile. "Not as excited as you, it seems."

"I really missed you today, more than usual, so yeah, I'm excited to see you. How's your morning been so far?"

She wrinkled her nose. "Unproductive. I'm fighting a massive dose of apathy. What have you been up to?" Another smile tried to make its way onto her lips, but seemed to falter halfway. "Saving the world?"

Something seemed off, but I couldn't quite pinpoint what, so I pushed aside my unease and answered her question. "Almost. I've been up to self-care, which helps me save the world. I went to the salon." I held up my fresh manicure. "You like the color?" I'd gone with *Vixen*, a gorgeous brown-plum shade, instead of my usual firmly-on-the-red-spectrum polish.

Sophia nodded enthusiastically. "I do. It suits you."

"What about my haircut?" I pulled the band from my hair to let my ponytailed hair fall free. Fluffing it out, I conceded, "I think you did a better hairdressing job that night in that hotel bath, but this one is still pretty good."

"It is." She smiled softly. "It's gorgeous, and so are you."

I hadn't been fishing for compliments, but you bet I was going to take that one. "Thank you." I crossed my legs and resettled the laptop on my inner thighs. "But, I'm sensing you're not as excited about my trip to the salon as I am."

"No, it's…I…you look incredible, hon. You always do."

"Okay," I said carefully. "Then what's wrong, sweetheart? You look like your fish died. Shit. Did your fish die?"

"No, my fish are great." Then, in typical Sophia fashion, once I'd offered her an opening, she ran straight through it. Her willingness and need to discuss her feelings both impressed and frightened me. Being honest and open was great, and obviously good for healthy relationships, but it highlighted my shortcomings and forced me to confront them, which wasn't so great for my self-confidence. My constant mental gymnastics to figure out what I needed to withhold from her were not fun.

She exhaled loudly. "I'm upset about what happened the other day. I know I shouldn't have, but I've spent way too much time Googling terrorist attacks all around the world that happened on Thursday. And the main thing I realized was this happens constantly in those areas where you might be." Her expression said what she hadn't verbalized: "If I actually knew where that is."

I licked my lips. "Yes it does."

She swallowed visibly, her mouth working open and closed before she asked, "Has it been happening where you are since you left?"

I paused for just a second before answering truthfully, "Yes."

Her entire face seemed to collapse in on itself. "And you didn't tell me because…?"

"Because of the look on your face right now," I said, gently. "Because it seemed pointless. Like…what would I even say? Oh yeah, at least once a week terrorists are attacking some place or some people nearby enough that I can hear it. But don't worry because it's not close enough to me to be a problem." Yet.

"I—" She frowned. "I just…" Sophia's cheeks puffed as she tried to work through her feelings. "I wish you hadn't kept this from me."

"I'm sorry." And I was. "I can see you're upset. It's just, I'm trying to…You made me promise to come home to you, and I have every intention of keeping that promise. But if you knew the reality of the situation here then you might worry that I'm not going to come home. And I need you to believe that I am coming home to you. Because I am."

"I know you are. That thought is what keeps me going." Sophia inhaled shakily. "It's all the other stuff that keeps getting in the way, the stuff I wish you would tell me. The stuff I wish you *could* tell me."

"I know, babe. I don't want this to be an issue, but at the same time, you know I can't share some things. And these, um…incidents are part of work and part of the way I think about my job, and you know where that lies on the 'Not Telling People Scale.'" I tried to sound teasing, but it felt hollow.

"Your job," Sophia said flatly. "Sometimes I really hate your job, even though I know how important it is."

"I know," I said quietly.

"You know that you not telling me about this won't make a bit of difference. I'm already worrying about you, Lexie. Knowing bad people are doing bad shit near you isn't going to change that worry." She inhaled deeply and a weak smile appeared at the corners of her mouth. "Remember that conversation we had early on? Before everything got all weird."

"Oh yeahhhh, I remember *that* conversation."

Sophia rolled her eyes. "You ass. The conversation about give-and-take. About the things we can compromise on and the ones we can't. About meeting each other either in the middle or sometimes more on the other's side, as long as it's not always one person coming across the line…" The way she trailed off made it clear she thought she was the only one going across the line of compromising. She wasn't exactly wrong.

"I remember." She'd been gentle, assuring me she understood that I had to be secretive with some parts of my life, but that she needed me to include her in everything else that I could. And I'd agreed, because it was an easy compromise, even as I'd known that so much of my life was secret and that she would likely be compromising more than me.

"This is me telling you what I need. More openness. And for you to come a little more on my side to tell me about things like this, and then you can stay on your side for the *specifics* of these things."

I huffed out a breath. "You're right, I'm wrong. And I'm sorry. I didn't think, it's as simple as that. I could have absolutely told you that we've had some…um, terrorism events here without giving away things I can't give away. Me not telling you had nothing to do with work, sweetheart. This was all me thinking I knew what you needed, thinking you shouldn't have to think about that stuff on top of everything else."

"And I appreciate that. But we've been through some heavy stuff together already. I'm a grown-up, I can handle knowing that things are dangerous around you. I want to know that. I want to support you while you're dealing with that." She laughed dryly. "Trust me, I don't think anything I've seen on the Internet during my downward spiral of panic is worse than my imagination."

"I know. And thank you. And I'm sorry."

"I'm sorry too. In amongst my own feelings, I forgot to check in with you." Sophia bit her lower lip. "You've got a bunch of bad shit going on around you. How's that feel? Do you need to unpack anything, love?" She was asking, without asking, if having semiregular terrorist attacks near me was dredging up anxiety relating to me being held hostage by terrorists.

I smiled at the endearment. *Love.* "I'm okay. I've got my coping toolbox. Yeah, sometimes it's…bad, and it's scary, but"—I shrugged— "it's kind of a different kind of bad and scary than 2017. And now, I have you. And honestly, nothing else matters."

CHAPTER TWENTY

Your Honor, I object

I took Sophia's feelings on board, and in the weeks that followed her request, I told her everything that was happening in my life, not just the non-scary events. I was thinking I should think about making dinner when my local cell phone rang. I saw Elaheh's name on the screen and froze. She'd never called before, and though we'd met up a handful of times, she'd only texted me twice to confirm the details. I tabbed over from the report I was reading to a fresh document for call notes. Wait a moment, don't be too quick to answer. Cheerful, but not too cheerful, aaannnd, "Hello?"

"Ellen, hello. It's Elaheh. I'm sorry to phone you instead of texting, but I haven't spoken to any adults at all today and honestly, I needed some spoken conversation." She said it laughingly, but there was an undercurrent of discomfort in the statement. Interesting.

"No apologies necessary," I said warmly. "It's always nice to hear from you. What can I do for you?"

"I'm very sorry for the late notice, but I will need to cancel our shopping outing tomorrow afternoon. Something has come up that I must attend to." She sounded genuinely apologetic.

"That's fine. No problem. Can we reschedule, or…?" I left it open, up to her to continue the contact, because I feared if I kept nagging her to spend time with me, she'd get uncomfortable and break off all contact completely.

Jeffrey's head popped over the divider, and he mouthed, "What are you doing?"

"How is Wednesday?" Elaheh asked as I wrote MY JOB? on a piece of paper and held it up to him. Duh.

"Wednesday is great. I'm flexible. Mostly, I'm just waiting around, interspersed with meetings and submitting paperwork and requests." Can't forget about the cover story.

"Wonderful. So, that's the same time, just on Wednesday?"

"Sounds great. I'll see you then."

We said our goodbyes and after I'd dropped my phone on my desk, Jeffrey came around to my side of the partition. "Organizing social events?" he asked dryly.

"Elaheh just called to tell me something's come up and she needed to reschedule our next social shopping and tea-drinking event."

"Something has come up," he repeated. "Something nefarious or something innocuous?"

"Unfortunately, that wasn't part of her explanation." I typed out some notes. "I've seen nothing that tells me they're mobilizing, so I don't fucking know. Maybe she's involved in a cell attack this weekend. Maybe she has to visit her family. Maybe her husband is taking her away for a nice, non-terrorist activity."

"Maybe. Let's tell the ops team, they might shake their talent a little and see what falls out of their pockets. See if they can spare one of their team for surveillance." Given how thinly the team was stretched, it would be part-time surveillance.

"She said something else, something weird. She hasn't spoken to any adults today, presumably meaning she's only spoken to her son. But she's married. Why hasn't she spoken to Mohammadzai? I haven't seen anything about him being out of the city. Are they fighting? Is he away, meeting someone?"

He held up both hands, obviously as in the dark as me but not willing to speculate, unlike me. "No clue."

I mmphed. "I'll send a report to the ops team. Maybe with our powers combined—"

"We can be the greatest intelligence superhero of all time?"

"I was going to say 'Avert another terrorist attack by a cell who are exceptionally good at covering up their planning tracks,' but sure, let's be an Intelligence Captain Planet or something."

"You're my hero," Jeffrey sang, off-key, to the tune of the *Captain Planet* theme song.

I tapped Sophia's Super Lexie drawing. "And don't you forget it."

Report written and disseminated. Dinner made and eaten. I'd just opened my laptop ready for my video call with Sophia when she texted *Sorry, something's come up and I won't make our call today.*

Everything okay? The last-second cancelation *was* odd but, given it was the middle of her workday, not worrying.

Yep.

Okey dokey. No worries, talk tomorrow. Love you.

No response. Something was coming up with everyone, it seemed. I put the laptop aside and rolled out my yoga mat for some presleep goodness.

As I was finishing my practice, I got the answer to what Sophia's *something* was when my Signal app alerted me to a call. Voice, not video call from Sophia. Something must have come down. I answered right away, flopping onto my bed. "Hey, babe," I said, unsurprised at how gooey I sounded. "This is a nice surprise. I didn't expect to talk to you tonight."

"Hi. I wasn't going to call, but then I realized that I shouldn't do this over email." Her flat voice got my attention a second before what she'd said registered.

My words came out haltingly. "Do…what over email?" The silence was so protracted that I prompted, "Sophia? You shouldn't do *what* over email?" There were only a few things I could think of that shouldn't be done over email. And I did not want any of them done to me.

Her shaky inhalation was audible, which didn't help my rising anxiety. She exhaled loudly. "Shit. I knew it wouldn't be easy, but I didn't think it would be so hard."

With a calmness I really didn't feel, I told her to, "Just say it. It's just me, Sophia, and you know you can say anything to me."

"Okay. Rip the Band-Aid off, right?" After a miniscule pause, she said something I never thought she'd say. "I think we should break up." After all that build-up, she actually sounded pretty relaxed about completely blindsiding me.

The goodness I'd just cultivated with my yoga practice left so quickly I would have been insulted if I wasn't so confused. Dinner churned in my stomach and I swallowed hard to try to calm the tumult rapidly spreading through my body. I… What? It isn't just me, right?

This really is batshit fucking crazy out of nowhere, isn't it? "You don't mean it," I blurted. "This is a joke."

Calmly, she said, "Yes, I do mean it. It's not a joke."

"I, but…I don't understand." I took a moment to push away the tremble in my voice. "Why? And why now, completely out of left field?"

Her voice remained impressively neutral and I wondered *how*. How was she so calm? "I'm sorry, Lexie. But this is how I feel. And we can talk in circles for hours, but it's not going to change how I feel or what I want."

"What about what *I* want?" Not that it mattered, really. I wasn't stupid enough to think I could make her stay with me. "Because a breakup is *not* what I want, not even in the realm of what I want. Is this because of the Internet cutting out during sex? Is it because I didn't tell you about the attacks? We've talked about that, I was trying to protect you." I tried very hard to not sound like I was a second away from crying.

"No, Lexie. It's not about any of those things. It's about *us*."

"What about us? I thought us was great, and this is the first I'm hearing that it hasn't been great." I waited for her to explain. Silence. "The only logical reason I can think of is that someone made you do this. Is there something going on with you or your family that you haven't told me about, sweetheart?" Sweetheart. It'd just slipped out, and seemed all wrong now.

"Nobody has made me do anything," she said evenly, but I heard the lies and pain in those six words.

They'd forced her, I was certain of it. If I set aside the actual breakup, which made less sense than a pickle and peanut butter sandwich, she said she was going to *email* me to break up? Who the fuck emails to break up with someone? A person who wanted to leave evidence of their actions for a shitty government intent on punishing one of their employees, that's who. Fine. That was fine. We could just pretend to be broken up. "I just…can…can you talk to me? Help me understand? I feel like this is a little drastic, to go from no issues that I can see, to broken up."

"I don't think talking about it is going to help. I've been talking to myself, here *by myself*, for nearly two months, Lexie, trying to talk myself through this, and this is what I want." Her exhalation was a sob and she faltered, then added, "So, we're done, it's over, we are no longer a couple, in a relationship." The formality stung coming from her, so completely out of character, as if she'd turned into someone I didn't know.

I knew exactly what she'd just said, what it meant. But I didn't want it. "I have to ask again, Sophia, because I just don't believe it. Are you really doing this or are you just pretending"—I lowered my voice to barely above a whisper—"for Them."

"It's real," she said steadily. "I want to break up with you," she added, as if I was unclear about anything she'd just said.

But I was very clear, so clear it felt like I was made of glass that might shatter at any moment. "Okay," I said because there was nothing else I could think of to say. A deep breath helped me find a few more words. Quiet, childlike words. "I still don't understand. Why? You've never said anything that was a major, breakup-worthy issue. Why not tell me you weren't happy? Why not let me try to fix what you're struggling with instead of just pulling the plug?"

"Because you can't fix it. This is your job. And it's *always* going to be like this. You're always going to hold things back from me."

She was right, and I felt myself slip a little further under. "But we've talked about that. You said you were okay with it, with the give-and-take, remember? Fuck, you reiterated that a few weeks ago."

"I did," she said. "But then I stopped and thought about it. Since you've been gone, I've been doing a lot of thinking about us, going around and around in circles, trying to figure out what I want and what I need and how that fits in with your wants and needs. And I've realized that we're not on the same page with this relationship. I think we moved too quickly after everything that happened around the events in Florida back in October. I love you, but I don't think this is leading to a place where I want to go or that it's going to end well for either of us, so I think we should do what's best for us, and that's a breakup."

Every time she said "breakup," I felt a little more of my composure cracking. How was I supposed to argue against this? I wasn't. She'd given me nothing, and I just had to accept it. "I wish you'd have said something to me instead of stewing on this. We could have worked through your problems with our relationship."

"I didn't think you'd listen." Ouch. That was cold.

When had I ever not listened to her? When had I ever not taken her feelings into consideration? I opened my mouth to snap at her, then closed it again. "I don't think that's a fair accusation," I said steadily, patting myself on the back for not giving in to the raging force of emotion swirling through me. The worst thing was knowing nothing I did or said was going to change this.

Instead of responding to me outright, she said, "I need to go. I, uh…if you could let me know when you get home? Even though we're not"—a hard swallow interrupted—"together. I'd appreciate it. Um, be safe." Her voice cracked up as she implored, "*Please.*"

The hurt, angry, cruel part of me wanted to ask her why she even cared now that she'd dumped me. Then I remembered *I love you, but…* Breaking up with someone you loved, over a few minor issues, seemed…well, it seemed completely wrong, and she'd sounded both certain and uncertain, like she thought it was the right thing but didn't want to actually do it. I held on to that tiny fragment of hope like it was the last bit of oxygen in the world, and decided that I'd lie down now, then get up and fight tomorrow. So, I agreed with a weary, "Sure."

Despite my conviction that there was more beneath the surface, something about the conversation felt…final. The fog of her accusations felt so heavy, I wondered if I'd ever see through it. I'd never felt like this after ending a relationship, and I was grateful for that because I honestly had no idea how I was going to stand up, and just go back to my life without her.

When she spoke again, her voice was steady—she'd found some steel. "Thank you. Okay. I need to go. Bye."

Then she was gone. Just like that. Leaving me with a casual "bye" and a hollowness that felt so vast that I thought I might involute and be sucked into a black hole of my own emotion. I calmly set the phone on my bedside table, slid under the covers, and pulled them up over my head.

Just a few weeks ago, when we'd talked about me not telling her about the horrible things that happened around me, she'd called me *love* as an endearment. Love. It'd stuck in my head, reminding me of the connection we had. How could we go from that to this? We couldn't. It wasn't logical. And I didn't know how to deal with things that weren't logical. So what the fuck was I supposed to do?

* * *

I woke to the call to morning prayers reverberating through the city, and tried to let myself be soothed by the recitations. Tried. Moderate success. Once the speakers were quiet again, I rolled out of bed and changed for a morning workout. I'd lain awake most of the night, thoughts circling like sharks, and the last thing I felt like doing was a yoga practice, meditation, calisthenics, or a treadmill session, even though I knew one, or some, or all, would make me feel better in mind and body.

I did feel better after calisthenics and yoga, and decided on a quick thirty minutes on the treadmill. But I needed my phone for that. My phone I'd been avoiding since about two a.m. after checking for texts, missed calls, and emails—and also checking my phone was working—every ten minutes, until I'd realized I was being obsessive and had put it in a drawer.

The email notification from Sophia felt like a slap. I almost didn't want to open it. But I had to know what else she had to say.

From: Sophia Flores
To: Lexie Martin
Subject: Our breakup

Lexie,
I'm sorry, I realize now that me breaking up with you last night must have felt abrupt and out of the blue for you. But for me, I've been thinking about this for a while, long before last night's call but I've been too much of a coward to do it before now. The situation between you and me, as a couple, isn't tenable any longer. I thought I could deal with you not being truthful, but I can't and I think we both know that's never going to change while you're doing the job you love and are so good at.

I meant what I said last night about breaking up with you. I'm sorry for not doing it earlier but I can't keep living like this, wondering what's going to happen and if you're going to have to do things that aren't good for us and then lie to me about it. I can't have people following me, contacting me because of something you've done or haven't done. That's not fair to me, and honestly? It's creepy.

I wish being in love was enough, but I don't think it is. If you care about me, please don't contact me about this anymore. Bombarding me isn't going to change anything. I wish you all the best, and please be safe over there and come home safely.
Please take care of yourself.
Sophia

The email confirmed my suspicions—this breakup wasn't her choice. She'd emailed me, even after deciding to not break up with me over email, because she knew that I suspected they were monitoring my personal as well as work emails, if not my other online communication like video calls. So now They knew that she and I were no longer together, she was free. Free of me. Free of Them and of having the constant worry about what they might do to her family, even though I'd given her my word that I could prevent that.

But maybe I couldn't prevent it.

The only positive in an entire ocean of negatives was that she was no longer something that would be held over my head as a threat to comply. A tiny, hopeful part of me thought she'd done this to protect me, and that was nice, but we were still broken up and that was not nice.

I read the email over and over, but I still didn't know for sure if it was real, if she really did have these issues with our relationship, or was just pretending for all the reasons that'd arisen because of the Kunduz Intelligence. If it was real, how had I not seen any of the issues she mentioned? If she was pretending, then she was a far better writer than I'd ever given her credit for. Her coolness and conviction emanated from every word.

It felt real. Fuck, please don't let it be real. My heart pounded so hard I felt like it was smothering me with every beat, and it took me almost thirty minutes to deep breathe my way out of what felt like the stirrings of an anxiety attack. I hadn't had one for years. When I finally emerged, later than usual and treadmill workout abandoned, Jeffrey didn't bother to hide his curiosity. "You okay?" he asked as he set his coffee mug in the sink and turned on the stove to boil the kettle for me.

"No," I said flatly as I spooned tea into my infuser. The infuser she'd bought me. Well, first thing I was doing today after breakfast was to shop for a new infuser and mug. "Sophia broke up with me last night."

"What?" he spluttered. "What the fuck? I—what? I don't understand."

I jammed my molars together, trying to stop my jaw from shaking. Deep breath. Let it out. "Honestly, neither do I."

Jeffrey leaned back against the kitchen counter. "Did she give any sort of reason as to why?"

"Yes. CliffsNotes version is that it's not working." I air-quoted those last three words. "And I have to say, I'm confident it was working. Before we left, everything was Hallmark-movie-level-love working. And I know things have been a little strained and weird at times since I left, but that's normal, right?"

He nodded. "In my experience, yes, things can get strained and weird when you're on an extended assignment."

"Yeah, but strained and weird isn't 'This isn't working, we're done.' So I just don't get it. Every time I've spoken to her this week, everything has been totally fine. Every time we've spoken before that? Fine. Not an inkling that she was unhappy at all, except with the low-level annoyances we've been dealing with. Which leads me to one logical conclusion. Someone made her do it to punish me, either by coercion or blackmail or something."

His expression softened to pity. "Lexie…that's a leap…"

"Is it?" I spat out. "The night before I left she told me how much she loved me and that I had to promise I was to come home safely to her. That she basically wanted to spend the rest of her life with me." I left off the part about how she'd implied she meant *fucking me*. "Every day, every conversation, every text—I love you, I need you, I miss you, I can't wait to see you in person again. How do you go from *that* to *this* in just a few months of no fighting, no animosity, just being apart, to 'we're done'?"

He shrugged. "I honestly don't know."

"Well I know. I know someone made her do this and the only reason would be to make my life even more miserable. Maybe the president threatened her and her dad again and she's trying to protect her family by breaking up with me. That makes sense, right?"

He made a sound that wasn't agreement or disagreement.

"Okay, so probably not the president personally, but someone on his behalf. That's the only thing that makes sense." I just could not believe, not after everything we'd shared, the love and connection we built every day, that she would break up with me. Not for the flimsy, bullshit reasons she'd given me. I slumped against the sink. "So this is what it came to, huh? Our tiny-dick president leveraging her to make sure I know he's the boss. Fuck him. I hope he falls into a fucking lava pit. I hope someone gets past the Secret Ser—"

Jeffrey's hand on my shoulder was gentle, but conveyed strength and support. "Lexie. Stop. Just stop."

I closed my mouth. He was right. Having those thoughts wasn't healthy. Verbalizing them where we might be monitored was dangerous. "Put yourself in my shoes, all of my shoes. What if out of the blue, Dominique told you she wanted to separate. Would you just accept it? Or would you look deeper? Especially if there's other factors at play, like the president personally threatening to upend your world."

Jeffrey's mouth thinned. "The president threatened you and Ms. Flores?"

"Yes. Not overtly, but there was a definite undertone of stay in line, or…"

He reached over to shut off the whistling kettle. Once I'd filled the mug—*the* mug, not Sophia's mug—and settled the infuser—*the* infuser, not Sophia's infuser—he crossed his arms over his chest. "I'm going to indulge you. Let's say you're right. Let's say that Ms. Flores hasn't suddenly realized that being with you isn't what she wants"— he held up both hands to ward off my death stare—"don't hate me, I'm just putting all the options out here, and someone, unspecified, has done something, unspecified, to force her to break up with you, against both your wishes. Why? What makes you so fucking special, excuse my French?"

"The Kunduz Intelligence," I said instantly. "I've already told you that I'm being punished for pursuing it, because pursuing it outed Berenson and outing Berenson embarrassed the president."

Jeffrey's face was the epitome of *ehhh, yeahhh, I guess?* "You know, it seems completely implausible, but…knowing the president, I think I could maybe believe it. Just. It still seems farfetched."

"Believe me, he's made it very clear what he thinks of me for doing my job and also what he thinks of me personally." I pulled the infuser out of the mug, and almost dropped it straight in the trash. Only the thought I might not find another one in time for my next tea craving stopped me. "So what do I do? He's using my job, and now my relationship to keep me in line."

"I've always found the best weapon against leverage, is leverage. It's what I'd use. It's what I considered using during our briefings until I was told Ms. Flores and her family really were off the table."

"You're such an honorable man," I deadpanned. "I don't have anything I can use as leverage. My arsenal is empty." I had nothing left in the tank at all, the president and his crew of cretins held all the power.

"No, it's not empty." Jeffrey's gaze was intense, measured.

"I don't understand."

"Think about it, and I'm sure it'll come to you. Are you going to let them drag you around by the things you love for the rest of your life, because of Kunduz? What if you and Ms. Flores reconcile? What if you meet another woman you want to spend the rest of your life with? What then? This same old merry-go-round?"

"We're not going to reconcile. She made that very clear." Everything he'd said made me feel sick. "I don't have a choice."

"You do," he quietly disagreed. "But maybe someone else will have to make it for you."

But when I pressed him as to what he meant, Jeffrey just shook his head and told me again to think about it, all of it, and that it would come to me. Why he wouldn't just tell me was beyond me, and also infuriating.

"I need to talk to Sophia again, I need to know what's really going on." She'd told me not to, but... I needed to know. I didn't know what cause of this breakup was worse—the real one or the fake one. "I don't even know if this is genuine or not, and I need to know."

"I would caution you against doing that. If she *has* been coerced into ending your relationship for whatever reason, then contacting her is going to draw attention to the fact you're clued into this and could make things worse for you, her, or both of you."

I hated that he was right. "So...what? I'm supposed to ride out the next four months like nothing happened?"

"What you do is up to you, Lexie. I'm just telling you what I think. But regardless, I'm here if you need me."

I will not cry. After swallowing hard, I managed a tight, "Thanks."

After picking at breakfast, I snuck back into my room to call Derek, even though it was sleep o'clock back in the States. But I needed to get this over and done with and him working on it as soon as possible.

"Wood," he answered groggily, the sound of sleep-clumsy feet on the floor echoing behind his answer.

"It's me. I'm sorry to wake you, please don't tell Roberta it was me. I don't want her giving me an earful about etiquette the next time I see her."

"She's still asleep and I'm hiding in the bathroom. Is everything okay?" he asked, the question laced with concern.

"I'm fine," I said quickly. "But I need a favor and I need it done off the books."

"If I can do it, I will."

"I know we told them to stop shadowing Sophia Flores." Saying her name didn't hurt as much as I'd thought it would. "Can you check and make sure they didn't sneakily start following her again after you told them not to. If you find any evidence of them making contact, in any way, even better."

"I'll look into it."

"Thank you."

There was an uncomfortably long pause. "Is there something you need to tell me, Martin?"

"I just need to know."

"Okay. And what would you like me to do once you know?"

"Nothing." There was nothing anyone could do. I thanked him again, and hung up.

My favorite part of the numbness was a call on the blue phone at lunchtime the day after The Breakup, right when I was wondering if asking to go home was an option. If I went home, then I'd be there with her, I could talk with her, and all her issues with my job and being here and all my issues I had with thinking she'd been blackmailed or coerced or whatever would be gone.

I'd only had sporadic contact from Lennon, mostly just him checking in, presumably making sure I was still alive and able to be "important" when I got home. But the timing of him calling less than a day after Sophia's bombshell was beyond suspicious. It also confirmed they were monitoring my emails. I answered with a short, "Yes?"

"Hello, Alexandra."

"Hello."

"How are you?" he asked after a long puff on his cigar.

"Fabulous."

"Are you sure?" He sounded almost singsong, and with that tone I knew right away that he knew.

"How did you find out?" I asked flatly.

"I find out everything, remember?"

"Right." How could I forget?

"Do you need anything?" The question was surprisingly gentle.

"Aside from my girlfriend back? No, I'm fine."

"Can I offer any mental health support?"

"Since when does Halcyon offer any sort of health service?" When I'd been injured during the Great Escape, it'd been radio silence from them. I'd had to take myself to an ER. And when I'd been stabbed et cetera in 2017, there was nothing aside from a perfunctory verbal check-in during my treatment.

"This is me offering, personally. I care about your well-being."

"Thank you, but my well-being is fine and I have a therapist I can call if I need to." A therapist I probably should call. But the prospect of therapy seemed utterly pointless. What was I going to say?

My girlfriend broke up with me.

That's terrible, you must be devastated.

I am.

Did she say why?

Yes, but I don't believe her and I think it's related to a thing I got tied up in a few months ago that made the VP resign and get arrested and oh, hey, I work for a secret government division so that's why I'm not in jail for that little extravaganza.

Let me just call the psych ward, Lexie…

Lennon hmmed. "If you're sure. I need you to take care of yourself, mind, body, and spirit, Alexandra. Don't forget, Halcyon will need you when you return to the States."

"How could I forget?" Whatever special thing he had lined up for me next had better be something fucking amazing to make up for what these jobs had cost me.

"Take care of yourself, I'll be in touch as needed."

We hung up, leaving me both confused and annoyed.

It took a few days for Derek to contact me to tell me that he could find no evidence of anyone having been in contact with Sophia from the White House, the agency, or Halcyon. He added that last one carefully.

I thanked him, then after a quick mental debate, said, "Quick question. Has Lennon ever offered you anything outside of the Division? Like health services."

"No. Why?"

"He offered to get me someone to talk to. On his own dime, it seemed."

"Must be nice being special and important," Derek teased.

"Believe me, it feels great," I deadpanned. "My life is wonderful right now. All because I'm so important."

* * *

After a week of my eternal downer, Jeffrey found me moping at the table and offered a friendly shoulder pat before he sat down. "Lexie," he said gently. "What can I do to ameliorate this situation?"

"You can't do anything," I said, not turning away from my phone screen. Hedgehogs attacking toys was great, so uplifting, super cute, big dose of serotonin. "There is no situation."

His response was a quiet, "Heartbreak doesn't last forever."

"I'm not heartbroken," I said flatly.

"Surrre you're not. So the crying and moping and every other cliché that you're displaying is just…what? For fun?"

"Pretty much. Thought I might be an actor if the intelligence analyst gig doesn't work out, so I'm working on my emotional range."

"Okay then. Based on what I've seen, you've got an Oscar incoming." His bantering face sobered. "I just wanted to check in and see how you were, make sure you're doing okay, or as okay as you can be given the circumstances."

"I appreciate your concern," I said flatly. I had to be flat or I was going to start bawling again. "I already went through the process of resigning myself to never seeing her again when I was considering turning myself in after the Kunduz Intelligence. I can do it again."

Something my father used to say had been pushing into my consciousness all week: *Don't set yourself on fire to keep someone else warm.* I couldn't expect Sophia to set fire to herself just for me. I couldn't expect her to stay just because I wanted her to be my partner. And the realization that I wasn't enough, that I, *me*, as a person, couldn't overcome those external and internal parts of my life, felt crushing.

"You're not fooling me, Lexie. Are you fooling yourself?"

I had to. Because I couldn't live with the alternative.

Jeffrey leaned forward. "Do you want to talk about it? I promise an unbiased ear, lots of nods and mhmms, and a hug if you really need it."

My teeth clenched and I made myself unclench them. "No. But thank you." He had turned into a friend, but not a friend with whom I wanted to discuss relationship complications. Ex-relationship complications. I didn't want to discuss that with anyone really, if I'd had someone I could discuss such things with, which I didn't. Maybe having friends was a good thing. Not that it would do me any good here. I didn't have close friends, partly by choice and partly because I'd never seemed to have an opportunity to cultivate them.

"Fair enough," he said amicably. "But the offer's always there. Any time, even when we've already gone home."

I rubbed my knuckles down my sternum, trying to smudge away the pain that sat there like a boulder. "Thanks. One day, I might take you up on that."

He smiled, the edges of his eyes crinkling softly. "Lexie, I really hope you do."

CHAPTER TWENTY-ONE

February

The situation between you and me, as a couple, isn't tenable any longer.

CHAPTER TWENTY-TWO

March

I meant what I said last night about breaking up with you.

CHAPTER TWENTY-THREE

April

I wish being in love was enough, but I don't think it is.

CHAPTER TWENTY-FOUR

Older, not much wiser

Jeffrey raised his coffee mug in a toast. "Happy birthday!"

"Thank you." I wasn't surprised he knew it was my birthday, but I'd been hoping to do what I usually did on that particular day—ignore it. I didn't hate getting older, not at all, but birthdays had always felt more like a day for my mom instead of me. Even as a child, the day that was supposed to be about celebrating me, became about how she wanted to celebrate *for* me. Even now, on my second birthday after her death, I couldn't shake the ingrained feeling that my birthday wasn't really mine.

He set the mug down and rubbed both hands together gleefully. "A day just for you, so what are we doing to celebrate? Are we working today or taking a birthday vacation? Do you want to go out for dinner? A long walk? It's your day, so it's your choice."

I smiled fleetingly. "It's just a regular day. So let's just do regular things. Actually, regular things, but I do want to go out for dinner."

"Copy that. I didn't get you a gift, but I will purchase something of your choice at the markets and wrap it for you."

Smiling, I assured him, "It's fine, but thank you."

"Do you need me to screen Ms. Flores's gift in case it's something super sentimental that's going to set you back on the path of mope?"

I paused longer than I wanted to. I'd spent the last three months working on my feelings about the breakup, and thought I'd been doing pretty well with not walking the path of mope. Full disclosure— sometimes I got close and walked alongside the path, but I managed to keep myself off it. When I got home, I was going to buy myself a trophy with WORLD'S BEST BREAKUP SURVIVOR on it.

"No, but thank you," I said calmly. "She didn't give me one. I...I didn't tell her when my birthday is." It was on my list of things to do once we'd been dating for a while, and because she hadn't pushed, I'd just let it slide.

Jeffrey eyed me for a few long moments before his expression softened. "Old habits can be hard to break."

"Yes they can," I murmured. Shrugging, I added, "Maybe that was part of the problem."

"Maybe," he said quietly. "However, from where I stood, what I witnessed, you and Ms. Flores had a solid relationship, where you both seemed to share the things that should be shared."

I considered it. "We did. So..." I inhaled and exhaled out all the air until my lungs relaxed and I could fill them even more deeply. "What can I say? My life was full and now it's empty. And I still don't know how to fill in the void. Am I even supposed to? Do I leave it gaping? Do I dig it deeper?"

"You do whatever you need to so you can move on with your life. Because if you believe in soulmates, then you've got someone waiting for you somewhere. If you don't, then spending your life mourning a lost relationship is incredibly unhealthy for you mentally, spiritually, emotionally, and physically." He gave me a pointed look. "Trust me. I had a very tumultuous five years in my twenties."

"Thanks, Dear Abby."

"Anytime."

"This is still weird, you giving me advice. Good advice at that."

He laughed. "I've lived a very interesting and varied life, Lexie. I've made mistakes and bad choices. But I've also made some good choices and I've learned that good choices always feel better, you should think carefully before your decisions."

"But the bad ones teach you what the good ones look like. Or so my mom used to say."

"I suppose that's also true."

"Does it get easier? We've been broken up now for longer than we were together." And it still hurt. Still felt unresolved. They knew Sophia was an effective leash for me, one they could use to yank me back every time they thought I was out of line. Maybe she realized that. Maybe she thought she was doing me a favor.

He nodded slowly. "Yes, it does, in my experience."

"Good. Because I can't fucking stand this, even after three months."

Sophia hadn't contacted me at all, and it was that complete lack of anything that had swayed my thinking about the breakup. Because if it wasn't really real, if They had blackmailed or coerced her into breaking up with me, then surely she would have found a way to contact me? And she hadn't. So, logically, it was really real, she hadn't been coerced, there was something about *us* that she couldn't live with or move forward with, and she'd done the best thing for her.

So, where did that leave me? In a deep well of devastation, because I'd been clinging to the belief she didn't actually want to break up with me, which meant the problem wasn't me or us, it was *Them* and it wasn't as personal. And maybe we could fix it once I got home. But once niggles about Sophia's reasoning had crept in, I'd crumbled, and now I was left with the sour taste of knowing the thing I thought we had, the incredible, deep, connected thing we were building was actually nothing.

I was also left with the discovery that I needed to work on myself. Work on being a person worthy of a relationship. Work on sharing myself more. And that was one positive thing, I supposed. But working on the less-good parts of myself was for when I got home and could employ my therapist to help me figure out how to be the person I should have been for Sophia.

Jeffrey gathered his mug and stood, stretching. "I have faith in you, Lexie. You'll be okay."

I forced a smile. "I'm glad someone thinks so." Sighing, I slumped back in my chair. "Well, at any rate, I guess the president got what he wanted. I'm fucking miserable."

His eyebrows scrunched together. "Has he contacted you again? You haven't mentioned anything…"

"No. Nothing. I've been forgotten. Discarded like a sock with a missing partner."

"Nice metaphor."

"Totally unintentional. And now I'm doubly miserable."

After breakfast, I excused myself to get changed, and when I came back out of my room, dressed in going-out clothes, lightly made-up and spritzed with perfume, Jeffrey raised his eyebrows. "Got a birthday date?" The moment he said it, his face wrinkled and he held up both hands. "Sorry, that just slipped out. That was tasteless."

"Just going to see Elaheh, remember?" I'd spent the past three months casually accepting invitations to join her for tea, both at her apartment and nearby cafés, getting our nails and hair done, and just… talking with her. It was clear she was lonely, as she had been when we'd first met, and was desperate to reconnect with me, if even just as friends. I'd picked up small hints of her other life, but she remained guarded even as she would accidentally let slip about something that would have been meaningless if I wasn't looking so carefully for information.

I'd asked Elaheh to meet for tea, with a side of light questioning, today. A junior member of the terrorist cell now headed by Basir Mohammadzai—congratulations on the promotion—had been arrested a few weeks back. He'd finally given us valuable information, like confirming there were five key members in his cell. We were close to having enough to tighten the net around the rest of them. Close. Not close enough. The ops team's assets had dried up, or been cut off from the flow of information, and I was running out of time. Unless I pushed Elaheh, the intelligence I needed to enact those arrests might never come. But if I pushed her too hard, too far, too fast, I could risk my life.

"Right." Jeffrey grinned. "That's much more innocent than a date," he said dryly.

I grinned back. "To her it is."

"Do you need me to come too?" He accompanied me, with his usual waiting in a nearby café, about fifty percent of the time, and even then it felt more like a desire to get out of the office rather than him thinking he could assist if the need arose.

"I'll be fine, but thanks."

"Okay. Be careful." He paused, licked his lower lip. "Do you think she's ever going to give you anything we can use? You've been working on her for four and a half months and it's almost time to go home."

I shrugged. I'd deciphered snippets from our conversations, but it was hard work because she'd never said anything outright. I'd give her one thing, she'd grown shrewd in her terrorist old age. "I haven't been working her *that* hard. She's smart, far smarter than she ever showed me before, far more guarded than she was back then. Maybe I'll get something. I really don't know. But I have to keep trying."

It felt a little like a sick joke by the universe, to force me to interact with Elaheh, but to get nothing I needed. I collected my handbag, double-checked I had all I needed, then tossed my phone in. "If nothing else, I can keep a line of communication open when I leave here and hope she trusts me enough to stay in contact."

Jeffrey looked dubious. "Stay in contact to say what? 'Hi, Ellen, I bought a nice scarf this week, got my nails painted real purty, and by the way I'm helping my husband execute a terrorist attack tomorrow'?" he deadpanned.

"I can dream."

I told him when to expect me back and when he should start panicking, then carefully arranged my headscarf around my hair and shoulders. The remnants of the winter had fallen away, and the short walk from my apartment to Elaheh's was warm and lightly breezy. I took my time, tuning out the catcalls and city noise and allowing myself the pleasure of being outside. If I could set aside the reason for being here, and everything that'd happened since I'd arrived, I'd probably be happy. But the prospect of another meeting with Elaheh, trying to ferret out secrets while pretending I wasn't trying to ferret out secrets, hung a shroud of apathy over me.

Sometimes with her, I felt like a hen pecking at the dirt long after the grain had been dispensed, hoping for a morsel to appear. But, in the absence of conversation with Sophia, I'd clung to Elaheh's company in a way that made me uncomfortable, given what she had done and what I knew her capable of doing. There was nothing remotely sexual about our meetings, and I felt less than no attraction to her, but long after I should have admitted that it was unlikely that she was going to yield any information, I was still clinging to hope.

She greeted me with her usual enthusiasm and ushered me inside. I still hadn't met her son or her husband, and I wondered who of the four of us she was protecting. I knew both existed and could think of no reason for this strange separation, other than she didn't trust either me or her family.

Elaheh set out her usual spread of cookies and tea, and I waited until she'd filled both our cups before picking up mine. "Thank you. Your tea and cookies are the perfect birthday gift."

"Today is your birthday?" she asked, eyebrows raised in surprise.

"Yes it is." I had no idea why I'd just shared that with Elaheh—not only that it was my birthday, but that it was really my actual birthday—when I'd never told Sophia. I didn't want to share things with Elaheh. I wanted to share with Sophia. I couldn't share with Sophia.

Her smile was full-watt as she reached out to take my hand, squeezing tightly. "Happy birthday."

"Thank you."

She gently fretted, "I'm sorry, I wish I'd known. I would have bought you a gift."

Smiling, I waved her off. "It's fine, really. I don't usually share my birthday with people. It just slipped out."

"Do you have anything special planned? Is…Mark taking you out for dinner?" There was an odd bite of acid in the question.

"He is."

"Where are you going?"

"I think we'll go to Khakestar Café."

"You've been there before, right?" she asked nonchalantly.

I paused a microsecond, and let my paranoia seep in at the nonchalance before I went over all the times we'd spoken. Eating at Khakestar had definitely come up in casual conversation. She wasn't following me. I showed my paranoia the exit. "Yes. It's one of our favorites." I bit back a snide, and antagonistic, comment about how I would have loved to try Aber before terrorists destroyed it. "I'm going to miss the cafés here when we leave."

"When *are* you leaving? It feels as if you've been here forever already."

"The end of the month." Shrugging, I corrected her *forever*. "We've been here for a little over five months already. Six is about standard for trying to set up a school. The wheels of bureaucracy turn very slowly, especially when you're a foreigner. Even if you're trying to grease the wheels."

"I see." Elaheh leveled a steady gaze at me. "And did you do what you came to do?"

"Mostly," I said honestly, before the not-so-honestly. "Hopefully our proposal and the promised financial incentive is solid enough and we can move forward with a school for girls in the city. If they agree, I'll be back." It felt horrible to lie to people, to young women, to build up their hopes for education, and then disappear like a bandit with their metaphorical jewels.

Though in this case, I would disappear and the ops team would move in and take over monitoring Mohammadzai and Elaheh and the other members of their cell. Maybe they'd just continue to use Elaheh and her husband until they led them to bigger fish, though Basir Mohammadzai was a decent catch. If pertinent intelligence with her name on it crossed my desk when I was back in the States, then I'd treat it as I did any other intel. But once I'd left, I would have nothing more to do with her personally. And that was best, for both of us.

Whatever happened, it wouldn't be my problem anymore. I had to believe that or it was going to eat at me because I *hadn't* made a difference here, not the way I'd thought I could when I'd first realized Elaheh was involved with one of the cells we were trying to track. I mean, yeah, I'd assisted the ops team with quick assessments, analyzed intelligence that helped bring in cell members, and forwarded pertinent intelligence to the agency. But I could have done that back in the States. I'd been handed a golden ticket with Elaheh, and I felt like I'd accidentally dropped it down a drain.

"That is just a few weeks away," she mused quietly. Her expression turned inward, eyebrows scrunching toward each other, forehead furrowed. I'd expected a commentary on my time in her city, but instead, she said quietly, "You seem...calmer. Almost like you're more at peace with yourself."

I masked my surprise at her observation. "I suppose I am. I've been reflecting a lot lately, natural when you're approaching adding another year to your age I guess, and I've come to realize some things about myself that I'm determined to change."

"Oh? Not that my opinion is important, but I think you're fine as you are. But I wish you all the best with whatever you're trying to accomplish."

"Thank you."

We made small talk for another few minutes before I decided to set up our next social event, hoping to fit in as many as I could before I left. "I'd like to get a haircut and manicure before I go. When suits you?" I asked, assuming that she'd accompany me as she had for all my other salon appointments.

Elaheh set down her tea, and I could sense her reluctance before she even said a word. "I don't believe we should meet again before you leave, Ellen. Basir is suspicious of me spending so much time out of the house, and having a visitor to our apartment so frequently. And more than that, I think it will be best for me too if we don't see each other again. It is...hard for me."

Fuck. Fuck. Fuck. Pushing back would only make her clam up, so I adopted my best sad-but-accepting expression. "Okay. I wish it weren't the case but if that's what's best for you and will keep a harmonious household, then I accept that."

"Thank you," she said, face pinched.

I sipped my tea, unsurprised when she topped it off again. Her discomfort when I'd mentioned a happy household made me a little bolder. "Can I just ask you, are you happy in this life, Elaheh? Really happy? Because you hardly speak about your family." It was a last-ditch, Hail Mary effort, but I had to try.

She didn't answer, and that was all the answer I needed. I leaned forward. "If you need help, if you need to leave, I can help you. I know people who could help you change your life, if that's what you want."

"I cannot leave. My son, my whole life is here. I'm...needed." No mention of whether or not this life she'd chosen was the one she wanted to be living.

"Needed for what?"

"Basir needs me," she said steadily. When she raised her gaze to find mine, her eyes were bright, almost feverish. "I once thought you needed me. I used to think you would take me with you, but now I know that was just a fantasy."

"I..." I inhaled slowly, trying to frame my answer in a way that wouldn't hurt her feelings. "You know that was never a possibility," I said gently.

"I know. But if you'd offered it to me, I would have accepted without hesitation and followed you back to America. Restarted my life there. With you. It took me a number of months to accept that you had broken off our affair and disappeared without saying goodbye. But now I know why you did it."

Doubtful, but if there was ever a time to play along, it was now. "Why?"

"To save me heartbreak. You knew what we had was temporary and by ending it when you did, you kept me from getting more attached than I already was."

I nodded once, as if confirming her thoughts. "I'm sorry. And I'm sorry we won't be able to see each other again. You can contact me at any time if you need anything or even if you just want to talk." The weight of that *talk* felt heavy, and I hoped she took it ambiguously.

"Thank you." She stood, eyes averted. "If you don't mind, I need to start preparing for our midday meal."

As far as Get The Fuck Out Of My House went, it was very gentle. I took the cue and stashed the rest of my questions away. "Thank you, as always, for the tea." I stood too. "And thank you for your friendship. Take care of yourself." There was so much more I wanted to say, but it was clear she was gone. Nothing I could say would matter now.

"And you too."

I nodded and, unsure if I should touch her, hug her, kiss her cheek, or do nothing, I stood there and let her decide.

Elaheh lightly held my shoulders, and kissed first my left then my right cheek. "Goodbye, Ellen. Perhaps fate will bring us together again in the future."

Elaheh's words stuck with me for the rest of the day, and though I hated to admit it—she'd gotten to me. I knew I'd never loved her, knew we would never be more than casual bedmates in my history, but her thinking that I had just left her with no regard to her feelings stung. Because it was true. Not *no* regard, but with very little because she was a complication that would be dangerous.

To save me heartbreak. I'd moved firmly into accepting-the-breakup territory, and it'd been a while since I'd felt optimistic about my chances at reconciling with Sophia, but that simple sentence, that knife under my armor, uttered by a woman who I'd held at arm's length, made me think about it now. Was Sophia just trying to save us both heartbreak down the line? Could she see something about where we were going as a couple that I hadn't been able to because I was so blinkered by the excitement of our relationship?

I wished I didn't care so much, but Sophia lingered everywhere, even as I'd tried to cleanse myself of the pain of losing what we'd had. But I was still holding on to parts of her, not just emotionally, but physically.

After the breakup, I'd quickly replaced the tea infuser and mug she'd bought me to remove the morning reminder of her, and thrown both things in the trash along with the octopus stress toy. A week after the breakup, when I'd moved past devastation and settled into resignation and profound sorrow, I'd taken down Sophia's Super Lexie drawing, the picture of us during the great Tampa burger expedition that Jeffrey had given me as a way to get into my head but which I'd actually loved once I'd gotten over him trying to be an asshole, and the naked drawing she'd given me for Christmas. They'd all gone into my suitcase along with the letters she'd sent me. Now that I thought about it, the Sophia Stash was a horrible surprise waiting to happen. I hadn't been at the "destroy everything" stage of devastation, but maybe now it was time to get rid of these final reminders of what I'd had.

I retrieved the photo, letters, and drawings—and I definitely did not look at the naked self-portrait—and carried them out to the kitchen. Jeffrey lounged on the couch with his bourbon, sipping like it was the last water on the planet.

"Could you please disconnect the smoke alarms for me?" At his raised-eyebrows silent query, I explained, "I need to set my past on fire."

He heaved himself up from the couch. "Is setting your past on fire going to set our dwelling on fire?"

"No. I'll do it on the stove or in the sink. It's my birthday and I'll burn all traces of my ex-girlfriend if I want to. Also, don't look. One of these is…an intimate self-portrait done by my ex." I didn't even want to look at it, didn't want to revive those memories.

"Got it." Once he'd pulled the battery from the smoke alarm, Jeffrey turned his back and dug in the junk drawer for a lighter, which he passed over his shoulder to me.

"Thanks." I crumpled the self-portrait, then tore the photo into six pieces. For some reason, it was harder to let go of the silly stick-figure drawing she'd done of me and I allowed myself a little indulgence, staring at it.

I'd spent three months running the gamut of feelings and concluded that all I'd done was waste my emotional energy on something I'd never be able to change. I'd loved someone with everything I had. I still loved her. I'd tried to share myself with her. But none of that was enough unless I changed the unhealthy aspects of myself. I crumpled up the drawing and dropped it into the pile of paper. Super Lexie is going to save the world. Regular Lexie couldn't even save her relationship.

I flicked the lighter and held it to an edge of paper. Time to move on. For good.

Lying in bed the next morning, I was congratulating myself for moving on when Jeffrey knocked on my bedroom door. "Lexie? You awake?"

"No."

"Then wake up. We just got a brief."

I rolled out of bed and opened the door. "About what?"

"Mohammadzai. Based on the months-long analysis of the lead-up to the explosion at Aber, Basir Mohammadzai, and two other members of the cell have been arrested."

Arrested. It was a start. My mouth was so dry I could barely ask, "What about Elaheh? Is she one of the 'two others'?" A group of five, with three arrested now and one already in custody, meant someone was still free.

Jeffrey's expression turned solemn and he shook his head. "No. She's gone. In the wind."

My stomach fell. "You're shitting me."

"Unfortunately, I'm not."

I sat heavily on my bed. Her goodbye had been goodbye for real.

CHAPTER TWENTY-FIVE

English rose

Now that the finish line was in sight, I could say without question that this had been the worst field assignment I'd ever had. And I make that assertion as someone who was held hostage, beaten, and stabbed multiple times on her last one. It was no contest, this one sucked more.

Let's recap...

Totally out of the blue, and after telling me every day since I left that she loved me, my girlfriend had dumped me not even two months into my new assignment. And I didn't know why. Maybe she didn't want to be with me. Maybe she'd been forced into it, to punish me for doing my job. Maybe I'd never know.

My ex-bedmate person was a terrorist married to an even worse terrorist, and after being implicated in recent attacks, had disappeared and despite me thinking she might contact me, hadn't. I'd spent months meeting up with her, battling nostalgia and the knowledge she wasn't the woman I'd once known, while I tried and failed to get a crumb of information from her. And since we'd farewelled each other a week ago, I'd seen and heard nothing from or about her.

That's about it, isn't it? Did I miss any of the bullshit? No, I think that about sums up my life.

Early on, I'd pictured this moment so frequently, imagining the joy of being so close to going home to Sophia. But now I knew I was going home to my old, empty life, I almost didn't want it. I couldn't stay here, of course, but maybe I could ask for a reassignment to another office. Maybe I should just take all the offshore high-interest-earning money I'd earned working for Halcyon and retire to a remote tropical island where I could live as a hermit with my horde of pet octopuses.

The only upside to this whole thing was the shift in my relationship with Jeffrey. Though he could still be a snide asshole, with a cutting sense of humor, I'd discovered that he was actually a decent guy, and I trusted him more than I'd ever considered I would. We weren't quite at "help me bury a body" friendship yet, but he was definitely at "take him shopping and trust his opinion on a dress" friendship.

Jeffrey peered over the top of the workspace divider. I was not going to miss him popping up unexpectedly like that. "Can I take you out to lunch?"

I glanced at the time. Noon on the dot. "Sure. What's the occasion?"

"I want to eat and I'm sick of being in this room."

I stared at the Airborne pictures I'd been going cross-eyed over all morning and saved my report. "All good points. Give me ten minutes to freshen up."

After changing into a brightly colored long-sleeved long tunic, I lightly made up my face, combed my hair, and arranged a blue silk headscarf around my head and shoulders, pinning a corner in place to keep it from flapping about as I walked. Jeffrey had swapped his polo shirt for a pale-yellow button-up and put on a jacket. He was stuffing his pockets with the usual men's detritus when I emerged. "Khakestar okay with you?" he asked.

"You need to ask?"

"Asking is the polite thing to do, but I assumed it was a given." He double-checked the door was locked tightly behind us, then with a light touch of fingertips to my shoulder blades, guided me to the elevator.

The moment the doors closed, I asked, "Have you started packing yet?"

"Of course not. We're here for another two weeks, Lexie. Why would I pack now? Who packs that early?"

I'd started organizing my packing cubes last week, filling them with cool-weather clothing I didn't think I'd need again before I left. "Anticipation. And *I* pack that early."

"I've got plenty of anticipation for going home. And of course you pack this early," he said teasingly.

"I cannot wait to get out of this place and back to a semblance of my normal life. This assignment has been…eye-opening for me. I'm even considering moving when I get home too, if the agency can place me somewhere not-shit. Fresh starts and all that."

"Oh? You've had a revelatory life experience here and want a change?"

"You could say that…"

As the elevator doors opened into the lobby, Jeffrey stuck his elbow out and jiggled it. I took the cue and tucked my hand into the crook of his arm, surprised by the comfort it brought. As much as I hated it, being a strong and independent woman and all that, having a man with me in an obvious companionship way meant I was less likely to be catcalled or annoyed by local men asking why I was alone.

"Don't tell Dominique I have another woman on my arm," Jeffrey murmured, as he always did when we walked hand in arm. He had a solid rotation of quips, most of which were mildly amusing, and I was surprised to realize I'd miss his humor.

And I answered the same way I always did. "Your secret is safe with me."

He laughed, sounding genuinely amused this time. "I think she'd actually be more likely to cut my balls off for *not* being a gentleman and/or keeping you safe." Jeffrey led us out the door and onto the bustling street, taking a moment to peer left and right before walking on.

"Every time you say something like that, I'm not sure if I should believe you or not."

"Believe it. In college she waited tables at a restaurant in Colorado, and they served Rocky Mountain Oysters. She knows how to cut off balls."

"I meant the keeping me safe."

His eyebrows shot upward. "No? I would never throw you to the wolves." He chuckled, and some of the asshole that'd faded over the past few months crept back in. "You can do that fine all by yourself."

"Thanks," I said dryly. "Just when I think we could be friends, you say something like that."

"I mean it. My job is to make sure you can do your job safely and unencumbered. It's not in my interests for you to be harmed in any way. Nor is it part of my personal pleasure list." He patted the hand I still had resting inside his arm, and the gesture felt at once condescending, comforting, and conciliatory.

We walked for another ten minutes in the midday heat toward the touristy café we frequented most, where we could eat together without fearing snarls—just stares—for sitting together. And, if he asked just right and the right person was working, a cold beer could magically appear for Jeffrey.

As we were shown to the table, Jeffrey glanced around the room, a habit I had too whenever I was out in public in this country. But where my glances were only when I didn't feel entirely comfortable, his were ingrained. His expression didn't change and I relaxed in the chair as he turned back to me. "Your usuals?"

"Yes please." I kept my eyes on him rather than looking around the room where I might accidentally catch the eyes of other patrons I knew were staring at me. Or rather, staring at me and Jeffrey eating together, despite the sign out front stating this was a mixed-dining café.

Jeffrey ordered my lemon rosewater shrub drink, as well as casually asking the owner whom he'd come to know well during our time here about beer. We sat in silence, surprisingly companionable, until our drinks were delivered and Jeffrey had ordered our meals. I sipped daintily from the sweating glass, even though it was so tasty I wanted to chug it down and order another. Jeffrey drank a hearty gulp of beer then set the glass carefully back onto the red-and-white-checked table covering. "Dominique and I almost divorced in 2019."

"Oh-kay. That's a random thing to bring up. I'm…sorry?"

"There hasn't really been an opening so I decided to create one before we leave. This is relevant to you, I promise, now that we're on our way home where you'll be settling back into a normal life and maybe a relationship in the future."

I made a *go on* gesture, even as I muttered, "No relationship."

After another, less enthusiastic, sip of beer, he wiped his mouth, apparently more for dramatic pause than beer foam. "After my discharge from the Marines, I was working for a private military contractor. Long hours, a lot of overseas travel, constant danger and uncertainty. She hated its unsavory aspects, such as the fact such companies can operate in gray legal areas. And if I'm honest, I didn't particularly enjoy not knowing where I'd be sent next month or if I was going to return at all. She…well, it wasn't an ultimatum as such, but she definitely let me know that if things didn't change, she couldn't go on as we were."

Sounded familiar, except I wasn't given an ultimatum. "So you quit your job to save your marriage?"

"That's the very simplified version. I moved into a job that was parallel to what I was already doing, but as an independent contractor. I was in charge of what I did or didn't take on. No more gray legal areas, just secrecy, which she can cope with. It wasn't difficult. What *was* difficult was realizing that one of the most important things in my life might not be there unless I made a change, that she'd been suffering in silence." He raised both hands in a gesture of placation. "Relationships are about compromise, about finding the common ground where you're both happy enough to be able to move forward. I don't believe any relationship is without issues, but it's how you approach the issues that makes the difference."

"I assume you're trying to bring this back to what's happened in my personal life the past few months?"

"Very perceptive of you." He held out the bread platter that had just been set between us.

"Why now? It's over and done with." I tore off a corner of the flatbread, and scooped up a healthy portion of yogurt dip, already salivating in anticipation of the tangy minty garlicky taste. "Long over and done with."

"Why *not* now? You're clearly still struggling with it."

I'd thought I'd been doing a pretty good job of pretending everything was A-okay. "I suppose I am," I admitted slowly. "I wish I wasn't."

He took his time tearing his bread into three pieces, using each bit to scoop up a portion of eggplant dip—told you I'd convert you, Jeffrey—yogurt dip, and green chutney. Once he'd finished his morsels, he finally deigned to enlighten me further on whatever point he was trying to make. "I know you've not had many interpersonal relationships in your life, Lexie, and even I, as an outsider blessed with some insider knowledge, could see how much she meant to you. That doesn't just go away."

I bit my lower lip, hoping it wasn't trembling as much as it felt like. "She did. Does."

"So are you going to just accept this?"

I almost snorted in disbelief. "I *have* accepted it because I don't have any choice. She said she's done, she said that months ago and hasn't contacted me in any way, shape, or form since telling me that she didn't want to be with me." Not even through the secret personal email account I'd created just before leaving the States that I'd given her for emergencies. Zip. Zilch. Zero. "So there's nothing I can do. And even if she did somehow decide to give it another shot, how can I change my life to make it what she's going to be comfortable with? I can't."

"Why not?"

"Because she was right, even if she wasn't speaking about her true feelings, and breaking up with me was forced on her by someone. I love my job, I'm very good at it, and what I do keeps millions of people safe. That's important to me."

"There are other job options for someone like you, where you could find some middle ground."

I shook my head. "Even if I move to an adjacent role, into contracting for private security or something, I'll still be dealing with secrets, and secrets are what ruined my relationship."

He raised his eyebrows, but aside from that, his expression was neutral.

"Besides," I continued, "if I give in to them now and quit my job, everything that happened in Florida was for nothing." Everything that had happened or would happen because of the Halcyon Protocol—the removal of Berenson, the tabling of beneficial legislations, the diplomatic strengthening—was for nothing. "Everything she was involved in, the support and kindness and...love she showed me during that time was all for naught."

Jeffrey shrugged. "Maybe. But maybe it's about drawing lines in the space where you're comfortable and absolutely will not cross. And maybe you have to draw multiple lines for different aspects of your life."

"Look, I know you're trying to help and I appreciate it. Really, I do. But I can't change my career." Even if I left my government job I still had to contend with my position in Halcyon Division.

"Can't, or won't? I mean, I don't want you to leave the agency. You're a damned fine analyst, but...I'm not sure you're going to be able to keep going like this, with her in the past, in the background of your job and the mess surrounding that. It's always going to color your opinion of the work." At my frowning stare, he smiled and assured me, "Just food for thought. Something to think about, either going back and begging her forgiveness, promising things will be different and meaning it, then finding a comfortable medium with her if you can. Or, leave it as it is now and figure out how to live with your big heavy bag of feelings."

My feelings sure were heavy. I sat with my thoughts during lunch, letting them marinate as I ate my spiced rice, and spinach and potato *perikee*. Jeffrey inhaled his lunch like a man starved, which meant conversation was sparse, suiting me just fine as I tried not to think about what he'd said. Why, just...*why* had he brought this up again now? I thought I'd cleared the emotional hurdle but I realized I was still struggling to clamber over it.

I wiped my mouth and set the napkin down. "I'm just going to the bathroom." Those shrub drinks went straight to my bladder. "Then I want dessert."

"Sure," he said, well used to my sweet tooth by now.

When I came back from the ladies' room, he was standing beside instead of sitting in his chair. Jeffrey peered around the room, his forehead crinkling. "I think it's time to go."

"What about my dessert?" Full or not, I could always eat a bowl of *shir berinj*. Though, going back to the apartment and to work might give me some respite from my brain, which was still being too introspective for even my tastes.

He gestured to one of the waitstaff. "I have a Snickers you can eat for dessert."

"Fine," I grumbled. "I'll eat your months-old Snickers."

"Great." A server appeared and before he could even show the bill, Jeffrey handed him some cash without thanking the guy. Rude. He slipped into his jacket, then took me by the arm and guided me through the café.

His unusually rushed demeanor made me pause. "Do *you* need to go to the bathroom? Are you suffering gastrointestinal distress? Is that why we're racing home? You want some privacy? I gotta say, if you shit—"

He cut me off with a terse, "My guts are fine."

We were halfway to the front door, weaving through tables when I became aware of it. Just a feeling, nothing concrete, but *something* felt out of place. I took a quick look around but couldn't see anything to back up my unease, and the low-level chatter in the dining room was easy and unbroken. Probably just ingrained paranoia making me think things were happening that weren't. Or his weird, suddenly frantic behavior making me extra paranoid.

Jeffrey sidestepped around me until he was behind me instead of me him and when I moved to get behind him again, I was blocked by another foot shuffle. "What are you doing?" I hissed under my breath.

If he'd had a sudden attack of chivalry, now was really not a great time. I could feel eyes on us at the fact I was ahead, but he refused to reverse our positions. I turned my head to quietly say, "Sending me into battle first." Charming.

"That's the exact opposite of what I'm doing, Lexie." Strong hands landed on my shoulders and I could feel the heat of him close behind me. I wanted to squirm from his touch but he pressed me forward. "Now let's go. *Quickly.*"

I squinted in the sudden bright light outside and fumbled for my sunglasses. I'd just gripped them when a woman, wearing a pale-gray embroidered niqab that covered her face, bar a gap for her eyes, pushed past me. The scent of English rose slapped me in the face first and a wave of recognition surged, followed quickly by unease.

I knew that perfume. I knew those eyes. "No, wait. I think—" I looked back. "Elaheh?"

She turned around, and the instant we made eye contact, I knew. I knew it was her, and I knew what I'd felt under her clothing as she'd brushed by me and I knew what she was doing there. Instinctively, I moved toward her, but Jeffrey gripped me by the arms, yanked me back into him then spun me around and propelled me forward, pushing us quickly away from the building. "We're leaving," he said, his tone making it absolutely clear that there was zero room for negotiation.

I barely managed to choke out, "But that was—" I couldn't finish the sentence. I'd seen the expression in her eyes change, just after the recognition. Resolute. And I knew exactly what was about to happen. "She's—" She's…she's… The thought stalled, even though I knew the truth of what she was doing.

"I know," he said. Then his voice firmed. "It doesn't matter now. You can't do anything. Lexie, move. *Now!*"

He'd barely gotten the last word out when the sounds of a woman yelling, then people screaming was cut short by a burst of heat and light and noise from behind us as the building exploded.

CHAPTER TWENTY-SIX

Gray silk rain

Come home safely.
Come home safely.
Come home safely.

That singular thought overlay the noise of the explosion, which sounded like ten thousand waiters dropping a whole city's worth of glasses and plates and cutlery onto the floor. Thrown forward by a gust of burning air from behind me, I tried to break my fall so I wouldn't slam face-first into the ground. Instead, I landed hard on my left wrist, sending searing pain up my arm, and slammed face-first into the ground anyway. The weight of Jeffrey landing on my back winded me so badly that I couldn't breathe, and the pain in my face was so blinding that I saw stars.

I blinked, opening and closing my jaw in an attempt to ease the high-pitched ringing blocking my ears. I tried to move my limbs, got vague responses from all four. I was injured. Not badly, but enough to add to the panic of knowing I'd barely escaped that café with my life. I finally managed to draw in an almost-full breath and let it out as a shaky sigh.

Jeffrey didn't move.

A new panic overrode the one currently coursing through my body. Jeffrey hadn't moved. My throat was choked with dust and fear, unable to ask if he was okay. I tried to shift from underneath him, but the dead weight pinned me down. Dead weight. Dead...weight. Is he dead?

Oh god. Oh god.

Every time I tried to shift myself to get out from underneath Jeffrey, I slipped and fell and failed. My breathing faltered and I realized that I was going to suffocate under him if I didn't get his corpse off me. I'd just freed my arm when the heavy press of Jeffrey's body eased. He emitted a low, loud groan as he fell off my back, elbowing me in the kidney in the process. Ouchhhh. But I'd take a bruised kidney in exchange for Jeffrey being alive.

I rolled until I lay on my back, staring up at the sky. Light debris rained down like snow, swirling around us. Pieces of gray silk fluttered in the wind rushing from the flame-fanned breeze and I rolled onto my side to stare at what remained of the café. Fire. So much fire.

I tried to get up, faltered, then finally got my feet under me. I had to stand with my hands on my knees to keep myself from falling over, but I was upright. Jeffrey had sat up and was hissing expletives as he got onto his hands and knees. Alive and moving. Good enough.

He pointed at me and made a thumbs-up. I nodded, then pointed to him. He gave another thumbs-up, followed by a wavering smile that leaned more toward a grimace. We were both alive and okay, relatively speaking. It was a start.

The rational part of my brain knew what had happened. Explosion. Injuries. Deaths. Destruction. Suicide bomber. Likely Elaheh... The emotional, illogical part of my brain screeched over and over that there were people inside the crumpled, burning shell. *She* was inside. No...she was...she was dead. But other people in there, people she'd injured, people she hadn't killed, needed help. I made it two steps before I tripped, this time managing to roll so I fell on my side instead of my face. It was only when I tried to get up again that I realized Jeffrey had tripped me.

"You asshole!" I screamed hoarsely at him, maneuvering myself onto an elbow and then pushing myself unsteadily back to my feet, teetering like a drunk failing a sobriety test. People rushed around us, some toward, some away. I looked. Saw things I didn't want to see. "They need help." Though what help I could give was questionable. My voice barely carried over the remnant sounds of the explosion, the screaming, the shouting. The heat felt like standing in front of an open kiln, but I still kept trying to rush forward, only to be shoved backward almost instantly by the intensity.

"She's in there," I coughed out. "It was her. She's in there." I cried those three words over and over. My legs shook so badly I had to lean forward to brace my hands on my knees again.

Jeffrey's voice rose roughly over the background noise and the clogged sensation in my ears. "She's *gone*, Lexie. That was her choice." He'd risen to his knees, and reached up to grip my wrist, again preventing me from moving, as much as I squirmed and tried to break free. "Lexie, look at me. Don't be so stupid. What's going to happen if you go in there? *If* you actually manage to make it more than one step inside that building, which you won't. You can't save them. They're all gone. What you'll do in the future is more important than the one life you *might* save right now. The trolley car, remember?" He seemed to realize that it'd come out as harsh and dispassionate and he softened his tone. "You're not the only bystander. Look. Nobody can help them."

I looked. Saw people standing by helplessly. Saw flaming shapes falling through a broken window. Then I saw more things I didn't want to and, like a coward, turned away. "Okay," I choked out, unsteadily.

"Okay," he agreed. "You've got a nosebleed," Jeffrey said absently as he stood up. "And a forehead bleed." He turned slowly around in place to survey the scene.

"And you've got…holes in your clothes," I answered dumbly, cupping my hands to my nose in a futile attempt to stop the blood. It was pointless because something above my eye was bleeding too, trickling down my face.

The back of his pants and jacket looked like someone had run them through a wood-chipper, and blood spotted and seeped through his tan jacket. I took a step forward, then realized I couldn't do anything for so many wounds. Not here where I had nothing but my two hands. His injuries seemed bad, but not *bad* and I felt so suddenly helpless that I was paralyzed and couldn't do anything to staunch the bleeding.

"Yeah." Jeffrey's voice was now completely steady as he reported, "I feel like I have a million shards of glass in my back and butt but I'm okay. We need to get somewhere secure and do damage control. Let's go before we get caught up in this." He started walking, paused, then backed up and slung an arm around my waist to bring me along with him. His arm was comforting, and I leaned into him.

"Back to the apartment?" My voice was muffled, and so nasal I would have laughed at myself if I wasn't trying so hard to not cry.

The commotion around us was deafening but it turned to white noise. I couldn't isolate voices. It was just yelling, screaming, crying, pain, horror, devastation.

"It's the best place for now. We'll call the agency when we get there and have a secure line. We'll need to contact the ops team too." He stopped walking and cupped my face, moving my hands away from my nose. His thumbs gently pressed against my cheeks, either side of my nose, which sent eye-watering pain through my face. "Sorry," he said soothingly. "It's bleeding, but not displaced."

"It's broken again, I can feel it." I placed my hand under my nostrils to try to stop blood trickling ticklingly over my lips.

"Yes, I think it is," Jeffrey agreed.

"What do you know about broken noses?"

"I've broken a lot of noses."

"You must have an incredible plastic surgeon, because it doesn't look like it."

He grinned crookedly. "I didn't say they were my noses…"

Again, I would have laughed, if I wasn't so afraid of the pain in my face. "Why is it every time I go overseas for…this job, I get a fucking broken nose?" What was worse—being held hostage by terrorists, or having your ex-ex-lover suicide bomb herself right in front of you?

"Continuity." Smiling a little, Jeffrey took my free hand and started pulling me up the street, dodging people rushing toward the burning building. "We'll just add your broken nose to the list of things we need to deal with. You're going to have to pick bits of stuff out of my ass and get me cleaned up." He turned to me and the light of the fire behind us flickered against the side of his face, making his smile seem both warm and wicked. "If that's okay?"

"I *have* seen a man's butt before." I tucked my hand into the crook of his elbow, pressing against him. My good friend Adrenaline had come out of retirement, and flooded my body with shakiness, and I leaned into the comfort of another person and the safety of him by my side as we fled the scene of…what had just happened.

"Oh? I'm sorry, I just assumed man-butts weren't your thing and thus you'd never laid eyes upon one."

"Man-butts definitely aren't my thing. It was Arnold Schwarzenegger in *The Terminator*," I clarified.

He laughed, bending forward to wheeze. "Oh god. No laughing. Oh god, that's uncomfortable." Jeffrey exhaled loudly, then straightened up again. Sweat beaded his forehead and trickled down his temples. "I'm afraid mine's nowhere near that caliber, but these are extenuating circumstances. All I ask is that you not make comparisons to Arnie while you're working on my ass." He inhaled quickly and sharply, then kept walking as if nothing were amiss.

For a man who had god knows how much glass and bits of building in his body, the only indication something was off—aside from the tattered back side of his clothes—was a slight stiffness to his gait. When this was all over, I was asking him for his mental tricks. I pressed against him again, pulled him to me. "You sure you're all right?"

"Big picture? Yes I'm all right. Or I will be, once I get this stuff out of my skin."

The wail of sirens cut through the screaming and shouting fading behind us, and Jeffrey glanced back before moving purposefully forward again. "That's our cue, time to skedaddle."

I agreed, except for a pressing issue I'd been trying to ignore until it became too urgent to ignore. I veered to my right. "One moment. I need to adrenaline puke." Every fucking time. I loved my good friend Adrenaline, but she could also turn on me without notice and go from helpful to not helpful.

Once I'd discreetly wasted my very nice lunch beside a building, Jeffrey offered me his handkerchief to wipe my mouth, then took my hand, tucking it reassuringly back into the crook of his elbow. The man was a saint, comforting me while he had pounds of debris stuck in his body. The flow of foot traffic was overwhelmingly leaving the scene and we blended into the stream of people rushing away. We weren't the only bloodied people, and nobody spared us a glance.

The walk home seemed to take forever, the silence making my anxiety spike even higher. Jeffrey's adrenaline seemed to drop after ten minutes, and he slowed a little, leaning more heavily on me. He looked pale and clammy. We made it to our building and the elevator without attracting any serious attention. I unlocked the front door and went to go inside first but he pulled me back. "Me first." He reached deep into his jacket, around his ribs and came back with his handgun.

I gaped. "You brought a gun to lunch?" The question made me realize he'd probably taken his gun every time he'd left our apartment in the past six months.

He scowled and made a *shut up* gesture. Oh right. Potential hostiles inside our apartment. Bastards. Or...potential bastards. I complied, reluctantly, and waited outside the door, slumped on the wall. A few minutes passed before Jeffrey stuck his head out of the door. "All clear."

I slipped inside the apartment, closed the door, then bolted and chained it. "Did you really think someone would be here, lying in wait?"

"No, but it was a possibility that what happened at the restaurant wasn't just some random attack. Slim, but a possibility nonetheless." Wincing, he eased out of his jacket and shoulder holster. "Always assume the worst and then you'll never be disappointed."

"Noted." My nose had begun to throb and I touched it as gently as I could. My eyes watered, and I closed them tightly. But the moment I did, I saw the woman…no, Elaheh…walking into the café. I forced them open again.

"Don't touch it," Jeffrey cautioned. "You'll just make it bleed again. You should put some ice on it."

"Can't, I need both hands to deal with all your injuries."

"Then we'll bandage it to your face. Funny and effective."

"Won't work. I'll need to wear my glasses to take care of all this glass." Oh wasn't that going to be fun, having glasses on my nose. That was it, as soon as I got home, I was getting contacts. My I-look-great-in-glasses vanity be damned.

"Fair point," he conceded. Jeffrey leaned closer. "You've got a cut above and through your eyebrow that looks like it needs stitches."

"No thank you. I'll just stick it closed."

"Okay. Anything else troubling you?"

"Wrist hurts, but all my fingers work so I'm assuming just a sprain or tiny fracture. Bit of gravel in my palms. Grazed knees I think. Nothing major."

"Let's get you fixed up first, quickly, so we can get this shit out of my skin, then we can make contact. Bathroom?"

"Mhmm," I agreed, following him.

Jeffrey flipped on the bathroom light and indicated with his chin to the cabinet under the sink. "First aid kit is there."

"Thanks. I was completely unaware of that fact." Upset, frightened, and on edge, I'd reverted to my base state of combative idiot.

Jeffrey, thankfully, chose to ignore my facetiousness.

I gritted my teeth as I leaned over the sink to clean my eyebrow gash and wash blood from my chin and under my nose. I submitted to his scrutiny to make sure the eyebrow cut was clean-clean, then raided the first aid kit for antiseptic and skin tape to close it up. Jeffrey cleaned grit from my palms and after gently moving my wrist and fingers around and taking note of my quiet "Ow," he applied antiseptic and bandaged my hand.

After a fistful of ibuprofen, I turned my attention to him. The back of his shirt was bloodied, large pools and small spots. His pants were black, but I was sure they'd look the same if they weren't dark. He turned away to unbutton his shirt. Very, very slowly. I busied myself stocktaking our first aid items. It was an impressive kit, filled with a stockpile of analgesics and antibiotics. The team who'd prepped the site for us apparently knew that going to a hospital here was not advised unless it was unavoidable.

"Stay here," I instructed. "I'm going to need some more water and towels."

"I'm not giving birth, Lexie," Jeffrey said around the chorus of grunts and groans as he worked his undershirt off.

My eye roll hurt my eyes. And my nose. "Take off your pants."

His tone was as dry as dust. "Does that line really work on women?"

"I don't know, I've never tried it." I hadn't used any lines on Sophia, just told her the truth of how I'd wanted to be intimate with her from almost the moment I'd seen her in person. I cleared my throat and reversed out of the room. "Back in a few minutes." As I left, I heard him opening a pill bottle.

When I returned with a jug of warm salty water, he was standing in the bath, bracing his hands on the wall, wearing nothing more than pale-green boxer briefs. Or rather, the small patches that weren't bloodied were pale green. Blood had trickled down the backs of his legs, leaving crimson streaks over his skin, but the bleeding seemed to have eased. A good sign, and we were due for one of those. I stared at all the pieces of metal and glass embedded in his skin like a porcupine's quills.

Most of the pieces were small, maybe a quarter of an inch at most and looked not all that deeply embedded, but there was one piece sticking out of his left buttock that was at least an inch long and god knew how much of it was in his butt. He was a fucking mess, and the feeling of inadequacy, of overwhelming helplessness smothered me until I felt like I couldn't breathe.

"I don't know where to start," I admitted in a small voice. "There's so much of it and a few that look like they might need sutures once the embedded stuff is unembedded."

"Then you'll steri-strip those closed. I'm not leaving this apartment until we're told it's safe. I want to go over everything we have about what just happened and how we didn't know about it in advance." There was no accusation, but I still felt the shame. It was Elaheh. I was sure of it. And I should have known. Jeffrey turned his head so he could look at me. The moment we made eye contact, his expression softened. "You'll be fine, I'll be fine. Let's just get this done. Oh, wait, can you take a photo first? Phone is in my pants. I want to see, and Dominique will be curious, once she gets over being upset and furious."

I obligingly snapped a photo and passed his phone back. He whistled through his teeth. "Shit. Yup, it looks as bad as it feels."

"Good to know." I exhaled, trying to release the tension under my skin. "Right. Okay. You ready?" At his nod, I advised, "I'm going to get the huge piece in your butt first."

"Please don't damage my ass any more than it already is. Dominique says it's my best feature," he deadpanned.

I carefully put my glasses on, adjusting them so they weren't jammed down on my nose. "Objectively, I can say it's a decent butt. Covered of course."

"Of course," he chuckled. "Sorry you'll have to see it uncovered."

It took almost an hour and a half with tweezers, gauze, saline, and towels to remove fifty-one pieces of glass and twenty-eight metal shards from Jeffrey's skin. After I'd used antiseptic solution to wash his back so I could see better, he took a few minutes to recompose himself and let loose with a hissed sequence of expletives. Other than that short break, he stood still the whole time I worked, and the only sounds he made in protest were grunts when I had to work a particularly recalcitrant piece from him. The only thing that bled with anything worth worrying about was that first, biggest piece—which earned me a good-natured sigh and a dry, "Isn't this off to a good start."

Once I'd thoroughly flushed all the wounds, applied antiseptic cream to what seemed like the entire surface of his back, carefully steri-stripped the big wounds closed, and placed adhesive bandages over everything that looked like it needed it, Jeffrey turned to face me, hands cupped in front of his crotch to protect his modesty. "Well. That's not something I ever thought we'd have to do, but feels like you did a good job."

I passed him a towel and turned away so he could wrap it around his waist. "Thanks," I said, crumpling up first aid debris and tossing it into the trash.

"I'm decent." When I turned around again, he stared at me, his expression radiating both concern and sympathy. "Are you okay?" asked the man with a zillion little wounds in his body.

"Physically or emotionally?"

"Both."

"No. To both."

"Do you want to talk about Elaheh? Assuming that was her. We'll know soon enough," he added, not unkindly.

"It was her," I said tightly. "I'm absolutely certain."

"I can't imagine how you're feeling about that."

"Well, you know, a woman I'd slept with killed herself and who knows how many others in the name of…fuck knows what, and had no qualms about doing it while I was right outside a café she *knew* I frequented, where I was minutes away from being *inside* the café where I could have been killed too. Probably would have been…" I swallowed hard to suppress my trembling nausea, crouching down to gather the piles of bloody gauze. "I think I need to stop dating. That's it. The last two women I've been with? Disastrous, on various levels."

His lips twitched. "Does joking about it help?"

"Yes. No."

"Well, whatever you need to do, I'm here. But for now, I'm going to take the last shred of dignity I have left after baring my ass to you, and get dressed." Jeffrey smiled and squeezed my shoulder in a way that felt both friendly and paternal. "Thank you. You did good."

"No problem. And…thank you for…you know. Dragging me out of the café and saving my life."

"Any time. It's what I'm here for." He winked. "I saved my own too, so it wasn't entirely selfless."

"Of course. How many years?" I asked, gesturing to his biceps where he had two tattoos—the Marines insignia on his left, and a skull on his right. I'd noticed them when he'd first removed his shirt but had been too stress-hyped and focused to ask.

"Fourteen. I was injured out."

"Stupid back?"

"Stupid back," he agreed, smiling.

He also had lines inked under the skull. I counted eleven and asked, "Kill count?"

"No," Jeffrey said instantly. "Men I knew from my time in service who are now gone. A few happened during ops, but…mostly after we came home."

"I'm so sorry."

"Me too. It's such a waste."

"You're a good man, Jeffrey Burton. I'm sorry I said you were the vilest thing to ever walk the Earth."

"You didn't—" He chuckled. "Oh."

"Yeah. I was pretty annoyed. I may have used a little hyperbole to get my point across to Sophia. It may take her some time to warm up to you if you meet—" I stopped short.

Sophia.

He would never meet her.

It still hurt.

Smiling gently, he gave me a quick, friendly hug, and I probably would have clung to him if not for the state of his back.

When he pulled back, Jeffrey sighed. "I'm going to lie down on the couch. Could you please pour me an inch of bourbon while I get dressed? I think this situation calls for a larger-than-usual ration, earlier than normal, and I may as well use it all now before we go home."

I did as he asked, then added ice and a small splash of bourbon to a second glass for me. It was time to ice my nose and wrist, though perhaps a little late, it was better now than not at all. Jeffrey emerged in sweatpants and a tattered AC/DC tee, walking like every part of him hurt. It probably did. He bit back a groan as he lay on his side, propped up on some pillows, and as I approached, he smiled and held out his hand for his bourbon. "Thank you." He clinked my glass. "To being alive. Always a good outcome."

I dropped onto one of the kitchen chairs I'd pulled over by the arm of the couch, and rested my wrist on my leg, balancing the icepack on top. This was going to take some coordination. After a sip of bourbon, I set the glass down and picked up the second icepack, wrapped in a dishtowel. "You knew, didn't you. That's why you kept pushing me in front of you when we were leaving." I pressed the icepack to the bridge of my nose, blinking away tears at the bite of pain and cold.

He sipped his drink, eyes closing in satisfaction. "I had a suspicion, yes."

"How?" My stomach turned uneasily at the thought that what'd happened today had been designed to *take care* of me. They'd employed the services of foreign players before, to test a chemical weapon. So why not do it again, this time for something I'd suspected they might do, but to me?

"While you were in the bathroom, someone came in to talk to the man at the table two over from us on the left."

"Who came to talk to him?"

"Mohammadzai's nephew," he murmured, raising the glass to his mouth. "Then they both left like someone had set their asses on fire." Jeffrey winced. "Bad analogy."

Closing my eyes, I tried to remember the occupants of the café, those who'd been sitting around me. It was just a bunch of random men, none of whom were on our watchlist. No reason to suspect anything. A sick realization came over me. "If you hadn't seen him…I…then…I…" I couldn't complete that thought.

"Lexie," he soothed. "This is what a team is about. Working together. Strengths and weaknesses, remember?" He smiled and raised his glass. "That's why we're partners, partner."

We sat quietly, and my thoughts inevitably and painfully returned to Elaheh. "I still can't believe she did it." And I still didn't know how I felt about it.

"Me either," he murmured. "Did she say anything to you? Was there any indication that they were planning the attack?"

I fought down the instinctive bristling at his implication that I wouldn't have reported such a thing. That I wouldn't have tried to stop her from…doing that. "No. No signs. I…" Frowning, I turned our last interaction over in my head. "Maybe she was a little more introspective when I saw her last, when she told me it was goodbye, but nothing that set off any warning bells."

"On your birthday?"

"Yes. But…she was always prone to it, self-reflection, introspection." I indulged in a bout of introspection myself, and hit upon an unpleasant realization I'd been trying not to think about. "I mentioned Khakestar, that we were having dinner there for my birthday, that we went there a little more regularly than to other cafés. But it's not like her eyes lit up villainously and she rubbed her hands together gleefully and said 'Oh good, then I might murder you there soon.' She seemed no more interested in that part of the conversation than she was other parts of our discourse. Do you think she would have done it if she'd seen me *in* the café?" I swallowed hard before forcing the words out. "The suicide bombing."

He didn't hesitate. "I don't know, and neither can you."

"She saw me outside, I know she did, and I know she recognized me. But she didn't say anything. I may as well have been a stranger." I paused to inhale a steadying breath. "I think she would have done it if she'd seen me in there. I kind of sensed that she'd made peace with it, that her new ideals were more important than her old life."

"You can spend your life driving yourself crazy trying to figure out the nuance of her actions, Lexie. Or…you can accept that she had reasons for doing what she did that you will never understand and that you may never get closure for."

"I don't want closure. This isn't open. I'm just…" I sighed. "I don't know what I am."

"You may never know how you feel about it."

I agreed with a nod, and left it there. "We still need to contact the office, let them know what happened." Derek was going to be upset. "And ask the ops team medic to come and check us out."

"We will. Once we've had a few minutes to equilibrate." He eyed me over the glass of greatly diminished bourbon. "Are you *sure* you're okay?"

I took a few moments to think about it, take stock, and nodded slowly. "I'm going to need to spend a thousand hours locked in my bedroom with yoga and meditation, but yeah…I think I am. Thanks again for saving my life."

He smiled, eyes creasing at the edges. "You're welcome. Thanks for teaching me to appreciate eggplant."

CHAPTER TWENTY-SEVEN

I'm special

Derek was indeed upset.

Jeffrey had gone into his bedroom to notify the ops team, leaving me at my desk to call Derek with the news of the day. "Please repeat that," he said tightly once I'd filled him in.

So I did. "So yeah, not a good day. But I think we're both okay. There's antibiotics in the kit so I'll shove those down Burton's throat ASAP just to be safe. And we're getting the ops team medic to come check out our patch-up jobs."

"Good. And you're sure it was Elaheh Ahsan?"

"As sure as I can be without DNA confirmation." And it would take some time to…scrape up bits of whatever remained for analysis. "I just know, Derek." Inhaling a shaky breath, I added, "Please, just trust me on this one."

"Okay," he agreed quietly. "I'm so sorry."

"Yeah, me too. I'll send through a preliminary report as soon as I can."

"When you can," Derek corrected me. "Take care of yourselves first."

"We will."

"After this, I think I'll put forth a request to clear you and Burton to come home early. Both the White House and the agency have been reading the status reports from you and Burton, and the ops team, and have decided this program is not worth allocating further resources to, and it's been scrapped. So there's no point in you staying on for another ten days, especially now after this incident."

"Yeah, no shit on the uselessness of this program." In my eyes, this entire assignment had been a failure. "We told you that six months ago."

Derek ignored my jab. "Assuming my request is accepted, it'll take a day or two to organize travel. I assume you're already starting your wind-up procedure, but maybe accelerate that, then get packed up and standby."

"Copy that, we are standing by to standby."

"Smart-ass," he muttered good-naturedly.

"If you could wrangle an upgrade to business class, I wouldn't complain. Jeffrey really needs some space to relax."

"I'll see what I can do. I'm sorry, Martin. This wasn't supposed to happen."

"I know, but it did and there's nothing we can do. I look forward to you calling later tonight to tell me I can come home early."

"Me too."

I put the kettle on, hoping a cup of tea might help settle my nerves, which had begun clinking against each other again. After collecting the tin of Oolong, I forced myself to slow down, to move through the calming ritual of making tea. A groaning huff made me look up.

Jeffrey had apparently started stiffening up and his gait resembled the Tin Man from *The Wizard of Oz* as he approached. "Everything okay?" he asked.

"Yep. Get packing, we might be going home early. The program's being discontinued, no surprises there."

He brightened instantly. "Well, that'll soften the blow of me telling Dominique I almost got killed."

"Glass half full, friend," I said, trying to ignore the fact I had nobody in my personal life who I could call to talk about what happened, and just how much that hurt. "Also…" I pushed the box of antibiotics and a glass of water over to him. "Take these. What did the ops team leader say?"

"Not much. He's shocked, glad we're okay, pissed it happened. The medic will be around soon to check us out. They're going to try to pressure the police to rush lab stuff to confirm one hundred percent that it was Elaheh, but they're also confident in your visual ID, so they're going after Mohammadzai. Hopefully this is enough to keep him locked away for a while, and maybe after a little time in incarceration he'll be more amenable to sharing his connections with the US."

"Hopefully. If he's still in prison, they must have had this one planned for a while." I exhaled. "Or she decided to go off on her own when the rest of the cell was picked up."

Jeffrey shrugged. "We'll know when we know." He popped a couple of capsules from the blister pack and swallowed them. "We're really going home early?"

"Good chance, yes. Told you that packing early was smart."

He nodded slowly. "Well, I'm glad. But I think I might miss you, Dr. Martin."

I smiled fondly. "I think I might miss you too, Mr. Smith."

* * *

Derek called back within three hours to confirm we were done, and we'd be flying out in three days.

Those last days blurred, much as my last days before leaving for this assignment. We spent most of our time moving slowly around the apartment with our respective injuries, packing up, moving data onto servers, shredding papers and wiping hard drives ready for the cleaning team to come in and take everything away like we were never there. The space would be returned to the ops team. The morning of our departure, Jeffrey shaved off his working-away-from-home beard, and I swear I heard sobbing.

And when I closed the door of that apartment for the last time, I felt...nothing.

I slept for most of the flights home—business class all the way, baby—grateful that Jeffrey was there to drag my groggy ass around airports and through Customs and Immigration lines. When we landed at our final destination to a gorgeous sunny late-spring day, I felt like I could finally take in a full, satisfying breath.

Once we'd collected our bags, Jeffrey and I both wandered through the airport together. I wasn't sure where we stood, what to say to him. Did I thank him for supporting me through the last half year? What was an appropriate amount of gratitude to show a man who'd saved your life? Should I suggest we stay in touch if we didn't see each other in a work-related scenario? In the end, I just asked, "Is Dominique picking you up?"

"No, I'll take Metro."

"Oh."

Smiling like he knew I just didn't quite know how to say goodbye, he said, "Let's take a stroll."

"I have an Uber coming."

"Cancel it. You can order another one."

His tone made it clear arguing was futile, so I canceled my ride and followed him for a lap around airport parking. When we were away from the main terminal building, he quietly spoke. "I know things didn't work out the way you wanted but we both made it home in one piece, Lexie, which was all I wanted."

"That was high on my list too."

He chuckled. "Good. I know the program was a failure, but it was never going to be allowed to succeed."

"Oh, I know. Its only purpose was to put me out on a brittle limb and nothing will convince me otherwise."

He nodded. "At the risk of sounding dramatic, I think you're right, and whatever this is, it really is bigger and more complex than you, or even I know."

"You do sound dramatic. What do you know?"

Jeffrey's expression slipped, unusual for him, and I wondered if he was going to give me a truth or a lie. "Not as much as I want to. Why do you think I was chosen to work this assignment with you, Lexie?"

"To annoy me into complying and to make this experience exceptionally miserable for me because the president is a whiny man-baby with the emotional intelligence of a sock and he wants to make me suffer. Oh, and to collect a little information around all of that."

"I was chosen to protect you, you blindworm." He laughed loudly, and genuinely. "For someone so clever, you really are an idiot sometimes. You're always so busy trying to save the world that you continuously forget to save yourself. That's where I come in." He paused and I could see him weighing up where we were and what he wanted to say.

"What's that supposed to mean? I don't need protection."

"Yes, you do, whether you think so or want it. I was asked to accompany you for multiple reasons—because I'm capable of doing this intelligence work and I was already aware of your situation after the Kunduz Intelligence incident. But my primary job was a bodyguard of sorts, for which I am also eminently qualified."

I was too tired to be shocked by his revelation. "You did do a very good job of keeping me from being exploded or kabobbed by glass and metal," I agreed. "So I got a bodyguard. Lucky me. But I'm starting to feel like the protagonist of a B-grade spy film. Are you a triple agent? Is your face real? Is this a mask?" I gripped his cheeks and pulled, only half-joking.

Laughing, he pulled my hands from his face. "Stop it. Do you know how to be serious at all?"

"I am being serious."

"I'm not any sort of agent, except a free one, and when someone with a bunch of legit highest-clearance credentials contacts you and offers you an assignment like this, for a ridiculously large sum of money, you do it and you don't ask questions."

"Oh?"

Jeffrey smiled indulgently. "Mr. Lennon said I might need to drop his name to get you to trust me on this one."

"Mr. Lennon?" I asked, feigning ignorance.

The smile turned to a smirk. "Mr. Lennon also said you'd pretend not to know who I was talking about. It's okay, Lexie, we'll pretend neither of us knows anything."

He was obviously more trustworthy than I thought, but how much did he know? He said *Lennon*, not Halcyon. If Jeffrey were part of Halcyon Division, he would have said so, or mentioned Halcyon in some capacity. But he hadn't. Which meant he didn't know about Halcyon. But instead of acknowledging what he'd revealed, I just nodded.

Jeffrey looked up as a plane roared overhead. "Have you ever considered your life, Lexie? I mean, seriously considered it and the events that have led you to this moment."

"Many times. I am a deep well of existential dread. Will you reach your point soon? This is one of the most tiring, confusing conversations I've ever had, and I once listened to a woman dissect every episode of *Stargate SG-1* on our first date."

"Oh, I fucking *love* that show," he enthused.

"Great. Totally relevant here."

"Sorry. I've saved your life, right?"

"Yes." Thinking about Elaheh's face made bile rise up my throat, and I swallowed hard.

"I was employed to keep you safe, at the behest of someone known to you. And I've saved your life, which means you should trust me on this. Think about it, Lexie. What you did would have had anyone else in a dungeon. So why not you? Why are you walking free, resuming life like nothing happened?"

"I'm special."

"But what is so special about you? Have you ever asked yourself that?"

I fluttered my eyelashes. "My good looks, intelligence, charm, and wit, obviously."

"Obviously," he said dryly. "Or...I think you have something that someone wants, something they need, something so important they'd bend the rules for you. I believe you hold power, Lexie. You just have to figure out what it is and how to use it to get what you want. I don't know of anyone who would get the concessions you have had, who would be assigned someone like me who has explicit instructions to bring you home not only alive, but healthy, even if it cost me my life." He was deadly serious. Bad analogy.

I spluttered out a laugh, which helped to hide some of the upset I felt that he might have literally put himself in front of a bullet for me. "You have got to be kidding me. What do I have?"

"I honestly don't know, and I have a feeling that neither do they. They just know you have something they need."

Uneasiness turned my stomach over. "How? And who?" For the millionth time, Halcyon's "important" echoed in my head.

"No idea. But my feeling is there's opposing sides. Because we know the president wanted you out of the picture. Heck, he threatened you, right? But someone else demanded you be freed and kept alive. There's a conflict somewhere. I'm just not sure who those opposing sides are."

It was easy to read between the lines he was drawing, even if he didn't realize exactly to whom those lines belonged.

So who did I trust?

I asked Jeffrey that exact question and he shrugged. "Whoever your gut tells you to trust."

At this moment, that was nobody. Except maybe Derek. And Jeffrey Burton.

I worked through the problem rationally. The government obviously knew about Halcyon Division, and my impression was they worked symbiotically. But what if they didn't? What if Halcyon was its own entity, working alongside, yet not always in sync with, the government. Was I working against the government and not even realizing it?

I held on to my anger, though all I wanted was to hurl something at the parked cars surrounding us. "Am I in danger?" I'd asked that question before, of Lennon, of Jeffrey, of Derek. Derek. Shit. He worked for Halcyon, but was he a good guy or a bad guy? Who even were the good guys and bad guys? Given what I'd seen my own president and ex-vice president do, the jury was out.

"No."

"What about when I give up this thing I have, whatever it is, to whoever it is?"

"I doubt it. Unless you do something they don't like. Then it's open season. You know that. They won't protect a liability once they no longer need you. It was hard enough to convince the president not to shoot you in the head, tie you to a bag of rocks and toss you into the ocean. For real, he said that's what he would have done with you if it were up to him," he added.

Oh I believed him. And it was now clear Jeffrey had no idea of Halcyon's existence, and seemed to think it was the government who wanted my important secret whatever-it-was. "People are so great," I drawled. "Why did you tell me all this instead of keeping me in the dark, or letting me figure it out, or letting them come grab me for..." Gesturing vaguely, I mumbled, "For whatever it is I know."

"Because I believe people should be masters of their own destiny. And because, contrary to what you might think, given the foot we got off on, I don't want you to get hurt." Jeffrey shrugged, the grin tugging at his mouth making him seem bashful and boyish. "And I'm a patriot, Lexie. My political affiliations aside, I want the best for this country, so its citizens get the best. If we can't take care of our own citizens, and be good allies, then what moral ground do we have to stand on?"

"None, I guess."

Jeffrey pulled me to a stop. "I knew the moment I was called in to debrief you back in October that something was off. I don't get called in for jobs that everyone knows about. I get called when people have something they want to hide. And when the White House brings you in for a job like that? Alarm bells. And because I knew something was off, I knew I had to pay attention from that moment on. So I did."

"You have a very strange job."

He snort-laughed. "Yes, I do. And *you* have the leverage here, Lexie. Not them. Remember that. And I'm here for you, no matter what you need."

"Tax fraud?"

"Yes."

"Burying a hit and run?"

"Yes."

"Dress shopping?"

"Yes."

"Why?"

"Because I think Ms. Flores was right. You're Super Lexie. You're going to save the world. We'll talk soon, I want you to come to my place for dinner and to meet Dominique."

"I'd really like that," I said honestly.

"Good." Jeffrey enfolded me in a warm, tight hug, kissed my cheek, then walked away.

Someone, probably Derek, had made sure my apartment was clean and my pantry and fridge stocked with enough food to last me a week. A stack of mail had been left on the kitchen counter, next to a cardboard box. After a quick peek inside the box I closed it back up again, then ignored it until I'd showered, unpacked everything from my time away, and started my first load of post-trip laundry.

The temptation to just toss the whole box of my things from Sophia's place into the spare closet was overwhelming, and I'd done just that when I realized there were things I'd left at her place that I wanted. I sorted through the box, deliberately not allowing myself to think too deeply about what I was doing. Just another form of unpacking, wasn't it?

I noticed she'd taken everything of hers, and her copy of my apartment key was in an addressed envelope on my mail stack. I'd imagined that being home, in the space I'd shared with her but was now without her, would be harder. But mostly I felt empty, as if I'd become incapable of accessing the emotion I felt about the breakup. To have felt so full but now feel so empty was crushing.

There. I'd found an emotion. Not one I wanted to accept or deal with, but it was what it was. I thought she might have left me a secret note explaining, either in that box or hidden somewhere in my apartment. But I looked everywhere I could think of, and all I found was disappointment.

Battling hellish jet lag, my recovering-from-an-explosion-and-long-flights body tired and sore, I was about to cave and take a nap. Instead, I changed clothes and with a heavy bass beat pounding in my ears to block out all thoughts, I went for a long walk. The city was exactly the same, and I allowed myself to soak in the vibe and appreciation of safety I felt being back here. I was going to be okay. Not right away, but I would be okay.

Maybe in a few months, once I'd settled back into my life, I'd open up the ol' dating site profile and try again. It'd worked once, right? No reason I couldn't find someone else to share my life with.

My phone, out of reach on the coffee table, rang while I was stretching post-walk. Thankfully, the quick nervous-excited jolt in my stomach that a call might be Sophia had stopped a few months ago. Derek. Voice mail. "Martin, it's me, just checking in on you. Let me know if you need anything. See you next Monday."

I deleted the message, and was about to hang up when I remembered something I should have forgotten. I stayed on the line as soothing voice mail lady told me, "You have no unheard messages. First message, sent twenty-fourth of November at 5:26 p.m."

Sophia's voice filled my ear. "Baby, it's me. I don't know why I'm calling because you're thirty-thousand feet above some ocean but I guess I wanted to hear your silly voice mail message. I miss you already, which is dumb because it's only been a few hours. Anyways, I'll talk to you soon and see that gorgeous face and hear your voice for real. I love you. Be safe."

Voice mail lady spoke too soon. "End of message. To delete this message, press seven; to save it in the archives, press nine; to replay this message, press four; to hear more options, press zero."

I pressed four.

"Baby it's me. ... I love you. Be safe."

"End of message. To delete this message, press seven; to save it in the archives, press nine—"

I stabbed a number with my forefinger and threw the phone down on the coffee table. Collapsing on the couch, I pulled the throw up over my head and lay there for hours until I could breathe again.

CHAPTER TWENTY-EIGHT

I am so sick of surprises

Technically, I still had a week left on my assignment, and I'd told Derek that I was taking that time off work, *not* to be taken from my PTO, and he'd agreed without argument. He'd been tiptoeing around me, probably because he was waiting for me to explode at him with some big "I fucking told you so" because of yet another less-than-positive experience in field assignments.

I spent my vacation week lounging around the apartment, taking short hikes and long slow runs as my body allowed, finally getting my butt to the yoga studio, and getting ready to go back to work. I'd sent all my work suits, blouses, and shirts to be dry-cleaned and on Sunday afternoon I drove to the dry cleaner's to collect the huge stash of clean clothes.

Olga, the elderly Ukrainian woman who owned the store, and who never seemed to take a day off, took her time going through my inventory while lamenting she hadn't seen me in "so very long" before she handed over a small slip of paper. "We found this in one of your pockets."

Probably a receipt I'd stuffed in there without thinking one day. "Thanks." I took the folded piece of paper and was about to crumple it into a ball to toss in the trash, when I realized it wasn't a receipt, but a piece torn from a pocket notebook. A quick glance at it made my heart race. Sophia's handwriting.

"Is everything okay?" Olga asked.

"Yes. Thanks. Just a phone number I thought I'd lost." I'd recognized the sequence as wrong for a phone number, but if she'd looked at the paper then my lie would appease her. I pushed the slip of paper deep into my jeans pocket.

Once I'd paid, I all but sprinted out of the dry cleaner's. I locked myself in the car and sat in the driver's seat, staring at Sophia's neat, rounded handwriting. It was only numbers, 13 of them, and nothing more.

Too short for a credit card—dammit, a free shopping spree would go down a treat right now.

Too long for a phone number.

Could be a bank account. But why? Was I supposed to send her money for something?

The most logical explanation was that it was some kind of code. I held in my sigh. Sophia adored puzzles and riddles and Sherlock-esque codes. I'd often had wry thoughts during our time in Florida when I was struggling to connect Berenson dots that I had someone who could help me but to whom I could never show my classified material.

I pulled out my phone and Googled "what has 13 digits." EAN bar codes. Old credit cards. Some Indian cell phone numbers. ISBNs.

ISBN. The unique number assigned to every published book.

Holding the paper at arm's length—must make optometrist appointment for maybe getting contacts—I typed the number into a new search and added "ISBN."

The result landed immediately. *Sinka's Sacrifice* by F. K. Loyes. Publication date, 2011.

I skimmed the blurb of what looked like a cheesy new adult romance, trying to suppress the sick feeling building in the pit of my stomach.

When Princess Sinka's father is kidnapped by rebel bandits and her homeland, Arind, invaded, Sinka's first thought is to be annoyed. With her impending wedding to Prince Theodore of Ilok just weeks away, the timing could not be worse. But Sinka soon realizes her wedding is the last thing she should be worried about.

Taken captive in her own castle, Sinka broods and schemes, especially when the rebel leader, Mikus, takes a fancy to her. And though it's the last choice she would have made for herself, Sinka reluctantly breaks off her engagement to Theodore and agrees to marry Mikus. After all—if she wants to keep both her paramour and her father safe, she's going to have to kick asses and take names, and what better place to do that than from within the rebel's ranks?

Sinka will do anything to save what she loves, even if she has to sacrifice herself.

The last choice she would have made for herself... Reluctantly breaks off her engagement... Sacrifice herself...

I would have laughed at the book if I wasn't currently freaking out. I read the blurb again more slowly, trying not to jump to conclusions. But I couldn't help it. Was Sophia trying to tell me she'd made a sacrifice and that she'd only broken up with me because she felt she had to for the greater good? She'd pushed the fat man? But if that were the case, why had there been no contact at all? It didn't make any sense. And I didn't actually know when that piece of paper had been left in my pocket. Maybe she'd left it there when we were still together to remind me to buy this book or for some other reason. But I'd worn this suit to work the week before I left, and I knew there had been nothing in the pocket.

I could have sat in the parking lot all night trying to figure this one out. Better to be at home where I could freak out in private. Before I started the car, I tried to purchase the book, but it was out of stock, and unavailable in eBook format. If she'd taken the time to lead me to this book, Sophia would have known it was unavailable. Maybe this blurb was all the answer I needed. Maybe there was a little hope.

My return to the office felt like coming back after a short vacation, nothing like when I'd returned after dealing with the Kunduz Intelligence. In the six months I'd been gone, nothing had changed. The same shitty commute. The same security around the complex. The same drab government building. The same trudge from "Parkistan." Oh, the concrete security bollards that were disguised as pretend planters now had flowers in them. I bent down. Real ones. There. Something new.

Sam cried more than someone at a funeral, then spent ten minutes scrolling through photos of Muffin, each one with commentary. He'd also snagged himself a boyfriend, who only earned six minutes' of showing off. Thankfully he was so absorbed in his own love life that he neglected to inquire about mine. Apparently emboldened by

Sam's display, my coworkers began to creep over to fill me in on their goings-on.

After about twenty minutes of catch-up, the crowd dispersed when Derek appeared at the edge of the circle. Murmured promises to talk later followed them as they left. Derek leaned down. "Martin, a word?"

I stood. "Yes, sir."

Derek gestured for me to follow him, keeping his voice low as we walked through the maze of cubicles. "Ears only, not to be repeated until the news goes wide, but the director has 'resigned' overnight and we have a new head of agency."

Resigned... "You mean our lovely head of State, President Fuckface, had him replaced?"

Derek nodded as he swept us into the hallway. "The new director has requested a meeting with you now and I'm to escort you up."

"Lucky me." I punched the elevator button with my forefinger. When we were inside the elevator, alone, I said, "But, you know what, I think I've earned a meeting with the director after everything that's happened to me since I started working here. Anything you want me to ask for? Better toilet paper in the men's room?"

He chuckled. "No. But thank you." His tone sobered. "I received a report overnight that I'll forward to you, but I wanted you to know that DNA and dental testing has confirmed the perpetrator of the bombing at Khakestar Café was Elaheh Ahsan. I'm so sorry, Martin."

"Thank you. And nothing to apologize for. I'm just sorry that I couldn't stop it." Sorry that I'd failed. That it had cost me so much.

He patted my back, then ushered me out of the elevator and up the hall. Derek knocked briskly on the door, then pushed it open. "Good luck."

"Thanks."

The overpowering scent of Faberge Brut twigged something from my memory, but I couldn't recall where or when it'd implanted in my brain. I closed the door behind myself, and the tall, solidly built man standing at the window turned around as I approached his desk.

There was...something...about...

I frowned, squinting, as pieces clicked into place. An uneasy feeling tightened my chest, and I looked around the office, noting a familiar figure in a photograph on the wall. My father.

I inhaled sharply. "Uncle Michael? What are you doing here?" In the big-boss office of my agency. Wearing a many-thousand-dollar suit instead of the casual pants, loafers, and short-sleeved button-up that was his uniform during my childhood.

He wasn't my real uncle—both my parents were only children—but he was my father's best friend, and for some unknown reason, as a child I'd always called him Uncle Michael. I hadn't seen him in at least thirty years. And I had no idea he worked in intelligence—I was a kid when we interacted sporadically, so why would I?—and definitely no idea that he was high up enough on the ladder to have snagged the director's role.

The voice that came out of his mouth wasn't the one I recalled from my fuzzy childhood memories. But it *was* intimately familiar. "Hello, Alexandra. It's good to see you again. It's been some time since we've seen each other in person, hasn't it?"

The chill running down my spine actually made me shudder, and I fumbled out one word. "Lennon...?"

"Yes," he said simply, smiling in a way that made me think of both the Cheshire Cat and Uncle Fester.

I collapsed into the leather chair on the other side of his desk. "You have got to be fucking kidding me."

Bella Books, Inc.

Women. Books. Even Better Together.

P.O. Box 10543

Tallahassee, FL 32302

Phone: (800) 729-4992

www.BellaBooks.com

More Titles from Bella Books

Mabel and Everything After – Hannah Safren
978-1-64247-390-2 I 274 pgs I paperback: $17.95 I eBook: $9.99
A law student and a wannabe brewery owner find that the path to a fairy tale happily-ever-after is often the long and scenic route.

To Be With You – TJ O'Shea
978-1-64247-419-0 I 348 pgs I paperback: $19.95 I eBook: $9.99
Sometimes the choice is between loving safely or loving bravely.

I Dare You to Love Me – Lori G. Matthews
978-1-64247-389-6 I 292 pgs I paperback: $18.95 I eBook: $9.99
An enemy-to-lovers romance about daring to follow your heart, even when it's the hardest thing to do.

The Lady Adventurers Club - Karen Frost
978-1-64247-414-5 I 300 pgs I paperback: $18.95 I eBook: $9.99
Four women. One undiscovered Egyptian tomb. One (maybe) angry Egyptian goddess. What could possibly go wrong?

Golden Hour - Kat Jackson
978-1-64247-397-1 I 250 pgs I paperback: $17.95 I eBook: $9.99
Life would be so much easier if Lina were afraid of something basic—like spiders—instead of something significant. Something like real, true, healthy love.

Schuss – E. J. Noyes
978-1-64247-430-5 I 276 pgs I paperback: $17.95 I eBook: $9.99
They're best friends who both want something more, but what if admitting it ruins the best friendship either of them have had?

Printed in the USA
CPSIA information can be obtained
at www.ICGtesting.com
JSHW08085026l023
50926JS00001B/2